FIUME
RESTORAL

FIUME RESTORAL

A NOVEL

RICHARD G. DENNIS

RUSHWOOD PRESS
Richmond Texas USA

FIUME RESTORAL

Copyright © 2023 by Richard G. Dennis

Published by
Rushwood Press
Richmond, Texas USA

This is a work of fiction. Names, characters, places, and incidents are either the invention of the author or are used fictitiously. Any resemblance to actual persons, alive or deceased, or events or locales is entirely coincidental.

Paperback ISBN: 979-8-9895995-0-9
Hardcover ISBN: 979-8-9895995-1-6
Ebook ISBN: 979-8-9895995-2-3

To Cheryl

Letter from Filippo Marinetti

October 16, 1919

Sean:

Week after week, your letters vex me with their embarrassing laments. You say your painting has suffered since the Great War, and you beg to rejoin our circle of Futurist artists. What place could there possibly be among us for one who trembles in thrall to the past?

How I loathe timid supplications such as yours. The war you blame could not possibly evoke in a Futurist anything other than belligerence and fervid joy. Nonetheless, in consideration of your service to Italy during the war, I shall grant you one chance to demonstrate you belong with us. The opportunity of which I speak awaits you in Fiume.

Does that astound you? It shouldn't. I will explain. Since the little city was occupied by D'Annunzio and his legionnaires last month, it has become the perfect laboratory to test our political program. Isolated from church and parliament, Fiume is ripe for artist-in-spired and artist-led change.

Our new political party shall reach beyond art, using dynamism and the beauty of machines and speed to animate even those who lack appreciation of the avant-garde. I have in mind our friends from the Arditi, those high-spirited, dagger-wielding young men whose vigor during the war crushed the enemy. In Fiume, we shall nurture in them and others a craving for the electric future that intoxicates us as artists.

In Fiume, you must prove to me you share that craving.

I will meet you outside Trieste railway station on Saturday morning with final instructions. Be there at half past nine. Come with bags packed for a long stay.

Until then,

Filippo

ONE

October 18, 1919

Sean Reilly arrived at the Trieste Centrale railway station at nine thirty, carrying a leather suitcase and a duffle bag holding paints and other art supplies. Standing outside, he scowled at its symmetrical two-story façade. Five semicircular arched openings, slightly recessed, stretched across the ground floor. Above each was a pair of round-headed windows, flanked by weathered pilasters. Alternating large and small stone quoins decorated the corners of both stories. A style he despised, dredged up from the past. The clock mounted in the middle of the upper story parapet was slow by more than an hour.

He dropped the bags on the front steps and wiped large beads of sweat from his forehead with a bandaged hand. It had been a long walk, almost two kilometers. He saw no sign of Filippo. Sean wasn't surprised. No one ever accused Filippo Marinetti of punctuality.

Men in uniform swaggered past Sean and disappeared into the shaded interior. They sported tunic collar patches of Bersaglieri light infantry units or Alpini mountain troops or Arditi special forces. Each wore a dagger hooked to his belt like a badge. Ready for action, headed off on a thrilling adventure. They, at least, seemed excited about getting on the train.

You don't want to go, do you?

The morning sun, relentless, glinted off cars drawing up to the station. Dizziness washed over him. He tried telling himself it was the sun or the long hike carrying those damn bags, probably both. Still no Marinetti. His patience eroded by the hike, Sean picked up his bags and followed men entering through the center portal.

Inside, he stopped a few meters from the platform. Uniforms, everywhere he looked. As an ambulance driver during the war, Sean had refused to put a uniform on. Here in the Trieste train station, his tan wool sack suit and straw hat stood out. Despite the warm weather, he felt chilled. His hand throbbed. Out on the track, a choking cloud of smoke puffed out of a locomotive's tall smokestack, trailed over the carriages, and spread out onto the platform in his direction. Sean coughed and covered his mouth. For a moment he longed for his old wartime mask. The soldiers, laughing and swearing and shoving each other, seemed unbothered as they boarded the train. The smoke swallowed them up until they became silhouettes behind a gray billowing curtain, not quite real.

Noises from the carriages grew in intensity. A voice shouted "D'Annunzio," and it was followed by the wartime chant, *"Eiya, Eiya, Allala."* Sean was familiar with the chant. He had heard men shout it often during the war before battles. They shouted it out before marching off to be slaughtered or maimed. He saw what was left of them after they were ripped apart by bullets or artillery shells, or were gassed or burned, or ravaged by frostbite or gangrene or dysentery. Many suffered tremors from shell shock that left them quivering and shaking and jerking their limbs without control. The lucky ones, and maybe they weren't so lucky after all, would hold on until he could load them into his ambulance and transport them to a field hospital. There would be no chanting or singing on that trip. Only curses and screams.

Marinetti wants you to go to Fiume, and you don't want to go, do you?

The men on the train shouted the war cry again and again as though it were 1915 all over again, as though the year since the armistice had wiped from their brains all memory of the agony and blood and death and destruction the war had caused. They clamored for action perhaps because they hadn't seen any, or because they had and were survivors and thus felt invincible and invulnerable. How could Sean talk to them about the future, when they were so eager to repeat the horrors of the past?

This was all a big mistake, coming here to the station. He didn't belong in Fiume with men so euphoric about fighting, so willing to ignore the war's bloody lessons. He'd been too distracted the previous evening by drink and by James's needling, to say nothing of the expensive minutes spent with Gretchen, to consider what it would feel like to mingle with such men. Marinetti must be outside the station by this time, he figured, but he didn't want to face the man who would prod him into boarding the train to a city where he didn't belong. Marinetti would of course be too proud to come inside the station looking for him. Sean picked up his bags and moved closer to the platform, closer to the train he refused to board.

The old black locomotive let out a loud whistle, drawing the last of the soldiers aboard. White hissing steam now poured from the smokestack and mingled with the gray smoke. Piston rods and connecting rods began pushing and pulling the steel wheels in slow rotation. "Fiume," somebody yelled, and another cheer went up inside the carriages. The train rattled forward with deliberate, unhurried momentum, its bulk covered with smoke, and vanished in a grove of oak trees. Sean picked up his bags and trudged outside.

He found Marinetti at the curb alongside a huge, gleaming automobile, polishing a chrome hood ornament in the shape of a winged man with arms raised. "Isotta Fraschini Tipo 8," Marinetti said without looking up. "The best car in the world and made in Italy. Fantastic. Eight-cylinder engine, and the chassis is mass-produced on an assembly line like in America. Are you listening, Sean? The body is custom, pure Italian design." He ran his hand over the gleaming metal. "Futurist art on wheels." Marinetti stuffed the rag into the back of the car and gestured for Sean's bags to go there as well.

"I'm not going to Fiume," Sean said.

"Get in," Marinetti said.

Sean got in the car. "I'm not going to Fiume," he repeated. "But I would like a ride back to my apartment."

The car pulled away from the station and quickly accelerated, a flash of scarlet metal and black rubber hurtling southward through an old stone-block street. "You were not outside where I told you to wait," Marinetti said. "Disappointing. I will need better from you in Fiume."

With a hand on his straw hat, Sean twisted around to make sure his bags remained secure in the back seat. "I thought about this, Filippo, and I'm not going. I'm sorry. The train has already left."

"Nonsense. Forget the train. I never intended for you to ride it. Americans can't get through the army checkpoint on the rail lines these days. The train station was merely a convenient place for us to meet."

The street by Sean's apartment would have been a lot more convenient, Sean thought.

"Your boat is on the south side," Marinetti said. "I told the captain you'd be there by eleven."

"I didn't get on the train, and I damn well won't get on any boat," Sean said. "You know I hate boats." At least the pier was only a few blocks from where he lived.

Marinetti shouted over the noise of the engine and the whipping wind. "I recently returned from an inspection of Fiume and found much to my liking." He handed Sean a copy of the journal *Roma futurista*. "In there, you'll find the Manifesto of the Futurist Political Party. It contains details you need to study. You remember Mario Carli, do you not? A brilliant theorist. He remains in Fiume, tailoring our political and cultural messages for the city. Simplifying it, you understand? You will help deliver those messages to the masses. I presume you can do that."

"I'm sure Carli can find someone else to help him," Sean said. He skimmed the manifesto, noting points about education, land reform, and industrial development. Nothing about helping blocked artists regain their abilities. "A brilliant man like him. There must be plenty of others already there in Fiume who could help. Please watch out for the corner up ahead. Do you not see the Grand Canal there?"

The car made a sharp turn, narrowly missing two pedestrians. Their curses were drowned by the roar of the car's engine. "Your job is to reach out to the legionnaires—that's what they are calling D'Annunzio's soldiers—and the local citizens. Carli will tell you what to say."

"He'll need to come to Trieste if he wants to talk to me," Sean said. "I'm not going to Fiume."

"Yet you brought your bags with you. I want you to create your own street events. Under Carli's supervision, of course. What did you do to your hand?"

"A wall was bothering me. Christ, Filippo, I drove ambulances in the war down icy mountain roads with heavy guns shooting at me and felt safer there than I do in this car. Would you please slow down?"

"Those bags of yours look heavy. Keep me informed about how ordinary people are reacting to D'Annunzio's Command. Find out what the Socialists are up to. The other Futurists in Fiume are too timid. You'll be a better representative."

The car raced past the Piazza dell'Unità. Marinetti nodded at the massive nineteenth-century palazzos framing it on three sides, icons of Trieste's Austro-Hungarian heritage. "Hovels of tradition," he said. "They should be torn down. You know, these legionnaires D'Annunzio took with him to Fiume, and the ones he's attracting now, even the Arditi, they find it hard to let go of such rubbish. They need the guiding light only artists and intellectuals can provide, and I have doubts about whether D'Annunzio is up to it. His mind, when not focused on copulation, is stuck on myths and old glories. He can't talk about airplanes without mentioning Icarus."

Sean leaned forward, hand gripping his hat. The October wind, though warm, stung his face as the car whipped along the road skirting the waterfront. To the right, dots of late morning sunshine sparkled in the blue waters of the Gulf. An old three-legged dog drifted in front of the car, causing Marinetti to swerve first left and then right, nearly dumping the car into the water.

"Move fast or stay out of the street, old dog," Marinetti shouted. "The future is coming at you. What do you say, Sean? Fiume is a dangerous place for an American. Perhaps I should send an Italian."

Sean knew the game. Marinetti constantly challenged all the artists around him. He'd praise them one minute and, in the next, threaten to replace their works in an upcoming show with those of someone manifestly inferior. In the days before the war, Sean was usually the threatened inferior replacement, which made him, the only American in the group, even more of an outsider. Boccioni taunted him often, saying it was the only reason Sean was allowed to stay with the group. In this case, Marinetti's ploy was misguided. Sean was happy to let someone else go in his place. "You should," he said.

"Funds have been wired to you in the care of Guido Keller," Marinetti said. "He's been in Fiume since the beginning of the occupation. I believe you two are acquainted."

Sean remembered Guido. He had carried the man in his ambulance during the war. Twice. Guido was a decent sort, though notoriously odd and impulsive. Someone who flew fighter planes wearing pajamas and drinking tea from a silver service. Sean couldn't picture Guido in a Futurist street event repeating Carli's words.

"I can't do this," Sean said. "Don't you understand? I'm not the man you need. I don't belong in Fiume. I hardly fit in here in Trieste. It's a bad time for me right now."

Marinetti skidded the Tipo 8 to a stop at the base of the pier, sending dirt flying on all sides. Sean climbed out and grabbed his bags. "Thanks for the ride," Sean said. "You can find someone better."

"Two of your friends are already in Fiume," Marinetti said. "Lorenzo Guidici and Thomas Delancy."

Sean halted midstride. He dropped his bags and returned to the car. "Renzo and Tom are there?"

For the first time since the train station, Marinetti looked him full in the face.

"Listen carefully. This mission in Fiume is a singular opportunity to redeem yourself and rejoin us. Only Futurism can revive your painting. You have competition, though. Many young artists throughout Italy—women, even—want to join our movement. We have limited room."

Marinetti let out the clutch of the Tipo 8. "Remember," he said, "only the explosive ideas of Futurism matter. Not the lives of Futurists." Tires spun in the loose dirt, spitting out a choking, brown cloud as the car drove off.

TWO

October 18, 1919. I'm writing this on the boat to Fiume but don't know if I'll be able to read it later. My handwriting is worse than usual, and the paper is getting wet from the damn spray. I hate boats.

I honestly meant to refuse this ridiculous trip to Fiume after seeing those soldiers at the train station. Joking, eager to fight, as if the war had not been enough fighting for them. Driving my ambulance, I saw more horror and destruction than any of them. The idea that the future will mirror the past is unbearable, yet that seemed to be what they clamored for. As much as I want to appease Marinetti and get my place back in his circle, this asked too much of me. What could Marinetti expect me to accomplish among the armed adventurers in Fiume?

Oh, yes. Become an errand boy for Carli. That is to be my role in Fiume. The brilliant Carli who, when not busy penning tepid poetry and an unreadable novel, recounts endless tales of his heroic Arditi days. I had never heard anyone besides Marinetti acclaim his profundity. Carli is just another soldier, like the chanting roughs I watched board the train. Not someone I care to be around.

But when Marinetti mentioned Tom and Renzo, it changed everything. I do so much want to see them again. Fiume can't be entirely bad with those two around.

THREE

From *Memories of a Fascist in Fiume*
by Tenente Lorenzo Guidici

Editor's note: This unpublished memoir was written by Lorenzo Guidici during his incarceration in the Regina Coeli prison in Rome. Years later, it was found in the warden's file cabinet. A cover note attached to the manuscript suggests the prisoner had intended that it be delivered to Mussolini.

Since the death of the agitator Matteotti, the Socialists and their friends have subjected those of us who love Italy to outrageous accusations and slander. The Duce, to maintain order for the good of the nation, acted quickly to apprehend those few individuals who may have overreacted to Socialist provocations, but justice, it seems, is not sufficient to appease the howling jackals who wish to poison our country with their defeatist ideology. Using their powerful unions and vicious press, they spread lies about Fascism, several of which target me for my actions during the heroic liberation of Italian Fiume. I am a patriot and a veteran, yet I sit locked in a cold prison cell, denied the opportunity to defend myself.

While I am not free to fight with dagger and gun against the enemies of my nation, I have been encouraged by friends to take up the pen. Heeding their advice, I shall set down my recollection of D'Annunzio's time in Fiume in 1919 and 1920, during the early days of our glorious Fascism, confining myself to matters in which I took an active part or have personal knowledge. What I am about to describe will spare no one, including myself. If I made mistakes, the reader will understand what I was thinking at the time my actions were taken and can judge whether, under the circumstances then existing, I made the right choices. It is a difficult story to tell, but it deserves telling. When the facts are revealed, I am confident my honorable contribution will be evident to all. And once the hysteria over Matteotti's death passes, our Duce will achieve the free hand he needs to lead our nation and no doubt put an end to my unjust incarceration.

Now, to my story. The city of Fiume, on the eastern Adriatic coast, is today proudly and irrevocably annexed to Italy, but in the months after our victory in the Great War, its status was contested by the Slavic heirs to the wreckage of the Austro-Hungarian empire. Reclaiming the city for Italy was the first step in reasserting Italy's stature in the modern world. I played a part in the city's rescue in a way that enhanced Italy's position in the world's eyes.

Make no mistake: in 1919, Italy's stature was under siege. People feared for their lives in those days. Anarchy prevailed. Riots were commonplace. Lawless workers occupied and shuttered the factories with gun battles, declaring strikes instead of producing desperately needed goods. Bandits, many of them foreigners, murdered, raped, and robbed with impunity. Peasants stormed the homes of their landlords. Veterans like me were assaulted and spit upon. Socialists, whose loyalties always lay beyond our borders, helped perpetuate these atrocities. The corrupt liberal government was powerless to stop them. In the absence of strong nationalist leadership, chaos reigned. Italy badly needed Fascism.

Internationally, things were even worse for Italy. France and Britain, the imperial powers who had been our allies during the Great War, betrayed us at Versailles. They wanted to deny us Fiume, a city that was indisputably Italian by history, character, and language, a city we had earned by our decisive intervention in the war and whose harbor was necessary for our country's defense. They tried to deny Italy and give it to the Croats, who fought with Austria on the losing side of the war. Did that make any sense? Our victory in the Great War was being mutilated because Italy was disrespected.

I was one of over a million veterans who had fought valiantly in the war but who, when the fighting ended and the enemy's guns were silenced, were cast loose by ungrateful politicians and shunned by others who had shirked military service. Civilians could comprehend neither the sacrifices we had made nor the dangers Italy faced in the postwar world. We veterans understood both. We were strong and well trained and eager to turn our fighting skills against internal and external adversaries. I myself had served in a fabled Arditi unit, one that took pride in carrying out the most daring and dangerous assignments. It was clear to me that spilling blood would be required to rid our country of the vices that tormented it. Only violent action could unite our citizens and harness the will and courage and pride that marked the greatness of our Italian race.

D'Annunzio was the man we first looked to for leadership in this fight. He had argued tirelessly back in 1915 for Italy's entry into the war and then, despite his age, fought bravely in air, land, and sea battles. He was magnificent then. If only you could have heard him speaking to the troops, raising morale, thrilling them even if they didn't quite understand much of what he was saying in that poetic style of his. They cheered him and raced out to fight with recharged Italian ferocity. We hoped for more of the same in the struggle for Fiume. But the war had extracted a heavy toll on the man. It took months of pleading to get D'Annunzio to lead the assault.

When D'Annunzio finally did agree to act, I happily joined him on the march to Fiume. In short order, we liberated the city in defiance of the cowardly liberals in Rome. Even then, however, I could see D'Annunzio lacked the focus and willpower to reach beyond Fiume and restore Italy to its legendary greatness. The future demanded younger men of steel.

Fortunately, there existed among us someone with the requisite strength and vision and will, someone who shared our pride in our heritage and our hunger for a new, more powerful Roman Empire. That man was Benito Mussolini.

I have never been in the presence of another man so imposing, so full of charisma and Latin virility. The first thing I noticed, even before his massive shoulders or his strong chin, were his eyes. They are huge and deep and mesmerizing, the eyes of a strong man who sees the country's sickness and is willing to do anything, however unpleasant, to deliver the required cure. I aligned myself with Mussolini and pledged to carry out his orders.

My story is about warriors who joined the struggle in Fiume to preserve and glorify the *patria*. Two of those warriors were Americans I knew from the Great War. Tom Delancy and Sean Reilly each saved my life on the battlefield. I shall forever be grateful and remember them as brothers. But this tale is also about making difficult choices in life for the greater good of the *patria*, even at the expense of those whom one most desires to protect.

Like the Duce, I am desperately Italian. I have faith in the genius of the Italian people, and in the destiny of our glorious nation. Those blessed with similar faith will, I believe, benefit from reading these recollections of mine about what transpired in those days in Fiume, and about the two Americans who played a not insignificant role in *l'impresa di Fiume*.

FOUR

October 17, 1919

Sean trudged past the cheaper brothels, following Via dei Capitelli uphill toward the section of Trieste where a relative sense of decorum and cleanliness prevailed. Cupping his left hand around the bandaged right fist to ease the throbbing, he halted at a corner and turned around. His friend, the Irishman, lagged several meters behind. "Hurry up, James, you sorry-ass beggar," Sean shouted by way of encouragement. "There'll be a line for Gretchen tonight."

James stumbled on uneven cobblestones and veered across to the sidewalk, stepping over a couple of supine drunks in the process. "For the love of Christ," he said, "forget Gretchen. Let us go to the Metro Cubo. We'd need not climb this bloody hill."

"The Metro is a filthy place," Sean said. "They've got diseases there no doctor can cure. Not for me, not on my last night in Trieste."

Having caught up, James reached out and landed a heavy arm on Sean's shoulder. Rapid puffs of wine-soaked breath landed squarely on his face. "You move too fast. Like all Americans. No bloody disease can catch up with you. Tell me, Sean Reilly, why would you want to leave fair Trieste?"

"I told you."

"That's right. You told me. Marinetti sent you a letter ordering you to go to Fiume. Did he ask you if you wanted to go?"

"I have to be a Futurist. Marinetti is the leader." Sean wondered if it had been a mistake to tell the Irishman about the letter. Leaving the city where he had come for artistic redemption—and found none—

without saying anything to anyone felt wrong but so what? Sean told James about the summons because James was a fellow artist, a literary one, with a published novel and a collection of short stories to his credit. He was the only person in Trieste who might appreciate why Sean had to go.

"Marinetti's a swine. And so are you." James had made an early start on the night's drinking, well before the two men met up. "Swine. Like all you Futurists. You lot are like the bloody Church. Scurry around like a priest and mutter unintelligible things, and then a bishop comes along and tells you where to go. All you need are vestments and a collection plate."

Sean said nothing. His right hand felt like it was on fire. The limited funds in his pocket would get him either half an hour with Gretchen, his girl of choice for the evening, or enough grappa for the Irishman to shut him up. Not both.

James took full advantage of Sean's poverty. "Futurism's a bunch of blather about speed and machines and manly fights, and a lot of nonsense about drowning museums and libraries," he said. "I went to one of Marinetti's little soirées here in Trieste, at the Rossetti Theatre. Eight, ten years ago. I don't know. Before the war. All I remember is a bunch of shouting and awful noise he called music and some paintings he tried to sell that looked like shite. Is that what your paintings look like? You've never let me see them."

Sean tried to put his arm under James's shoulder, but the man ignored the proffered help and slid down into a sitting position, his back against the flaking stucco of a tenement. Across the narrow street, the door of a tavern burst open, and two sailors spilled out, one of whom promptly threw up. The smell of vomit crept across the street, arriving seconds ahead of the sour aroma of cheap tavern spirits and cigarette smoke. "Marinetti tells you to go to Fiume for the sake of Futurism," James said. "How noble. And you do what he says. Yet you don't want to go. Do you? You know fuck-all about Fiume."

"You're wrong," Sean said. "Fiume's a proving ground these days. It's where I will become a great artist."

James laughed, then coughed. He spit something green and vile onto the cobblestones, where it sat erect like a tiny monument.

Sean couldn't let this contempt go unaddressed. "Futurism is more than machines and speed. It's painting and sculpture and literature and music. Eliminating space between objects and their surroundings. Elapsed time captured in simultaneity. Everything in motion. The running horse has not four legs, but twenty."

"What in hell are you saying? Do you even understand it?"

"A little." Sean should have stopped there, he knew. "It's dynamic sensation, drawing out the force lines that exist in everything. And not only art. Futurism will improve the whole society. A whole different and better way of seeing the modern world, and we need a new way because the old way was pretty fucked, wasn't it? They had a big war. You may have heard." It was a cheap shot, but Sean wanted to get moving. Gretchen was a popular girl. She had once told him his brown eyes were like smoldering velvet.

"I heard about the war," James said, nibbling at the bait without swallowing the hook. "That's why I moved to Switzerland until the armistice."

"Well, I stayed in Italy, and I saw the war up close. It was fucked."

"Marinetti's poetry is going to unfuck the world, that's what you imagine? I've read it, my boy. Quite honestly, it's shite. There's no substance. Oh, he does write with a little style these days, doesn't he? All feverish and wild. The syntax is original, I'll grant you. Somebody could spin gold with that. Not him, but somebody."

The gas lamps lining the street cast an orange-yellow glow on the stucco walls and on the Irishman.

"I do like D'Annunzio, on the other hand," James said. "He acts like a bloody clown, but his writing is good. Decadent, sure. But knows his classics. People will be reading decadent D'Annunzio a hundred years from now. Nobody will read Futurist Marinetti, who's all style and blather and tells folks where to go and they go, leaving their friends behind. You're an apostate, Sean Reilly. Let's get one drink before we go shagging."

The evening breeze swept a damp chill through the streets of the quarter, bathing them in salty Adriatic air. Shouts and laughter from the tavern drifted into the street. A woman leaned out of a window above them and shouted for quiet. Sean tried again to rouse James to his feet, without success.

"Marinetti wants you to go to Fiume, and you don't want to go, do you?" James's head was tilted downward slightly, lips crooked and eyes opened wide behind the thick lenses of his black-rimmed spectacles. He could be a smug little bastard at times, Sean thought, this being one of those occasions. "The Holy Bishop of Futurism wants a missionary for his Futurist church. But Sean Reilly is a bloody parish priest. Father Sean prefers to worship with the already converted." He leaned over and spat again into the street. "The future. What blather. It won't be any different. We're all the same bloody yahoos we were before the war, and we will be the same tomorrow, no matter if we live in Trieste or go running off to Fiume. Take Ireland, for instance. Are you *au courant* about the land of your ancestors?"

Sean did not want to hear yet again about Dublin and its feuds and Parnell and all the chumps who had their heads up their arses and couldn't manage to keep their eyes on the real problems before they started accusing each other of terrible treacheries. Probably all true but beside the point. "Spare me tonight, will you?"

"Ireland eats its own young, you see," James said. "And Dublin's worst of all. Every one of those buggers will tell you a bright new day is coming if only the rest of the dumb fucks would follow him. They're all headed off a cliff. Trust me, in a year, you won't—"

"What I fear most is spending another year in Trieste listening to you whine about Dublin." *And not being able to paint.* Sean stood up. This wasn't a talk he wanted to have on his last night in Trieste. *I want to go to Fiume. Even with all the soldiers there.* "Now get up, damn you. Paradise awaits me, and it won't wait all night."

James rose unsteadily to his feet. "Your expectations are too high, my friend. Mutton dressed as lamb." His eyes narrowed. "You're not a priest, Sean Reilly. More like an altar boy. But you've a mind made up." He started to sing:

> The harlot's cry from street to street
> Shall weave Old Ireland's winding-sheet.

He sighed and made the sign of the cross with his right hand. "Paradise looms like death, Sean, and draws us near."

The two resumed working their way uphill, skirting drunks occupying choice spots on the sidewalk. "Weep not for me, you daughters of Trieste," James said as they passed another of his favored whorehouses, voice laced with melancholy. "But tell me, Sean. Why is Marinetti making you walk all that long way to meet him at the train station, instead of at your apartment?"

Good question, but not the right one. The real question was why Marinetti chose him in the first place to go to Fiume. *Sean Reilly, a man who wants desperately to become a great painter but can't paint worth a shit anymore.* A man who brought disgrace to Futurism in a single tragic day during the war. He let James's question linger in the air untouched.

"An altar boy is what you are," James said. "Not even a priest."

An altar boy. Who sends an altar boy to a city teeming with soldiers? Sean felt his gut tightening. "*Et cum spiritu tuo,*" he said, and pushed James up the hill. Only one thing could silence these questions, and it wasn't drink or stories about Dublin.

FIᴗE

October 18, 1919. Still on the boat. This voyage feels like it will never end. The waves are getting worse. I just threw up for the second time.

At least I'm out of Trieste. Who could paint like a Futurist in a city like that? Marinetti was right. It is a hovel of tradition.

Yesterday, before I got the letter, I tried to paint. The day began with sunlight and ambition like all the other mornings. I stared at the canvas on my easel, brush in hand. How else does one become a great painter? When I tired of waiting, I slashed a few wild streaks of blue paint on the white surface, stopped, and looked at what I did. And groaned. Memories of the war tumbled through my head, along with thoughts of Paris and Milan, jokes, faces of people I dreaded seeing again, fantasies, old art lessons, things I should have said in arguments over things that weren't worth arguing about, embarrassing things I did say. I got up, shuffled to the back window of the apartment, and peered out at the squalid courtyard. I started over, red this time instead of blue. Four or five streaks and mix in green. "Your art is crap," I shouted to the walls, venting my worst fears. "It will never get any better."

After mutilating the canvas, I stood up and pounded my fist against the wall, not stopping when the neighbors pounded back, not letting up until blood dripped onto the floor. Then I laid back down in my bed, hoping to sleep until it was time to meet up with James. It was so different before the war. Sure, there were times back then I felt blocked, but they would pass. I used to believe in the future, the power of machines and speed. That old optimism seems pretty remote now.

My rest was disturbed by a dirty little boy who couldn't have been more than ten. He handed me Marinetti's letter and held his dirty little hand out for a tip. I grabbed the letter and slammed the door in his face.

Trieste had done that to me. Perhaps Fiume can provide a fix.

SIX

From INTERVIEW WITH DUŠAN KCLEŽA (1992)
[UNEDITED TRANSCRIPT]

Hello, everyone. My name is Jakov Horvat, and I am the assistant director of the Oral History Division of the Croatian State Archives. I'm here today in the small port city of Rijeka, a jewel on the Adriatic between Dalmatia and the Istrian peninsula, which some may remember by its old Italian name, Fiume.

With me this afternoon, as we proudly celebrate Croatia's international diplomatic recognition as an independent nation, is one of the city's most honored sons, Dušan Kcleža. Mr. Kcleža is best known today as one of the fearless Partisans who fought with Marshal Tito against the German and Italian Fascists in World War II. But not many remember that he was a warrior two decades earlier when still in his teens.

Back in 1919, the eyes of the world were focused on this city. In those chaotic days after World War I, Gabriele D'Annunzio, the notorious Italian poet and demagogue, marched in with a ragtag troop of unemployed veterans and army deserters and illegally occupied the city from 10 September 1919 until 6 January 1921. Mr. Kcleža played a major role in the resistance to this occupation and has agreed to share his story with us.

Mr. Kcleža, thank you so much for agreeing to sit for this interview. It is a privilege to hear about the Rijeka struggle from a hero who began his fighting here.

DK: I'm happy to be here. I wasn't sure I would live long enough to see this day when we can celebrate Croatia's independence. Call me Dušan, please.

JH: Certainly, Dušan. You have lived through so much, the entire twentieth century almost, and seen so much bitter action. But you always fought back. What has kept you going?

DK: I fight for my people, for Croatia, for our thousand-year-old dream of independence. Italians, Germans, and Serbs, one after the other, they occupied our land. Exploited us, stole from us, and mistreated our people. Fighting them made us all stronger and brought us together, closer as a people.

And let's remember we're not finished fighting yet, even today. Serb soldiers continue to violate our Croatian land. They killed nine more this past week in the Krajina territory. That will not stand. Like I said to President Tudman at breakfast last week, I'm ninety-two years old, but I'll pick up a gun again if I have to. This country belongs to us. All of it.

JH: We are fortunate to have men like you defending our nation. Let me go back, if I may, to your early days in Fiume. You grew up in the Old Town section of Fiume, correct?

DK: That's right. Two blocks north of the Corso. It was an old building. My father had his first restaurant on the ground floor, and we lived in an apartment on the floor above. My brother, Veselko, and I shared a tiny room.

JH: Can you speak about what life was like in Fiume before D'Annunzio and his mob invaded?

DK: I'll tell you what it was like. I went to schools where only Italian was spoken. Think about it. I couldn't read or say anything in class in my own language. All the Fiume schools were like that. The newspapers and magazines, too. Anything Slavic was confiscated and burned. If you put a picture of any Croatian hero in your window, the window got broken. Everywhere you looked, you saw these hateful slogans and phrases. Somebody painted on the side of the Capuchin

Church, "Croatian Imperial and Royal Whorehouse." Right on the church. They would do anything to degrade us. They were trying to put us in our place. And we hated them. You bet we hated them.

JH: It sounds like you had a hard time.

DK: Nothing was ever easy back in those days. The Italians controlled the police and the municipal government, even back in the days when we had a Hungarian governor. Fiume was part of the Empire before the Great War. A young fellow like yourself, you probably don't even know about the Austro-Hungarian Empire.

JH: Not as much as I probably should. If you could point to one thing that turned you into a resistance fighter, what would it be?

DK: After I got expelled from high school, for the second time, actually, I went to work at my father's restaurant. Every night, it seemed, another incident happened somewhere on the Corso.

Roving bands of young thugs took over the streets, you see? They were members of this gang which they pretended was a gymnastic club for young men. They didn't even pretend very well. The club gave them rifles and grenades. Did you ever hear about gymnasts with weapons? These guys made a lot of noise about annexing the city to Italy. If they saw you on the street, you had better run for it if you were a Croat. The police protected them and let them do whatever they wanted against us Croats.

One night they came to my father's restaurant—ten or fifteen of them. The minute they entered, I knew there would be trouble. I could hardly breathe. Does that make sense? These thugs burst in, chanting "Italia o morte!" and positioned themselves around the dining room. They started singing the Italian national anthem and made all the patrons stand up and sing. As soon as it was over and people sat down, it started over again. They dared people not to join in. The customers were amused at first, and then some got irritated, even the Italian ones. When they stopped singing, it got worse. They wandered around, picking on Croatians, anybody not wearing those stupid Italian colors. One guy picked up a lady's plate, spat on the food, and then handed it back to her. Another poured a man's wine right on his meal, and then turned the plate upside down, all over the table. Fucking animals. They got in people's faces. This one ugly brute, he leaned over an old man, his face right next to the old guy's, and started talking gibberish, like he was imitating our language but with made-up words and sounds. Like we were the barbarians. It was sickening.

JH: You must have felt awful. The indignity of all that.

DK: You said the right word. It was a crime against our dignity. They didn't see us as human beings who deserved any respect. I kept telling myself this cannot be happening. Even after all the other things I had seen, you know, stuff in school and on the streets, the newspapers and all. My hands gripped the tray I was carrying so hard I thought I might break it. My ears were pounding. You know how that happens when you get so mad? Well, mine pounded like somebody was playing drums in my head. My teeth were grinding so hard my jaw started to hurt.

JH: Did you recognize any of these hooligans?

DK: Yeah. I knew a few of them from the Italian school I had gone to. They didn't recognize me, thank goodness, or at least they didn't say anything if they did. I stood over by my father and begged him to do something, say something, confront these thugs. The old man refused. He submitted to the Italian rabble like older Croats had been doing in Fiume for forty years. He said he would take care of it his way. Finally, the thugs left, promising to return the next evening.

JH: Did they come back?

DK: I didn't wait to see. I quit that night.

SEVEN

October 18, 1919

With Trieste and James left behind, Sean tottered to the front of the boat, clutching the rail. Currents pitched the small vessel in all directions, even sideways. Closing his eyes made things worse. His legs buckled and his feet slid on the deck, much to the loud amusement of the crew. He found a small place to sit and write in his journal.

The boat reached the Fiume harbor just as he was about to get sick for the third time. It docked in between two Italian warships.

Renzo greeted him on the quay. A trim man slightly taller than Sean, he had dark eyes shadowed by the visor of a kepi cap and a coal-black pencil mustache at odds with his welcoming smile. Dressed in the crisp gray-green tunic, white shirt, and black necktie of an Arditi officer, and with a long dagger fixed to his belt, he might have stepped out of a recruiting poster.

"Welcome to Fiume, my friend," Renzo said after they embraced. "I received word only yesterday you were coming. I couldn't believe it."

Sean gazed at the piazza, where a bustling festival was in progress. Women in loose flapper-like outfits—necklines cut low at the top and more than a little leg showing at the bottom—danced with civilians in tweed jackets and legionnaires in uniform. The legionnaires, Sean noted, were adorned with badges, medals, scarves, feathers, and even flowers, their daggers proudly displayed. "I didn't expect you to throw a party for me," he said. "What's all this? Did they just now learn the war ended?"

Renzo slapped him on the back and unleashed a long laugh. "This is nothing. In a few hours, the festival will get wild. Much like your St. Patrick's Day, Tom tells me."

"They take St. Patrick's Day more seriously where Tom's from. Where is he?"

"You can find him there in the piazza, chasing after the local lovelies. Fiume women love soldiers. They love artists, too, as you will soon learn. Ah, excuse me for a minute. I see a young lady who requires my attention. You must room at the barracks until you find a place. My driver will take your bags."

Freed of his suitcase and duffle bag, Sean stood at the edge of the festivities and drank in the scene in the piazza. Men and women danced everywhere, in the street and on the narrow abutting sidewalks and shaded patios on either side, swaying, embracing, and laughing, many with a drink in hand. In one not quite concealed recess, he spotted a man grinding away on a woman whose dress was hiked above her waist.

Banners stretched above the dancers' heads, tied to the hotels and office buildings on either side of the piazza. Colored lanterns hung suspended from balconies. Music came from somewhere he couldn't see, cresting over the cacophony of shouts and laughter. People sang, badly and with passion. They swirled around and around in untamed revelry, free of rules or decorum. Sean was entranced. Shadows darted in all directions, split by the lanterns and the afternoon sun into multiple sparring phantoms, making up in violent motion what they lacked in substance. He thought of all the Futurist paintings that tried to capture the magic of speed and motion with blurs and force lines and superimposed images. Here in Fiume, real Futurist dynamism took on flesh and blood in front of him on this sunny festival afternoon.

Sean spotted a large white building halfway up the hill beyond the piazza. In contrast to the crowd around him, the structure seemed firmly rooted in space and time, glowering downhill like a disapproving grandfather. Those dancing paid it no mind.

Sean found a small gap in the swarm of gyrating bodies and went searching for Tom. Around him, dancers waved their arms and kicked out their legs and bumped into one another without taking notice. It seemed the gods of dance had taken possession of human bodies.

Not all of those gods were in a pleasant mood. A man in a soiled gray tunic staggered backward in Sean's direction, waving a bottle over his head. Drops of wine flew from the bottle and landed on revelers around him, none of whom appeared to mind. Sean veered to avoid the man, but they both moved in the same direction and collided. The bottle dropped from his hand and shattered on impact with the street. "My wine," the man cried. His head whirled around, bloodshot eyes darting in every direction before he spotted Sean. "Look what you did, you piece of shit."

"It wasn't my fault," Sean said. "You should watch where you're going."

"American!" the man roared. Dancers surrounding them stopped and crowded around. "Americans are pigs," the man said. "Worse than the French. I killed a French pig, do you know? I found him hiding in a whorehouse. Where have you been hiding?"

The man unsheathed a dagger from his belt and waved it like a flag. The blade was dull and dirty, much like its owner. Sean glanced left and right, searching for some escape, but the onlookers were packed together tightly, jeering like spectators in the Colosseum and locking him in. The man stepped forward and put the dagger to Sean's cheek. Despite having no desire to be a gladiator, Sean slapped the man's hand away. It was instinct more than anything, like swatting a bee. The man stumbled and fell. The dagger landed a few feet away. For a few seconds, the man lay still, perhaps trying to understand how he got to that position. Then, scrambling to his feet, he collected the dagger. "You will pay for that," the man said and moved straight toward him. Sean swung wildly, eyes shut, hitting nothing but air. Then he heard a scream.

When he opened his eyes, the attacker stood close by with his arm twisted behind his back. The dagger fell from his hand. A short, stocky man caught the dagger before it hit the ground and stepped out from behind the attacker. "Trouble, Sean?"

"Tom?" Sean said. "Oh, thank God."

"My arm," the attacker cried. "Ahhhh!" He gasped for breath. "Help me," he pleaded to the crowd. No one moved.

"No," Tom said. "They ain't gonna help you. Unlike you, I know how to use a knife. You don't hold the dagger like this." Tom imitated the attacker's grip. "That's the way you hold your dick." Tom tossed the dagger up and caught it in midair. "See? My thumb's up near the blade."

"There you are, Sean," Renzo said, pushing his way through the circle of onlookers. "Ah, I see you found Tom."

Tom twisted the attacker's arm higher. "Say hello to the lieutenant," he ordered.

"Please sir," the man said to Renzo. "These Americans attacked me. They are enemies of Italy. They spit on our flag."

"Oh, let the fool go," Renzo said. Tom released him, aiming a kick at the man's behind as he ran off. Sean was mildly disappointed he didn't get a chance to punch the man a few times while Tom held him. In the company of Tom and Renzo, Sean felt a lot braver.

"Don't tell me," Renzo said. "I don't even want to know."

"Where are these pretend soldiers coming from?" Tom asked. "Can't fight worth a shit. Even Sean could've handled this one."

Before he could take proper offense to this slight, a woman with a camera and a seductive British accent called out, "Hello. Can I take a photo of you American cowboys?"

EIGHT

From SEAN REILLY'S JOURNAL

October 18, 1919. That goddamn boat ride. My head is killing me (maybe the wine has something to do with that) and the dizziness hasn't completely gone away. The sea always disagrees with me. Marinetti used to sing its glory in his poetry days. The "mother of revolutions," he called the sea. An odd metaphor, to my way of thinking. The sea is cold, dark, deep, and violent but hardly revolutionary. Nothing good comes from the sea except food one can eat sitting on dry land.

It was great seeing Tom and Renzo today. Of all the wounded I carried in my ambulance, these two were special. True friends.

The festival surprised me. Apart from a little altercation, it was grand. I enjoyed myself for several hours, dancing and drinking. Then Renzo brought me to the barracks and made introductions. The other legionnaires greeted Renzo with serious respect, I noticed. More like awe.

The men who came by the train from Trieste filtered in while I was getting settled. Everyone seemed in a good mood. One of them recognized me from my ambulance days. "You're the American who drove crazy fast and never wore a uniform," he said. Lots of laughter. Good fun. They passed around bottles of grappa and cigarettes, and we all told stories and lies. Maybe I can interest them in the future.

NINE

From *Memories of a Fascist in Fiume*
by Tenente Lorenzo Guidici

Much has been written about the march from Ronchi and our liberation of Fiume from the foreign armies that had occupied it. I see no reason to repeat the details here. Suffice it to say, we entered the city and took control. That was the easy part. For the next sixteen months, we faced the more difficult task of defending it.

Fascism, then in its early days, attracted men for different reasons. Some like me wanted to purge our enemies and build a new, stronger Italy. Others sought power or wealth or wanted to settle old scores. Some just liked excitement and violence. To build our movement, the Duce found a place for all of these.

Squadrismo had proved an enormously successful tactic in both the cities and rural areas of the mainland, at its best when truckloads of men armed with guns and clubs raced into an area and over-whelmed the local Socialists and strikers. As I said, it was a difficult time, and our homeland needed Fascists to defend it, tough men for a tough job. Fiume, too, needed tough men.

While I was delighted to see my friend Sean Reilly once again, other matters demanded my attention. I became aware of a theft problem around the barracks. Petty things at first, but the larceny soon grew more serious. Our trucks were parked in a dirt field on the north side. After the second one was stolen, a guard was posted. When the third one disappeared—the guard had no explanation and lied that he had been awake for his entire watch—I took charge of security. I had the trucks repositioned so that exit from the field could only proceed through one narrow lane, and I blocked that lane by disabling the lead truck.

That night I caught the thief trying to start it.

"Looking for this?" I demanded. The man was forced to his knees, arms pinned by two burly legionnaires. He wore a filthy soldier's tunic that was far too large for his lanky frame. All of the regimental patches had been ripped off, leaving ragged holes. I waved the truck's magneto in the man's face.

The thief twisted his head to the side and said nothing. One of the legionnaires slapped him on the back of the head.

"That's enough," I said. "Take him to the police. Tell the sergeant I'll be over in the morning with details for the charge."

The thief grunted and spit. "I'm not going to that fucking jail," he said. The legionnaire hit him again.

I watched the man's rapid breathing. He reminded me of a Rottweiler, a skinny, hungry one, waiting for an opportunity to run away or, more likely, attack. A man like that, if harnessed and properly trained, could be useful but left on his own was dangerous. I instructed the legionnaires to tie the thief's hands and then dismissed them, saying I'd changed my mind and would take the prisoner to the jail myself.

Once the legionnaires were gone, I marched the thief to a small alley on the eastern edge of the parking field. "Don't try anything," I said. "If you run, I'll shoot you and then finish you off with the dagger." We reached a spot behind an abandoned building, where I ordered him to halt.

"You don't want to go to jail. Why not? You must have been in many jails, from the looks of you."

The thief said nothing. He squinted up at the sky.

I rested a hand on the grip of my dagger. This thief was a perfect example of the worst part of Italian society, lacking in rudimentary elements of discipline and honor, not to mention cleanliness. I decided to make something of him, something worthwhile and productive. "You're not going to jail. I'm going to ask you a few questions. If I don't get the right answers, you'll wish you were in jail. Now tell me, what else have you been doing here besides stealing military trucks?"

The thief studied me. "I'm not going to jail?" He glanced at my hands and exhaled. "Stealing, mostly. Sometimes, me and a few others go out and knock people down, take what we can get. Croats, most of the time. The police don't care if it's just them we hit. But if you put me in jail with Croats, they'll kill me."

"Very likely. What else?"

"Once in a while, somebody gives us money to steal something they want or bust up a person they don't like."

"Who gives you money?"

"For one, this guy up at the big palace. Wickson, I think his name is. Slimy little shit, but he pays us in cash."

I lifted my dagger from its sheath and put it to the thief's throat. "Don't move," I said, my voice hard and low. "I want you to listen. From now on, you don't steal from the barracks or legionnaires or any Italians unless I tell you. Meet me here, right where we're standing, two days from now, at noon. I may have some work for you." I pulled the dagger back, holding it in front of the thief's eyes. "Do not fuck with me, understand? Now, get out of here."

"What about my hands? Cut the rope, eh?"

I took two steps away and wheeled around to face the thief. Training him, it was clear, would require considerable effort on my part. "I said to get out of here. I don't like to say things twice."

TEN

October 20, 1919

S ean rented an apartment in a cheerless building on Via Giuseppe Parini only a few blocks from the barracks where he had been staying. The building's façade featured a jumble of large square stones mixed with smaller ones the size of rocks. Sean guessed the builders ran out of good material and filled in with whatever they could find. The thin coat of stucco that once covered the hodgepodge was falling away in chips. Most of the ground floor was occupied by a grocery store. Signs on either side of its doors had been freshly painted but did little to dispel the shabbiness of the structure.

Inside, the apartment was small, but the light was decent, at least until midafternoon. He'd have to get started on his painting earlier in the day than he had in Trieste. It had a small kitchen area and a bathroom with a tub, the latter a legacy of the prior occupant, who owned the grocery store. Such luxury could not be found in any other lodging Sean could afford. The place suited his purposes. He didn't require a palace.

Soon after he moved in, Tom came to visit him. Sean had news to share. "When I was in Philadelphia after the armistice, I visited your sister, Gen. Nice lady. She had a baby last year. So you're an uncle. Here's a picture."

That earned Sean the reaction he hoped for. With eyes and mouth opened wide, Tom looked like a kid getting a new bicycle. "Baby's name is Rita," Sean said.

He let Tom ponder the picture and the good tidings for a moment, then apologized for not being able to offer him a drink to celebrate. That earned Sean a frown. "I guess you'll get the place stocked by tomorrow," Tom said, in a tone that sounded like an order. He glanced around. "This place is decent, though. Beats the barracks."

Tom had a large, moon-round head topped by thinning black hair. His face was lined and reddish from too much time in the sun. With his stubble beard and grease-marked jumpsuit, he was the opposite of Renzo in nearly every respect, at least in appearance. When Sean knew Tom during the war, he seemed always in a good mood, joking, playing practical jokes, losing at cards, drinking and telling stories about his days in Mexico, when he rode with Pancho Villa, and before that, when he fought under Black Jack Pershing in the Philippines. People said Tom smuggled rifles to the Irish Republican Brotherhood before their Easter uprising. Sean believed the stories.

"What have you been up to?" Tom asked. "Last I heard, you was pretty busted up. Those damn airplanes are dangerous. You'll never get me up in one of them."

"Says the man who engages in machine gun battles for a living," Sean said.

"Says the man who finds big rocks to hide behind when he shoots and keeps both feet on the ground. And I don't let nobody shoot at my back."

"You don't understand how much fun flying is, Uncle," Sean said. "I bet Rita will love it. But you're correct about me getting hurt. Right before the war ended, I finally got to fly an ambulance plane, and it crashed. When the plane flipped over, I figured I was a dead man. After I came to, I couldn't eat, couldn't shit right. My right leg hurts even today. After two miserable months in the hospital, I took a quick trip to Philly to see my parents. That's when I saw your sister. Then I came back to Italy, to Trieste, where I painted, got bored, and heard about Fiume. One nauseating boat ride later, here I am."

"And got into a fight within five minutes. At this rate, you won't get bored in Fiume. Why did you come here?"

It was Sean's turn to frown. He was getting tired of these questions about his motives. "I'm an artist these days. A Futurist painter. We believe Fiume is going to help forge a magnificent future."

He should have known better.

"Here?" Tom shook his head, his lips curled. Sean might as well have said he planned to build spaceships in Fiume and travel to the moon. "Just since we been here, the Torpedo Works and a bunch of other businesses closed down. Some poor jerk got the castor oil treatment last week near the garage where I work. They poured a whole bottle down his throat and watched him shit himself almost to death. He wasn't the first, neither. And a Croat business in the old section was torched the day before yesterday."

Marinetti hadn't said anything about violence in Fiume. Nor had the newspapers in Trieste made any mention. "What's going on?"

"I don't know the whole story. It goes way back, I hear. Renzo says the Hungarians ran the city for a long time, and they brought in people from Italy to piss off the Croats who lived here. Now that the war's over and the Hungarians are gone, the Italians outnumber the Croats and want the city to become part of Italy. The Croats are all upset. It's a mess. So tell me, what's your real reason for coming here?"

Sean fixed his eyes on the ribs of the steam radiator, which had begun to hiss. He told Tom he was working for a rich Italian who paid him to come here for reasons he couldn't divulge. Then he tried to change the subject. "Why did you come to Fiume?"

"Me? I'm a dope. My sister must've told you."

"Gen thinks the world of you. She did have a few tales, though."

"I guess she did. OK, I came here with D'Annunzio and Renzo and the rest of them. They reckoned there might be a big fight to take Fiume and then defend it. I'm a fighter who can handle a machine gun, so they called me."

"You're a fighter."

"Yeah. That's one way to put it."

"You're a lot more than a fighter."

"No, I'm not. Not much good at anything else. I tried other stuff before the war."

"You tried other stuff. Like what?"

"Stuff. Like driving a taxi, for instance. I got a little crazy."

"Don't you want to accomplish something grander? Like making the world a better place?"

"If I shoot enough bad guys, that should make the world better. I'll let smart guys like you point out who the bad ones are."

"That's it?"

"If I gotta be honest, I'm not exactly welcome in a lot of places. Long story. But you didn't answer my question. Why come here, and am I gonna have to keep taking knives away from drunks you piss off?"

"I hope not, but it's nice to know you're looking out for me."

It was soon time for Tom to get back to work. They walked out together and proceeded to the Corso. A dozen fez-wearing soldiers passed, their arms swinging smartly right to left. Tom gave them a sour look. "These guys love to march up and down the streets in front of everybody, like that makes them real soldiers. Then they go off in the woods and wander around naked. They eat berries and climb trees, for Chrissake. A bunch of them dress like women."

Tom, the unconventional soldier, had fixed ideas of how soldiers should conduct themselves. Sean had similar ideas during the war about his fellow ambulance drivers. Even though he refused to wear the uniform, he had found fault with those drivers whose hygiene and commitment did not measure up to his standards.

Afternoon shadows fell on Tom and Sean as they waded through the shoppers filing in and out of the Corso's clothiers, hatters, stationers, booksellers, apothecaries, *patisseries*, and tobacco shops. Loud conversations and passionate arguments spilled out from café patios in Italian, Hungarian, Croatian, French, and English. Tom halted midway in front of a tall, yellow tower whose four sides were each adorned by a large white clock face. On the side facing the Corso, the city's coat of arms had been sculpted in high relief. Two legionnaires and a young woman passed them. The woman, in the middle, had her arms wrapped around an elbow of each man. One of the men said something, and all three laughed. The woman pulled out her arm, slapped the man in the face, then took his elbow again, all without missing a step.

"My garage is down that street," Tom said, pointing south. "Renzo says he's gonna take us to this good restaurant, and he'll invite that lady photographer, too. Yeah, I seen the way you looked at her. She's been here in Fiume for a couple of weeks and takes lots of pictures. Maybe she can get you to spill the real reason you came here. Because how I see things, the future will need more machine guns than paintbrushes."

ELEVEN

October 20, 1919. Why are my motives for coming to Fiume so fascinating to other people? First James and now Tom. I don't want to keep explaining myself. I'm here, all right? I want to paint. I saw things in the war and now I want to help make a better future so I don't have to think about them anymore. Seems simple enough to me. Tom wouldn't understand, though. Not that he is dumb. Anyone, especially an American, who survived fighting with Pancho Villa and later with the Arditi, has to be plenty smart. Or exceptionally lucky. Having seen Tom play cards, I know luck rarely favors him. But Tom's clever survival skills would not help him appreciate what a painter needs.

In my case, I need Futurism if I am to become a great painter. Other art seems lifeless and boring.

I don't know quite what to make of Tom's comments about the city. He seemed to have a harsh view of what goes on here. Italians and Slavs not getting along? Nothing new. If it is so bad, why has he stayed? I didn't ask. I am determined to form my own judgments about the place.

Marinetti once drove his car into a ditch and bragged about it in *Le Figaro.* The article started an international art movement. When I was in high school, I drove a car halfway up a tree and put another one in the Schuylkill River. My father spent a fortune to keep my peccadillos out of the newspapers. Even so, he couldn't keep me from becoming a Futurist, and neither will Tom or James.

TWELVE

From INTERVIEW WITH DUŠAN KCLEŽA (1992)
[UNEDITED TRANSCRIPT]

JH: What effect did D'Annunzio's occupation have on the city?

DK: You're shitting me, right? What do you think? It made things worse. The Rome government put up a blockade around the city because D'Annunzio was an embarrassment to them. It wasn't a very good blockade, but even so, it killed off most of the industry in Fiume. The city lost businesses and jobs. Most never came back, even after all these years.

But somehow the blockade managed to let in a bunch of drunks, drug addicts, and criminals. They roamed the city, sang muddle-brained tributes to the Italian homeland, and beat up people.

JH: Didn't the police do anything to stop the beatings?

DK: Ha. They wouldn't lift a finger to help Croats. They were busy harassing us. I'll give you an example. A friend of mine, a young man I grew up with, he was out for a walk with some buddies by the canal and said something about how Fiume was Croatian, not Italian. Which anybody with a brain knew was true. Anyway, two big Italian policemen ran over and grabbed the boy and started punching him in the face, right there on the street. They took him to the police station and kept him there for two days. He had bruises all over him when he got out. True story. And it happened to a lot more people. If you said anything or if you got attacked and tried to fight back, you either got beaten or put in jail or deported. Sometimes all three.

That's the way Italian justice worked in Fiume. It pisses me off even now when I remember those days. It didn't stop, even after D'Annunzio left, until the end of the Second World War. After that, we had to make the Italians all leave so we could finally have peace.

JH: Why all this disrespect?

DK: I never spent much time talking to them, but if you ask me, they were jealous of us Croatians. We have a long history of culture and civilization. Italians hadn't had anything to speak of since Michelangelo. Their idea of culture in 1919 was D'Annunzio, who wrote filthy trash and acted like a clown. Italy was a backward, miserable country, full of illiterate peasants, oppressed factory workers, and crooks. Lots of poverty and crime and such. Yet they behaved like they were superior. Always bragging about ancient Rome and Venice.

JH: And Vittorio Veneto.

DK: Oh yeah, the glorious battle where brave Italian troops routed the Austrian army. They forget to mention that Austria was in the process of surrendering before the battle started. How glorious was it to shoot men who had already laid down their guns and were trying to go home?

JH: How did it make you feel, with D'Annunzio set up in the Governor's Palace and his legions rampaging all over the city?

DK: You are shitting me, aren't you? Yeah. I hated it. They were like that mob at the restaurant, only a lot more of them, and better armed. I knew even then I had to do something.

JH: What did you do?

DK: I went looking for guns.

THIRTEEN

1910–1915

As an only child, Sean understood that expectations for him were high. His father was a successful businessman, remarkable in Philadelphia for an Irish immigrant in the closing years of the nineteenth century, and he moved the family from their Fishtown tenement to a posh Center City townhouse. People told Sean repeatedly that he was exceptional. But being neither studious nor particularly athletic, he had difficulty finding the right thing to be exceptional at.

His teenage years were filled with opportunities available through wealth. He owned a car—several of them, in fact—and raced up Chestnut Street past the Gas Works and across the Schuylkill River, or out in Fairmount Park on dirt near the reservoir. Nothing could match the thrill of a fast automobile until he discovered airplanes. After persistent badgering, his terrified parents reluctantly paid for flying lessons.

They were both gratified and relieved when Sean showed an interest in art. With his customary enthusiasm, he threw himself into painting. Art classes were arranged and private tutors engaged. His technique improved. Some observers, perhaps currying favor with his father, called him a prodigy. His parents enrolled him at the Pennsylvania Academy of Fine Arts, whose alumni included Mary Cassatt and Thomas Eakins.

Mary Cassatt stopped by the Academy on one of her rare trips outside Paris, and before leaving Philadelphia she passed wordlessly through the cavernous open room where students labored to capture an image of lilacs arranged in a tall glass vase. Sweeping past row after row, she made no comments. Her footsteps gained speed, the swift pace suggesting a hurry to catch the afternoon train to New York and board the next ship to France. She stopped behind Sean. He had been struggling for hours with the light on the petals and was too intimidated to turn around. A wrinkled hand reached over his shoulder, pointing a finger at a smeared spot on the canvas. After a short grunt, she moved on.

What to make of that bony finger and that sound? Sean knew immediately. He had been singled out, although not in so many words. No words at all, admittedly. It was his first public recognition, and more were bound to follow. From that day forward, his devotion to painting soared. He dug out and read the art history texts he had previously ignored. He made regular pilgrimages to the art gallery in Memorial Hall and took the train to New York to visit its museums and galleries. He began to feel a connection to the great painters, with a special affinity for those bold ones who broke new ground. The Impressionists became his heroes. Hadn't Mary Cassatt herself achieved her breakthrough after joining them? Degas had befriended her, and soon after, she received the recognition she deserved. The great ones knew greatness, spotted it quickly and decisively.

Sean dreamed of having a studio in Paris, where he could mingle with other great artists who would drop by to offer words of encouragement or to seek advice. He grew impatient with his classes at the Academy. Mary Cassatt had anointed him. Paris was where he needed to go to realize his ambition, his destiny.

Sending their only son across the Atlantic to study art was not what his loving parents had in mind for him, but reluctantly they gave in, hoping that, even if Paris didn't advance Sean in the business career they planned for him, at least it might keep him out of airplanes. They agreed to finance his studies abroad. In Paris, Sean found an art instructor, and then another. He went through several more before he figured out the problem. These instructors did not see his great potential, because they lacked greatness themselves. Of course. Cassatt saw instantly how gifted he was. He needed to associate with artists of her stature.

Sean made discrete inquiries and waited for replies. He painted day and night. One of his works was chosen for the Salon of 1911, confirming for Sean his ascension into the ranks of great artists. Except, it hadn't. After the Salon, nothing. No invitations were forthcoming from the artists to whom he addressed letters. No dealers or customers sought his paintings or commissioned new ones. He was compelled to look critically at the works he had created. Landscapes and nudes and bowls of fruit and flowers in vases. Faultless, but why did modernity, that lifeblood of the new century, not reveal itself in his painting? Where was the energy of automobiles and airplanes?

Cubism interested him briefly, but that style merely broke things down and reassembled them in static form. Modern, yes, but lifeless. What did it matter if the fruit bowl were broken into pieces? It was still a bowl, and who cared? Besides, Cubists had made rude comments about his piece at the Salon and snubbed him in the cafés.

Then Filippo Marinetti led a coterie of Futurist painters to Paris for their 1912 show at the Galerie Bernheim-Jeune. Sean was dumbstruck. He attended the show each night, captivated by Marinetti's grandiloquence and by the works of Boccioni, Severini, Carrà, and the others. Strong, garish colors suggested raw states of anguish and excitement and anger. These Futurists shared Sean's infatuation with new technology and powerful machines and, most of all, speed. Marinetti railed against tradition and worship of the past. He was loud, rude, arrogant, vulgar, passionate, bombastic, furious, and thrilling. Sean loved it. Art connecting to life. Life exploding with potential and electricity and violence. Exactly what he longed for and what he needed to become a great painter.

"From where does art derive its *vitalité*, its *ardeur*?" Marinetti demanded. "Only from its surrounding environment. Not from academies. Destroy those swamps! Banish your banal landscapes and nudes. Originality is what we seek, however daring, however violent." He seemed to enjoy the shocked looks in his audience. "The miracles of contemporary life quicken our pulses, unleash our spirit. We worship the beauty of those marvelous machines whose flights furrow the skies and those mighty vessels that tame the oceans. Their fumes fuel our art. We inhale the frenetic life of our great cities, from their smoking factories to the streets full of belching automobiles." It sounded like sweet music to Sean.

Boccioni moved over to one of his works and picked up where Marinetti left off. "Our paintings center the viewer in our art. Here is an example. I call it *The Street Enters the House.* The woman on the balcony looks out from inside the room. But we see so much more than what she can see from her window. I show everything she experiences, all her sensations. What she sees and hears and what she remembers. The balcony rail, the multitude assembled in the street, rows of houses in the distance, and those right beside her, dismembered and scattered and then fused. Sounds of men working, disturbing her peace. Neighbors shouting. Life. Not vapid water lilies. Futurist originality captures life, the synchronousness of elements in her mind. This reveals the intoxicating telos of my art." Sean drank the telos each night and became thoroughly intoxicated.

On the last evening of the exhibition, an obnoxious visitor shouted that the Futurist works were simply watered-down Cubism, compensating for lack of competent technique with an excess of grotesque colors. He and Sean traded insults and began shoving each other, knocking over a refreshment table in the process. When they were separated, Marinetti took Sean aside and invited him to continue his art studies in Milan with the Futurists.

Sean moved to Milan and began his next step toward greatness. Marinetti gave him a place to stay and paint in. He took Sean to Venice with the other artists, where they climbed to the top of St. Marks and shouted out rhetoric and insults to churchgoers below exiting Mass.

He participated in the Futurist Evenings, events that mixed talk, art display, and riot, held throughout Italy. And he painted under the critical eyes of Marinetti and the artists. Progress came painfully. He had to learn new concepts, like how vibration and motion endlessly multiply each object. "*Scemo!*" Boccioni yelled at him repeatedly. "*Idiota.* Do you not see? A running horse has twenty legs, not four." Sean studied examples of dynamic sensation and divisionism. He drew force lines of objects to reveal their essences. He absorbed the constant criticism and painted. He was becoming a great painter, he could tell. Then came the Great War.

FOURTEEN

October 21, 1919. Men and women flooded the Corso this evening, full of excitement after the *Comandante*'s latest speech at the Governor's Palace. They swept past me on their way to the cafés and clubs on the Corso or onto side streets for the taverns and brothels and private parties. The more sober and better dressed headed to the Teatro Giuseppe Verdi to enjoy a production of *Francesca da Rimini.*

While I walked, I thought about my conversation the previous day with Tom. He had penetrated right to the heart of the matter. What would bring a Futurist painter, especially one who lost his sunny outlook about the future during three and a half years of the war, to a city during a quasi-military occupation opposed by the leaders of virtually every country in the world, including Italy? What I need is optimism, not adventure.

Fiume isn't a bad place to paint, I have to admit. Although I have only been here a few days, it seems rich with promise despite what Tom said. It reeks of stimulation and energy I haven't experienced since the early days of Futurism. That vision of the dancing I had on the day I arrived here was a breakthrough for me that I could not have imagined possible back in Trieste. Will it let me paint? I don't know yet. But I sense a spirit, a roar, an odor—I can't really say what—that struck me when I stood at the edge of Piazza Dante. If only I could get it down on canvas.

FIFTEEN

From *Memories of a Fascist in Fiume*
by Tenente Lorenzo Guidici

Two days after my encounter with the thief, I stood in the alley, waiting for his return. He showed up twenty minutes late and halted a few meters away. I closed the gap between us without greeting him and punched him in the kidney, dropping him to the ground. I kicked him onto his back and rested a boot on the man's chest. Harsh, but one must be harsh to tame a wild thief. What else would he respect? "You're late," I said. "Tell me your name."

He struggled to get up but halted at the sight of my pistol aimed at his head. "Fuck you," the thief said. "Let me up."

I moved my boot to the man's head and pointed the pistol at his crotch. "Luigi, isn't it? I don't care what your family name is or whether this is even your real Christian name. It's what I will call you, assuming we come to an understanding. And by that, I mean when I tell you to do something at a certain time, you do it, and you do it on time." I watched the man reach for the boot. "If you touch it, I will cut off your hands. Imagine trying to steal a truck without hands. Or even take a piss, for that matter."

The thief stopped struggling. "Yeah, I'm Luigi. What do you want?"

This was progress. Luigi had a wildness about him that I admired. It could be useful if properly directed. "I will ask the questions, Luigi. I won't ask many, but when I do, I expect answers without bullshit. Now, where have you been living? Not at the Hotel Europa, I'm guessing."

I followed him to an abandoned warehouse at the western edge of the quay, near the train yard. Inside I beheld a throng of thirty or more men, some of them little older than boys, dressed in rags, unwashed. The stench of stale urine hung over the building. In one corner were the remains of crates and old furniture consumed by a fire. In another, several would-be mechanics attempted to pry parts from a truck, one I recognized as having been stolen from the barracks. Elsewhere men were shouting, wrestling, and throwing things at each other. A few managed to climb up the walls and were hurling themselves onto old mattresses laid out on the floor.

Near their landing spot, a huge individual sat undisturbed, amusing himself by smashing an exhaust pipe from the truck with a hammer, flattening it inch by inch. A fight broke out a short distance to his right; he took no notice. The stone wall behind him was pitted with holes from grenades.

This is how men without discipline live. Worse than apes. They won't improve if left to themselves or coddled by liberal democracy. Men like this don't need the vote. They need to be ruled. And used.

"You must have had helpers when you roughed up your targets," I said. "I assume they are here. Bring them outside." I stepped out the door and waited. Luigi soon returned with three men. Like him, they were thin and filthy.

I made them all an offer. They would carry out my orders. In exchange, I would arrange for them a more comfortable place to live, a steady diet of proper targets to harass, and protection from the authorities in the event they were caught. If they chose not to accept, I would deliver them first to the legionnaires for stealing the trucks and then to the Croats. They quickly accepted.

You may wonder what purpose I might have in mind for such a motley group. The truth is that, as of that moment, I had no specific plans for them. I only knew that when I received my instructions from Mussolini, I would need the services of men loyal to me who would carry out the tasks I assigned them without qualm or question, regardless of the risk. In their current state, with no goals beyond their immediate gratification, they were just animals fighting for bigger servings of garbage. I intended to make them instruments for a higher purpose, for Fascism.

One piece was still missing. These four, while evidently capable of petty theft and occasional assaults, were likely to shrink away from certain actions that might be necessary. They needed someone to make them more fearsome. "Go get the big fellow, and bring him out here," I ordered.

Nobody moved. "We don't talk to him," said one of the four. He was coatless and shivering. "We give him food when we got it. Otherwise, we stay the fuck out of reach. I'll take my chances with the legionnaires and Croats before I cross him. One guy was bugging him, called him a *baggiano*. The big fellow took that fucking hammer and smashed every bone in the guy's body. Slowly, like he had all the time in the world and wanted to make sure he did it right. That was a week ago, I think, and I can still hear the screaming."

"I want to talk to him," I said. "What's his name?"

"Ugo," Luigi said. "Let me try."

SIXTEEN

1915–1917

Once Italy entered the Great War in 1915, most Futurists enlisted in the army. War was the cleansing hygiene of the world, according to the original Futurist Manifesto back in 1909. Marinetti made clear to Sean that his nationality did not excuse him from the duty to join in the cleansing. Sean went to the crowded enlistment station and followed the signs to the tent for volunteer ambulance drivers.

Ambulance driving had an appeal. Sean pictured himself behind the wheel of a truck racing furiously through all kinds of obstacles. After passing the brief but thoroughly invasive physical exam, he put his clothes back on and shuffled out to the sunbaked ground outside the tents, where the new ambulance drivers sat separated from the newly enlisted army privates. The latter amused themselves with loud expressions of their contempt for ambulance drivers in general and Sean in particular. He let it all pass. Pretending he couldn't understand Italian, he sat near the other drivers and smiled. They didn't smile back.

For three and a half years Sean drove a battlefield ambulance. He dodged shells from the enemy's big guns and the craters in the roads they caused. He drove at night with the car lights off, past makeshift grave sites that had received the dead only to be blown up again, the shells disturbing what was supposed to be a final resting place. Poison gas often forced him to don a mask; from the odor of rotting flesh and burning wood, however, there was no relief. When he finished his assigned runs, he cleaned blood and vomit out of the ambulance. Not infrequently he slept on one of the stretchers stored in it.

He had no time to miss painting. His job was to transport those who survived the butchery of battle. He carried them off, their screams audible above the ambulance engine's roar. However traumatic death might be, it was no match for dying.

He didn't fraternize with the other drivers, and he refused to wear the uniform offered to him. He followed orders, most of them anyway, and drove where he was told to go. Exasperated officers harassed him about his refusal to wear the uniform, but there was little they could do. He was a volunteer and by far the most fearless driver. Six months into the war, he came up with an idea to improve the evacuation of the injured. Modern technology had made the war more horrific. He saw a way it could be used to reduce suffering.

He was on leave in Milan when Captain Fabi sent for him. Sean waited an hour outside the captain's office before being ushered in. "You are not in uniform, I see," the captain said. "It seems the reports I heard about you are correct. You lack respect for the army."

"I'm not in the army," Sean said. "I'm a volunteer driver. Besides, I'm on leave."

The captain rose and leaned over the desk, his hands balled into fists that left dents on the layers of papers. He tilted a little to the left. War injury? That would explain why the captain was in Milan and not at the front. "I summoned you because of the noise you made at Udine," he said. "A lot of nonsense about flying an airplane. An 'ambulance plane.' Your superiors tell me you will not stop badgering them."

Badgering his superiors worked for Sean before. During the first three months after he signed up, he had only been allowed to ferry patients from one military hospital to another. A taxi driver, that's all they wanted him for, far from the front lines. Useful for propaganda, to show that America was supporting Italy's war effort even though it hadn't yet joined the war. But after much pleading, arguing, and, yes, badgering, along with a few veiled threats to leave Italy for France and join the American Ambulance Field Service, he prevailed. He was permitted to drive up to the dressing stations near the front, and the authorities ignored his insolence in not wearing their uniform.

"It isn't nonsense, Captain. Let me have one of the reconnaissance planes. Even an old, slow one. It could cut the time for getting wounded to the field hospitals by half, maybe two-thirds. Consider how many lives we could save."

The captain picked up a file from his desk, gripped it tightly for a few seconds, and then threw it down, sending several papers fluttering to the floor. "Here's what I will consider. We have enough injured and dead already. We don't need to kill more off by putting them in those damn airplanes." He sat down. Streams of sunlight creased the whiteness of the captain's face and highlighted the baggy folds under his eyes. "I'm beginning to think I made a mistake allowing an American to drive so close to the front. Americans are sure they know everything. You feel compelled to share your wisdom with those of us who have been doing the actual fighting and dying in a war your country has not seen fit to join."

Sean knew the interview with the captain was about over. He had one last card to play. "Two weeks ago, I carried a senior officer, a major, in my ambulance. I told them at the clearing station when I loaded him in the ambulance that the major would never make it to Udine. A three-hour drive, minimum, in all the mud. I'm no doctor, but I knew he wouldn't make it. I asked for a plane to fly him out. One was right there. I could see it from the window. If they had let me, I could have used the plane and got him to Udine or even Milan and brought the plane back in less than two hours. It might have saved his life. But they said no. So three hours later I delivered a corpse to Udine."

"Major Longo."

"Yes. Did you know him?"

The captain bent over to pick up one of the papers from the floor. A short gasp escaped him. His face was red. "I knew him. What you ask is impossible. We cannot allow people to take joy rides over a war sector while battles are being fought on the ground. This is a warning to you. Stop the agitation and do the tasks assigned to you. I will see if I can get you a faster ambulance. Although from what they tell me, your driving already scares the men worse than Austrian artillery. You are dismissed."

Sean fumed for the rest of his leave. The captain was wrong, the whole army was shortsighted, and men died needlessly because their leaders, safe in offices far behind the lines, could not see like a Futurist. The airplane was the future of war and medical care, too. Planes could fly over the battlefields, over roads covered with mud or ice or clogged with dead horses and overturned lorries, over terrified civilian refugees with their carts full of whatever few belongings they could salvage, over blood and stench and shit and vomit, over pig-headed officers and compliant peasant soldiers who followed orders and ran straight into machine gun fury, over earth blasted by artillery shells until nothing could ever grow or be built there again, over every manifestation of man's stupidity and desecration.

But no, the army clung as ferociously to the procedures and protocols of the past as it did to the uniform even though the war proved over and over that following the past without learning its lessons led to disaster. War might not be the hygiene of the world Marinetti envisioned, Sean lamented, but it did a superb job of highlighting the tragic consequences of the army's old rules.

SEVENTEEN

From SEAN REILLY'S JOURNAL

October 26, 1919. I have devoted myself to painting since I landed in Fiume. The apartment yields four hours of decent natural light, starting in late morning when I finally get out of bed. Regrettably, the painting problems I experienced in Trieste have followed me here. I am not surprised. It wasn't only the Fiume sun that I needed, of course. Something is missing. The canvas doesn't lie.

The future, the future. What kind of future can come out of a world war?

One day, late in the war, I was sitting in the garden of a little cottage that had been blown to bits by one side or the other. A bench was set against a bed of purple and yellow primroses that had somehow survived, and from there I had a clear view of the dirt road that led to the front. A pair of trucks rolled past, filled with soldiers. They looked tired to me although, at that distance, I couldn't be certain. They were quiet, at any rate. The trucks stirred up a whole cloud of dirt that lingered for some minutes after they passed. For reasons I still don't completely understand, the sight bothered me more than anything, more than the dead and wounded I had to touch every day. These men were quiet and maybe tired, and soon most of them would be dead or wounded, and all I could do from that bench in that living garden was watch them disappear into the cloud.

The future, the future.

I once assumed everyone was like me, anxious for the Great War to end, ready to get back to living. Even Futurists, who babbled about how glorious war was. This Great War proved different. After it was over, the world would be a better place. We would be better people making up for lost time, embracing all the happiness and creativity we could find. Enjoying things we had previously not even noticed.

But those trucks just keep rolling, don't they?

Do I feel sorry for myself? Sure, I guess. But that isn't it or, at least, not all. Am I embarrassed about not getting killed in the war like a self-respecting Futurist, like Boccioni and Sant'Elia? Maybe a little. But that's not all of it either. I am sick of the questions I can't find answers to.

You didn't want to go to Fiume, did you?

I did. It's just, I don't know.

Why do you stay in Fiume, if you don't want to be here?

I do want to be here. But I can't do what I've been asked to do.

You're an altar boy. What are you doing here? Altar boys are good for snuffing out candles, but not much else. You and your Marinetti catechism. Why don't you leave?

Maybe I can accomplish something. I don't know what.

But you're afraid to find out, aren't you, altar boy?

In the past week, I have prowled the streets at night in search of drink and sex. Neither is hard to find, this being a port city like Trieste. Fiume girls are easy to meet, as Renzo promised, and easy to bed. Afterward, they seemed as eager to be finished with me as I am of them. Not surprisingly, none of this has helped my painting.

EIGHTEEN

From INTERVIEW WITH DUŠAN KCLEŽA (1992)
[UNEDITED TRANSCRIPT]

JH: How did you find weapons in Fiume?

DK: It wasn't easy, I'll tell you. I asked around. Somebody—I forget who, it was a long time ago—told me about somebody else, who gave me another name, and so on. I met the seller at the Mercato. It was a perfect place for the meeting. A big, busy place where so much was going on, nobody would pay any attention to you, and lots of escape routes should one become necessary. I had gone there many times with my father when I was a kid. It's where he got all the meat and fish and vegetables for his restaurant. Everything had to be fresh every day. Yeah.

The seller was an Italian. I didn't know him at the time. He agreed to sell me the weapons I wanted, and the price was reasonable. Then he made me promise to use them only against Serbs. I guess he needed something for his conscience, if you can believe a gun seller could have a conscience. Especially an Italian one. Seriously, what could the man have supposed would happen with the weapons? Anyway, he said I would have them in a few weeks.

When I left there, I went through the Old Town neighborhoods. To this day, I love to roam those streets, especially the narrow ones with the tiny squares and the cobblestones that hurt your feet. And you have to walk in the street because the buildings come right down to the edge, you see? No sidewalks. No room for them. These streets were so narrow they stayed dark even during the day because the sun can't get down there except for a few minutes.

JH: You felt safe there? Safer than other parts of Fiume?

DK: You bet. It was all Croatians in Old Town. The shops and taverns and cafés were on the street level, and the people lived on the upper floors, where they would hang out laundry and yell at the neighbors, who were so close they could almost reach over and touch them. This was the original heart of Fiume. The walls were stone and brick and stucco. Everything built to last and patched up as needed.

I wandered around past St. Vitus Church and finally made my way up to the main cross street leading to the bridge to Sušak. As I got to the corner, I saw five men across the street beating up two guys. I recognized the victims. Croats I knew from school. Blood was pouring from the nose of one of them, and the other was clutching his ribs before being knocked to the ground by the fist of a huge guy. I saw one of the other attackers pull a bottle from his pocket and open it. The man grabbed the fallen Croat by the hair and poured the contents into his throat. I moved back into the shadows of a doorway.

JH: Wasn't there anything you could do?

DK: I was a rebel, but back then I was young and inexperienced. To tell you the truth, I was scared. Five against two. Nothing I could do. Five against two or five against three—what difference would it make? My getting involved would not change the outcome, especially with that huge gorilla on their side. So, yeah, I hid in the shadows. But not far enough, it turned out.

A glass bottle came crashing into the doorway over my head. The Italians had spotted me. I jumped out of the doorway and ran back toward the church. Behind me I could hear shouts and laughter. I reached the church and hurried in. Once inside, I wiped the liquid from my hair and could smell castor oil.

Do you see why I wanted guns?

NINETEEN

Out on the Corso, a pack of young legionnaires swaggered past Sean, shoving and cursing at one another and singing a trench song from the war:

When you are behind that little wall,
Young soldier you can't talk anymore.

Ta pum ta pum ta pum . . .
Ta pum ta pum ta pum . . .

I left my mother,
To become a soldier.

Ta pum ta pum ta pum . . .
Ta pum ta pum ta pum . . .

Behind the bridge, there's a graveyard,
A graveyard for us soldiers.

Ta pum ta pum ta pum . . .
Ta pum ta pum ta pum . . .

A graveyard for us soldiers,
Maybe one day I will come find you.

Ta pum ta pum ta pum . . .
Ta pum ta pum ta pum . . .

They sang proudly and badly, bestowing on each verse a dose of sentimentality that Sean had to admit he liked even though it contrasted with their rowdy deportment and with the Futurist paeans to war. Most of these men looked too young to have fought in the Great War or, at most, only saw limited action at the end. He wondered if any of them had even seen a soldiers' graveyard.

He trailed behind them, matching their pace until he reached the restaurant where Renzo had made the reservations. A line stretched outside, but following Tom's advice, he ignored the queue and went straight through the door.

Inside, customers were crammed together at tables covered with red-and-white or blue-and-white linen. They blew translucent cigarette smoke into the warm air, where it mixed with the aroma of garlic and onions. The din of ardent conversations resounded off walls displaying framed photographs of local people and places. Sean scanned the room for a moment before he spotted Renzo seated at a table with Tom and the female photographer. Even at a distance, her striking beauty mesmerized him.

Renzo was chatting with a plump balding man in a black vest and multicolored bow tie, sporting a huge smile that seemed never to quit. "Ah, at last," Renzo said when Sean fought his way to the table. "Welcome, my friend. We have just been seated." He turned to the man in the vest. "Gaj, this is our guest, the man I told you about."

"Have a seat, please, Mr. Reilly. You are most welcome to my restaurant," Gaj said, with a slight bow. "Tenente Guidici has been telling me about how you saved his life in your ambulance."

Renzo clapped Sean's arm and shook his hand. "And you've already met Chesa Rei, back at the festival," he said.

"Saved mine, too," Tom said. "I thought I was done for before he come along."

"So nice to see you again," Chesa said. "It seems you are quite the hero." Her eyes, emerald green and piercing under the electric lights, stared right at him. No false modesty, no coyness. If there were other women in the restaurant, Sean didn't notice.

"I drove an ambulance," Sean said, seating himself next to her. "These guys did the heroic stuff." With his head humbly angled down, he stole a glance at Chesa. "Did Renzo tell you how he saved me from getting shot?"

"I would love to hear every detail," Gaj said. "But please let me take your orders. For the appetizer, I recommend the octopus salad tonight. Very tender, very fresh. And for the entrées, I have something special in mind for you. May I surprise you?"

"That sounds delightful," Chesa said.

Renzo ordered two bottles of the house wine, and Gaj went off to the kitchen. More customers squeezed into the restaurant. Sean could feel sweat beading on his forehead. Renzo, in contrast, appeared perfectly comfortable in his white shirt and wool tunic.

"Gaj is a good man," Renzo said. "Runs a nice little restaurant."

"So you drove an ambulance during the war," Chesa said to Sean. "You must tell me about it."

Renzo fixed his eyes on her from across the table while Tom, on his left, talked to him about Fords. Sean stared at her too. She had a delicately sculptured face with high cheekbones that a goddess would envy, a slightly turned-up nose, and ripe red lips. She wore her long chestnut hair tied in a chignon at the nape of her neck, in a way that made her look both casual and elegant at the same time.

"Not much to tell," he said. It occurred to him that if he had a model like her in Paris, he might never have left his studies there. "I picked up wounded from the field stations and brought them to the hospitals."

"He drove like a demon," Tom said. "Like a demon racing through artillery fire."

"Brilliant," she said. "Weren't you frightened, at least a little bit?"

He did not want to talk about ambulance driving, notwithstanding the lady's keen interest in the topic. He preferred to discuss art. "Renzo tells me you are a busy photographer," he said. "You must enjoy the quiescence of the studio."

"I prefer the drama of the streets, personally. Unlike Futurists, I believe photography can be art."

Before he could ask more about her photography, Gaj returned with the appetizers, assisted by a young man sporting a clean kitchen apron. "Who is the handsome young man with you?" Chesa said to Gaj. "Your son?"

"Ah, the beautiful lady is very observant," Gaj said, his smile getting broader until it looked as though it might sever his lower jaw from the rest of his face. "What a dangerous combination."

"True," Renzo said.

Gaj put his arm around the young man. "Yes, this is my younger boy, Veselko. He helps me out. Almost finished school, so I'm afraid he will soon leave me, like his brother. But he is a good help. And very smart."

"I daresay the young ladies of Fiume have discovered him already," Chesa said.

"Very probably, but what boy tells his father?" He rubbed his son's hair. "There will be time later for the ladies. Most important for him now is education. But I talk too much. Please enjoy the octopus. Very tender tonight. I shall return with your entrées straight away."

Chesa and Sean resumed their conversation and Tom tried to capture Renzo's attention. "Nothing beats a Ford," Tom said for the third time. "The new ones have—"

"Chesa," Renzo said, "you asked me earlier about the march from Ronchi that brought us to Fiume. Would you like to hear the story?"

"Why, yes, if you'd be so kind." Without taking her eyes off Renzo, she draped a languorous hand on Sean's. He wondered if his conversation had been *that* compelling.

"I'd be delighted, since you asked," Renzo said. "At that time, Fiume was occupied by four armies: British, French, American, and Italian. We, who proposed to liberate the city, gathered in Ronchi, 187 strong. No, I shouldn't say strong. Some of us were Arditi—the special forces—or trustworthy veterans like Tom and Guido Keller, but most came from the Sardinian Grenadiers that marched out of Fiume two weeks before. An unimpressive lot. They had grown soft. *Beh*. No surprise, after months of enjoying good food and the company of beautiful Fiume girls. I warned Guido we were in trouble."

A piece of octopus from Tom's plate found its way onto Renzo's sleeve, drawing a breathless gasp from Chesa. Without looking down, Renzo brushed the errant food off with his napkin and continued the story. Tom took no note. He continued to eat with the same ferocity Sean imagined he must employ in combat.

"We stood there waiting for D'Annunzio to show up and lead the march. It was getting cold, and the wind picked up, and we hadn't seen him or the trucks to carry us. None of us wanted to march a hundred kilometers to Fiume, I assure you. Finally, D'Annunzio arrives in the back seat of a sporty Fiat, looking like a man heading out to a dog track for the races instead of joining a military march. He practically fell out of the car and started wobbling like a drunk. He staggered around and fell flat on top of an outdoor table, knocking dishes and cups everywhere. Sick as a dog, face pale and sweating, and making these ghastly moans. An old peasant woman tiptoed up from who knows where, put a wet rag on his forehead, and left him a drink, but I doubt he even had the strength to pick it up.

"We had no trucks, a commanding officer who looked like he was going to die, and a squad of soldiers who wouldn't scare a pack of schoolchildren. I said to Guido, 'If we don't get moving soon, our little band of volunteers is going to run off and rob a bakery.' He smiled at me and shook his head up and down like one of those jack-in-the-box toys. Then he hopped in D'Annunzio's car and yelled for thirty men to follow him. I had no idea what was going on. A half-hour later I heard the sound of motors, and I thought, it's an army coming to arrest us, but are they Italian or Jugoslav? Then I spotted Guido in the Fiat leading a parade of army trucks. He got out and told me he 'persuaded' the captain at the Ronchi military depot to donate the trucks to our cause. Apparently, the persuasion involved a bag of grenades and a submachine gun. I never heard whether he traded the weapons or threatened to use them.

"So there we waited in Ronchi with our trucks, ready to move out, but burdened with a sick leader. At the sound of the trucks, D'Annunzio roused himself enough to make his way to the Fiat and flop into the back seat, groaning all the way. Guido and I looked at each other and shook our heads."

"Wait," Chesa said. "I don't understand. How could 187 men who couldn't scare schoolchildren manage to invade and take over a city guarded by four armies?"

Renzo pounced like he had been waiting for this question. "The simple answer is our little band grew along the way. Every soldier we met on the road ended up joining us, even the regular army troops sent to intercept us. We numbered over two thousand by the time we got to Fiume. When we were about ten kilometers from the city, this old army general drove out to stop us. General Pittaluga. He had a company of terrified regular army with him. He told us—I'm in a truck at the front—to turn around and go back to Ronchi. I told him to get the hell out of our way, we were on a mission to liberate Fiume. The general knew D'Annunzio rode with us but couldn't see him, because D'Annunzio was in the Fiat somewhere in the middle of the convoy, probably throwing up. The general said we needed to make D'Annunzio stop the march, and he told his soldiers to shoot D'Annunzio if necessary. We laughed. He got mad and drove around us. I followed him, figuring once the general saw how pathetic our leader looked, I could convince him we needed to get D'Annunzio to a hospital in Fiume before he died. By the time I caught up, the general had gotten out of his car and stood next to it with his mouth wide open.

"D'Annunzio was standing on the front seat of the Fiat. He whipped off his overcoat so everybody could see all the medals on his tunic—the Gold and Silver Medals of Valor and a host of others—and he said to the general, 'Go ahead. All you need do is order the troops to open fire on me.'

"What a sight! Understand, back in Ronchi the man had to be helped into the car, and here he stood like Napoleon facing down Royalist troops on his return from exile. If this occurred in an opera, you would laugh. But in real life, the effect was nothing short of magnificent. D'Annunzio called the general's bluff—the Rome government's bluff, you might say—and won. They were afraid the entire regular army might mutiny, rally behind D'Annunzio and head to Rome next. D'Annunzio told the general to return to his car and follow us into the city. And the general obeyed! He *apologized* to D'Annunzio. I didn't know whether to laugh or cheer. We had no more resistance from the army after that. We marched into the city. The foreign armies saw us coming, and they packed up and left. D'Annunzio was acclaimed *Comandante* of Fiume."

Tom helped himself to more wine and said, "See what you missed?"

"I can't be around to save your lives all the time," Sean said.

"Ah, we could have used your flying ambulance," Renzo said. "I thought for a while we might be forced to drop D'Annunzio off at an army hospital, and I couldn't decide which would be worse: Italian or Jugoslav."

"I could have flown him out and brought in Marinetti to replace him," Sean said, leaping at the chance to deliver the Futurist message even though the present company bore no resemblance to the masses. "That would have made things interesting."

"Marinetti tries too hard to make things interesting," Chesa said. "As though he could change the world by acting cheeky. I knew him in Florence. The avant-garde there couldn't stand him. They called him a cultural despot and an insincere one, at that." She picked up her wine glass, twirled it, and set it down without taking a drink. "Obsessed with nationalist pride but at the same time he hated tradition. I mean, what is Italy without tradition?"

"Hideous thought, Marinetti as *Comandante*," Renzo said. His eyes narrowed and the smile on display for the story faded. Sean remembered seeing that look from Renzo before, at the military hospital during the war, when his coffee was not brought quickly enough.

Sean's thoughts returned to Chesa. *What to make of her?* She knew Marinetti. Knew him well, it was obvious. With a few cutting words, she had laid him open like an earthworm pinned to a dissecting table.

"What a fantastic story, Renzo," Chesa said. "You told it so well." Her hand remained atop Sean's. "But I'm trying to picture Filippo Marinetti standing out on the balcony of the Governor's Palace speaking to the crowd. What would they make of him here?"

"They might take him more seriously than D'Annunzio," Sean said. After an impetuous sidelong glance at Chesa, looking in vain for her approval or at least support, he took a long drink of wine, which left him coughing. "I heard the *Comandante* makes up nicknames for his enemies. What is a '*caioga*' anyway?"

"It's like a bag of shit," Renzo said. "Just a name he uses for Prime Minister Nitti. Chesa, I saw you over by the barracks today. Did you get many good photos?"

"Yes. No. Oh, I'm not sure. It's a new camera. From America. It has a range finder and a premium lens I have to get used to." She pushed a chunk of octopus around her plate with a fork. "I took a lot of photos but haven't developed them yet. Ask me in a few days."

"Marinetti should return here," Sean said. "Think about it."

"Marinetti's a provocateur, that's all," Renzo said. "Producing all those manifestos for the arts and now politics. He was amusing when he first started this Futurist business, and I admit he helped rally people for the war in 1915. But it's time for him to go back to his poetry. Today we need fighters, not entertainers."

"So you think poetry and art are mere entertainment," Sean said.

"You missed Marinetti's battles with the editors of *Lacerba*," Chesa said. She twisted in her seat to face Sean squarely. Her lips were pinched tight. "I was trying to get my photos included in the journal, and he wanted the whole issue to be about himself. He had quite a fight with Papini."

Renzo leaned forward. "Did he regale you with his comments about scorn for women? I'll wager that got his face slapped more than a few times in Florence. Here in Fiume, Marinetti spoke out too much, getting the population upset and angry. He interfered with the message D'Annunzio is trying to send."

Chesa's gaze fixed on the wall behind Renzo's head. "I like those framed photographs." She drew back and regarded Sean. "In Florence, D'Annunzio's messages were mostly aimed at luring women to his bed."

Sean shifted his body to get a better view of this woman. She kept elite company in Florence, well out of his league. But here in Fiume, her hand rested on his. Her fingers were soft, but the grip firm. He was afraid she could feel him quivering. She must be trying to drive Renzo crazy, he thought. Either that, or she had an unfathomable obsession with artists.

Both of Renzo's hands remained free, and he used them to make his point. "Only one message matters today. Fiume must be annexed to Italy. It is an Italian city. The people here are Italian and need to be brought into our united country. Marinetti wants to make the occupation about something nobody except a few artists can understand."

"This is about more than conquering another city," Sean said. "Fiume represents the electricity of the future, shaking off the past. Artists and intellectuals will lead the way with the Futurist political program. Can't you see? The war started the demolition of old institutions and now we are—"

The entrées arrived before he could finish. They ate in awkward silence for a few minutes. "This mackerel is delicious," Chesa said, finally, covering her mouth as she spoke. "I love all the spices and garlic."

"Gaj has put together a hybrid cuisine," Renzo said. "The fish is grilled the Croatian way, with old recipes. He bastes it with rosemary and thyme and paprika and olive oil and who knows what else. He adds Italian pasta and his own red sauces that are better than you can get anywhere outside of Bologna."

"What a fabulous combination," Chesa said. "No wonder the restaurant is so popular."

"Marinetti thought highly of this place," Renzo said. "I hear he is currently at work on a Manifesto of Futurist Seafood."

"Don't make fun of him," Sean said. "His vision will change everything. A blast will shake people up."

Chesa turned to face the wall behind her. "These photographs are quite good, too," she said, putting an end to the debate. "Do you think Gaj took them?"

After the meal was over, they stood outside the restaurant, chilled by the night air. Pedestrians strolled the Corso, stopping for ices or coffee or vermouth. Stars filled the crisp sky. Sean told Chesa of his interest in airplanes and his attempts to bring them to life in paintings, while Renzo and Tom discussed machine guns. Two young women, distinguishable from one another solely by their different colored silk headbands, sauntered by in the company of two legionnaires. The women had pretty, well-scrubbed faces, highlighted by mouths painted a brilliant red. Their short dresses of black velvet and gold metallic lace matched perfectly, as did their evening wraps.

The legionnaires saluted Renzo and glanced nervously at the young women, who fixed their attention on Tom and Sean. "Hi, Renzo," said the young woman in the blue headband. "And hello Tom. I haven't seen you in a while."

Tom, whom Sean had never seen blush, even when "entertaining" nurses in the military hospital, flamed red like a schoolboy. "Hi, Capricia. Good to see you. And your sister, too."

"Aren't you going to introduce us to your pretty lady friend?" Capricia asked.

"Forgive me," Renzo said. "Capricia and Annalisa, this is Chesa Rei. She's a photographer who has come to capture the city. And next to her is Sean Reilly, an artist friend who arrived a few days ago."

"It's a pleasure to meet you," Chesa said. "You both look lovely tonight."

"Artist," Annalisa repeated, staring at Sean. The word was drawn out with a piquant flourish. "You must need a model." She removed her red headband, shook her long auburn hair, and assumed a pose: back arched, one hand pushing her hips to the right, the other raised to her forehead, dangling the headband over the side of her face. Not exactly classical form, Sean noted, but the pose had its merits. "I'm ready to model whenever you want me," she said, her voice a dusky half whisper. "Just let me know."

Sean struggled for a response. When the twins departed, Chesa looked hard at Sean, then at Renzo and Tom, and then burst out laughing. "I can't wait to see that painting. 'Just let me know when you want me, Sean.' She'll be draped over an airplane, no doubt. Wings spread, so to speak. Will she be wearing anything besides a cap and goggles?"

"Knowing Sean," Renzo said, "most likely not."

TWENTY

November 1, 1919. This morning I woke early, alone in my bed. Head fuzzy from the previous night's drinking, I rose and decided to follow an impulse. Go outside, young man, and see what Fiume looks like at dawn. I went down the steps of my building and stood in front of the grocery store, which had yet to open. I could hear the owner and his wife inside, talking and doing whatever shop owners had to do in the morning to get ready for customers. The sun's rays warmed my face, a nice contrast to the chill of the evening air. I drifted in the direction of the sun.

My steps took me past the Capuchin Church, where the morning light greeted its façade. I hoped the glow of its colors might give me some ideas for my painting. The church has bands of white stone separated by rows of red brick for a dramatic, rusticated look. Construction continues on the upper level, but no work marred this Saturday morning. A voice behind me said, "Looks quite different at this time of day, doesn't it?"

When I turned around, I saw Chesa. She held her Kodak camera chest high, bellows out, the lens trained on the hood molding over the entrance to the upper church that was still under construction. She tilted her head down to peer into the camera's viewfinder, hiding her delicious eyes, but those cheekbones and that mouth were unforgettable. I know it's not polite to gape, but since her attention was focused on photographing the church, I dared. She looked every bit as stunning as on the evening of the dinner. Her bright red jacket and loose white slacks made her appear taller.

We talked. She tried to get me to pose in front of the church but I declined, politely. The façade was Gothic, not something I care to be associated with. The upper part is closed off. She disappeared through the carved wood doors of the lower church, and I followed her inside. The church was empty, and the sound of our voices bounced off the vaulted ceiling. Not much sunlight penetrated the nave. It has heavy walls, thick piers, and massive round arches that all seemed designed to sober visitors. One could imagine early Christians worshipping in a place like this. I wonder if she found it as oppressive as I did. Eight or nine rows of pews faced an altar topped by a carved statue of Mary. We switched to whispers, like we were children playing in a place where we shouldn't have been.

Chesa walked over to a tiny chapel hidden off one of the side aisles and took pictures of the tall stained-glass windows. Suddenly she swung around and pointed the camera in my direction. I dove into a pew to hide. She laughed and called for me to come out. Said she would count to five. I stood up at three, to be safe. A bunch of silliness, really. It was fun. "Come on," she said. "It's such a beautiful morning. Too nice to be hiding inside."

She moved quickly and gracefully out into the piazza in front of the church, forcing me to scramble after her. We crossed through the piazza, passing benches where I would have preferred to sit with her, stopping only when we reached an open spot on the quay. Thanks to the blustering winds of the bora, the islands out in the bay stood out with unusual clarity. She took several photos and said she had to go.

"Can't you stay a little longer?" I pleaded. I was—and remain—willing to act like a clown for a lot more pictures if she would let me. "How about coffee?"

"Sorry. I've more photos to take." Apparently, she meant photos elsewhere, not involving my antics. She signaled the finality of her words by collapsing the shutter and bellows back into the camera body and latching the cover in place. I really didn't want her to go.

"I know this charming little café."

She gave me a look that was either a playful smile or a sarcastic rebuke. It was hard to tell which. "I'm sure you do. But no. I'm already dreadfully late."

I can't understand what anyone could be dreadfully late for on a lazy Fiume Saturday morning, but she took off without waiting for any more of my protests.

"Wait," I shouted after her. "Will I get to see your photos?"

"Perhaps," she said. "Will I see your paintings?" She didn't slow down for my answer.

TWENTY-ONE

From *Memories of a Fascist in Fiume*
by Tenente Lorenzo Guidici

In early November 1919, I received a letter from Mussolini telling me a shipment of guns would be arriving in the city by plane. The letter told me where and when to meet the plane. I was also instructed to make arrangements for the disposition of the weapons.

Those arrangements were easily concluded. I had my choice from a number of potential buyers, but one stood out—a young Croat with a hot temper and a big mouth. In his hands, the weapons caused a great deal of trouble. This point needs to be clear, though—I did not tell him what to do with the guns or incite him to perpetrate the violent acts for which he and his friends were later responsible. He asked me for weapons; I simply provided them. He was looking for guns before I ever met him and would have found them somewhere else had I not stepped in. At least my merchandise was unlike any other in Fiume, so it could be traced back to this young man, and the people of Italy could see beyond any doubt how ruthless and dangerous the Croats were.

A few days later, I set off to the landing strip to collect the weapons. My drive was quite pleasant. It took me on the main road out of Fiume, northwest, following the curve of the bay. Little waves from the blue water dashed themselves on small rocks littering the beach. To my right, I could see a gently sloping terrain, with brown hills rising behind it. Looking up, I spotted an airplane flying over my head.

After another few kilometers, I turned the car onto a small road. It was little more than a path through a thicket of beech and fir trees, unmarked by any sign. Tall weeds on either side of the path brushed against my vehicle. Finally, it opened up into a large clearing. A small single-wing plane sat at the far end, turned so that it faced away from the trees, positioned for takeoff. I parked the car in front of the plane's propeller right as the pilot climbed out of the cockpit. He pulled out a package of cigarettes from a pocket of his grease-stained jumpsuit, lit one, and looked up.

"Finally," he said. "Where the fuck have you been?"

"Santo, Santo," I said. "You haven't been here long. I saw your plane come in. Have you brought the items?"

"Ah, first you are late, and now you are in a hurry." Santo flaunted a brazen familiarity that he had done little thus far to earn. I was not pleased. "I've got your supplies," he said, "and a little something extra." He flicked the cigarette away and retrieved a small glass vial from inside the plane. "For you, my friend."

I took the vial of cocaine and unscrewed the tin lid. "How thoughtful of you," I said. Santo did have some redeeming qualities. "Can you get more? There are several others here who would make excellent customers." Our *Comandante's* appetite was well known, and I saw an opportunity to make some much-needed money in selling to him. My pay was military-grade, which is to say quite low.

Santo told me he could bring enough on the next trip to keep all my friends happy. "But it will cost." He was ever the hustler. Before I could respond, we heard a truck. I replaced the lid and put the vial in the inside pocket of my tunic. The truck emerged from the path into the clearing and sped over to the plane, skidding to a stop near the wing.

"Jesus Christ," Santo said. He pointed a long yellow finger at the truck. "They nearly hit the plane. Where did you find these guys?"

"You don't want to know," I said. "One cannot be too choosy these days. The lads are sometimes a little awkward, but they mean well. I shall have a word with them about their driving, though." I marched over to the truck.

The driver and his oversized passenger were getting out as I approached. They glanced around at the plane with doltish smiles on their faces. I stepped over to the driver and admonished him like a parent disciplining a child. "You worthless pigs." Their mirth disappeared. "Do you know what that would have meant if you hit the airplane? Of course not. You are not nearly bright enough to understand what a little damage to the wing would have done. I'd have had to shoot you." It was the only way to instruct people like these.

The driver started to protest but thought better of it when I rested my hand on my pistol. I shook my head. "Go ahead, unload the plane," I told them.

Inside the fuselage lay twenty-five Russian-made Mosin-Nagant rifles and fifty boxes of ammunition. The helpers loaded the items into the back of the truck and covered them with several blankets. Piles of old clothes were then heaped on top. When they were finished, Santo reached inside the plane and slowly removed a small package wrapped in plain brown paper. He handed it carefully to me. "Gelignite. I hope you know how to handle it."

I gave the package to the driver and took the detonators to my car, where I laid them carefully inside.

"Get moving," I said to the two men. "Take the rifles to our warehouse. Park the truck inside. Don't unload it. We will take care of that later. And be careful. If you hit the plane, I will shoot you. Seriously."

When the two had driven away, Santo turned to me and said, "I don't understand why you need rifles. I heard you guys hijacked a ship full of them."

If Santo hadn't been trusted with the details in Milan, I certainly wasn't going to share any in Fiume. "Don't ask questions," I said. "I'll see you here next month." Trust is something more precious than gelignite and should be shared just as sparingly.

TWENTY-TWO

November 6, 1919

An enchanting twist of chestnut hair escaped the chignon and dangled over the side of Chesa's face. Sean watched it drop, little by little, alongside her cheek until she swept it back with her hand. "What are you staring at?" she demanded.

He blushed like a schoolboy at her challenge. "Sorry. Please go on. I just, oh . . ."

"What was I saying?"

"You were describing your tour of the city with the enchanting Capricia and Annalisa."

"Enchanting, indeed. If I have to listen one more time to Annalisa's wistful little sighs about posing for the handsome American artist, I might scream. But I must say they are fun companions, and they gave me the inside story on everyone of importance in Fiume, from D'Annunzio and the Command to the city's Italian National Council and the police chief."

It sounded to Sean like the sisters' knowledge of the Fiume elite rivaled Chesa's familiarity with the literary *beau-monde* of Florence. He wondered if the twins met Marinetti on his visit here.

In the days after their morning at the Capuchin Church, Sean had persuaded Chesa to join him for coffee at a café by the Piazza Cesare Battisti, where she showed him the photos she had taken on that Saturday. He had made a few honest comments, but perhaps had not delivered them as diplomatically as he could have. Somewhat to his surprise, she agreed to have dinner with him the following evening. Now they were enjoying a meal at a quiet little *trattoria* off the Corso.

"I learned these young girls go unescorted to the *Comandante's* rallies at the Governor's Palace and even to the festivals," Chesa said. "By the way, there's another festival this weekend, in celebration of God knows what. Anyway, the girls go in pairs or in packs, where they rub shoulders and much else with strange men." She raised a hand to her cheek in mock horror. "Oh, and Capricia told me women enjoy the vote in Fiume, and divorce is legal. There's a whole plank of your Futurist political program right there, already in place. What do you say?"

"Yes."

"Yes, what? Are you listening, Sean?"

He was, but his thoughts kept wandering. Chesa's voice had a lyrical quality, like a piano sonata played *andante*. He knew she found D'Annunzio interesting, Gaj's son handsome, Renzo fascinating, and the twins amusing. But what thoughts did she entertain about him? He couldn't tell.

"The twins played a part in the success of D'Annunzio's occupation," she went on. "On the night before his arrival, they and their girlfriends descended upon Piazza Dante with rifles and knives. Yes, put that in one of your paintings, will you? Annalisa with her dagger at the ready.

"As it turned out, their knife-fighting services were not needed but they found another way to aid the cause. They went off to entertain the sailors of the *Dante Alighieri*. The ship had been ordered to sail away that night. I asked if by 'entertain' they meant singing and dancing, and amidst riotous laughter, the girls said things got a wee bit more intimate. Whatever they did, the ship remained in the Fiume harbor. I took a photograph of it there today."

They finished the meal and waited for the espresso. Sean had a number of questions he wanted to ask this enigmatic photographer from England who knew all the leading art figures in Florence and made friends easily here in Fiume and who, for some reason he didn't understand, seemed interested in him. Instead, neither of them spoke. Around them, forks touched plates, cups settled in saucers, chairs scraped the floor. Conversation buzzed from other tables.

"Tell me about your ambulance driving," Chesa said at last. Her tone had kindness buried in it, all but irresistible.

Of all the things to talk about. Not his paintings or Futurism or fast machines that will change the world. Or America or even his friends Tom and Renzo. No, the ambulance.

"I don't talk much about those days," he said.

"I understand. Seeing all those poor men hurt so badly must have been quite terrible."

He stared at a table of legionnaires and young women off to his left and closed his eyes for a second before turning back to her. "I'll tell you about my ambulance, shall I?"

"That would be lovely," she said, her voice almost a whisper.

"The truck they gave me at first was an old prewar Fiat. It carried cans of extra gasoline and a set of tools, tubes for the tires and a pump, spark plugs, chains, rope, anything you might need to fix your vehicle in the field because you couldn't count on getting any help. I drove it through all kinds of weather, and when I wasn't driving, I worked on it."

He stopped, afraid he sounded like Tom going on about Fords. To his relief, her eyes were still bright and focused on him. "It sounds like you were quite attached to the ambulance."

"It was my home. My suit of armor. It sheltered me and whisked me out of trouble. Other times, though, it got me into trouble. The truck had these big headlights that didn't always work and these skinny tires that went flat all the time. And brakes that didn't grab going down the sides of mountains."

"Good Lord. I'm sure that demanded quite a bit of courage. Did you go near the fighting?"

"Yeah. That's where they needed me. One minute I'd be behind the lines in a safe quiet area with old villas and nice shops and cafés, and then I'd get the call and have to dodge artillery shells and phosgene gas and drive past all the rubble and wreckage, all the ruined houses and villages."

"Oh, how awful. It must have been quite a shock, going from one to the other. What kind of injuries did you see?"

He hadn't expected her to return to the topic so quickly. "Listen, I'm not . . . I can't. Don't make me think about the wounded and the dead. Even if I could describe it, you wouldn't understand. Not just you. Anybody who didn't see it. All I can say is, you do what you can. Help load the injured into little hammocks in the back of the ambulance as quickly as you can so you can get them—and yourself—out of the area. You want to push the truck hard, but you can't go too fast, because of those damn brakes, and besides, you're dodging the holes in the roads and the debris that's scattered all over." He paused. "Those guys in the back had a hard time with all the bumps."

Chesa laid her hand on Sean's as she had at the restaurant on the evening with Renzo and Tom. The hand felt warmer this time, passing on a message through her fingers.

"Well. Here's to Sean," she said, "for all those boys in the back who survived because of him." She picked up her coffee cup. "I wish we had some wine left to do a proper toast, but we've polished that bottle off, haven't we?"

They strolled along the Corso to a little side street near the far end. Her hotel was nestled in between a couple of larger apartment buildings. At the door, she asked Sean if he wanted to come up.

"Are you serious?" He wondered if his mind was playing tricks on him, scrambled by the wine, the yellow light from the streetlamps, and the damp breeze rolling in from the bay. Unlike on the boat, the sea air had a mellowing effect, but could he trust it?

"Don't make me work so hard, will you?" she said. "It's been a long day, and I'm tired. Come up if you want. If not, I'll see you in a few days."

The door of her room had hardly closed when he pulled her close. She grasped the back of his head and ground her lips to his. They fell onto her bed and made love until both were exhausted.

He rolled over on his back while she curled up beside him. He could hear the pounding of his pulse, which continued to race even as his breathing slowed. In the dim light, he saw the shadowed profiles of the wardrobe and dressing table, along with the fine upholstered armchair. Every piece of furniture stood sturdy and graceful, like her, with clean straight lines. He wanted to preserve the moment but feared losing it if he remained quiet and fell asleep.

"Do you think I am crazy?" he asked. He knew it was an asinine thing to say, but he was anxious to hear her answer.

"Definitely crazy. You're Irish and American. You can't help it."

"Seriously."

"You want to talk seriously now? All right. Take your hand off my thigh."

He relocated the hand to her breasts.

"Fantastic," she said. "Real improvement."

He pulled his arm away. "What I said about Marinetti the other night at dinner."

"I'm teasing you," she said, climbing on top of him. "So you are wondering if Renzo is bang on about frivolous Futurists needing to get out of the way of the righteous fighting Arditi."

She got to the point quickly, he noted. Like Tom. He gave her a long kiss and stroked her hair, which hung down and brushed against his chest.

"That was mercilessly put," he said, "but yes. Am I crazy to suppose artists and poets should be in charge of trying to make the world a better place? Or is Renzo right?"

She drew a finger across his lips. "Art and soldiering each have their place."

"Shit," he said. "I thought you would give me an answer."

Chesa pulled her head up, arched her back. Her eyes fixed on his. "I haven't known you long, so I'm not certain how honest you want me to be. I'll be straight with you, though. I am brutal. If someone asks me a question and they're serious, I give them the God's honest truth." She paused. "I like you, Sean. A lot. But if you ask me again, I won't spare you."

"I'll risk the God's honest truth," he said, although truth was not exactly what he had in mind. He was hoping for confirmation of his views. Maybe a few verses from the prayer book of Futurism—Marinetti's catechism, as James called it—to bolster his faith. And, if he were lucky, more compliments. The whole evening to this point had seemed like a fantasy.

Chesa's tone changed. "As you wish. You see Fiume as an epic story. It's not. This ridiculous march into the city is hardly the stuff of the *Iliad*. It's farce. D'Annunzio leads these soldiers on a parade into an undefended city when the other armies decide they'd rather go home. Once he takes over, he and his friends treat the Croatians who live here like shit. D'Annunzio, of all people, is proclaimed *Comandante*. I know he's supposed to be irresistible to us women, but what's your excuse? D'Annunzio's the leader of your new order?"

"But that's not the point," Sean said. "I was talking about Marinetti. He sees Fiume as a start, a foundation for Futurism to build on."

"You see Marinetti as a visionary. I see someone who took a good idea—using progressive art to shape Italian culture for the modern world—and twisted it into a histrionic excuse for war. In your mind, D'Annunzio and Marinetti are changing the world. I see two pompous, puffed-up literary windbags calling attention to themselves. I go out in the street and look at the city through my camera lens, and I see men in funny uniforms prancing around, waving daggers, pretending to be heroes, acting like they did something noble. Have they? I'll answer that. No, they have not.

They're like schoolboys on a holiday, who bullied their way into the younger children's playground and made a shambles of the place. How long before they're beating each other up or stabbing people with those daggers? Marinetti may fancy this as the foundation for his Futurist wonderland, but all I see is barbarians egged on by an empty-headed audience."

Sean's hands dropped to the bed. Chesa rolled onto her back. They lay silent, side by side, for several minutes.

"Do you hate me now?" she asked.

"No. No. Of course not. I'm just, uh, surprised you see things that way. I mean, I didn't figure you were that cynical."

"You don't know the half of it," she said. She twisted her body toward him. "When I used to paint, I saw great beauty in my subjects at first glance, but then I learned to look closer."

"Closer at what? And when did you paint?" Another layer of mystery about Miss Chesa Rei had been revealed. How many more were there?

"Not now. It's not something I want to talk about. The point is you and I look at things differently. You see the world like a painter, like artists have been doing for thousands of years. You pick a subject, even the future, and you are moved and want to pack all your other ideas and hopes and dreams into a picture. And you are a Futurist, so your bag of ideas and hopes and dreams of the future is enormous. Am I not right? You want to show dynamism—whatever that is— and electricity and airplanes and all the energy of the new age. And it's great for your art. I'm sure all that adds nobility and spirit to your painting. But that's not life. Life is shit. You lose the smell in painting, but it's there in life."

"And is the shit in your photographs? I suppose the modern camera captures what the old-fashioned canvas cannot." It was an ugly, imprudent thing to say, he realized immediately. Impulsive. She hadn't asked for the God's honest truth from him. But the whole evening had a dreamlike quality, over which he felt little control.

"Wind your neck in, Sean. You're changing the subject." Quiet seconds drifted by in the darkness. "Yes, there is shit in my photographs. You drove an ambulance, so you know how awful life is. Put paradise in your paintings. That's where it belongs. You'll not find paradise here in Fiume."

TWENTY-THREE

From SEAN REILLY'S JOURNAL

November 7, 1919. What was I thinking? In bed with a goddess, her warm body resting on mine, shifting slowly and rhythmically, and I asked her about Futurism. And then said what I said about her photographs. What a fucking idiot I am.

Chesa kept asking about my ambulance driving. I found it hard to talk about it, but part of me felt captivated by her request. Reminds me of *Othello*:

> She loved me for the dangers I had past,
> And I loved her that she did pity them.

That didn't end all that well for the Moor or Desdemona, but I'll keep my wits about me.

She wouldn't let me stay the night but agreed to meet for a drink in a few days, after D'Annunzio's speech at the Governor's Palace. She wants to photograph the *Comandante* in action, she said.

I wish I could paint Chesa's portrait. Get her to sit still and close so I could gawk at her without embarrassment. Perhaps then I might understand what makes her so—I don't know what—enchanting? Bewitching? Intriguing, certainly. A painter who traded paint brushes for a camera, a woman who tore me to pieces with a few words yet left me feeling more attracted to her.

Not that I could ever do her justice in a painting. Boccioni used to say that painting a portrait showed the artist's mental cowardice. I guess that's why the few humans displayed in his paintings showed up as grotesque-looking figures. Even when he included his mother. Especially his mother.

Well, Boccioni never met Chesa. At least I don't think he did. Who knows, with her, though? To have her sit near me, giving me an excuse to study her, would be sublime. I could paint anything I wanted during the sitting. I'd never show the painting to her.

November 8, 1919. Still thinking about Chesa. Before I left her the other night, I asked her why she wanted to photograph D'Annunzio. The pictures she has shown me are mostly streets and buildings, and besides, she thinks he is a pompous windbag. She just smiled and said good night.

Maybe this will do her good. If she included a few people in her pictures, she might have a better attitude toward art and life. Less cynical, anyway. I certainly want life in my art.

My art. What a joke. What life can I put in my painting? Mangled bodies and shattered buildings come to mind. The hygiene of the world. Right.

It occurs to me that Chesa's expensive camera lens can show only what was actually there at the instant the shutter opened and closed. Her Kodak can never go beyond the reality of the present. Never glimpse the future, never find anything better. In contrast, my painting—if I were able to paint—would go far beyond the present, like she said. Everything is out there available for me, objects and their surroundings, the present, and the better future, all viewable with the wide lens of my imagination. And the Futurist imagination is the widest of the wide lenses. If only I could focus that lens.

I started a new painting of airplanes in flight today. In a flash of illumination, I perceived the fusing of visual and auditory sensations of flying as experienced by the pilot and simultaneously by people on the ground who see the airplane hurtling toward them. But I had trouble reducing the idea to canvas, and soon the image in my head melted away.

TWENTY-FOUR

From INTERVIEW WITH DUŠAN KCLEŽA (1992)
[UNEDITED TRANSCRIPT]

JH: I can appreciate how much these indignities you suffered must have motivated you. You needed weapons. Where did you get the money for the guns? From your father?

DK: Oh, I tried him. Listen. My memory isn't always so good these days about some things, but I can tell you about what happened that day like it was yesterday. I waited by the door until he arrived at the restaurant. It was not yet seven. I knew my father would be there early. He always was.

Inside, the place was spotless. Every dish and pan had been washed, dried, and put away the night before. Tablecloths had been removed and chairs placed upside down on the tabletops. The floor swept clean. My father's rule was, the workday is not over until everything is ready for the next day. Except for the purchase of food supplies, of course. He always headed to the Mercato early after a quick stop at the restaurant to check on the place.

He looked surprised to see me. "You must be in trouble," he said first thing when I greeted him. "I haven't seen you in months. What do you need now?"

You see, with anybody else, he was mild-mannered and kind and patient. He wanted to be friends with the whole world. Not with me, though.

"Always suspicious, Father," I said. "Instead of a welcome."

You know how fathers act when they don't have time for you?

He hardly looked at me. "I am busy, Dušan. Tell me your business quickly."

I knew this was going to be difficult, but who else could I ask? I followed him into the kitchen. The odor of cleaning solutions brought back memories of my days helping out at the restaurant. Like when I was twelve and I dropped a tray of dishes. Other days when I screwed up. And the night those Italians invaded the restaurant and forced everyone to stand and sing, when I called my father a coward.

Now here I was, hitting him up for money. "What makes you think I need something?" I asked.

JH: And what was his reaction?

DK: He looked at me now. He gave me the father's look of judgment. Had the room been pitch black, I would have felt it. I said to him, "In the last month, two Croat grocery stores and a warehouse were robbed at night. Last night three of our people were attacked on the street. You know who is responsible. This is how they keep their occupation of our city going. They prey on anything that's not defended. The people—your people, your friends—need protection."

He kept giving me that whammy father's eye, letting me know I didn't have much time. "What is it you want, Dušan?" he said. It was like he was talking through his teeth.

"See," I said. "You don't dispute what I say. You know it's true. Yet you don't care." I wasn't going to stop, no matter how tough he acted. "It's all the same to you, whether you buy your supplies from your countryman or from the scum who steal from them. You're happy as long as you get your goods."

He said, "I don't need lectures from you about what goes on in this city. I'm late already, and you haven't gotten to the point. Finish what you have to say."

I told him I wanted a contribution from him because some of us were going to defend Croats from these predators, and we needed funds.

"Guns," he said. "That's what you want, isn't it? Money for guns?"

JH: He obviously had other ideas.

DK: He had other ideas, you're right. He was nobody's fool. My father could always scrub clean down to the bare surface of the truth, no matter how many layers of dirt were piled on.

"We need funds for protection," I said. "All kinds of things. For our people. Consider them once in a while, won't you? All you ever worry about is your customers. Think of your family, for once."

He took a step toward me and stopped. "Get out," he ordered. "Now. I give no money for guns. I think always about my family, and I will not contribute to your suicide. If you want to make things better for our people, then get a job. Work."

JH: He refused your request for defense funds and told you to get a job? That must have been hard on you, coming from your father.

DK: It was my father's answer to every concern. Work. Job. Was work going to bring relief from the invaders who ruled Fiume and robbed us? Would all the shame, the daily humiliations, the fear of being assaulted, all the messages screamed at us that we were crude barbarians unfit to rule or even live in the city that was rightfully ours—would all that go away if we minded our manners and stayed in our places and bowed our heads while we cleaned dishes or served meals to disgusting, ungrateful people, grinning the whole time? No, I knew work was not the answer in those days, if it ever was.

JH: Why did he feel that way? He must have had some reason.

DK: It's the kind of person he was. New Testament, love thy neighbor. My father wanted to get along with these people and have a better life for himself and his family. I had bigger dreams. I didn't want to serve meals to the Italians. I didn't even want to sit down at the table with them. I wanted to kick them the hell out, take their place at the table, make it a table just for Croatians. The angry prophet from the Old Testament, that was me, calling down judgment on sinners.

In the meantime, our people needed protection. And protection meant weapons. If my father would not finance what was needed, then my friends and I would get the money in the only other way possible. Stealing from the thieves.

The way I looked at it, Italian laws didn't apply to Croats. Stealing from Italians wasn't a crime. It was an act of liberation. The crime was when they stole from us.

TWENTY-FIVE

November 11, 1919

Sean heard the story about the Governor's Palace several times, from different people. The Palace had been built in the 1890s at great pains and greater expense for the city's Hungarian governor, but he resigned from his position before he could move in. The governor who came after him complained the Palace was too big. The first one replied, "No, it is you who are too small."

So how ironic was it that the diminutive D'Annunzio, who according to Marinetti had never found any edifice too large or too extravagant, made the Palace his residence and headquarters promptly upon his arrival in the city?

D'Annunzio. Renzo spoke of him in flattering terms, although mostly in the past tense. D'Annunzio was Italy's finest poet since Dante. He published his first book of poems when he was sixteen. His novels and plays were translated into French and many other languages and were acclaimed around the world. The most famous and beautiful women in the world literally begged for a chance to sleep with him. In 1915 he gave up a life of ease in Paris and returned to Italy so he could preach for intervention in the war. Huge crowds came to hear him speak. Once Italy entered the war, he joined the military even though he was well past fighting age. His bravery in the war was legendary. He accompanied the army on ground attacks. He prepared leaflets telling the enemy to surrender their hopeless cause, and braved antiaircraft guns to fly over Vienna and drop them. And he sailed into hostile waters in a small swift boat, firing torpedoes at Austrian ships. D'Annunzio became Italy's most decorated veteran of the war.

Not everybody was impressed. Some, including Marinetti, argued that D'Annunzio's fame rested on his decadent poetry and scandalous prose, the huge debts he incurred and then evaded by fleeing to Paris, and his talent for seducing and quickly abandoning beautiful women after which he wrote about them most cruelly. Always trying to be clever, always dreaming of turning the world upside down with a well-turned phrase.

Sean figured it was time to go to one of the *Comandante's* speeches and hear those phrases. He arrived early at the Governor's Palace and found a spot on the grass inside the fencing. The Palace gleamed white under the late afternoon sun. His close-up view confirmed the observation he made on the day he arrived. Two-story pilasters on the white stone façade, elaborate entablature, and grotesque little animal heads all over the front. Ugly Neo-Renaissance, a style that confused symmetry with elegance and fell into decline even before the building's construction was completed. The little *Comandante* lived in a big, atavistic toy: a *bon mot* Sean resolved to include in his next letter to Marinetti.

Five thousand or more filled the grounds of the Palace and spilled out beyond the stone fence into the street. They waited. Like Marinetti, D'Annunzio appeared to have little respect for punctuality. Or perhaps the crowd wasn't yet large enough for his ego. Sean debated whether to leave.

Finally, D'Annunzio stepped out onto the balcony protruding over the Palace's portico. He had an egg-shaped face with a small mustache and a pointed beard. His tunic displayed promotion badges on the cuff and flaunted a peacockish array of decorations and medals on his chest. He wore a gleaming dagger on his Sam Browne belt, white gloves on his hands, and an Alpini hat on his head. Sean could picture this man at a reception greeting King Victor Emmanuel but not rising from a trench to face machine guns or climbing a hill in pursuit of the enemy. To the crowd here in Fiume, however, D'Annunzio was the picture of a mighty military hero.

A long and loud wave of cheers greeted the *Comandante*. Behind him, the balcony was packed with taller men in uniform. D'Annunzio lifted his hands, causing an awesome and immediate silence to descend upon those on the ground. No one spoke or moved or even seemed to breathe. Even birds and horses hushed. The air itself was stilled. D'Annunzio gazed out at the people, letting the silence linger.

"Italian Fiume!" he began. Those two words threw the crowd into a frenzy. Men waved their caps or straw hats, women their scarves or handkerchiefs, all of them driven to ecstasy by this simple phrase linking Fiume to the home country. "Fiume is today the apotheosis of liberty, the cynosure to the shackled. Let vain cowards quiver and hide in Stygian blackness, banished there by a flaming sword. For those with the courage of Roland, there is one pure light, one truth: Fiume!"

A well-turned phrase, indeed. As far as Sean could see, the world remained right side up. He couldn't deny the effect on the crowd, however. All, even those out in the street beyond the Palace's stone fence, were captivated by the sound of the *Comandante*'s voice. He was a preacher demanding the attention of congregants in the last row, a stage actor declaiming for patrons in the balcony. Deathly silence prevailed when he spoke; wild shouts took over when he paused. For each rhetorical question he hurled out at them, they returned a thunderous "Sì" or "No." He wondered where in the crowd Chesa was, and whether she was chanting with everyone else.

D'Annunzio laid out his version of Fiume's proud but tortured history under Austro-Hungarian rule and how evil powers at the Paris Peace Conference plotted to deny the city its freedom. Eloquent, but Sean heard nothing new in what he said. Nothing about the future. D'Annunzio, the decadent poet, dwelt in the past, like Marinetti warned. Bored, Sean surveyed the crowd scouting for Chesa who, he figured, must be darting around, searching for the perfect camera angle. Sean's legs were tired from all the standing, and his back ached, another legacy from his plane crash.

D'Annunzio continued talking about the Great War and the importance of reclaiming for Italy the territories rightfully belonging to her as a matter of reward for her heroic and decisive intervention in the war. Some of the women in the crowd were really pretty, Sean noted.

"Annexation of Fiume to Italy is merely the beginning of our magnificent struggle," the *Comandante* said. "The spirit of Fiume is the spirit of immortality. *Dulce et decorum est pro patria mori.* We may all perish, but the spirit will survive, ever vigilant, ever strong." Sean sensed a change in tone and refocused his attention on the balcony.

"Fiume heralds a new crusade of poor and free men against the wealthy predators who waged war yesterday so they could exploit peace today. This new crusade will resurrect justice. Our enemy is nothing less than the evil of the world. The oppressed of all races and religions shall be consecrated with Fiumean blood!"

The words froze Sean. He struggled to unscramble what he'd just heard. D'Annunzio called for a new crusade after all the sacrifice and destruction and agony of the war. A crusade for justice. Something worth fighting for. Not for some notion of world hygiene, like Marinetti had so cavalierly proclaimed in his manifestos. Not for glory or empire. For a better world. A fight against domineering world powers that schemed for oil and profit. D'Annunzio seriously planned to turn the world upside down, and not merely with words. And he had the crowd with him. People cheered him on.

The *Comandante* wasn't done. "This contest is an act of expression, a labor of creation. It matters not if blood is spilled so long as the struggle is carried forward to the future. For you Italians of Fiume, the hour has come to fly to your destiny."

Sean took off his straw boater and waved it wildly, shouting as loud as he could until his throat ached.

TWENTY-SIX

From SEAN REILLY'S JOURNAL

November 11, 1919. One year has passed since the armistice shut down the war's big guns. One year, but the killing goes on. Fighting in Russia, Hungary, Germany, and even the Baltics. Strikes and riots everywhere while the politicians squabble. The Great Powers expand their empires, just like before the war. Is there any hope for the world? If there is, maybe it starts in Fiume. D'Annunzio's words about the future were magic language to me, the words I longed to hear. The future matters above all. And the "act of expression" he mentioned had to be art. A "labor of creation," I understood immediately, could be nothing other than a Futurist life of speed and aggression. It was Futurism in a nutshell, and D'Annunzio had expressed the concept from a balcony in Fiume, taking it a step further. The *Comandante's* future went beyond machines, beyond art, and beyond the borders of Italy and sought to make the world better for all.

That new crusade will, of course, need the benefit of Futurist ideas to liberate itself completely from the tyranny of the old order. That's the message I should be delivering to the masses. Tear down the walls of the oppressors. Time to fly toward the future.

Chesa found me after the speech was over and most of the crowd had melted away. She took my photograph. "You look like a little boy on Christmas morning," she said. "Like you saw Santa Claus."

What I saw was a path to the future, to Fiume's destiny.

TWENTY-SEVEN

From *Memories of a Fascist in Fiume*
by Tenente Lorenzo Guidici

In the middle of November, I received a note from one of Mussolini's deputies. It said Chesa Rei was spying for the Ministry of the Interior. That wasn't even her real name. Chesa Rei was in fact Marian Lomask, née Troutman.

The woman was everything one would want in a covert agent: beautiful, articulate, sophisticated, engaging. Made friends easily. And as a photographer, she had the perfect cover for her movements around the city. I hadn't suspected her at first. Then I saw her photographs of strategic locations in the city including the docks and the barracks. I passed my suspicions on to Milan, and confirmation arrived soon after.

Her path to becoming an informant for the Rome government was quite unique. Back in Florence before the war, she had become friends with Nina Giovanitti, the author of a scandalous popular novel about a woman who is raped by a family friend and is forced to marry him. Not my taste in reading, I'm afraid. Chesa and Nina shared stories about their lives and troubled marriages—yes, Chesa had been married and had a daughter, something I doubt Sean ever knew—and their respective love affairs with various art figures in Florence. When the war ended, Nina went to Rome and became a newspaper journalist, writing inflammatory articles about poor women in rural areas. She made a crude bargain with the government: they funded a few schools and other improvements, and in return, she agreed to pass on things she learned from time to time, especially anything involving Fascists. The interior minister asked her to go to Fiume to keep an eye on D'Annunzio. Nina declined but suggested Chesa, who, being British and not a journalist, would arouse less suspicion. Nina got together with Chesa, filled her head with tales of atrocities supposedly committed by Fascists, and explained that keeping an eye on D'Annunzio was critical because, if he fell in with the Fascists, poor women would suffer the most. It wasn't clear why or how they would supposedly suffer, but with women, of course, details like that were not important. Chesa took some convincing, but in the end, after an ugly scene where her estranged and spiteful husband came to Florence and claimed sole custody of their daughter, she agreed to Nina's request. Soon photographs and letters were flowing from Chesa in Fiume to Nina in Rome, and then from Nina to the Ministry.

I was instructed to monitor her intelligence gathering without interfering, a task I found not in the least unpleasant.

The letter also brought news about the November election on the mainland, which had not gone well for us. Despite the combined effort of Mussolini and Marinetti—the two put aside personality issues long enough to campaign together—the Fascist candidates received far fewer votes than expected. Even though the *squadrismo* actions against Socialists were popular with the industrialists and the big landowners, not to mention the police and the army, the attacks on an internal enemy didn't appear to excite the masses. Only when the anti-Socialist message was coupled with railing against our external enemies, particularly Slavs, did the Fascists score with voters.

To become a dominant force in Italian affairs, Fascism needed to tailor its message to different audiences. Marinetti's intellectual approach was not likely to appeal to more than a few, so it was mostly discarded. Many people didn't understand this. My friend Sean, for example. He believed that Futurist ideas mattered.

There was so much Sean never understood.

TWENTY-EIGHT

The cheers for D'Annunzio echoed in Sean's mind. The time had come to follow up on D'Annunzio's start. Time for a Futurist street rally.

Carli gave him a list of known Futurists in the city. Sean sent them word to meet on the Corso by the City Tower. Only four showed up: three men and one woman. The brilliant Mario Carli was not among them. Sean hadn't counted on him to appear although it would have been nice.

One of the men produced a script authored by Carli and a sack of leaflets. He explained that Marinetti arranged for their printing during his stay in Fiume and entrusted them to Piero.

"Piero Terruzzi?"

"Do you know him?"

"Yes." Sean knew him in Milan, before the war. Like Sean, he was an artist trying to work his way into Marinetti's inner circle. Piero enjoyed the dubious honor of receiving Boccioni's direct tutelage, together with all the abuse that entailed. Piero and Sean were not exactly friends—more like competitors for crumbs tossed by the masters—but Sean didn't dislike him. Nobody did. Tall, broad-shouldered, with a large head topped by wavy black hair, he was fierce-looking and loud but surprisingly gentle. Piero desperately wanted to learn English, so Sean helped him with a few phrases. Someone, probably Boccioni, told Piero the English equivalent for *Piacere* was "Fuck you, buddy." Piero would say it to everyone, men and women alike, and because of his size, no one challenged him. Of course, it didn't help his socializing. Marinetti and the others thought it hilarious.

A German gas attack during the Caporetto debacle left him nearly blinded and ended his artistic ambitions. *Piacere,* said the ungrateful nation. Fuck you, buddy.

"Marinetti brought him to Fiume," the woman said, "to deliver the Futurist message to the people. Piero tried hard."

"Where is Piero?" Sean asked.

"He's dead. The police said he fell off a ledge or slipped on the rocks while hiking in the hills north of the city. The day before Marinetti left."

That didn't sound possible to Sean. Piero was an experienced and careful hiker. He enlisted in the Alpini because he loved climbing mountains and could scale them blindfolded. Sean found it curious, to say the least, that Marinetti neglected to mention Piero's presence in Fiume or his fate.

The morning traffic on the Corso began under light rain. The aroma of warm, buttery bread and pastries wafted out of the *patisseries.* Sean and the others grabbed leaflets from the sack and began handing them out. One of the men rang a loud schoolyard bell.

Most of the leaflets ended up tossed to the wet pavement. Sean moved out into the flow of pedestrians, reading from Carli's script. "People of Fiume, listen to me. I will educate you about Futurism, about the multicolored polyphonic tides of revolution, the destruction of space and time, and the creation of eternal, omnipresent speed." One of the leaflets, crumpled up, hit him in the face. Hardly the reception D'Annunzio got to his speech, Sean thought.

"We, the Futurists, will lead Fiume from the stinking cemeteries of stale ideas, from the traditions and institutions that buried you in their putrid filth, from the rotting gangrene of the professors, lawyers, tourist guides, and antiquaries. Here are the seven elements of our challenge:

"First, a complete modernization of the social structure, including full and equal rights for women and an end to the institution of marriage.

"Second, a new era of avant-garde individualism, with artists and intellectuals leading the masses into a mechanical age, bringing about a life of wealth and aggression.

"Third, a ceaseless battle against tyranny, *promoting equality for people of all nationalities, including Slavic peoples.*" Sean added that last part himself, with D'Annunzio's crusade in mind.

"Fourth, shutting down the churches and an end to—"

"Equality," a voice shouted out. An old man in a long overcoat stepped forward, staring at Sean. He began speaking in Croatian. Sean had no idea what the man said but waved for him to come closer and get a copy of the leaflet. The man took but one step before being intercepted. Three men, one of them huge, knocked him down and began kicking him. The Futurists, including Sean, watched in horror and then scattered like dead leaves in a winter wind. Sean grabbed the sack of leaflets before fleeing.

Chesa came to his apartment that evening and planted herself in the worn stuffed chair by the window. He picked up a bottle of whiskey and looked around for a clean glass. Not finding any, he sat on the bed, held the bottle up, and took a drink.

"It didn't go well, did it?"

"No," he said. "It did not." He forced another swallow down his throat.

"Thanks. I'd love some."

He held the bottle out to her.

"Such a gentleman," she said, reaching for the bottle. She took a long drink and handed it back to him, coughing. "Nasty stuff, that."

They sat without speaking for a few minutes. He held the bottle and glanced over at the painting he had been proud of as recently as that morning. Under the yellow light from the old table lamp, it looked shallow and artless. He regretted not covering it before she showed up.

"Do you want to talk about what happened or should I go?" she asked.

"No. Please stay." He sat up straight and gave her the details.

"Dear God. Did you help the fellow? You got him some medical attention, I trust."

Sean shook his head.

"You left him?" She leaned forward, hands raised on either side of her head. "I can't believe you. The poor bloke was lying there, possibly bleeding to death, and you left him?"

"What the fuck was I supposed to do?" He took another drink and held the bottle without offering to share. "Get in a fight with the three gangsters who knocked him down? Or wait around until the guy's Croat buddies showed up and found their friend bleeding all over the street and me standing next to him? You know how those people are. Or maybe you don't. I didn't like my chances with them, either."

"Pass the bottle here, will you?" Chesa said, stretching out her hand. "I want to drink to 'those people,' if you don't mind."

He gave her the bottle and reclaimed it after she had her drink. "I saw Renzo later and told him about the whole thing. He didn't even blink. He asked me whose side was I on." Sean realized he shouldn't have told her that. Chesa needed no additional evidence of Fiumean depravity.

"I don't understand," she said. "You go out and make silly noises with your tiny group, then these hooligans bash an innocent old man and you leave him there, and Renzo berates you because you express concern? Welcome to your paradise of the future, Sean. I can't wait to see what happens next."

She came over and sat on the floor by his side, her back against the bed. He slid down beside her and offered her the bottle, but she declined.

"Look," he said, "this is not our idea of the future. It's the dirty work of somebody trying to stop Futurism. The shit that your camera picks up." He told her about Piero. Another swallow, followed by a cough. "Renzo, well, he's a soldier, and that's the way his mind works. You point him at the enemy, and he'll fight to the death. Like Tom. But a guy who falls off a hill or a Croat who gets beat up, it's not his problem. It's just something that happens. Listen, I was just an ambulance driver. Maybe he's right. Maybe I do need to pick sides. What do I know?"

She took the bottle from him for a long drink. "Here," she said, handing it back. She wiped her lips with the back of her hand. "Polish it off. Now listen to me, please. Being an ambulance driver is a beautiful thing, not anything to apologize for. And you are an artist. You're different. You possess vision that soldiers don't. That's what sets you apart."

"Yeah, I'm different. You can say that again. I'm a Futurist. So was Piero and look what happened to him. He got killed. So I got sent here, Marinetti's second choice. Or third, maybe. Who knows?"

"You're also a pilot," Chesa said. "You are trying valiantly to reach people with your message, but at some personal risk, to say nothing of the safety of those who might listen to you. Why not get an airplane and drop your leaflets on their heads? You could be like D'Annunzio during the war, except nobody will be shooting at you. I hope."

"And who would give me an airplane?"

"You're a war hero, are you not? You drove an ambulance at the front and saved lives. A friend of Tenente Renzo Guidici and Guido Keller. What did they do at Ronchi when the trucks didn't show up? Renzo said they went out and took them. So, go to wherever they keep the planes and demand one. And if nobody will give you an airplane, take one."

TWENTY-NINE

From SEAN REILLY'S JOURNAL

November 14, 1919. The day started so well. I was painting with a passion I hadn't felt in a long time. Slashed lines of red and blue and green. Force-lines. Concrete images broken up, mixed with abstract forms. Dynamic and chaotic. The torrent of impressions came in such a rush that my brain had no chance to censor them.

It had been like this since I heard D'Annunzio speak. I ate little, drank less, and blocked out all sounds from the neighboring apartments and the store below. I kept no track of time.

While I was working, a thought made me smile. Marinetti sent me to Fiume to bring the Futurist message to the masses. But D'Annunzio, for whom Marinetti had nothing but ill-disguised contempt, had done that splendidly from his balcony. D'Annunzio sketched a better future and shared it with everyone. Now, I thought, I only needed to fill in the colors of D'Annunzio's sketch—the details of Futurism to make that future possible. I figured I could do that on the Corso.

That was this morning. Then Fiume taught me what a chucklehead I am.

I can't get over how Marinetti has never mentioned Piero. The fact that a good man who was doing what I was sent here to do got murdered must have slipped his mind. Right.

I'm glad Chesa came round this evening, but to tell the truth, I was tempted to send her packing a couple of times. She says these things that drive me crazy. She tells me I am an artist and have vision that sets me apart. What good is vision if nobody pays attention to what I'm saying? Artists are supposed to grab the attention of the people. I told her I must be one shitty artist, and an expendable one, too.

Chesa says I'm a fine artist, but how she can say that, I don't know. I hide my paintings whenever she comes to my place, except tonight I neglected to cover a couple of them, and they're pretty awful. Even the one I was so proud of this morning.

She urged me to drop the leaflets from the sky. I told her it was impossible. But she had a point. If I could get in the air, I could reach everyone in the whole city. The perfect way to promote Futurism: from a machine moving at great speed. That woman is a Daniel come to judgment. Or Deirdre, the beauty who brings tragedy. One or the other. I can't figure out which.

She offered to lend me her camera. "The photographs could be quite smashing," she said.

I told her thanks, but no. I'm afraid I might drop it. "I might hurt someone, and you would hurt me."

She jabbed me in the ribs. "Yes, I would. I would hurt you badly. So, are you going to do this?"

She is relentless. And as good as they come.

"I am," I told her. "Tomorrow morning. 'Viva la revolution,' as Tom says. The Futurist will take to the skies."

"That sounds wonderful." Then she lay out flat on the floor. "Sean," she called.

Oh, yes, Chesa, oh yes.

THIRTY

From INTERVIEW WITH DUŠAN KCLEŽA (1992)
[UNEDITED TRANSCRIPT]

JH: You mentioned the blockade and how it didn't keep out the criminals and undesirables. Some celebrities also managed to get in. Toscanini, Marconi, to name a couple.

DK: Yeah. Some blockade, wasn't it?

JH: Filippo Marinetti was here for a short time as well, wasn't he?

DK: Who?

JH: The leader of the Futurist art movement. At the time, Futurism was popularized as something new, celebrating machines and speed, and turning its back on tradition. Did their idea of progress mean anything to you or the other Croatian people in Fiume?

DK: No. Should it? This Futurism, what I knew about it, had nothing to offer me. Futurism, D'Annunzio, Fascism, they were all the same, as far as I was concerned. Anything new they wanted was bad news for us Croats. All they cared about was Italy, Italy, Italy. I cared about Croatia. The progress I wanted was freedom from our oppressors.

JH: Futurism featured a number of prominent artists. Painters, especially. They liked to mix war ideas with their art. Did you—

DK: Listen. I didn't give a shit about art. I'm a fighter and always have been. I know some people get all excited about paintings and statues and such, but not me. What's the point? Somebody paints a picture and they hang it on a wall. What good is that if you're not free? How's that help feed your family when you're hungry because somebody is stealing your food?

JH: Who was stealing your food?

DK: Are you serious?

JH: Sorry. I assume you are referring to the blockade. It didn't keep people out, but it did have an effect on food and other necessities coming in.

DK: Some of it got through. For the rest, the Italians used to go out on raids and steal. That's how they got their food and coal and other essentials. They stole everything. First, they took the provisions that the French army had left behind under lock and key. After they cleaned all that out, they would go out at night, usually by boat like pirates, and steal from the Italian Army depots. And the army let them. D'Annunzio's people, a lot of them, had been in the army and some were still on active duty, technically, so the soldiers who were supposed to be guarding the supplies wouldn't shoot at them. The army let the pirates have everything and pretended they couldn't do anything about it. Then one night, I don't know why, somebody got excited and shot one of the pirates. There was a big commotion and a lot of yelling and crying in Fiume, so D'Annunzio decided that instead of stealing from the army, which had lots of guns, they would steal from Croatians, who didn't.

JH: Steal from the Croatians in Fiume?

DK: No, Croats in Fiume didn't have much left, except my father, and nobody would steal from him. He was too popular, even with the Italians. But in Sušak, businesses were flourishing. The Italians hadn't managed to screw those up yet. So the pirates came across the river to take from Croats in Sušak.

It was their old arrogance and insolence and contempt for us. They could steal whatever they wanted, and we were supposed to stand by helplessly and watch. They were in control, and we were unprotected.

JH: Until you acted to provide that protection. How many did you have in your group of freedom fighters?

DK: It varied. Up to fifteen, maybe twenty, at first, when we weren't doing anything but talking. After we got the weapons, maybe seven. After we used them once, even fewer. At one point it was me. Only me.

JH: By yourself? Oh, my. Did you ever have doubts about whether you would succeed?

DK: Do you think I'm a pussy?

JH: No, certainly not. I wasn't implying anything of the sort. It's just that the odds were against you with so few fighting at your side. Why didn't more Croatians join you?

DK: I don't know the answer to that. It seems like everybody's a patriot until you ask them to do something, and then you can't find them. There should have been more. It's a big sore point with me.

It's like when I was with Tito and the Partisans, and we fought the Italians and Germans in the Second World War. I fought against the Ustashe, too. People need to remember that. The Ustashe, they were Croatian, but they were Fascist puppets of the Italians and the Nazis. What they did to the Jews, even to the Serbs, that was awful. They disgraced Croatia. We're not like that, most of us. I joined the Partisans and we fought against the Ustashe and the Fascists. Tito was a Croat, and he knew how to fight. He kept everybody in line, then and afterward.

Ah, it's too much. I could talk all day about that. Just say I fought against everybody who tried to keep Croatia from being free. And there have never been all that many of us doing the fighting.

THIRTY-ONE

November 15, 1919

Sean stood at the far edge of the macadam runway, admiring the three biplanes. He was sweating. The tram had carried him less than halfway to the airport, making him walk the remaining kilometers on an airless dirt road.

He shifted the strap on the bag of leaflets to his other shoulder and advanced toward the planes. They were parked by a small wooden shack. One man stood guard in the doorway of the shack while another circled the planes. Both carried army-issue rifles.

"Hello, Mr. Reilly," shouted the guard by the planes. "It's me, Antonio. Private Cabiati. Remember? I helped you load wounded in your ambulance at Tre Monti."

Sean remembered him. Tre Monti was where he rescued Renzo and Tom. He was relieved to see a familiar face, one who might smooth Sean's gaining access to a plane.

Antonio told him about getting discharged from the army and how he had been eager to follow Renzo—Tenente Guidici, he called him—to Ronchi for the march. Sean asked Antonio to give him a hand with one of the planes, a pristine-looking Nieuport 17 with a black prancing horse painted on the fuselage. He couldn't wait to get it in the air.

"Sorry, Mr. Reilly," Antonio said. "Nobody touches the airplanes. Orders."

"Orders? Who grounds three perfectly usable planes?"

"Mr. Wickson. From the Command, sir." Antonio moved closer

to the plane. "Nobody gets in the planes unless I see an order from Mr. Wickson."

Sean hadn't come all the way out to the airfield with a heavy sack of leaflets only to be sent away because some Luddite at the Command didn't like planes. He was hot and tired. The people of Fiume needed the Futurist message dropped on them.

He went over to the Nieuport and squatted by the wheels. "Look, Antonio. I have orders also. Mine came directly from *Comandante* D'Annunzio. He assigned me a mission, for which I need this plane. Help me with these wheel blocks, would you?"

"Stay back, Mr. Reilly. Nobody is allowed to touch the airplanes without a written order signed by Mr. Wickson. He came out here and showed me an instruction signed by the *Comandante.*"

Sean reached down and pulled out the wood blocks surrounding the left wheel. The guard slouching in the doorway straightened up and inspected his rifle. "It's all right, Antonio," Sean said. "I understand your orders. We had orders at Tre Monti, didn't we? You'd help if you could. How about if you and your friend go around the back and take a leak? You didn't see anything until it was too late to stop me."

Antonio smiled. "No, I can't do that, sir. Please step away from the airplane."

Sean circled to the other side of the airplane and removed the remaining blocks. Straightening up, he tugged at the cables running to the rudder and strode forward, running his hands over the struts connecting the upper and lower wings. From the corner of his eye, he could see the other guard drawing closer.

"Mr. Reilly, you need to stop," Antonio said. "I can't let you do this." The smile remained in place, but the tone of his voice had frost in it.

"You want me to shoot this guy, Antonio?" the other guard said. He positioned himself next to Antonio.

Sean began his inspection of the engine, tugging each of the wires. Satisfied, he leaned back and grabbed the propeller.

"Move away from the plane," Antonio said, shaking his head slowly. He rotated the rifle in his hands.

"Hey moron, are you fucking deaf?" the other guard said. "Get lost." He spat on the ground. "Antonio, let me shoot him."

Sean pulled on the propeller. No time to check inside the cockpit.

"You better listen to him, asshole," the other guard said.

Sean pulled once more on the propeller and raced around the wings to the fuselage. Before he could climb up into the pilot's seat, a sharp pain exploded in his head.

Sean woke up on a small cot in a room reeking of industrial grease and oil. His head ached horribly. He sat up and surveyed the room. The scuff-marked walls were bare save for a calendar with a suggestive picture of a scantily clad young woman.

Standing up, a dizzy feeling flushed into his head. He staggered outside. Antonio and the other guard stood in the shadow of the building, their backs to the door. He headed quietly in the opposite direction, toward the dirt road. A brown cloud rose above the trees lining the road.

It didn't take long for the guards to spot him. "Mr. Reilly. Hey, come on back, sir," Antonio called.

"Where the fuck is he going?" the other guard said. "I told you, you should've let me shoot him."

Sean began to run. The pain in his head grew more intense. That cloud, he figured, was dirt stirred up by a car coming to pick him up. Take him somewhere and finish him off. Like Piero. It seemed crazy to go straight at the car, but what other choice did he have? Without cover in any other direction, he would be an easy target for the guards' rifles. His only chance was to get to the trees and the dirt cloud, where he could hide. Besides, the car could not turn around on the narrow dirt road, so he would enjoy a temporary advantage.

The guards' footsteps quickened. Sean lowered his head to go faster.

"Mr. Reilly," Antonio yelled. "Look out."

The automobile burst out onto the runway and skidded to a stop. With his head down Sean ran straight into the front grill and fell backward, landing at the feet of the two guards.

"Shit," the driver said as he climbed out of the car. He hurried to the front and squatted. "Jesus, Mary and Joseph, and all the saints and apostles."

Sean closed his eyes tight. Pain shot through his brain like it wanted to burst out his eyeballs. When he opened his eyes, Tom's face emerged as a blur. Sean groaned. "Tom? Is that you? What are you doing here?"

"Antonio rang me at the garage and asked if I'd come get you. He told me you was acting crazy trying to take one of the airplanes, and he had to knock you out. Only way to stop you. I said to him, 'Yep, sounds like Sean.' Can you get up?"

Antonio squatted next to Tom. "Sir, we were trying to get him to come back and wait for you, but he ran away and wouldn't stop."

Sean rose, slowly, using the car fender for support. "I need to go to the Governor's Palace," he said as he eased himself into Tom's car. "I need to talk with D'Annunzio about getting to use a plane." As soon as the car began to move, a nauseous feeling swept over Sean. "Can you slow down? Bad enough you ran over me. Now you're going to hit somebody else."

"I didn't hit you, you dumb shit. The car was stopped. You ran into me. If I had hit you, you'd be in the trunk, not the front seat. Why'd you run? Antonio said you was waiting for me."

"He almost took my damn head off," Sean said. "Antonio or the other guy. I don't know him."

"I seen him before. He goes on the raids."

Sean had no idea what raids Tom meant but did not bother to ask. "One of them whacked me from behind, and when I woke up, I couldn't tell what was going on. I wanted to get out of there. This is bullshit. Where are we going?"

"You are going home, buddy. And you're gonna stay there, understand? You're in no shape to tangle with anyone at the Palace. That head of yours will hurt for a couple of days."

"What am I supposed to do at home?"

"Sleep. Do your painting. Christ, I don't know. Jerk off. Do you have any more of that whiskey I gave you?"

"No," Sean said. "Chesa and I polished the bottle off last night. The girl can drink. Do you have any more? Preferably something that tastes like whiskey?"

Tom reached behind the passenger seat and picked up a bottle. He examined the label in the manner of one retrieving a fine wine from the cellar vault, and then handed the bottle to Sean. A few minutes later, he stopped the car in front of Sean's building. "Thanks for the ride," Sean said. "Glad I ran into you." He started to laugh, but the act triggered a shooting ache in his head.

He climbed the narrow stairs, pausing outside his room to drink from the bottle. The stairway stank of boiled cabbage. Upon entering his apartment he set the bottle carefully on the chest and lay on the bed. The room was cold. Sounds of customers laughing and arguing in the store below floated up through the ancient wood floor.

In the apartment above his, children screamed and adults argued. Sean got up and pounded the ceiling with the handle of a broom, knowing the effort was futile. Finally, the entire family grew quiet either from exhaustion or because they were dead, perhaps from the cabbage. He frankly didn't care.

A new sound greeted him from the other apartment on his floor, with which he shared a wall. A young couple had recently moved in. They made noisy love for hours.

THIRTY-TWO

November 15, 1919. My first two attempts at spreading the message have not gone well. Marinetti will no doubt be losing patience. What am I doing here in Fiume, the city where drunks bump into people and then want to cut them with daggers, where thugs stomp on an old man for speaking Croatian, and where young guys in uniforms defend unused airplanes with rifle butts?

Marinetti exalts war as something heroic. The world's only hygiene, he calls it. What bullshit. I saw a lot more of the war than he ever did. There's nothing heroic about bombs dropped from planes or shells fired from miles away.

He thinks artists can lead the masses by mouthing some rousing words. Maybe silver-tongued D'Annunzio can, but he's unique and not burdened with Futurist bombast. D'Annunzio gets people's attention with his nationalist rhetoric and his reputation. I am not D'Annunzio.

I remember Tom's prediction. Maybe machine guns are the future. What if the postwar life is simply going to be a continuation of all the stupidity and violence of the past? What if art and machines and electricity and speed can't bring civility and progress?

I can't accept that. How can a Futurist paint with such thoughts?

November 16, 1919. All morning, I lay in bed awake, smelling that fucking cabbage. The couple upstairs, very much alive and having packed their children off to school, picked up their argument from the previous evening or perhaps started a new one. The hostility penetrated their floor and my ceiling like an unorthodox music score—loud then muted, high-pitched then low, following no established tempo. Futurist music: the art of noisy argument.

I can't get over the situation at the airport. Antonio said Wickson showed him a note signed by the *Comandante* grounding the airplanes. Why would D'Annunzio, of all people, stop planes from flying? There must be a mistake. Whoever this Wickson is, he can't be expressing the wishes of the man I heard speak from the balcony of the Governor's Palace. Is this not the place where the Italians of Fiume fly to their destiny? They'll get there a lot faster in airplanes.

When I finally got up, I made some tea and settled into the stuffed chair. The afternoon sunlight poured in the two windows of my studio and bounced off my latest creation. A sleek biplane hurtles upward and banks to the left corner of the canvas, its silver wings gleaming in the sun. The pilot's profile is visible but fades at a sharp angle. Lines of paint stream from the wings in ways that are intended to convey speed. The only thing conveyed, I'm afraid, is my inadequacy as a painter.

November 17, 1919. Lots of good stuff to write about today.

I slept all morning and into the afternoon and tried to ignore the knock on my door. "Open up, goddamn it," Chesa shouted, so I let her in. She breezed in with a plate topped by a tin cover. "Grilled lamb from Gaj's," she said. "Because I know you haven't been eating."

The aroma quickly took over the whole room, driving out all trace of stairway cabbage. "How did you know?" I asked.

"I ran into Tom, and he told me about your bruising experience at the airport. I was afraid something had gone wrong when I didn't hear from you."

"Did he tell you I ran into him too? Literally?" Pathetic attempt at humor, I know. Tom hadn't thought it was funny either.

She mumbled something she obviously didn't want me to hear and then said, "He did mention that. Yes. He's a bit coarse, but I like him. The stories he told at lunch about his soldier days with Pancho Villa all sounded fantastic."

"So you and Tom dined together," I said. "How nice. Sounds like a romantic time." It was an obnoxious thing to say, but I couldn't help it. Renzo's attention to Chesa was threatening enough, without my having to worry about Tom as a rival.

"It was delightful," Chesa said. "Look at this." She set the plate on the small wood table, swept aside the clutter of my paintbrushes and old newspapers, and pulled the cover off the plate. "Gaj prepared it for you. He doesn't normally let food leave the restaurant, but when we told him you weren't feeling well—and don't worry, we didn't tell him you got bashed for trying to steal an airplane—he insisted I bring this to you. He is such a nice man."

I hurried over to salvage the paintbrushes and then went to fetch my stool from in front of the easel. "So you and Tom—"

"Oh, stop, will you?" She wasn't offended, thankfully, even with my being a jerk. She rummaged around looking for a knife and fork. "We had the twins with us, too. Frisky things, they are. Capricia draped herself over Tom like an old cape, and Annalisa couldn't stop talking about you. She says you are a handsome gentleman and a great artist. She wants so badly to model for you. Yes, well. I'm the one who deserves to be jealous. This smells absolutely smashing and it's warm. I nearly burned my bloody hands off getting the plate here." She found the utensils at last and went to wash them in the sink. I wish my sink were a bit cleaner.

"Tom said to tell you they are having a big to-do at the Governor's Palace a couple weeks from now," she said over the noise of the running water. "He says you might find it easier to talk to the right people there if you still want to fly an airplane." She came back and handed me the clean knife and fork. "Here. Go ahead and eat." She dropped herself into the stuffed chair.

I devoured the food like an animal, like someone who hadn't had a decent meal in days. Which was precisely the case. My mouth was too full to speak. Fortunately.

"I feel bad about what happened to you," she said to my great surprise. "It was my suggestion that you demand the plane and take it. My imprudence got the best of me."

"No," I reassured her after swallowing too large a bite and almost choking. "It was a good idea. During the war, I wanted to use a plane for an ambulance, but they didn't let me for a long time. If I had taken one back when I first asked for it, I could have saved more lives."

Chesa got up and came over to me. She stood behind me and squeezed my shoulder. That felt so good. "You're a good man," she said. "You did save a lot of lives."

I could have told her what happened when I finally was allowed to fly the ambulance plane, and about the two lives that didn't get saved. I could have, yes. "The lamb is really delicious," I said.

She waited until I finished eating and then asked if I would look at some photos she had taken the previous week. We shifted to the floor where the declining sunlight better illuminated the photos. Our backs rested against the edge of the bed. I reached over to put my arm around her, but she pulled away. She had other ideas.

"The photographs, please, big boy," she said. "I want your critique as an artist. Be brutal. Yes, you can be exceptionally and exquisitely brutal. It is quite shattering. But I need an honest opinion, so I'll risk it."

The pictures were hard to look at. Legionnaires marching in drills outside the barracks. What was she doing by the barracks, anyway? Others showed men and women at the Mercato, picking out meats and vegetables. The pictures did not look posed. These subjects were ordinary, unsuspecting shoppers, and she had invaded their lives. Some of the people struck me as quite ugly or even deformed, but nothing in the pictures made me feel anything for those people. Chesa merely displayed them as she found them. *Look at these and don't wince,* the pictures seem to be saying. *Life is shit, don't you see?*

I didn't wince or feel any other emotional response. "Nice to see humans in your pictures," I said, and yawned.

"You don't care for those," she said. "Neither did Nina."

The photo critique couldn't end soon enough. I don't know who Nina is or how she got to see the pictures and don't care. Didn't ask. Chesa looked strangely anxious for a second but then relaxed as I continued through the pile.

One photograph stood out. "This one is, oh, what is his name? Gaj's son?" This subject had happily posed for her. I could see a real connection between him and her. The difference came out in the way she caught his eyes, gazing forward with the natural impudence of a thoroughly agreeable and guileless youth.

"Veselko." She seemed happy I recognized him.

"The picture shows me his humanity," I told her. "Those eyes. It's a little too dark, though. Too obscure for a young kid like him. Plus he's just standing there. Where's the energy, the life?"

"He's a young man, not an airplane," she said. She got up on her knees and leaned closer to me. She felt warm. The trek from the restaurant to my place carrying the food had made her sweat. "But I take your point. This is helpful. Exactly what I need."

I flipped through the rest of the photographs, commenting on each one. More men and women and a few distant shots of legionnaires on the march. A couple of cannons. I tried to be constructive, but it wasn't easy. The last was a street scene, taken from above. "Where did you take this one from? I recognize the streets but you are shooting from elevation. And you are looking into the sun because the picture has a washed-out effect. Very nice. In this case, it really works."

Chesa put one arm around my back and squeezed me close. "I took that one especially for you," she said.

"The framing, the focus on the church on one side, the balance, with a little tension. I love it. Stones on the street on the left fade and blur as you move out to the right. A lot is going on here. The shadows are creeping towards you. This has dynamism."

I gave the photographs back to her. "You are doing so well here," I said. "That's great."

"Now, are you going to show me the paintings you've been working on?"

"Not a chance," I said. She left soon after.

This evening, I dragged my stool back to the easel and began slashing colors, red and brown, on the canvas with short, quick brush strokes. Streaks of green, too, for reasons I couldn't explain. Must be from an impulse somewhere deep beyond my brain, beyond the critic that always condemns my work.

Chesa Rei. Bearer of food, messenger of hope. She sought my opinion of her art. Me. D'Annunzio had it wrong. In this crazy world, there is one pure thing, one truth, but it's not Fiume. It is Chesa Rei.

November 18, 1919. Making progress on my latest painting, but it's hard to get into that frame of mind without a visit from Chesa. Hope to see her tonight.

Tom's suggestion is a good one. At the Palace, I might get close to D'Annunzio. I do want the plane, more than ever. Besides dropping the leaflets, I want to take a look at those hills where Piero had been hiking. I have trouble believing he accidentally fell.

THIRTY-THREE

Letter from Filippo Marinetti

November 15, 1919

Sean:

Your recent letter has occasioned in me more than a modicum of concern. Street brawls with drunken festival revelers are always to be avoided. I would have thought that obvious and not require my explicit instruction. While you managed to escape without harm, I cannot imagine any circumstance in which this will further our cause. You were involved in enough battles during our Futurist Evenings to know that we do not run from confrontation—we seek it, with open embrace—but at the right time and the place of our choosing. I trust you will be more judicious in your choice of venue for your next fight.

Carli tells me your efforts to promote Futurism in Fiume have been negligible. How can that be? He also advised of your plan to drop leaflets from an airplane. It sounds so D'Annunzian. While the *"Comandante"* loves to tell the story of his flight over Vienna, especially to women he is seducing, it did nothing to win the war. Futurists need to engage people face to face, with shouts and music and, yes, fists. You need to stay on the ground.

Filippo

THIRTY-FOUR

From *Memories of a Fascist in Fiume*
by Tenente Lorenzo Guidici

In the aftermath of the November 1919 elections, Mussolini was challenged for leadership of the Fascist organization he had built. Some wanted more compromise with the other political parties, while others insisted on turning up the violence of the squads. Never was a great leader under such pressure. He had to walk a fine line to keep the Fascist movement from falling apart, all while trying to find the right message to the masses.

In Fiume, the two Americans were becoming a nuisance. My friend Sean Reilly was possessed by some misguided notion to unlawfully take one of the Command's airplanes. I'm afraid all he received for his efforts was a headache.

Tom Delancy didn't do anything imprudent, but he would not stop complaining. "I only work part time lately. There ain't enough trucks to fix, and we don't got parts for those. Even when I get paid, it's with this worthless Fiume scrip that nobody takes unless you make a big stink and threaten to shoot them." Tom was not wrong, but I had grown weary of his litany of woes.

He and I stood on the parade ground on the south side of the barracks one morning, watching a squad of legionnaire recruits stumble through basic drills in the rain while their instructor shouted and swore at every mistake. The marchers, replacements for men who had recently left Fiume, showed little interest in mastering the art of moving in harmony.

"These guys," Tom said. "They wouldn't have lasted a day in Mexico."

"Pancho Villa was not indulgent?"

"That's one way to put it. When somebody didn't measure up, the rest of us had to clean the mess."

I enjoyed listening to Tom's stories about Mexico. Tom was a warrior, underneath his unkempt attire. And his observations about these new men were on target. Wearisome, though. "They're anxious to get to grenade practice," I said.

"I wouldn't trust them with rocks. How many have been hurt with the grenades?"

"About twenty or so." That was Guido Keller's fault. Keller loved playing with grenades, so who could stop legionnaires from following his example? We had to set up a little hospital adjacent to the barracks.

Small pools of water collected on the field. One of the marchers turned the wrong way, leading four men behind him to fall out of the formation. One of them fell into the mud puddle, drawing laughter from the rest. The gray-bearded instructor screamed at them again, this time with vulgar insinuations about the men's sexual history.

"I don't figure these clowns can fuck any better than they drill," Tom said.

"They might do better than you suppose. But to your point, they would find a way to foul things up immediately afterward. Let me tell you a little story. One of those men out there, one of the better ones, as a matter of fact, sent a letter home to his fiancée. 'Everything's wonderful here in Fiume,' he wrote. 'The food is great, the people are friendly, and the girls are not at all difficult.' This, to his fiancée, mind you. The girl's father is an infantry captain, a friend of mine. He asked me to cripple the soldier. I tell you, Tom, many people are too dimwitted to be trusted with any decision-making. They must be given orders and trained to follow them."

Tom nodded.

"Are you still seeing Capricia?" I asked. The happy look on Tom's face answered the question. For all his skills and experiences, Tom could never quite hide his emotions for long. It's one reason he always lost at cards.

"Quite a spirited girl, that one," I said. "How about our friend Sean? I haven't seen him in weeks."

"I went to his place yesterday. He says he's fine, painting and whatnot. The only thing he talks about is this world crusade D'Annunzio is supposed to lead."

Yes, I thought, that sounded like Sean, embracing Marinetti's infatuation with fast machines and now D'Annunzio's insufferable quest. Aesthetes, the three of them, in a time when hard work needed to be done. At least Marinetti and D'Annunzio shared a common nationalism, no matter how much they despised each other. But I wasn't sure Sean felt the same way.

"How about you, Tom? Would you consider going to Milan or Turin to help with the fight against Socialism? A man with your skills would be invaluable there. And amply rewarded."

Tom nodded toward the drilling legionnaires. "Leave the city defended by these?"

I admired Tom's loyalty. During the Great War, many cowards abandoned the fighting after the disaster of Caporetto. Not Tom. He never left his fellow soldiers in the middle of a fight. But I hoped he might consider shifting the venue of his fighting to a place where he could be more useful.

The trainees looked miserable, but soldiers must learn to endure rain and worse. They need discipline, something many people don't understand. "The Socialists want to put men like these in charge of the country," I said. "Those of us who believe in freedom, in the greatness of Italy, we can't let that happen."

"So why do you stick around here?" It was a fair question, but the success of my work in Fiume required keeping some things secret. That is the way battles are won.

I walked out in the rain toward the marching legionnaires, whose drill had degenerated into noisy squabbling. Halfway out, I stopped and wheeled around. "Not for the League of Fiume," I called back.

THIRTY-FIVE

November 25, 1919

Sean stood back from the painting he had been working on for the past week. *Not finished yet, by any means.* His starting point had been the street scene in Chesa's photo of the church and the creeping shadows. He added a campanile by the church and had it leaning over at an acute angle to make it look passionate and dynamic, like Carrà taught back in Milan. Then he included a crowd of stooping figures seen from behind as they pitched forward in the direction of the campanile. He liked the composition, but it still lacked the heightened simultaneity that Futurism demanded. Sean mulled adding an automobile with blurred force-lines. That would have to wait until the next day, however, and better light. He donned his coat and headed out to seek help getting an airplane, notwithstanding the rebuke in Marinetti's letter.

The weekly meeting of the Union of Free Spirits Tending Towards Perfection was underway when Sean got there. Twenty men and women, most of them young, sat in the gardens once belonging to an Austrian archduke, surrounded by autumn remnants of agaves, camellias, yucca, irises, rosemary, cherry laurels, and other plants Sean couldn't identify. Bare-limbed trees towered over them, and piles of dead leaves lay scattered on the ground. Guido Keller, the man Sean came to see, was not present.

Sean settled in to listen to a debate on the merits of creating a new world through unrestrained sexual love. He thought that a worthy topic, especially as one of the most active speakers was a comely young woman. To his deep disappointment, she took the contrarian view.

"Your views on women," she said, addressing a bearded man, "reek of the same puerile impulses that have fueled centuries of women's enslavement. Not to mention our boredom. Your idea of liberation for the female sex is nothing more than a plan to add to the chains already binding women and make us more widely available for your insatiable carnal appetites."

"Not true," the young man cried. "I want to elevate the spirit of lust among all people, regardless of gender. It is the sentimentality, the jealousy, the artificial boundaries and rules that must be cast away so man and woman can realize their true essence and achieve their potential. The current ideal of woman as a fragile, tragic plaything was invented by bad poets. But the political role you seek is simply another side of the same farce. You are too excited about elected office, as though politics meant anything. In your haste to join the execrable sophistry of modern democracy, you underestimate the need to first suffer the many years of bad learning that have afflicted the male sex and reduced us to the heap of corruption in which we find ourselves today. Women should preserve their ignorance and naïveté. Use those qualities to help men overcome the dung heap of modern philistinism and machine worship, and return us to simple agrarian paradise guided by mystical—"

"Your mystical paradise rests on the bodies of women," she said. "Women who, while not on their backs pleasing you men, are forced to clean your houses, cook your meals, and rear your children. Now you want us to plow your fields while you amuse yourselves by plowing us. Keep your spiritualism and your farms if you wish. Enjoy mystical pleasures with the goats, for all we care. For myself, and for all women, I want full political engagement and power. Moving, living, destroying, and creating. That is what we demand."

Keller arrived and took a seat on the grass without interrupting the discussion. He had black hair and a dark, satanic-looking beard.

Sean was anxious to hear his comments on the battle of the sexes. Unfortunately, the group's conversation shifted abruptly to a new topic, the abolition of prisons. Keller offered occasional cryptic comments with a wry smile. "Dionysian spirit is based on chaos," he reminded the group, and the Free Spirits honored Dionysus by escalating the passion and volume of the discussion.

When he could restrain himself no longer, Sean spoke up in defense of Futurism. "Machines and speed are the keys to progressive development and the solution to the postwar malaise," he said. This earned him rude responses from several of the members, including the two who had been arguing over the role of women.

"Your machines and speed achieved little besides a calamitous war and mass extermination," the bearded man said.

"Those airplanes endanger us all, dropping out of the sky and crashing," the young woman said. "Consider what happened to those two pilots last month."

The reference to pilots stopped Sean before he could retort. He demanded to know what she meant. Keller answered. "A plane crashed in early October before you got here. Aldo Bini and Giovanni Zeppegno. Bini was thrown from the plane and impaled on a church fence. We had a big funeral, and D'Annunzio gave a good eulogy."

The news silenced Sean.

The Free Spirits' conversation pushed ahead, touching on the abolition of currency and the abandonment of cities. Nothing about machines or dynamism or reaching out to the oppressed around the world. Nothing more about the dead pilots. Preoccupied with his own thoughts, Sean stopped paying attention.

After the meeting ended, he stayed behind to speak with Keller. "I need an airplane," he said. "To drop some leaflets. Marinetti asked me to keep Futurist activity going in Fiume and maintain visibility of our presence. He suggested you could help me get in the air."

"Leaflets from an airplane," Keller said. He laughed, but the sound was a strange one, like a combination of cough and throat clearing mixed with a sneeze. "You Futurists haven't had an original idea since 1909. You want to mimic D'Annunzio's wartime flight over Vienna."

"Marinetti sent me here to—"

"Marinetti's an elitist who fancies himself above elitism," Keller said. "He's a rich man who wants to destroy everything traditional except his privilege. It's one reason why D'Annunzio deported him. Surprised?"

Sean was indeed surprised to learn Marinetti had been forced to leave Fiume. But it didn't change what he had come to Keller for. "Would you put in a word for me with Wickson about the plane?"

Keller shook his head. "I don't talk to Wickson unless I absolutely must. The man is a pervert, and I mean that literally. He likes young boys more than D'Annunzio likes women."

Sean glanced over at the flower beds, where remnants of the summer's blooms had withered. "How did someone like him get to Fiume?"

"D'Annunzio hired him. From what I hear, he was a clerk at one of the lesser British banking houses until his bad accounting and worse social habits were exposed. He barely made it out of London alive and somehow found his way to Fiume to keep D'Annunzio's books. Honestly, of all the strange characters the *Comandante* has collected at the Command, Wickson is the worst."

"I'm surprised you and Renzo haven't—"

"The finance guy, Conte, is nearly as bad. He pimped for the generals during the war, in a nice office as far from the fighting as he could manage. Made sure they had plenty of wine and meat and girls. Pocketed a lot of easy cash that way. These days he's the designated fundraiser for Fiume. I don't talk to him either."

"So you won't help?"

Keller shook his head again. "If Marinetti really wants you to fly, tell him to ask Mussolini for a plane. They're such good buddies now. Maybe there's a Fascist plane you could fly." With another freakish laugh, he strolled away, leaving Sean speechless.

THIRTY-SIX

From SEAN REILLY'S JOURNAL

November 25, 1919. In my short time in Fiume, I have gazed upon the awesome diversity of the city's population. The streets teem with drug users, nudists, naturalists, vegetarians, communists, syndicalists, Socialists, anarchists, Fascists, monarchists, mystics and other fanatics, crossdressers, priests who demand the right to marry, soldiers who play with live grenades for sport, and men and women who are addicted to the pleasures of orgies. Then I met the Free Spirits, who weren't merely different. They seemed to have landed here from another planet. I wish Chesa had been there with me, but she was off photographing the city streets, as usual. I'd love to hear what she thought of these characters.

Their conversation was intriguing at first, but when I heard them speak of the plane crash, I felt nauseated. Bini and Zeppegno dead. Both were decorated fighter pilots during the war. They were heroes to someone like me who aspired to fly. Especially Bini. I remember the day I met him. I was waiting in my ambulance near the front and watched as three Austrian planes came out of the clouds and started toying with an Italian reconnaissance plane that was trying to land. Bini's machine appeared from out of nowhere. He shot down one enemy plane and chased the other two off. When Bini landed, I ran over and congratulated him. He accepted my congratulations stiffly, as one might entertain the gratitude of a beggar after giving him a coin. I took no offense. Now he's dead.

Here in Fiume, some people want to transform Bini's legacy of courage and daring into a halt to aviation. Stopping flight seems like stopping destiny, stopping Futurism.

The other shock was learning Marinetti had been deported from Fiume. Marinetti never said anything to me about being forced to leave. One more little deception, one more omission of a crucial fact, like not telling me about Piero's presence in Fiume or his violent death.

Keller's lack of enthusiasm for promoting the Futurist cause puzzles me, like his sharp comments about Marinetti himself. Admittedly, I shaded the truth about what Marinetti said regarding leaflets being dropped from the sky. But no matter how it looks in Milan, anyone here in Fiume can see that it's the best way to deliver the political message to the masses. The only way, really. I think Marinetti overestimated the extent of Futurist influence in the city. Carli has offered me little assistance, and Keller seems completely indifferent.

Fly a Fascist plane? I don't get Keller's sense of humor.

THIRTY-SEVEN

From INTERVIEW WITH DUŠAN KCLEŽA (1992)
[UNEDITED TRANSCRIPT]

JH: Was it only Croatians who faced these atrocities at the hands of the occupation forces, or did they pick on others as well?

DK: Mostly Croatians, I'd say. One American I can think of, though.

You're familiar with St. Jerome's, right? You should be. Everybody should be. The church goes back to the fourteenth century. Beautiful little church, right by the old administration building on the western edge of the Old Town. Now if you go around behind the church, you get a wonderful view of its oldest part, where these stone—what do you call them, buttresses?—stone buttresses are sticking out from the walls, which had to be repaired with concrete and so because we have had tough times here in Rijeka over the years, earthquakes and a lot of fighting.

Where was I?

JH: You said there was an attack on an American. Was this in the Old Town section?

DK: Ah. That's how I got started on St. Jerome's. No, I didn't actually see the American get attacked, but I saw the result, if you get my meaning. I was wandering through the Old Town streets late one night. Early December, if I remember correctly. We had been out, my friends and me, raising what we needed to buy the weapons. Like I said before, it wasn't really stealing, the way I looked at it. We were simply reclaiming assets for our community.

We had done a few jobs and were finished for the night, except I didn't feel like going home. I wanted to walk around by myself.

JH: And this is where you saw the American get attacked, on one of these little streets?

DK: No. I just told you I didn't see it. Listen to me, will you? I went to the little square behind St. Jerome's, where there's grass and old pine trees. In the center of the square there used to be a fountain and a round concrete pool about three or four meters in diameter, with water coming up from inside this figure of Saint Somebody, I forget which. No benches or anything to sit on, but it had a little stone ruin at one end.

So I'm coming from the east side of this square, from the old streets, and I hear somebody coming from the other direction. That was unusual, because the Italians never came that way, especially at night. This was our ground, you see? But this guy, I could tell he was by himself and headed my way. He staggered, almost crawling, over to the fountain, fell down by the side of the pool, and started drinking from it. He wasn't dressed like one of those legionnaires, you know, with the crazy uniforms they wore and the daggers and feathers and such, so I guessed he might be American. He scooped up handfuls of water to drink and didn't pay me no mind. I moved closer and thought maybe I should help the guy out.

I could barely see him, it was so dark. There were no streetlamps there. He started washing himself in the pool. All of a sudden, the rotten shit smell hit me good. I mean to tell you, it was unbelievable. I thought I was going to get sick. So I went back the way I came, back to my streets. I don't know where this guy went next.

Maybe you think I should have done something to help him. It's easy to judge, here in this studio. But the stink of this man, it was terrible. That's what castor oil will do to a person, and I could tell he had gotten a serious dose.

This wasn't the last time I saw the American, by the way. Had I known then what I learned later, I would have smashed his head on the fountain that night and drowned him in the pool.

THIRTY-EIGHT

December 6–7, 1919

The Governor's Palace exuded elegance. In the ballroom, ladies in floor-length silk or satin gowns adorned with ropes of pearls mingled under crystal chandeliers with men in dress uniforms and white gloves. The dancing was slow and graceful, unlike anything Sean had seen at the festivals. A small orchestra played music of Vivaldi and Toscanini. It seemed like the Palace had cast a spell and transported everyone to the nineteenth century. The old Hungarian governors, even the small one, would not have felt out of place.

Sean, who did feel out of place in his sack suit, had gained entrance to the Palace by posing as a photographer, using Chesa's camera. He found Keller standing with two other officers and asked where he could find D'Annunzio.

"You missed him," Keller said. "He's gone upstairs to his quarters. Plotting our next adventure, probably, now that he has decided to take on the whole world."

"Plotting his next conquest, you mean," said the officer on his right.

"I need to talk to him," Sean said.

"Is this about the airplane? Sorry, Sean. Like I told you, you need to go through Wickson." The other officers snickered. "We all do. Today it pleases the *Comandante* to place this man at our forefront. Tomorrow, perhaps, the veterans will again lead the way."

"Dragging the little shit behind us in chains, I hope," said the other officer, who wore captain's stripes. "On a leash."

A young man in a spotless tunic came up the marble stairs from the ground floor and halted at the edge of the ballroom. A woman followed close behind him. When she reached his side, he opened a door to another stairway to his left. The woman nodded to the young man as she swept past and climbed the stairs.

"Looks like the *Comandante* has his evening entertainment arranged," the captain said. "Not bad. Not bad at all."

Keller continued talking. "There's no other way, I'm afraid. Wickson's in his office, down the hall." Keller pointed to the hallway on the east side of the atrium. "Conte is with him. If we're lucky, Conte brought lots of cash, and cash will loosen things up." Keller looked like he wanted to spit on the marble floor.

The door to the stairway closed and the aide disappeared. Sean rubbed the side of his head with a shaking hand. His face felt hot. *Chesa, going to D'Annunzio's private rooms. Impossible.* But he had just witnessed it.

"Did you get a photo of that?" the captain asked.

Clutching the open camera with a loose, one-handed grip, Sean stormed off toward the hallway Keller had indicated. He needed to put distance between himself and what he had seen. Wickson might be an ass about the airplane, but at least dealing with him would clear away thoughts of Chesa. Outside Wickson's office, he stopped and fumbled with the camera, trying to close it up. The slide for the shutter and bellows proved balky. In exasperation, he was ready to dash the Kodak against the wall. He remembered the instructions Chesa had given him and worked the slide back into the frame. Once folded, the camera fit in the pocket of his jacket. The resulting bulge hardly showed. He knocked on the heavy door of Wickson's office and, without waiting for a response, marched in. "I'm looking for Mr. Wickson," he said.

The man behind a desk glared at him, eyes reddened and lips drawn tightly together. His face was pinched and taut, giving the appearance of not enough skin to cover his skull completely. But what stood out was the uneven cut to his greasy hair, as though no barber would deign to touch it, forcing him to cut the mess himself, likely without benefit of a mirror. "Yes. And who are you?"

"Sean Reilly. I need to use an airplane, and I understand you are the one to approve it."

Wickson leaned back in his chair and blinked. Another man, whom Sean hadn't initially noticed, stood by the desk cracking his knuckles. Tall and thin, he had a long face topped by black slicked-back hair and wore an expensive-looking blue suit. He scrutinized Sean the way one would look at an alien form of life. Shifting his gaze to Wickson, the standing man said, "Do you have any airplanes here?"

"No, Mr. Conte, I do not," Wickson said. He crossed his arms over his chest.

The finance man, Sean thought. Keller said he was a bad one.

"He doesn't have any airplanes here," Conte said. "Go look someplace else. We're busy."

Sean wanted nothing more than to go someplace else, away from these two, away from this office, the whole Palace. Far away from the room where Chesa was currently being entertained by D'Annunzio, the world-famous lover. He tried to make it quick. "The guards out at the airfield said I needed a note authorizing the release of a plane to me." He felt ridiculous saying this, like being in high school again. "Can you write a note to that effect? Then I'll be on my way."

"You must be the one who tried to steal the plane," Wickson said.

"Steal a plane?" Conte said. He sat on the edge of the desk. "Don't they shoot criminals for things like that? He sounds like an American. They shoot people in America for stealing horses."

"I believe you're right," Wickson said. "I can't entrust any of our valuable airplanes to a thief."

Sean felt blood throbbing in his head. "Just give me the authorization, and I will go and not bother you again. The plane will be returned safely in an hour. OK?"

"No, it is not *OK*." Wickson mimicked Sean's pronunciation.

"I've had my fill of your demands. We have nothing more to discuss. Get out of my office."

Sean wasn't ready to go yet, although he did not know what else to do. Renzo would have known. Tom, too. But Tom's way would leave too much blood on the walls. Sean thought of Piero falling helplessly down the hill onto the rocks and boulders, his bones smashed.

"There's something else I can do in the air. I can look over the spot in the hills where Piero Terruzzi was climbing when somebody killed him. Maybe I'll figure out what he saw that got him killed."

Both Wickson and Conte leaped to their feet. "Get the hell out," Wickson said.

Sean backed toward the door. "Might be pretty embarrassing for some folks." He wasn't exactly sure what he meant but couldn't stand to leave without a retort to these two. Without waiting for an answer, he stormed out of the office and out of the Palace.

He lingered for a while under the Palace portico. Wickson's reaction when he mentioned Piero troubled him. The man had been odious and disagreeable from the moment Sean entered his office, but only after Sean mentioned Piero did he become threatening. What connected Wickson to Piero? What did he know about Piero's death? And why did he refuse to grant anyone permission to fly? Those were perfectly good airplanes out at the airfield.

Music and human voices flowed up the hill. Sean considered losing himself in a serious night of drink and debauchery. He walked down to the Corso but changed his mind. He didn't want to be around people. Best to go home. Besides, he had Chesa's camera in his jacket. She had some explaining to do when they next met. Losing or damaging her precious Kodak would only complicate the discussion.

He retraced his steps and turned onto Via de Amicus, a side street dark like his mood. He had gone a short distance when he heard a noise behind him. He looked around. Five men in black clothing and balaclavas suddenly surrounded him. Just like in Piazza Dante that first day, he saw no path to escape. He had to force his way out. What would Tom do? The school on the right, if he could get to it, might offer safety or something he could use as a weapon to defend himself. Picking out the smallest of the five men circling him, Sean darted directly at him, dropping him with an elbow to the throat. He sprinted toward the open gate adjacent to the school and raced through it down a long ramp to a fenced-in playground. The pursuit was close behind. He reached the door of the schoolhouse and pulled on it. To his horror, it was locked.

The men caught him and dragged him to the center of the pitch-dark playground. Two men pinned his arms behind him while two others began punching him in the ribs and solar plexus. The final blow went to his head, bloodying his nose.

"This asshole is bleeding all over me," a voice said. "Give me the castor oil, quick."

A bottle was pressed against Sean's lips. He kept his mouth closed tight. One of the men punched him in the gut while another held his nose. Sean's mouth burst open and immediately the bottle was shoved in. A foul-tasting liquid raced down his throat. He couldn't see anything in the blackness. He squirmed the best he could and kicked blindly, hitting the man who held the bottle. A foot crashed into the back of Sean's leg, forcing him to his knees. The bottle never came out.

"It's empty," the voice said. "Bring me the other one."

"The boss said he don't want us to use gasoline."

"I didn't get the message," the first voice said. "Get the other fucking bottle."

Sean could already feel the effects of the liquid in his guts. A hand he never saw pulled the empty bottle from his mouth and held a second one to his face.

"This ain't right," said one of the others.

"Shut the fuck up. Now shove it in his mouth." The man who spoke lit a cigarette and flicked the spent match at Sean. The bottle was put to his lips. Even though he closed his mouth tight again, the foul taste seeped in. He began convulsing from the mixture of gasoline and castor oil.

"Open up and drink," the leader said, "or I'll pour it over your head and light you up like a candle."

Before Sean could react, a gleam from an electric torch broke through the darkness, shining down from the street above. "Police. What's going on here?"

The attackers let go of Sean, and he fell forward onto the unforgiving cement of the playground. He heard feet running away. Two policemen came down to the playground and shined the torch on him. Sean did not move or say anything. He couldn't explain why, but he was sure it was safest.

The castor oil had begun working seriously by this time. "God, does he stink," one of the policemen said. "Look, he's shit himself. Is he dead?"

"He made somebody mad," the other said. "I counted five of them." He leaned over and picked up a cork off the ground. "Smells like gasoline."

"Gasoline? That's not just mad. They wanted him dead. Here's what I say. Let's leave him. If this was done by who I think, I don't want to mess with it. Let the stink blow off. We'll come back in an hour, and if he's here we can arrest him for public intoxication. If he's alive." He chuckled and dropped the cork on Sean's back.

Sean sat up after he was sure the policemen were gone. His head, ribs, knees, and gut all ached. He had a violent thirst, and his bowels relinquished all semblance of control. He was surprised and relieved to find the camera in his jacket pocket. But he had other worries. Where could he go? Returning to his apartment was out of the question. His assailants might know where he lived and be waiting for him there to finish the job. He couldn't stay out in the street. He had to find shelter and desperately needed to clean himself and get fluids. He was too embarrassed to let anyone at the barracks see him like this, and that included Tom and

Renzo. Struggling to his feet, he stumbled in the direction of the hotel where Chesa lived.

Walking was agony. He stayed in the shadows of the small dark streets, where the stench and stain of his fouled pants would not be obvious. In the vacant gloom behind a church, he came upon a small fountain with a round pool. He staggered over to it and fell on his knees. Cupping his hands, he drank from the dark water like a man in a desert who'd found an oasis. His thirst seemed unquenchable. When he had drunk all he could, he leaned away and took a deep breath. Thinking he heard somebody, he remained still for a moment before nausea hit him like one of those punches. He barely had time to draw his head away from the pool before vomiting.

After the gagging let up, he leaned over the pool again and splashed water on his face. He rose slowly, bent over to relieve the dizziness. He listened for footsteps. Not hearing any, he started moving again. He stopped frequently to rest, leaning up against whatever wall or building was handy, progressing slowly until he arrived at the entrance to Chesa's hotel.

The window of her room was dark. Sean slid into the alley across the street from the hotel and vomited again. Wiping his mouth with his sleeve, he scanned the street to make sure no one could see him and then stole across and entered the hotel lobby.

The night clerk was a young man of twenty, an art student during the day. Sean had often chatted with him about painting when he came to visit Chesa. The clerk had his head buried in a book when Sean staggered in. He glanced up and flinched at the sight.

"Sweet Jesus. What happened to you, Mr. Reilly?" He ran out from behind the desk and put an arm under Sean's shoulder. "Sweet Jesus," he said again. "You got it bad."

"I need help, Paolo," Sean said, breathing heavily. The odor from his clothes overpowered the small lobby. "Is Miss Rei in her room?"

"No," Paolo said. "She hasn't come back yet. You want to go up and wait for her, Mr. Reilly?"

Once in her room, Sean set the camera on the dresser and sat on the bathroom floor. He forced himself to drink cup after cup of water. Then he rose, filled the tub with water, and threw all of his clothes in. While they soaked, he examined his reflection in the small bathroom mirror. Dried blood had caked under his nose, and his cheeks were swollen. He swayed unsteadily, exhausted.

He retrieved his clothes from the bathtub, squeezed out all the water he could, and laid them on the radiator. Returning to the bathroom, he feared he might vomit again but nothing was left inside. He refilled the tub and climbed in. The warm water felt good, and he relaxed. When he got out, he made a brief effort to clean the bathroom so Chesa wouldn't have a fit when she returned. Then he crawled into bed to wait for her.

In the morning he woke up alone. It took him a moment to get oriented and to recognize something was wrong. She wasn't there. His body hurt all over. He grabbed his still-damp clothes from the radiator and dressed.

At the front desk, Sean asked the day clerk for the house phone. Soon a car pulled up to the hotel. He climbed into the passenger seat.

"Christ Almighty," Tom said. "What happened to you?"

"Just drive," Sean said. "To my apartment. Please don't ask questions."

Tom shrugged and put the car in gear. Soon it was parked by Sean's building.

"Thanks for coming to get me," Sean said. "I appreciate it. I got the castor oil treatment last night. Real bad. I'm gonna drop out of sight for a while."

Sean didn't wait for an answer. He climbed out of the car and slowly mounted the stairs to his room. Once inside, he opened the window, letting cold air blow in. Then he went over to the unfinished canvas that rested on the big easel—his painting of the church and creeping shadows and the angled campanile leaning over dark figures. He kicked the easel with all his remaining strength.

THIRTY-NINE

Letter from Filippo Marinetti

January 30, 1920

Sean:

Carli tells me he has neither seen nor heard from you in months. How can that be?

I have a new task for you. Your assignment is to pen a manifesto about the Fiume experience. I intended to have Carli write this, but he is presently occupied with censorship authorities who are giving him trouble about his journal.

Think of this as one of the *Comandante*'s speeches but presented in a coherent essay. You should focus on how Fiume provides the flame, as D'Annunzio so quaintly put it, to light the future. I understand that Léon Kochnitzky is heading back to Fiume shortly to resume work on this so-called League of Fiume. He's a Belgian poet of minor renown and less talent, but D'Annunzio seems to like him. Meet with the man and find out what the plans are for spreading this "flame" around the world.

I shall send you helpful books. I want to see drafts quickly so I can monitor your progress.

Filippo

FORTY

From **SEAN REILLY'S JOURNAL**

January 12, 1920. After more than a month, I finally feel like writing in this journal again.

The sight of Chesa being herded to D'Annunzio's rooms tore me up like nothing ever before. It was like giant hands squeezed the breath out of me. The feeling gets me even now. She knew I was coming to the Palace, did she not? Loaned me her fucking camera so I could get in. She would never go to D'Annunzio's rooms, given her opinion of the man. He was a pompous, arrogant windbag, only after one thing from women. Were those not her very words? I wanted to run after her and drag her off those stairs, but I didn't move. I couldn't. Why not? I don't know. She kept climbing and I stood frozen, not breathing.

We've known each other for a short time, only a few months, but the relationship was so intense—at least on my part and, I imagine or had imagined, on hers as well—that the idea of her with another man, particularly one like D'Annunzio, is beyond bearing. How could she do this to me, right in front of me?

And then, not be around later when I needed her most?

When I woke up at her place and she still hadn't come home, I was confused. Everything that happened the previous evening came to me in flashes, unconnected at first. The beating and the castor oil, mostly. Lately, the thing that stays with me most is Chesa heading to D'Annunzio's rooms.

The fucking bitch and her fucking camera. Why did she loan it to me? Maybe she wanted me to take pictures of her going to D'Annunzio.

I'm feeling sick again as I write this.

January 20, 1920. What is my life like these days? Oh, just delightful. In the mornings, I turn and toss in the bed and roll over. Lay the pillow over my head, then pull it off and start punching it. I punch the bed. I pound away, wishing I had the guts to punch myself. I stay in bed until I cannot stand it anymore.

Once up, I sit before the mended easel, staring at a white canvas. I wrack my brain for a subject to paint. If ideas come, I reject them one after the other. They are stupid or insignificant. Or too difficult for me to paint. No one would ever want to see my work, much less give it the acclaim I crave. Great painter? Why do I even try? I block out memories of my ambulance and force myself to recite the principles of Futurist painting. Then I rise from my stool without touching a brush. It's like Trieste, but worse.

I take afternoon walks to the train station, where I stand across the street under a leafless oak tree and watch people. Most days, it rains. The people come and go, scurrying as though nothing bad had happened: no Wickson, no castor oil, no Chesa at the Palace. Cold raindrops run down my collar and onto my back. I resolve to get on one of those trains and leave Fiume, but where would I go? Back to Trieste? And what would I tell Marinetti? My bags never come with me to the station. I don't deserve to leave.

When I've had enough of the trains, I go over to Piazza Cesare Battisti by the Capuchin Church. The grimy little square looks even worse in the winter gloom. I sit on a bench watching seagulls fight over scraps of food they scavenge from somewhere. At least they can fly. I can't. I listen to voices and machine sounds that drift over from the piers. In the center of the piazza, a fountain launches a feeble spray of water half a meter into the air. Rain or not, I'll sit there for an hour or two or three and then head back to my rooms.

January 23, 1920. Yesterday, I forced myself to go out and spread the gospel to the public. Alone. None of the Futurists dared accompany me. I went to the Mercato, in the early morning when the eager shoppers congregate. No one stopped or listened to me. Today I tried the afternoon crowd at the Piazza Regina Elena, with the same lack of success. After an hour, I laid the sack of leaflets, still almost full, in the middle of the Piazza and walked away. Another validation, as if I needed more, of my former plan to drop leaflets from the air. Nobody reads the paper I try to hand them, but if it came from the sky, I'll bet it would have been irresistible.

The air drop was Chesa's idea, and like her, it's now gone forever.

February 5, 1920. Marinetti wants me to write a manifesto about Fiume because brilliant Carli is too busy. Wonderful. Something else for me to fail at. Write about the Fiume experience? I could describe the taste of castor oil and how it felt to shit all over myself while D'Annunzio was fucking my woman, and how nobody listened or cared about me or Futurism. Would that make a good manifesto?

My problem is the world—at least the small portion residing in Fiume—isn't really interested in the future. That's what is holding me back. From what I've seen, only D'Annunzio and a few Futurists care about making the world better, while everyone else wants to keep things the same or make them worse. Oh, the people go to the rallies at the Governor's Palace and they cheer for the *Comandante,* but afterward, they retreat to the usual rounds of drinking and fighting and fucking. And then I think, what does it matter what I think? I was Marinetti's second choice for writing the manifesto, like I was his second choice, behind Piero, for coming to Fiume and spreading the word to the masses. Perhaps I should count myself fortunate. Piero was killed for his efforts. I only had to drink castor oil and shit myself.

Violence hangs over the city. The League of Fiume is, for me, the sole redeeming aspect of the Fiume experience, but little news of its progress has emerged. Perhaps this Kochnitzky fellow can get it moving again. I will talk to him. Maybe he can explain how the flame of Fiume could be spread to the world when it appeared to be burning itself out here.

February 10, 1920. The books Marinetti promised have arrived. I stacked them under the bed where I'm not forced to look at them.

FORTY-ONE

From *Memories of a Fascist in Fiume*
by Tenente Lorenzo Guidici

By early January, I had grown weary of Fiume and its clownish *Comandante* and longed to return to Milan, where the real fight was taking shape. My return was destined to be delayed for another year, however. The work demanded of me in Fiume was crucial to the later triumph of the Fascist Party. Nonetheless, I was by nature eager to share in the more physical battles taking place back home. I was, after all, an Arditi.

The weeks leading up to Christmas had witnessed the absurd spectacle of a public vote in Fiume on the *modus vivendi*, the Rome government's plan to end the occupation. Early reports indicated that it was going to pass, but D'Annunzio decided on his own to scrap the referendum and reject the plan. He had something else in mind, some greater purpose for Fiume.

The instructions I received from Milan indicated that Mussolini, too, had something else in mind, but it wasn't quite the same as what D'Annunzio wanted. I received my orders on a cold afternoon in early January. I can recall precisely where: across from the train station on Viale XVII Novembre, in a little row building. It was marked by a weathered wood door with carved lion's heads on the side panels. A tiny sign advertised the address as "22." I remember it so well because I rented it.

When I walked in, the men inside flinched. "Christ, don't you ever knock?" Wickson said. "You're fortunate I didn't shoot you."

Wickson was a creature whom I found thoroughly repulsive. "You, with a gun? That is a funny joke," I said. "Have you ever shot one? Conte, here, would be in more danger if you tried. Shall we get to business?"

Wickson started to speak. Conte said, "Shut up, Wickson," and handed me a white envelope. "You better open it now and read it."

I read the typewritten letter in silence. When I finished, I stuffed the letter into my tunic pocket. The other two waited for me to divulge its contents. The Duce's decision to increase focus on the Slavic menace meant my work in Fiume was about to get more active. But these men didn't need to hear that. I looked over at Conte. "It said I need to pound a few things into Wickson's head. About the money. And about not being stupid."

"The latter will be especially difficult," Conte said.

I pivoted to face Wickson. It was painful to look at the man. "Listen carefully. There will be more funds coming in soon. Mussolini says to use the cash to keep the city alive, but don't let the *Comandante* give it away for this League of Fiume. We're not interested in starting another world war."

"Why doesn't Mussolini get rid of that old windbag?" Wickson asked, scribbling on a pad. "And those others, too. Clean out the lot of them."

"Nothing in the letter asked for your suggestions," I said. "It did say, 'Make sure Wickson quits stealing so much.' Mussolini can add and subtract, even if D'Annunzio can't."

The point on Wickson's pencil broke. He threw the pencil across the room in disgust. "Speaking of subtracting," he said, "I saw your mate, the artist, on the way here."

I was in no mood to tolerate such insolence. I grabbed Wickson by the neck and slammed him against the wall, pinning him with one hand. Wickson gasped for breath, his eyes open wide. I slapped him twice across the face. He deserved much worse for his part in the castor oil attack on my friend Sean.

"That American is my friend," I said. "If anything else happens to him, I will drop you out of an airplane. With a rope around your neck. After I hurt you. Are we clear?"

Wickson did not respond. I slapped him again, harder.

"Yes, yes. I hear you," Wickson said. I let go and shoved him over toward his chair. Wickson stumbled backward and fell, knocking over the chair on his way to the floor. "You are crazy," he said. He wiped his hand over his mouth, smearing blood. "What did you hit me for?"

"I slapped you," I said, and smoothed out my tunic. "If you were a man, I would have hit you."

FORTY-TWO

February 14, 1920

Renzo escorted Sean to the door of a pleasant but unpretentious three-story building, distinguished by the heavily draped Venetian-style windows on the upper floors and the absence of any windows at all on the ground floor. They gained admittance and stood in the vestibule. "I don't need this," Sean said, eyeing the trompe l'oeil of unclothed nymphs staring down at him from the ceiling of the great room. "I'm fine. Perfect." He was perspiring.

"You need this," Renzo said. "Maybe try a little less cocaine next time."

Two young women approached, clad in diaphanous white lingerie. Renzo provided the introductions. "This is Zoe and the other is . . ."

"Mona."

"Mona," Renzo said. "How could I forget? The loud one, aren't you?"

"You don't look like a Mona," Sean said warily. "Renzo, I can't feel my face."

"She wasn't last week," said Zoe. "Her name changes more often than her underwear."

"Are those ostrich feathers on your boa?" Sean asked Mona.

"I'm not all that loud," Mona said. She stuck her tongue out at Zoe.

"Did you bring your little vial, Renzo?" Zoe asked. She dropped a thin strap off her shoulder.

"Ladies, ladies, give us a chance," Renzo said. "This is my friend's first time in an establishment of this nature." Whispering in a stentorian voice to the women: "I suspect he's a virgin. Like me."

"So am I," Mona said, dragging the boa across Sean's chest and twisting her body sideways. "This is my first day on the job."

"It's gonna be your last if you don't get your ass upstairs soon," said a stocky, heavily made-up woman who joined them. Her plunging neckline revealed more ragged cleavage than Sean cared to see. "Renzo, you evil man. You didn't tell me your artist friend was so handsome."

"A thousand apologies, my good woman. Sean, allow me to introduce Madam Christina."

"A pleasure," Sean said. He caught himself as he was about to bow.

"Welcome to Casa Piacere," Madam Christina said. Sean almost choked suppressing a laugh.

"The house is busy tonight." Renzo surveyed the crowd. "Enough here for a referendum. Shall we hold a vote? Who's for annexation?"

"It would pass easily this evening," Madam Christina said. "I count seven from the Command so far. Eight, if you include that little one over there by the divan flitting around in the kimono. Did you bring your precious vial, Renzo?"

The kimono-clad one, sporting enough rouge and white powder to make a geisha blush, smiled from across the room. "That's . . ." Sean struggled to finish the sentence and then gave up. The object of his consternation was D'Annunzio's young aide, the one who led visitors, especially nocturnal ones, to the *Comandante's* quarters at the Palace.

"Madam Christina," Renzo said. "Sean needs the full experience of your house. And I'm afraid I will require the tenderness of at least two of your ladies tonight."

"Cheeky," Zoe and Mona said in unison.

"We don't double up on virgins," Zoe said, raising her chin and stretching out a long, pale neck, "unless they're artists."

Mona drew the boa languorously across Sean's face. "You're an artist. I heard about you. Do you need a model? I'll bet you need a model to pose for you."

"I don't need—"

"What Sean means to say is that he is exploring his options. The lad recently had his heart broken." Renzo bit his lip.

Sean gave him a dirty look.

"I'll show both of you around," Madam Christina said, grabbing each man by an arm. "What we have here will cure anything that ails him."

Sean stopped to look at a painting on the wall flaunting a pyramid of naked men and women engaged in group sexual activities from positions that seemed physically impossible or, at the very least, painful. "Lust is the exalting of the flesh, reclaimed as a creative work of art," he muttered. "Futurist lust on display in Fiume."

Renzo shook his head.

"Step away from the painting, Mr. Reilly," a familiar voice behind them said. After a pause, laughter.

"Antonio?" Sean said. "What the hell?"

"Like at the airport, huh, Mr. Reilly?"

Madam Christina dragged Antonio away. Renzo found an open space on the divan near the stairs and soon had a girl sitting on his lap. Sean stood by himself, sneaking peeks back at the pyramid painting.

"Haven't found what you're looking for?" The speaker's face seemed vaguely familiar. Long eyelashes, dark eyes, impossibly red lips, hair wrapped in a purple silk scarf. Tall, in high heels like the rest of the girls, but unlike them fully dressed in a shimmering, gossamer gown, accented by an unlit cigarette at the end of an arms-length holder. "So much to see. So much to choose from. If you know what you want." A languid sigh punctuated the remark. "A gentleman would offer me a light."

"What do you think I want?" Sean asked, searching his pockets for matches. Failing to find any, he offered a lit candle. "I was telling them, I don't need—"

"Oh honey, don't even talk about need. Not in this place. Those officers over there, they take what they need. But artists enjoy what they want. Aren't you an artist?"

"I'm a great artist," Sean said, "and I stand on the promontory of centuries. Shall we go upstairs? I'll show you."

"Are you sure you want to do this?"

Sean paid the fee. "An artist does what he wants. A great artist does what he must."

"You are a great artist. I can tell by the way you move. Kiss me."

He did. Their kiss was long, wet, tobacco-spiced.

They went upstairs and entered a room with mirrors on all sides. The bed was in the middle, beside a tall mahogany chest. On top of the chest stood a washbowl, a towel, a bar of Lysoform soap, a tin of talcum powder, and a box of prophylactics. Incense burned somewhere Sean couldn't see.

"Get undressed." The order came out low and breathy. "And then you can undress me."

"I'm fine, you see," Sean said as he obediently removed his pants. "Renzo thought I needed something. But I'm perfectly fine."

"Perfectly. A great artist. Now reach under and pull my dress up."

Sean did. What he found was not what he envisaged. He shrieked.

"Good lord. You're louder than Mona. Do you want to scare the entire house?"

"But you're a . . . You're not—"

"And you're not a great artist if you can't appreciate real beauty."

Sean fled down the stairs, dressing as he ran, thinking: *I know that face. Captain somebody. He was talking to Guido when I saw Chesa at the Governor's Palace. Oh shit.*

"Leaving already?" asked the kimono-clad aide, who met him at the bottom of the stairs. "There's spirited group action up on the third floor. Like in the painting you kept looking at but with incense and candles and bear rugs. I believe tonight they're doing satanic."

Sean bolted toward the door.

"Was that you making all that noise?" Zoe asked as he rushed past.

"He's louder than me," Mona said.

"Wait," Antonio hollered. "Come back, Mr. Reilly. Watch out for that car." He and the girls laughed and laughed.

FORTY-THREE

February 16, 1920. Renzo surprised me today. I was seated at my usual bench in Piazza Cesare Battisti when he came up. We didn't get much chance to talk at Madam Christina's. "I had to leave early," I said. Like he hadn't seen the whole fiasco. "I wasn't feeling well."

"I'm sorry about that," Renzo said. "I thought you would find it amusing. He's done this many times, and usually it gets a good laugh. D'Annunzio thinks it's hilarious."

"Tell me the truth," I said. "Was that really Captain—?"

"Yes. And you have to admit, he did look good in that dress. D'Annunzio himself would have been all over her. Him. That face would have lured any man in Fiume, I'll wager."

Watching D'Annunzio pounce on the captain, now that would have been amusing. I wonder how many men the captain has kissed and with such passion. I feel a little ashamed of my outburst at Casa Piacere. The joke was crude, but so is much other Fiume humor. The captain pretended to be a woman. Well, in a whorehouse, everyone is pretending. The girls pretend to like their customers, and the customers imagine the attention they are getting isn't just for their money.

I don't know what to make of that kiss, though.

"Mona and Zoe were disappointed when you left," Renzo told me. "Mona says she wants to model for you, if you are interested. But enough of that. I have some news for you. We found out who was responsible for attacking you. It was that *stronzetto* from the airport, the one with Antonio the day you went out there. He and a few of his friends. You must have said something to make him so mad. But don't worry. We took care of him. He is no longer in the city."

"Good," I said. Renzo's words did not make me feel any better. How many more like him lurked out there on the streets of Fiume? I didn't ask.

Renzo nodded. He probably expected a better reaction from me. Too bad. I hoped he was not going to suggest another evening at Casa Piacere. He had something else in mind, it turned out. "The quality of men we have to work with today, it's not like the old days. Many good people have left Fiume. It is hard to find the right men for the *colpi di mano* these days."

I told him I had no idea what he was talking about.

"*Colpi di mano*. Officially it's the Office of Armed Coups. Another of Keller's little projects. Since Rome imposed a blockade around Fiume, we steal from the army to get what we need. The *colpi di mano* raids their depots outside the city."

Raids. Tom had once mentioned something to me about raids.

"We need people who understand discipline and can stay under control," Renzo said. "Like you, Sean."

That struck me as laughable. Me? The one who tried to steal an airplane? "I've been accused of many things," I said, "but not discipline. I have a problem with authority."

Renzo nodded. "Yes, you do. But you are smart, and you can function under pressure. Like you did during the war."

I did not want to entertain thoughts about what I did in the war. I go to that piazza to escape memories. "That was a long time ago," I said. "Right now, all I want to do is paint and write."

He said he didn't know I was writing, and asked me about it. Two seagulls landed in front of us and started fighting noisily over a scrap of bread. I told him I'm working on a manifesto of Fiume politics. "It's been tough getting started but I'm making progress." A complete lie.

He sounded happy to hear that but said, "It must be difficult to write perceptively about a community without functioning as a part of it. Something has to be missing, no?"

A larger gull landed nearby with a loud squawk and a great show of flapping its wings. The other two backed off and watched the large newcomer devour the scrap.

"During the war," Renzo said, "no matter how bad things got, even during those awful winters, I couldn't let my country down or my soldier brothers. You felt the same way. That day at Tre Monti, when I saw you drive your ambulance through the artillery barrage, I thought to myself, That driver has the heart of a Roman warrior. With men like him on our side, we can't lose."

He stood up and all the birds scattered. "Join us on the raids, Sean," he said. "Like the poet says:

How dull it is to pause, to make an end,

To rust unburnish'd, not to shine in use!

Did I say that right?"

I got to my feet and embraced him. I told him he never ceased to amaze me, and that I would consider what he said.

"You know where to find me," he said. "*Ciao.*"

I sat back down on the bench in a deep slump. Despite Renzo's little encouraging talk—which I appreciated—I am not ready to help Fiume steal its way to a utopian future. And seriously, no one, not even Renzo, has ever confused me with a Roman warrior. Especially not Renzo. Rusting unburnished sounds to me like a better option, Tennyson notwithstanding.

Funny. People always seem sure about what I need, and often it means my joining some group I do not want to be a part of. Like the Red Cross.

FORTY-FOUR

From INTERVIEW WITH DUŠAN KCLEŽA (1992)
[UNEDITED TRANSCRIPT]

JH: I want to go back to something you mentioned earlier. You agreed to buy guns from that man you met at the Mercato. How did that go?

DK: It went off without any problem. The delivery took place over by the old French depot. I tried to bargain with the guy for a cheaper price. He wouldn't go for it, but he threw in two sticks of gelignite and a couple of detonators. I handed over the full amount.

Once I paid him and got the weapons, the man's smile disappeared. I thought, *Oh shit, here it comes,* and I looked around for I don't know what. The man said, "Forget where you got these from, and my associates and I will forget who I sold them to. Understand?"

I understood. Me and my friends packed the weapons and ammunition in some carts we brought, covered them up, and got out of there as fast as we could. We didn't want to meet his associates, whoever they were. At least not until we had a chance to load the weapons and learn how to use them.

JH: Did you suspect D'Annunzio was behind the sale?

DK: I honestly didn't know at that point. If I had to guess back then, I would have said this was some slicker peddling black market stuff. Later I started to wonder if D'Annunzio and his underlings were involved and maybe the guns wouldn't work. It wasn't until a couple weeks before D'Annunzio left that I discovered it was somebody a lot smarter and a lot worse. Somebody who wanted to use us in a bad way.

JH: Who was that?

DK: Slow down, young man. I'll get to that.

JH: By all means, keep us in suspense. You mentioned before that you had a core of solid supporters, at least initially. Were they all young like you?

DK: Mostly. We had one older guy, a man named Andrej. He was always reminding us how he fought with the Austrian Army against the Russians in the first Brusilov offensive in 1916. But we all knew the Austrian Army did not exactly distinguish itself in that campaign. Over a hundred thousand Austrians surrendered. Maybe more. It shows you what happens when you conscript people and send them far away from their homeland to fight for something they don't understand. Like America did in Vietnam.

JH: Even so, I imagine Andrej was a big help to your group, with things like tactics and logistics.

DK: Andrej was a royal pain in the ass the entire time. He stood a head taller than me, and he had this long jaw covered by a white beard. That and his silver hair made him look old and wise, like maybe he knew more than the rest of us. When I showed the group the Mosin-Nagant rifles, what does he say? "These are Russian rifles. I thought you said they were French."

"No, Andrej," I say to him. "I told you I was picking them up at the old French supply depot. Do you have a problem with Russian guns?"

"French ones are better," Andrej says. "These, I don't know. I collected a couple of Russian guns at Lutsk. They were crap."

I was in no mood to listen. I told him, "There were a lot of other guns on the ground at Lutsk, I hear, because the Austrian soldiers dropped theirs and ran away." Oh, he didn't like that at all. He gave me a nasty look.

"I wished you had picked up some food," a young guy next to Andrej said. You see, once Andrej started complaining, the others joined in.

JH: Where was your hideout?

DK: In Sušak. A small, abandoned store near the pier.

JH: So, back in Sušak, your comrades see the guns. Aside from Andrej, what was their reaction?

DK: Most of them couldn't wait to get their hands on the rifles. They were like children in a toy store. One guy sitting on the floor tried to load his rifle while it was pointed at Andrej's head. Andrej cursed him and showed him how to do it properly. Then he said, "None of you know what the fuck you're doing, do you? A bunch of babies and misfits." He turned to me. "What are your plans, assuming you have any? Before we end up shooting each other."

I knew he would challenge me. He was the only veteran in our group, and his war experience was, like you said, an asset, but I was the organizer of the group and the architect of our strategy. I was the one who brought in the weapons that no one else had been able to procure. And another card I held: my private source of intelligence. I knew where the Fiume pirates were planning to strike. Most of the time. I told the others which stores and warehouses to guard.

Also, I had the gelignite, but I didn't say anything about it right then. There are some things that not everybody needs to know, and that is more true than ever when you are in a fight. Somebody tells a friend, and the friend says something to somebody else, and next thing people get killed. Things like that you learn in troubled times. I've seen a lot of troubled times.

"We're going to drill," I said to the group. "Over on Krk island. There's a spot on the far side where we won't be seen. We can go over there at night."

"Wonderful," Andrej said. "If we don't get killed on the rocks when we land on the island, we can practice shooting each other in the dark."

What was I supposed to do with him? Leadership is so hard.

FORTY-FIVE

October 1917

Early in Sean's third year of ambulance service, Captain Fabi wanted to see him again. This time Sean didn't have to wait long in the hallway.

"Good morning, *Signor* Reilly," the captain said. "You are having a pleasant rest break, I hope."

"Yes, Captain. As usual." No point in telling senior officers about the feelings he had when he wasn't busy driving. Who knew what they might do?

"Good, good. I hope you will say good things about us after you leave."

"Leave?"

"When you join the American Red Cross. Now that they have finally deployed here in Italy, you must be anxious to serve with them."

"Have I not done good work here?"

"You are an excellent driver. No one has more courage when it comes to driving. But you must want to be with your countrymen."

An aide scurried in with papers needing immediate signature. Sean waited in silence until the aide left.

"I have no desire to sign up with the Red Cross. In France, the American volunteer drivers are being forced into the US Army as privates. I figure it's only a matter of time before they do that here. They will make me drill and wear a uniform."

"I see. You prefer the more informal ways we permit you. I won't ask why. Our other drivers love their uniforms. But you have been telling your superiors for months that you were ready to join—"

"That was before the volunteer units were militarized. Anyway, I was bluffing because I want to fly an airplane. I still do. The Red Cross will never let me. Maybe one day you will."

"Unlikely," Captain Fabi said. He rose from his chair. "Come. Let me show you something."

Sean followed the captain outside to a paved parking area where a line of new ambulances sat, immaculate, undented, and freshly painted. Each had a red cross on a white background on the side of the wood body and a spare tire thoughtfully strapped to the roof.

"Ford trucks," the captain said. "The first installment. We are promised twenty-five more, at least. The latest American technology. Lighter and faster than our Fiats. Only Red Cross drivers will be allowed behind the wheel. Are you tempted to put on that uniform now?"

Sean liked the looks of the trucks, shorter than the Fiats and with higher ground clearance. He allowed himself a few seconds to imagine driving one, feeling the power of the American engine. Then he shook his head. "No. I'll stay where I am unless you force me to quit."

"You are a peculiar man, *Signor* Reilly. It won't be easy keeping the predators from the American Red Cross away. They insist on taking over the ambulance business, and they possess money and connections in Rome. They will not be happy to learn of an American driving with us who goes almost to the front."

"Not almost. I've been all the way."

"Yes. All the way to the front. I want to keep you. But that won't be easy."

"So don't tell the Red Cross about me. I won't tell them."

They returned to his office. The captain showed Sean a map of the upper Asiago region. "The Red Cross has no interest in this sector. I can move you there, and you can continue to dress like a peasant. I'll even try to get you one of the Fords. But you will find it more difficult to drive on those mountain roads."

Sean didn't mind driving difficult roads, but the future flew over them. "Will you try to get me the ambulance airplane?"

FORTY-SIX

From SEAN REILLY'S JOURNAL

February 20, 1920. Renzo asked me again about the raids. I told him again I was still considering it. He doesn't understand my reluctance. All he remembers is how I drove during the war. He remembers Tre Monti. So do I, but I also remember lots of other days. I remember picking up the corporal. Twice. After that, I tried not to think about the men in the back of the ambulance.

The injured soldiers were humans, with lives and families, but I needed to distance myself. I don't apologize for doing it. To me they were nameless bodies, injured and needing care, and I was the best driver to get them to that care. Always bring in the wounded. No excuses. I brought them in and didn't need to see them again. Didn't want to. Other bodies soon took their places. Some died, some went home, some got patched up and sent back to the front. I had to go out the next day or the day after and rescue more. I couldn't do that unless I kept them at arm's length. Not Tom and not Renzo but the rest of them. Only on leave, when I was away from my ambulance, did I start to contemplate soldiers as people. It got to the point where I hated to see them getting on those trucks bound for the front. So many of them would have no future at all. Those memories made me drink.

I meant to write "think," but yes, drink.

February 23, 1920. I tried to work on the manifesto. It seemed a way I could promote Futurism with less risk of injury to my person. The people of Fiume can read, at their leisure and in the safety of their own homes or favorite cafés, about Fiume's role in nurturing Futurism, and Futurism's shepherding of Fiume and the rest of the world into a bright tomorrow. Whatever I achieve with a pen and paper might carry over to sessions with a paintbrush and canvas.

The idea wasn't bad. Execution is another matter. It seems the altar boy can't even light the candles anymore.

After several hours trying to write, I feel the walls of the apartment closing in. My neighbors make their usual noises, and the radiator clanks like someone is hitting it over and over with a large hammer. My jaw aches. I need some kind of respite.

FORTY-SEVEN

From *Memories of a Fascist in Fiume*
by Tenente Lorenzo Guidici

Last night, my prison cell was colder than usual and my cell-mates more annoying. I would have no reluctance to silence one or two of them, but since I share these filthy quarters with eight others, I am forced to endure their whining. To take my mind off my prison environment, I find it pleasant to detail in this memoir some of the more amusing moments of my time in Fiume. Like the day I came up with the idea for the Castle of Love.

I left the barracks early that morning and went to see Guido Keller. The Action Secretary of the Fiume Command was sitting in a tree in a secluded part of town, carrying on a spirited conversation. Not until I got close did I notice Guido was talking to an owl.

"I've got an idea," I said. I stood by the trunk, enjoying the bite of the February morning air on my face. "You might find it amusing."

"I'm listening." Guido made no move to climb down.

"You want to get rid of D'Annunzio's mistress, I assume."

"Which one? If you mean Luisa Baccara, certainly." The woman in question was the *Comandante*'s latest great love, a pianist whom he had installed in the Palace. She quickly became unpopular with everyone in the Command, pestering all of us to limit his activities and trying with little success to fend off his other girls. "What is your idea?"

"The Castle of Love," I said.

Guido dropped out of the tree, narrowly missing my head on the way down. He was clothed only in a blanket. "The Castle of Love? Isn't there enough love in Fiume already? A little too much, perhaps."

Guido's blanket flapped open in the breeze. I discreetly looked away while I unfolded my idea. "In Treviso, in medieval days, they held a festival—Lord knows we're no stranger to those here—where they gathered all the prettiest girls and put them in a wooden castle, and the men attacked by tossing food and coins and flowers at them. Gently, of course. Then the men stormed the castle. After the battle was over and the castle was liberated, they had a wild love fest."

"This is your great idea? A food fight followed by an orgy? Sounds rather tame by Fiume standards. No grenades?"

"Hear me out, Guido. We set up the castle at the beach and make Luisa Baccara the queen. When the battle is at its peak and the men are rushing in and the ladies are swooning, a few trustworthy Arditi grab her, put her on a boat—preferably in a cage—and push it out into the bay, where somebody tows the boat to one of the islands or up the coast to Trieste."

"You are a sick bastard," Guido said. "Have I told you before?"

"Once or twice," I admitted. "Here's another idea. We put Wickson and Kochnitzky and a couple others in a second boat and maybe this one doesn't get towed very far. Maybe it has a hole in the bottom."

"Now you're getting crazy," Guido said. "But I like the first idea. Let me talk to D'Annunzio about the Castle. It sounds like something he'd enjoy."

Leaving Guido to his owl, I returned to the center of the city. I was getting concerned about Sean. The raid was scheduled for the following week, and I wanted him to join the crew. At lunchtime, I decided to try Gaj's. I spotted Chesa seated at a table in the rear, deep in conversation with the twins. To me, it had the makings of a perfect meal: excellent food enjoyed with three lovely women and no other men to distract me with talk of politics or trucks. I went directly to their table.

Chesa welcomed me. "You must join us," she said. "It's terribly crowded today. We were having a little girl talk, but you are welcome to listen. This is how I find out what's going on in Fiume. These young ladies know everything and everybody."

I seated myself next to Chesa. "Please continue," I said. "I would love to hear what is going on. Not much news reaches me these days."

"I'll tell you," said Annalisa, beaming. "The *Comandante* will travel to Zara a couple of days from now. Luisa Baccara is furious. She demanded that he not go. She says it's not safe. They had quite a row. The *Comandante* ordered everybody out of the room, which was silly because we stood outside in the hall and could hear everything."

Chesa turned to me. "This is why I love these girls. One can't get scoops like this anywhere else."

"I couldn't agree with you more," I said. Each of the twins, I noted, pinned her hair in a knot at the nape of her neck, like Chesa. Quite becoming. "But may I caution you all? The trip to Zara is not public information. For security reasons, you understand. Let's keep the secret to ourselves, please. Now, where is Gaj? Service seems slow today. Ah, here he comes."

Gaj hurried over, sporting his customary smile. "Good afternoon. Ladies, I see you are joined by a distinguished guest. Tenente, you are a lucky, lucky man to dine with such beauties. Someday you must tell me your secret."

"You are the lucky one, Gaj," I said. "These three angels chose your place. Me? I'm simply a poor wretch they took pity on because of the crowd."

Gaj roared with his cheery laugh. "My friends, I am happy to see you all. And do you know who was here earlier? The *Comandante* himself! With Miss Baccara. He told me he is going to Zara next week and wanted a good meal before he left."

Annalisa kicked me under the table.

"The lunch took much effort," Gaj said, "but the meal panned out beautifully. The *Comandante* told Veselko it was the best he's eaten since coming to Fiume. Can you imagine?"

"That's brilliant," Chesa said, clapping her hands. "Congratulations. But where is your son? The girls were keen on talking to him."

"I am sorry to disappoint you. He worked so hard serving the *Comandante,* I gave him a little vacation." Gaj glanced over at me. "The boy stood around staring at these women. I told him, 'Go on. Go home. You're useless now.' A father has got to protect his young son from temptation. Besides, his exams are soon. I gave him the week off."

"Gaj, you are terrible," Chesa said. "Look at these poor girls. They're wretched."

"No," I said. "Gaj is absolutely right. A father must do what he can to keep his boy safe from the dangers of the world."

Gaj roared again, with the ease of someone unaware of how close danger lurked. If only he had known. "You understand me perfectly. Now, may I take your orders?"

When Gaj had gone to the kitchen, I asked Chesa if she knew where I could find Sean. I was pretty sure they were not back together as lovers, but it was possible she might have run into him during one of her spying expeditions around the city. She said she had not seen him in several weeks but did not elaborate.

The convivial banter with the twins continued. Gaj returned carrying the meals himself. "Enjoy," he said. "I must get back to the kitchen. Why did I ever let that boy go home?"

"Delightful man," said Chesa after he left. "And his son is so much like him. Quite the charmer. Gaj is right to shield him from you two vampires, though."

"What about Gaj's other son, the older one?" I asked. "I don't recall ever meeting him. One never sees him around the restaurant."

"I knew him in high school," Annalisa said. "His name is Dušan. He was cute. Tall and skinny, shaggy dark hair, a little awkward. Pretty wild, as I remember."

"Dušan might be a more suitable target for you girls," Chesa said. "What man could possibly hope to resist either of you?"

"The *Comandante* has been holding out so far," Capricia said, "but mostly due to that witch Luisa Baccara, who watches him like a mother hen. She tries to chase all the girls away."

Chesa's face flushed red. I wondered, had the mother hen spotted Chesa sporting with the rooster? It was none of my business, but I felt sorry for poor Sean. "I was hoping you had seen Sean," I said to her, "since you go all over the city to take your photographs. Where have you gone lately?"

"All over," Chesa said. "Here and there."

Yes, I thought, *all over*. Even after I had tried to warn her. The spy with her camera. I ate quickly and stood up. "Most reluctantly, I must leave you ladies. Please accept my apologies and continue with your meal. To make up for my untimely departure, lunch will be my treat." I laid a pile of notes on the table and leaned over toward Chesa. "If you happen to see Sean, please ask him to get in touch with me. I have a special invitation for him."

Chesa stared straight ahead in the direction of the twins. She nodded her head slightly.

"When you find Sean," the irrepressible Annalisa said, "tell him my invitation is open, too."

On my return to the Governor's Palace, I found Guido descending the staircase, having traded his towel for tunic and puttees.

"I was looking for you," Guido said. "Do you have a full crew for the Sušak raid next week? You will need at least eight men. Good ones, please. No crazies. We don't want any trouble."

"It's a good crew and a good plan. I'm not worried. We'll get in, clean out the warehouse, and be gone before anyone knows what hit them. Much easier than an army depot."

"Excellent," Guido said. "One more thing. I spoke to the *Comandante* about your Castle of Love plan. He laughed and laughed. I thought for a moment he might go for it. But then he said no because it would be, get this, too decadent. Right. He said the Castle was 'too D'Annunzian.'"

Too D'Annunzian, indeed. Had the Castle been implemented, who can say what the effect on D'Annunzio might have been? Perhaps his time in Fiume might have been shortened, and the emergence of Fascism on the mainland might have been accelerated. Here in my crowded cell, I have plenty of time to speculate on how things might have turned out differently, for Fascism and for me. But I am writing a factual account, so I will spare the reader any more of my conjecture.

FORTY-EIGHT

February 24, 1920

The morning rain had let up, leaving only a few clouds to mar the sky. *Forget painting or writing for the day,* Sean decided. *Strain the body instead. The mind will come around when it's ready.* It was time to tackle the ancient stone stairs up to Trsat Castle. All 560 steps.

Sean went outside and swallowed deep breaths of fresh air. He began to relax. At the bridge into Sušak, a sullen guard examined his papers and waved him through. He crossed the river and soon found the tiny Baroque chapel marking the entrance to the stairs. The chapel was open in front and back and quite small, allowing him to traverse its entirety with four or five decent steps. It reminded Sean of a pedestrian toll booth. He walked through and beheld a long, intimidating climb.

Get going, he told himself. *Not too fast.* He mounted the first steps free of any thought of Futurism or Fiume. Small landings broke off at ten-step intervals. He stopped at the fifth landing and did a self-evaluation. Fifty steps, more or less. *Not bad.* Breathing was a little heavier, but his legs were not tired. He went on.

On some of the landings, gates led to houses built right against the stairs or to paths that went off and quickly disappeared. At others, small stone chapels had been erected. He paused at one to look in through an open iron door. Fresh-cut red and purple flowers and a wooden cross adorned a tiny marble altar. A small oil painting of the Holy Family hung on the wall.

The steps narrowed as he climbed higher. He had to stop again soon to slow his breathing. Sweat formed on his forehead. An old woman in a black coat and wool cap passed him on the stairs without stopping or speaking. She carried two sacks filled with groceries.

He looked ahead as far as he could and observed how the stairs tapered off to a point. Aiming for that spot, he pressed on, but before he reached it the stairs curved to the right and continued to another vanishing point that also faded as he approached. Wild ideas came to him for his manifesto about the role of art in the vanguard of the new order being created in Fiume. An international league of Futurist artist-governors leads the world upward on a perpetual climb out of the fetid cesspools of tradition and war and usurping world powers. The climb never ends. Younger and stronger men take over and throw the older ones aside like bad paintings and useless manuscripts, locking their predecessors in deconsecrated chapels. The ghosts of the war are silenced in a new era of pulsing creativity. He put a hand to his forehead. Ideas collided without connecting, getting him nowhere. Pushing onward, he fixed on the latest vanishing point. This one didn't go away. He hurried up the steps and stopped.

A dirt road lay before him. Beyond, to his dismay but not surprise, rose another set of steps. He glanced around while catching his breath. A few meters to his left, a woman with a camera stood by a stone railing, focusing on the landscape below. Chesa.

She did not turn around or even look up, but he didn't need to see her face. He instantly recognized the baggy white pants and blazing red coat, her distinctive working-photographer outfit.

"Hello, stranger," she called out. "Come all the way up these stairs to see me?"

"No," he said and moved on to the next flight of stairs. He heard her call his name but didn't stop.

The manifesto, he told himself as he climbed. *Concentrate.* Reconcile burgeoning nationalism with artist-inspired revolution under a new global system rising in challenge to the old colonial powers and what the hell was she doing up here taking pictures, today of all days? Were there not any other buildings or people she could capture in her bleak photos? Abruptly, the steps ended. He had reached the summit.

He didn't see the castle. A few hundred meters ahead stood a peculiar looking church. Its two-story cream-colored façade was topped by a curved crown, with a tall bell tower sticking up in the middle. It resembled the bell the nuns used in the schoolyard at his elementary school to summon the children.

A voice behind him asked, "Do you know the story of this church?"

Chesa again. He did not feel like any playful banter, and it was neither the time nor the place for a confrontation. "No," he said. "But I'm sure you'll tell me."

If she heard the edge to his reply, she did not react. "This is the Church of Our Lady of Trsat. Back in the late thirteenth century, the site was the location of the house of the Virgin Mary. Angels moved it here from Nazareth. I guess they were just resting because three years later they picked it up again and moved the whole thing to Loreto. I'm not sure if it's still there. Could be in Cornwall by now for all I know, or maybe Texas. Anyway, this church was built on the spot where Mary's house used to be. Then some sixty or seventy years later the Pope felt sorry for the locals and for the pilgrims who visited from all over the world and were no doubt disappointed not to find Mary's house up here after climbing all those damned steps, so he gave the church a painting of Mary to cheer them up. It's hanging inside there today."

"Sad story," Sean said. "One day you have the Mother of God's house on your hill, and the next, it's flown away to Italy, and you're stuck with a consolation painting."

"The part I like best," Chesa said, "is that people keep coming here on pilgrimages to see where the house used to be. Shall we go on to the castle?"

She knew the way, unlike him. They strolled together in silence, as two strangers might transit the same city sidewalk at the same time linked by nothing more than coincidence. The narrow dirt path curved along a tangle of low scrub before opening into a sunbaked meadow bordered on their left by a row of hedges. A light breeze stirred the grass. The ground sloped upward gently. Sean tried to think of something appropriate to say, but before he could come up with anything, the path veered sharply left and cut through a gap in the hedges. From the other side, the upper elevation of the castle loomed over a small cluster of pine trees. A few minutes later they stood before its walls.

"This is so perfect," Chesa said. "It has everything a good castle needs: massive walls, turrets, and a tower with little pointed roofs. The only thing missing is the dragon."

"And a princess," Sean said. Chesa smiled and curtsied. They stood close, each studying the other's face. Her eyes—beautiful emerald eyes that always seemed brazen, fiery, intense even when she smiled—those eyes looked different now. Searching instead of sending out signals.

He turned away, and they resumed walking. The path led them to an unadorned wood door between two columns. "The place is a mish-mash of styles and shapes," she said as they entered the courtyard.

"Hardly fit for a princess," Sean said.

The wood door was locked. She located an open stairway farther on. They climbed it and emerged onto a stone patio. A small temple-like building with formal columns and pediment squatted between a fat round tower and a tall bastion with a pointed top.

Chesa disappeared inside the tower. Sean lingered on the patio and looked down on both Sušak and Fiume. The structures behind him brought to mind a metaphor for the manifesto: art occupied the center and the military rose high, off to the side, looking over . . . over what? And the fat tower: what did it signify? Wealth? Industry? A unity of diverse elements, all organized around . . . something. His train of thought slipped away at the sound of Chesa's voice from high above.

"Sean," she called out from the parapet. "Look up."

He stood motionless, eyes shut.

"Come on up, please. You've got to see this."

"I'm enjoying the view right here."

"Oh. Sorry." She was silent for a few seconds. "I'll be up here taking photos. Splendid view, really, in all directions."

He moved to the edge of the patio and leaned on the railing. *Leave,* he told himself. *Now. This minute. You've had your exercise. The castle gave you an idea for your manifesto. Don't let it get away.* He stepped away from the railing and headed in the direction of the stairs on which they had come up. Like Orpheus, he knew the danger of looking back.

"Are you leaving?" Chesa called out. "Pity. You can see things here you can't see from anywhere else." He glanced up and spotted her through one of the crenels. "At least come say goodbye, would you? Please?"

Orpheus surrendered to temptation. He entered the tower and climbed the stairs. He noted the narrow treads, less than a meter wide, and risers of varying heights, all designed to give an advantage in a swordfight to the defenders at the top. Something else to be worked into the manifesto, somehow.

Chesa greeted him from her spot on the parapet. "You made it. I'm glad. It's so different up here. I can't wait to develop these photographs." She pulled down the locking lever on her camera and used it to steady the lens on the battlement. Long strands of her hair escaped the little knot in the back and fell across her cheek. She brushed them away with a free hand.

Sean drifted lazily to his right until he faced due west. In the distance, he spotted the street where he suffered the castor oil attack. It brought back a memory he had no wish to entertain.

He looked farther north in the general direction of where Piero must have been hiking. The brown-and-gray hillside rose sharply behind the castle, hiding from his sight the villages and hamlets that lay in the valley immediately beyond.

As he started to turn away, a tiny shape caught his eye, a wrinkle that marred an otherwise unblemished hill. At such a distance, he could not make out any more detail. It was a smudge out of place on the slope. Not something he would likely have noticed had he not been thinking of Piero. He asked Chesa if she had taken any photos in that direction.

"Not yet. Working my way around. Didn't I tell you this was fantastic?"

"No. You said it was splendid." He continued staring at the spot where he had seen the mysterious shape. A few patches of green sprouted amid limestone and browned scrub on either side. "Could you bring your camera over here, please?"

"Give me a sec," she said. A rough grunt followed the metallic click and dull thud of the shutter. "Got it," she said and came over to where he stood.

"Are you able to enlarge photographs?" he asked.

"Yes. Some. Gaj may be able to help if I can't. His darkroom is better equipped than mine. But the enlarged photos won't be very clear if the object is too far away. What am I shooting at?"

Sean pointed, guiding her as she photographed the spot from several angles and at different speeds and aperture openings. Behind him, he could hear the panting voices of fresh visitors to the parapet. He ignored them and focused on Chesa. Her movements with the camera could not honestly be called graceful. Professional, unquestionably. He had often seen her more beautiful, more elegantly dressed and made up. But never had she appeared more desirable. He could not take his eyes off her. He wanted her touch. He craved her smell, her breath. She stood and faced him before he was ready.

"You look like you're studying a painting," she said. "Let me get a photo of you." Without pausing to refocus, she snapped the photograph. As the shutter clicked, a voice behind him cried out, "My hat!"

He spun around. A woman with one hand on her head pointed with the other at a red hat skidding toward the edge of the parapet.

Sean ran after the hat and captured it seconds before the wind could blow it over the side.

"I believe I've caught a hero in action," she said after he returned the hat to its owner. "Oh Sean, you should have seen your face when you heard the lady scream. I captured you right as the excitement started. I even snapped one as you almost went over the edge after the hat. It was priceless."

"I'm sure it was," Sean said.

"You will have to visit me, to see the photos. Won't you?"

FORTY-NINE

From SEAN REILLY'S JOURNAL

February 24, 1920. I spent the whole afternoon exploring Trsat Castle with Chesa Rei, the woman who betrayed me. I cannot tell you why, any more than I can explain why I have remained in Fiume after all that has happened. For a short time up there it felt like that day when we explored the Capuchin Church. It seems so long ago. I feel like one of those pilgrims who climb the stairs to visit a sacred house that isn't there anymore.

I am anxious to see the photos Chesa took of the area beyond the castle. Perhaps they will provide a clue to what happened to Piero. I suppose I could hike out there myself, but those hills are steep and unforgiving. If Piero couldn't survive out there, as good a hiker as he was, it's no place for me. Funny, if there were a road there for me to drive, I wouldn't hesitate for a minute. If I had a car, that is. But I don't.

She promised the photos would be developed in a few days. By that time I should have my feelings once again under control. Orpheus will lead again, facing forward, stronger after a few days' rest. Meanwhile, I have important manifesto work to get on with. Despite our amiable interaction at the castle, I cannot forget she betrayed me. Up there on the castle tower, her camera may have caught me, but that was just on film.

FIFTY

From INTERVIEW WITH DUŠAN KCLEŽA (1992)
[UNEDITED TRANSCRIPT]

JH: Around the time you bought the rifles, D'Annunzio began preaching to the world about the League of Fiume. He had this farfetched idea to lead a multinational battle—a "crusade" he called it—against the more powerful countries. He even targeted the Serbs. Did that have any attraction for you?

DK: No. The idea was crazy stupid. Anybody could see that. Except him, apparently. He didn't know that some of his trusted Italian friends were working against him, behind the scenes. Laughing at him, probably. I'll never understand why anybody thought he was worthy of respect.

If he wanted to fight Serbs, he didn't have to go far or recruit any other countries. The Serbs were right there, north of the city. He could have sent those legionnaires of his after them. What I think is, he didn't want to fight anybody. He just wanted to be the *Comandante* and live in the Governor's Palace and screw all the women. He told everybody about this crusade to make himself look important but didn't believe it himself. At least, that's what I heard.

JH: You talked earlier about the pirate raids the Italians conducted and how you were getting information in advance about where these raids were going. Can you tell us from whom, or would that betray some confidence?

DK: I can tell you now. My brother heard things, working in the restaurant. The customers, especially those Italian legionnaires, they saw him waiting on tables and didn't think nothing of him. He was just another smiling face, understand? So they would drink and talk and he would listen. Then he would tell me things. Not all of it useful, of course. But sometimes he would hear about some action they were going to take, and we'd make sure that when the time came, our people were there first. With guns.

JH: Quite courageous of your brother. Is he older or younger? I don't recall hearing much about him.

DK: Younger. His name was Veselko, and he died too young. Over seventy years ago. I miss him every day.

JH: You were close.

DK: As kids, we were. Then as I grew older, I was, you know, the oldest son. I had a lot of pressure on me from my father, and I didn't like that. Plus I was politically aware and always speaking out, especially in school. I was the troublemaker, and Veselko was the good little boy, the golden child. My parents fussed all over him. But it wasn't his fault.

FIFTY-ONE

February 27, 1920

Sean waited in the dimly lit hallway outside Kochnitzky's office at the Palace, wrestling with how to fit the League of Fiume into his manifesto.

"What is the purpose of your visit?" Kochnitzky demanded when he finally let Sean in. The man looked to be in his late twenties, much younger than Sean envisioned. He had a soft, boyish face topped by a mass of thick black hair. His eyes, in contrast, were dark and shadowed by heavy lids, like an old man's. Sean described his work on a manifesto about Fiume and said Marinetti recommended him as a good person to talk with. Flattery didn't work with Kochnitzky, or perhaps Sean hadn't employed a sufficient quantity.

"Another Futurist. It seems Marinetti cannot get enough of Fiume. I had rather thought he might lose interest after he was deported. But no, he sends one of his myrmidons. An American." He said the last word with obvious distaste.

"An American, yes. I'm also an artist who painted in Paris and Italy before serving with the Italian Army during the war." Sean didn't clarify that his service had been limited to ambulances. He figured the Belgian spent the war hiding in a library somewhere safe.

"The League of Fiume unites peoples of all nations, races, tribes, et cetera," Kochnitzky said. "Ours is an anti-League of Nations, organized to support the victims of French, British, and American imperialist avarice. Now, if you will excuse me, I must prepare for an important meeting with the *Comandante*."

Sean, too, had an important meeting awaiting him. Chesa had developed the photographs she took at the castle. But he was not ready to leave, not without more details for his manifesto.

"Why hasn't there been more progress with the League?" he asked. A fair question, if somewhat aggressive. "I heard the *Comandante* talk in October about reaching out to oppressed people. What action, if any, has there been since then?"

The reaction was quick and sharp. Sean was obviously not the first to press the Belgian on the slow pace. "Matters of diplomacy are complex," Kochnitzky said, in a voice that exploded like an old shotgun. "It may be hard for painters to understand, but negotiating international agreements is more difficult than slapping paint on canvas or penning manifestos. I assure you there has been significant progress, but I am not at liberty to discuss it with you."

It surprised Sean to hear a poet make such a distinction between art and politics and then emphasize the complexity of the latter in contrast to the former. Did he seriously believe creating art was easier than chatting with politicians? He decided to switch topics on Kochnitzky before coming back to the League. "Piero Terruzzi, a prominent Futurist, was murdered in the hills above the city last year. What has been done to solve the crime?"

"How should I know? You said you wanted to talk about the League. This is the Office of External Relations, not the police. Go ask them."

"I did. Piero was a good hiker and an effective voice for Futurism here in Fiume. Someone silenced him. The murder was investigated, was it not?"

Kochnitzky stood up and opened the window, letting in cold air. "I know nothing about the dead man. I can tell you many people want to silence me and put an end to my work in Fiume. Do you know why?"

Sean didn't answer. He sensed Kochnitzky, despite his abrupt demeanor, wanted to talk.

"We, D'Annunzio's Command, are an embarrassment to the Italian government, Mr. Reilly. They hate us because D'Annunzio marched when they feared to act. The Serbs hate us because they want the city and the port for themselves. The Croats do not want us or the Serbs here and cannot make up their minds which of us they loathe more. Your American president and the other leaders of the so-called Great Powers try to impose their League of Nations on the world so they can oppress everyone else. The Socialists in Rome don't want Fiume to succeed because they are confident only they know all the answers, and the veterans' groups look at Fiume as a distraction from the coronation of Mussolini. Does any of that relate to your friend's death? I cannot begin to speculate."

Good material, but Sean wanted more. "Perhaps the *Comandante's* message is too confusing. At times he sounds like an ardent nationalist, making the occupation all about Italy. Then he declares he wants to lead the world or, at least, the less developed part. Does the League need a man with more diplomatic experience to help the *Comandante*?" If Kochnitzky had a problem with American artists, Sean wanted him to understand that Belgian poets were vulnerable too.

Kochnitzky glared at him like he wanted to spit. "Are you familiar with the works of Giuseppe Mazzini, the intellectual father of Italy's independence? Probably not. If you were, you would appreciate the century-old dream of a strong Italy uniting other peoples in a Third Rome. I have neither the time nor the inclination to explain history to you. Perhaps Mr. Marinetti can make a few reading recommendations when he is not busy crashing his automobiles into ditches."

Sean made a note to read up on Mazzini in the books Marinetti had sent and forged on. "When I listen to the *Comandante* speak, I hear great things. His speech about the crusade was inspiring. But meanwhile here in Fiume, on the streets, folks aren't safe. One evening at the Governor's Palace I said something about Piero Terruzzi to the wrong people, and that night I got the castor oil treatment. How is the League going to improve things in the world at large when right here in Fiume Piero gets murdered and people like me who ask questions get assaulted?"

Kochnitzky stood again and this time darted to the door, opened it, and glanced up and down the hallway. He closed the door quietly and came back but remained on his feet. "Who did you direct your questions to? Did they say anything about money?"

"Good guess. But I am not at liberty to say more." This was starting to be fun.

"Progress comes at a high cost, and we are beset with a cash problem. Donors make financial commitments to help the League but never come through with the cash. Our enemies are hard at work. They make us look bad. D'Annunzio is unable to deliver on his promises. The League of Fiume can unite the oppressed but only if it can dispense funds."

Once the man got started, the words came flowing out like water after a sluice had been opened. Sean scribbled notes furiously on his pad. "You're saying you need to bribe the oppressed peoples to rally them. Why?"

"That is the world we live in. It runs on money. Not electricity. And for reasons I don't fully understand, money doesn't make its way to Fiume. Are Futurists willing to contribute? Or do you just talk?"

"What is the League's position regarding Croatians? Are they considered oppressed people whom the League is willing to help, and if so, who are they being oppressed by?"

"The League is glad to help anyone battle Serbian aggression, the same as we would help anyone trying to free themselves from the French or the British. But all that has nothing to do with Italian Fiume." He was silent for a moment, contemplating papers on his desk. "What have you heard about the League from Marinetti? Is support for D'Annunzio strong in Milan? Would they object to giving if they knew a portion of the funds went to, say, communists?"

"Those I talk with expressed mixed feelings. They need to understand the enterprise better."

Kochnitzky fixed his eyes on Sean, and for the first time since Sean entered the man's office, he felt noticed. "We face enemies here in the city who want the League to fail. Enemies I cannot yet identify. Perhaps you and I can help each other."

Sean put his pen down. No one in Fiume had asked him for help before, other than Renzo, and that was for a raid.

"Mr. Reilly," Kochnitzky said, slowly, "I need information. Apart from D'Annunzio, few at the Command speak to me. But you, with your friends here at the Palace, you may hear things. Let me know what they are saying about the League. And about Fiume and its future. Who supports the League and who doesn't. Where has the money gone? I will see what I can learn about your friend."

The audacity of the suggestion left Sean dumbstruck. "You are asking me to spy for you?"

"Something is going on, Mr. Reilly," he said. "I can feel it."

FIFTY-TWO

From SEAN REILLY'S JOURNAL

February 27, 1920. Visited the Palace today. First time since that night.

I took an instant and intense dislike to Kochnitzky and everything about him: his elegant black suit and starched white collar, his sanctimonious air, his funny accent, his smug tone that made clear he had tolerated my presence long enough, and his shallow two-sentence summary of the League I could have gotten from any newspaper. Even his hair annoyed me, thick and black and piled up impossibly high on his head.

At least he wasn't as bad as Wickson. And he did, finally, take an interest in what I said about Piero and promised to help, although at a price. He wants me to feed him information about what people in the Command are saying about the League. How ridiculous is that, me as a spy? He's the one who works right there in the Governor's Palace, not me.

I left Kochnitzky's office feeling disturbed. His paranoia sounds ridiculous, except that I share the fear.

FIFTY-THREE

From *Memories of a Fascist in Fiume*
by Tenente Lorenzo Guidici

If asked at what point *l'impresa di Fiume* devolved into *la tragedia di Fiume*, I would say mid-January, when Léon Kochnitzky returned to the city, this time as the head of the Foreign Office. It was pretentious for D'Annunzio to create a Foreign Office for this sleepy little town in the first place and simply preposterous to let that Belgian communist run it.

As much as D'Annunzio seemed to enjoy being the *Comandante*, it was obvious by this time he had tired of the hard work required. He spent most of his days visiting the barracks in the mornings to chat with the legionnaires and then, in the afternoons, taking naps or giving speeches or entertaining the stream of visitors at the Palace. His nights were spent in vintage D'Annunzian fashion with the ladies. Not much work got done.

In that vacuum, Kochnitzky got started right away. I will give him credit for that. Despite little money and only a few helpers, he reached out to every communist and leftist and anarchist from Ireland, Hungary, Germany, Morocco, China and everywhere else. His project was the League of Fiume, and any terrorist was welcome as long as he had a grudge against the British or the French. Even Bolsheviks were courted. Fiume was going to lead them. Which, of course, was madness. Who but a poet would even consider associating with these people? What Italy needed was the elimination of social conflicts, not alignment with more troublemakers.

FIFTY-FOUR

February 27, 1920

Sean sat on the floor of Chesa's hotel room with a stack of photographs on his lap, shifting his body around until he found the best natural light for viewing. He tried not to think of the last time he had been in this room. Chesa sat beside him.

They started with the photographs she took of the hills behind the castle. "I can't do much with these," she said. "Sorry they're so blurry. I've already enlarged the photographs as much as I can without turning them into mush." She went through the pile and picked out two. "I'll see if Gaj can help with these."

The mystery in the hills refused to give up its secrets. Sean thanked her for the work she did and sat patiently while she flipped through the other photographs she had taken that day. They were nice but not especially arresting. Shots of the quay and the roads leading into the city from the north. He complimented them anyway. "You're too kind," she said, and then leaned over and kissed him.

He wanted her. Right then, there on the floor or on the bed, it didn't matter. All notion of resisting her dissolved. He felt himself sliding down a slick tube, heading for a place his head kept telling him he shouldn't go.

"Here's something I don't understand," he said to arrest the slide. He picked up the photograph of him and the lady who lost her hat. "I swear she was a couple meters behind me. How come we're both perfectly in focus?"

She took the photograph and examined it. "The circle of confusion," she said. "I'll give you a quick lesson. It's a bit arcane, but here goes. Keep in mind photographs are two-dimensional, not three. What you see here is the result of light going through a lens and hitting the film. Light comes into the lens in the form of a cone—big object, tiny lens opening. It expands on the other side of the lens somewhat to hit the film. There's a spot where the focus point lines up with the focal plane. You're not following this at all, are you?"

He reached over, grabbed her blouse to pull her close, and kissed her, a long warm kiss like they used to share. She didn't stop him. His slide picked up speed. She pulled her head back and retrieved the photograph from where it had fallen from her hand.

"Now what in Christ's name was I going on about? Oh yes. Some points of light make dots on the film that are too big, some too small. Others fit just right." She giggled. He started to make a joke but she cut him off. "Hush. Let me make this simple. If the aperture is large, only a subject located the perfect distance away will be in focus. If the aperture is small, a lot more points of light can play tricks on us and look like they are in focus."

"But the larger opening is best for objects closer in, correct? If you want to capture a subject far away, you need a small lens opening."

"Bang on." She gave his leg a playful squeeze. "Yes, it's a trade-off. When you open the aperture, that gives you a more accurate photograph but it's limited. Only a few objects are captured in focus. When you narrow it, you get more information because more dots are in focus, but you lose accuracy of depth perception. In effect, the photo starts to tell lies. I had stopped down the aperture to take the photos you wanted of the hills. I didn't get a chance to open it up when the hat flew away. That's why you seem dark in the photograph but everything is in focus, both you and the lady. It told a lie."

"So what is the circle of confusion?" he asked. "The little dots on the film or the whole area that's in focus?" He never did get an answer. The lesson was over. She slid over and straddled him, pressing her mouth over his. Within seconds her clothes were draped on the chair, his heaped on the floor.

He dropped onto his back, scattering the photographs as he pulled her on top of him. She lowered herself onto his cock and began rocking, her back arched. Her gyrations were fast. She grabbed the back of his head with one hand and with the other pulled him deeper into her. Something felt different, though, not like it used to be. His fault, hers? He rolled her over on her back and pinned her hands to the floor. She had climbed the stairs to D'Annunzio's rooms, scurried up them to spend the night there, and he hadn't done anything to stop her. He used his weight to slow the pace of her writhing movements, forcing them to match his. Light filtered in from the open curtains and fell across the white skin of her face. The image of her on those stairs wouldn't leave his brain. She groaned, calling his name. Her eyes were closed. He slowed his thrusts even more, in and out, making them harder, more punishing. He wanted the pounding to dim all thoughts in his head of that night at the Palace. Her arm and leg muscles began clenching. She was close, her face flushed and serious. He let go of her hands and reached under her back. Squeezing her hard, he emptied himself into her with a violence he had never before dared. She shuddered, mouth open, marking her climax with her nails dug into his back.

When they were both spent, she pushed him onto his side. The afternoon light had vanished. Voices from the street below floated up, laughter and shouts. Had he crossed a line with her? D'Annunzio would have been gentler. And used cushions instead of the floor. She climbed the stairs at the Palace to D'Annunzio but came down the Trsat stairs to Sean. They didn't kiss. She lay next to him, stroking his forehead. He traced a finger over her collarbone and breasts. "I have a present for you," she whispered.

After a while, she scurried off to the bathroom. He could hear water running. She returned wearing a soft red velvet robe. Wide lapels crossed her chest, and lines of loose pleats fell to her ankles. Sean sat up. In her hands she carried a second robe, matching in style but royal blue. "This is for you. Sorry it's not wrapped with a bow, but

I didn't know if . . ." He stood and slipped the robe on. It felt yielding and snug like a blanket against his warm and sweating skin. Chesa pulled the sides together and tied the belt for him. She stepped back and studied him. "Beautiful," she said.

She squatted and scooped up the photographs that lay scattered on the floor. "Now that we're decent, tell me about what Léon Kochnitzky had to say. Is he steadfast in his enthusiasm about the League to rule the world?"

Her questions caught Sean by surprise. Who asks about international politics after a fucking like they just had? He buried his hands in the robe's deep pockets and recounted his discussion with Kochnitzky. When he came to the part where Kochnitzky asked him to gather information, Chesa shook her head.

"You declined, of course," she said. "What an outrageous thing to ask."

"I said I would let him know if I hear anything he should be aware of. I plan to go out on those raids with Renzo and Tom, a few times, anyway, so I may learn a thing or two. The raids should help my writing. Futurist manifestos are most authentic when the writer is active in fomenting the change he is trying to describe."

"Oh, please." She threw herself on the bed, pulling the red robe tightly around her. "Spare me. Let's call it what it is. You're going to go steal from people you don't know and tattle on your friends while you do it. All for the glory of the *Comandante* and his League of Oppressed Whatever. Plenty of Futurist honor there, surely." She brought her feet onto the bed and curled into a fetal position. "Sorry. I warned you I'm brutal. Read me your manifesto, please. I want to understand you."

He sat cross-legged on the floor and opened his notebook. She closed her eyes while he read. Each time he glanced up from his notes, he observed an ugly grimace marring her face. The muscles in her cheeks tightened, and her lips compressed like she tasted something awful. When he finished, she lay there and didn't say anything.

"Was it that bad?" he asked. "No need for God's honest truth tonight." A little joke, a throwback to a more innocent time.

"It's tripe. All this rubbish about artist-governors leading the world and perpetual creative whatever. And that part about art in between the towers of industry and the military—what in God's name is that supposed to mean? Even allowing for the usual hyperbole, it's painful to listen to. You want heroes and epics, and you are convinced you see them when you're only looking at mirages. It reminds me of the times when I take photographs and think, oh, that looks nice, but later, when I develop them, all I see are old buildings in a dirty city."

"And dirty people. Yet you keep taking photographs. So you must find some things worth seeing and preserving."

"It would seem so," she said.

"And you didn't see any problem taking pictures of the *Comandante* at his rallies."

"What's your point?" Her tone sharpened, like a dog's growling when it senses trouble.

"The *Comandante* must have looked awfully heroic when you went to his rooms and spent the night with him."

"You ass." She sat up. Her face flushed red, almost the color of her robe. "I should have guessed this was coming when I criticized your precious writing. Yes, I went to his rooms that evening and I fucked him. I fucked him all night. I know he's had thousands of women, but that night he made me feel like I was the only one, in a special place where no woman had ever been taken before. Is he heroic? No. But the sex was sublime. Better than . . ."

"Better than what?"

"Never mind."

"I know what you were going to say. About tonight?"

"It doesn't matter. I slept with your *Comandante*. That's all I'm going to say."

"Oh, it matters. It matters a lot. But all right, we can let that go for now. But tell me. When you were with the sublime lover, did you think about me at all?"

"No," she said. Her lips compressed into a dark frown. "I didn't think about you until I got back here and found the mess you made in my room. Listen to me. I will sleep with whomever I want, whenever I want. I'm not letting you or any other man put a leash on me. If you want me, you better get used to it."

"Do I have to get in line?"

"Oh." She exhaled and folded her arms. "Why do you make this so hard? You want me to throw myself at your feet and beg forgiveness? Tell you how ashamed I am? If that's what you want, you'll be sadly disappointed."

He stood up and stepped over to the window, his back to her. "I was disappointed. Badly. That night I saw you in the Palace heading upstairs to him."

"Oh, which night was that?"

"Of course. There must have been several. What color was his robe? Or did he give this one back when he got tired of you?"

"Get out!" She shrieked so loud he imagined people in the lobby or on the street heard her. "Get the fuck out of my room."

He didn't say anything. He took off the robe and dropped it on the floor. His hands shook as he put on his clothes. At the door, he stopped and spun around. "Seeing you get delivered to D'Annunzio's room like a package, it made you look common, like just another of his tarts."

Chesa stretched out on the bed, face buried in her pillow. "Poor Sean. He can't decide whether to worship his bloody *Comandante* for fucking so many women or despise the women who were fucked. Maybe you can figure out how to do both. But tell me, Sean. If you thought I was such a slag when you saw me go to him, why did you come to my room that night?"

"Good question." He leaned against the wall. "I wasn't thinking too clearly after what happened to me, I guess. I told myself you'd make it a short night with him and come back here, in case I might be waiting for you. Absurd, wasn't it? To imagine my goddess would sacrifice any part of her night with the legendary lover. Like I was somebody special. I did feel special with you. Until you didn't come back that night." He glanced at the photographs stacked on her nightstand. "This was a bad idea, my coming here."

Chesa had not moved. "Bad?" she repeated. "How's that? You saw the photographs. We fucked. Was I supposed to cook dinner too?"

"That's not what I meant."

She sat up, clutching the pillow to her chest. "Your problem is this epic male artist fantasy. You have this idea of me, and I don't want to live up to it, even if I could. Don't you get it? I am no more a goddess than D'Annunzio is a world savior. People are small. But you can't accept that. You need big ideas, big events, big actors."

As he closed the door, she concluded the second lesson of the evening: "But those only exist in bad manifestos. They're not real."

FIFTY-FIVE

Letter from Filippo Marinetti

February 25, 1920
Sean:

Your draft of the manifesto I asked you to write is, to put it charitably, shit. If I wanted something sounding like D'Annunzio, I would have asked prostitutes here in Milan to write it. I suspect they have authored more than one of his speeches and certainly several of his plays.

There is nothing in it about the Church or marriage or lawyers or the academies. What are you thinking? I begin to wonder if it is within the power of an American to capture the true Futurist meaning of Fiume. Thus far you have failed to convince me otherwise.

You need to toss every scrap of your draft into the trash and start over. Immerse yourself in the books I sent you. More are on the way.

I await a new draft. Do not disappoint me again. I will remind you that your success in Fiume is a precondition for any further association with Futurism.
Filippo

FIFTY-SIX

From SEAN REILLY'S JOURNAL

February 28, 1920. I burned that bridge, didn't I? The minute I first mentioned the Comandante, I should have stopped and changed the subject, or fucked her again, or got dressed and gone home. Even castor oil would have been preferable to what came next.

It was madness to persuade myself something was still there between Chesa and me, that anything of our relationship could be salvaged. What's dead is dead. I learned that in my ambulance driving days. In Fiume, what's dead is us. Wishing doesn't help when the patient has expired.

I can't even write a straightforward journal entry.

March 9, 1920. My draft of the manifesto, scorned by Chesa, has not pleased Marinetti either. I tore his letter into hundreds of tiny pieces and dropped them in the waste can.

I have accomplished nothing here in Fiume to promote Futurism or to discover who killed Piero. The legionnaires haven't talked to me since I moved out of the barracks, and the Futurists here continue to avoid me. I drink more than I should, and I still can't paint. Neither Tom nor Renzo would understand, and my friend James is far away in Trieste, mad that I left. I know only one person in Fiume who might listen.

I went to his restaurant in the last minutes of the lunch serving. Gaj must have seen that I wanted to talk. When he brought my food, he carried a plate for himself and sat at my table.

We ate in silence for most of the meal. Gaj finally broke through. "You don't want to be here in Fiume. Do you?" James's challenge again.

"Of course I do. It's just . . . well, it's not easy to say." *Say it*, I told myself. *That's why you came to the restaurant.* "Things are all fucked up. When I came to Fiume, the idea was to help Futurists spread their message here so they would let me back in their good graces."

"And they do not let you into their graces?"

"They avoid me like I suffer from the plague."

Gaj's fingers, stained red with dried tomato sauce, rested on the table. At first, I mistook it for blood. "Chesa has talked about your painting," Gaj said. "She says you are very passionate about your ambitions."

"Can we please not talk about her?"

"As you wish. What a charming lady she is, though. You were a daring ambulance driver, and now you want to be a great painter. That is admirable. And you decided to be a Futurist and came to Fiume to achieve your goal. What stops you?"

"Lately, everything about Fiume gets in the way. The whole experience here hasn't worked out the way I anticipated. Fiume has become a dirty, violent place. Trash on the streets and broken windows and empty shops. People getting assaulted." I shoved my plate forward. "The city doesn't inspire me like I thought it would."

Gaj picked up my plate and put it atop his, but did not get up. He pulled two cigars from his pocket and offered one to me. I declined it. Gaj eased his chair a few inches from the table and lit his. I felt guilty about sharing my troubles and taking up his time.

"Some people are doing fine," I said. I shifted my weight in the hard chair. "Renzo is a rising star in the Command, and Tom has a job and a girlfriend, Capricia, who he is crazy about. They're doing good things for themselves and Fiume. For the world, too."

"What is different about them?" Gaj blew smoke politely away from me. "How is it they find . . . contentment here, and not you?"

"I'm not sure. They are fighters; they struggled to get where they are."

Renzo and Tom had moved on from the war and were now fighting for Fiume by going on raids. That struggle was the real difference between them and me. They didn't wait around for Futurism to cure the city's ills or to improve their lot in life. They didn't look to others for support or comfort. I didn't want to mention the raids to Gaj, however. An army depot was involved. Best not to talk about it.

"Let me ask you," Gaj said, "do you need to be a Futurist to paint? Why can't you just paint? Forget about the parades and the airplanes and rallies and fights. Paint. And find a job. Do some good work like you did in your ambulance, and let it inspire you."

I wish it were that easy.

March 24, 1920. I have been reading, or at least skimming, the books Marinetti sent. Something in Mazzini's writings made me think. He really wanted a literary career but felt compelled instead to take up an active political role in the struggle for Italy's independence. He gave up art for politics. I don't think I could do that.

March 25, 1920. Gaj extolled the benefits of work. Well, a little raid to feed the city sounds like work to me.

FIFTY-SEVEN

From INTERVIEW WITH DUŠAN KCLEŽA (1992)
[UNEDITED TRANSCRIPT]

JH: Toward the end of March 1920, there was a pirate raid by the Italian legionnaires into Sušak that resulted in tragedy. Tell us about that.

DK: I don't want to talk about it. Ask something else.

JH: Oh. As you wish. Perhaps you could describe briefly how you prepared that night to defend against attacks. You knew where their target was, right?

DK: This is hard for me, I'm telling you. I'll try. We knew where they were going, like you say. It was a warehouse over on Kumičićeva, in the industrial sector. The building isn't there anymore. Got leveled in, I forget which war. We went to the warehouse early, right at dusk. Six of us. Is that right, six? Yeah. We were all carrying the Russian rifles, except Andrej. He had an old shotgun. He didn't like the Russian weapons. I think he didn't like them because I bought them. The man was a mean bastard.

My brother showed up a little later. He didn't have any weapon. He shouldn't have been there at all.

JH: What was your plan? Patrol around the building to discourage an attack?

DK: That was what I wanted to do. I figured once the Italians saw Croats with guns, they would run away. Go back to stealing from their army depots. But Andrej said we should hide. He said six Croats wouldn't scare them. It would make us easy targets. I argued, but he was the veteran, and the others looked up to him, especially about tactics. Remember, I was just twenty years old back then.

This warehouse was an old stone building, nothing much to look at. Windows bricked up, all except for one on the south side. Big, heavy wood door in the front that a tank couldn't knock down. We had a key, so Andrej let himself in, and the rest of us looked for places where we could wait and not be seen. I told them the idea was dangerous.

Other than some bushes off to the left of the door, there was not a tree or rock or anything else a man could hide behind. I told my brother to hide in those bushes and made him promise not to move. I waited there with him and the others for the Italians to show up. They did, and I couldn't stop my brother. He ran out and they shot him.

JH: How awful. Your younger brother was killed over a warehouse raid?

DK: He died defending Croatia. He got killed because he believed in our right to be free. Listen, I can't do this no more. Turn the tape off.

FIFTY-EIGHT

March 25, 1920

om's face was buried under the hood of a Ford. He didn't look up. "What the fuck do you want a gun for? Do you know how to use one?"

"I don't plan on using it," Sean said. "I'm just a little uneasy, especially at night. I'd feel more comfortable if I had a weapon. I don't even need any bullets."

Tom stood up straight and shook his head. "Never carry a firearm unless you are prepared to use it. And you can't use a gun if you don't have ammunition. Don't be stupid. Do you want the gun or not?"

He did. Tom disappeared into the rear of the garage and came out with a revolver. He handed it to Sean along with a small box of ammunition. "This is a Bodeo, an old Italian Army service piece. Accurate and dependable. You need to go practice. There's a place near the drill area that the legionnaires use."

Sean promised he would and meant to do so.

That evening, he showed up late. The designated meeting spot was a small woodshed at the edge of a pier crowded with fishing boats. Tom looked surprised to see him, and not happy.

Renzo, on the other hand, greeted him warmly. "You will be a great help this evening. And I see you came armed. Good." He handed Sean a balaclava and briefed him on the objective for the evening. The rest of the crew stood outside, masked, having already received their instructions. Tom was assigned to drive the truck. Renzo and the rest would go by boat to a pier a few blocks from the target and meet up with him. Sean was in high spirits. Unlike the day at the Trieste train station when he watched men in uniform from a distance, this time he was with them. Instead of smoke and steam, he saw only darkness, and it enveloped all of them.

Almost immediately things went wrong. The engine of the boat they intended to use for the short trip refused to start. The crew had to commandeer an old fishing vessel for transport. Gasoline odor mixed badly with the stench from the day's catch. The boat rocked like the one Sean took from Trieste to Fiume, and the noise of the motor made talking impossible.

Once the boat docked at the Sušak pier, they disembarked and waited a quarter of an hour before the truck approached. Renzo was not happy. "Border guards," Tom explained.

Renzo told the group to get going. Tom handed the truck over to one of the other men with orders to drive it up to the warehouse but not until the others secured access to the building and opened the front door. The group marched in tense silence. Tom was beside Sean.

"Bad start, huh?" Sean said.

"Not good. Be careful and stay alert."

"I thought the target was an army depot. But now I hear we're going to a Croat warehouse."

"Change of plans. The last time we tried a depot, the army started shooting at us. Tonight is supposed to be easier. You need to be quiet."

Sean stayed close to Tom and followed his lead. They crossed a deserted boulevard away from the streetlights before turning onto a small lane. The warehouse loomed at its end.

Renzo signaled for Sean and two others to go to the rear of the building and for Tom to try the window on the side. The men hurried to their positions. Sean leaned around the corner to watch Tom. One of the men behind Sean said he hoped they would get the chance to capture a Croat guard.

"Quiet," Sean warned. The muscles in his arms began twitching. He waited in black silence, listening for any indication Tom had made it inside. His mouth was dry, and the stress made him sweat. Time seemed to stop. He reached down and rested his fingers on the Bodeo's pistol grip.

A different voice close behind him spoke up. "If we do get one, I'm gonna pour gasoline on him and light him up like a candle."

Sean froze. He knew that voice and those words. Before he could react, the night exploded.

The truck came racing up, headlights on. The driver hadn't waited as he'd been instructed. The headlights pointed at the window and lit up Tom's body like the spotlight in a theater. Sean heard shouts from Renzo and others at the front. Then a shotgun blast shattered the window.

Tom lay stretched out on the ground. Sean ran over to him. Shouts and gunshots rang out from the front of the warehouse. Another blast came through the window, showering glass and wood splinters down on both of them. Sean heard more shouting and spotted a figure running toward him. It was happening so fast. "Get him," somebody cried out. Sean fired the pistol and the running man fell over. Sean crouched, ready for more attackers. None came.

The sounds of the skirmishing at the front of the warehouse tapered off. Renzo called out, "They're gone. Anybody hurt back there?"

"Tom's been hit," Sean yelled. "Shotgun from inside the window. I'm pretty sure I got one of them, right where you're standing."

"We better get out of here. I'll take Tom in the truck." Renzo lit a match and studied the body at his feet. A pool of blood collected on the hard ground. He squatted and held the match above the face. "Christ," he said. "You shot Veselko."

FIFTY-NINE

From SEAN REILLY'S JOURNAL

March 27, 1920. The devil has collected on the Faustian bargain I made to improve my manifesto. What separates me from the hoodlums with their castor oil? The fact that I paint? That I drove an ambulance years ago? Here in Fiume, in the *danse macabre* that began when I borrowed the gun from Tom, I discovered that I can kill.

When did Futurism become a license to steal and to kill? Chesa could answer that.

There are moments when I think perhaps it never happened, that it wasn't me who fired the fatal bullet. I never handled a weapon before, so how likely is it that I could have hit anything I was aiming at?

I saw Tom on the ground, bleeding, and it was like the war all over again, except this time it wasn't some anonymous soldier I could just carry in my ambulance and let others worry about. This was Tom, my friend. He was lying there wounded, and my reaction was to shoot and kill a boy. An unarmed boy. I can't make sense of what I did.

SIXTY

From *Memories of a Fascist in Fiume*
by Tenente Lorenzo Guidici

On one of the night excursions of the *colpi di mano*, my American friend Sean Reilly fired a gun, probably for the first time in his life, and killed the son of the much beloved Fiume restaurateur Gaj Kcleža. As a soldier I knew the risk of violence on our raids; as an officer, I accepted that there would be casualties. My concern was always for the men who served under and alongside me, not for the enemy. This was Gaj's son, though. I had often seen him in the restaurant, and he seemed like a decent young man. But at that moment, I had other things to worry about. My other American friend, Tom Delancy, had been shot and lay bleeding on the ground, in a hostile neighborhood. We needed to get out of Sušak fast.

I called off the raid and, with Sean's help, loaded Tom into the truck. The others returned to the boat. I drove the truck, while Sean rode in the back with Tom. No words were spoken. Just groans of pain from Tom whenever the truck hit a bump. We got back into Fiume without further incident. My uniform and rank kept us from any trouble with the border guards. It was late, and the streets inside Fiume were empty. I stopped to pick up the army surgeon at his home and then drove straight to the hospital adjacent to the barracks. Sean and I carried Tom inside and laid him on a table in the operating room.

"This doesn't look too bad," the surgeon said after a brief examination. He asked us to step out into the hall. That was certainly good advice. Neither Sean's experience as an ambulance driver nor my time as a soldier prepared us to contribute anything of value to the surgery.

We moved outside into a darkened hallway—there was nobody else in the infirmary at that hour—and I made Sean tell me what happened. He was virtually incoherent. "The truck made all that noise. Those fucking headlights. I heard the shotgun, and then I saw Tom was hit, and a guy was running right at us. Somebody said, 'Here they come,' or 'Shoot him,' or something. I don't remember what. I couldn't see because of those lights. I pulled the trigger. Are you sure it was Veselko?"

"Yes," I said. "It was him. Did you hear any other shots? Anybody else fire at the boy?"

He looked miserable. "No. I don't think so. It all happened so fast. Christ, why him?" He ran to the bathroom.

While Sean was in there vomiting, the surgeon came out into the hallway and gave me a report on Tom. The news was good. The pellets had not hit anything vital. He said Tom would need to rest for a couple of weeks but nothing to worry about. I passed the news on to Sean when he came out.

I was confident Tom would recover. Bullet wounds were nothing new to him. Sean was another matter entirely. He was not a soldier and did not possess the mental strength to put the unfortunate death into its proper perspective. I tried to comfort him. I reminded him that he was protecting Tom when he fired the gun and that these things happen in the heat of battle. Armed Croats should not have been there at the warehouse. I do not believe it brought him any relief.

As for me, I mourned Veselko's death and expressed my condolences to Gaj. I even attended the funeral.

SIXTY-ONE

March 29–April 9, 1920

The summons brought Sean to the pier where a large cruiser, the pride of the *Comandante's* burgeoning navy, was docked. Renzo met him on the quay, just as he had in happier days when Sean first arrived in Fiume. He escorted Sean aboard the ship and immediately disembarked, with no explanation. Sean stood by the rail, shivering in the cold morning air, fighting panic. He wished he could climb into an airplane and fly somewhere.

He felt a polite tap on his shoulder. "Mr. Reilly?" a young man said, the same young man who led Chesa to D'Annunzio's lair last November. The kimono guy at Madam Christina's. "You'll be coming with us to Zara," the young man said. "The *Comandante's* orders are that you remain there under the supervision of Admiral Millo. Arrangements will be made to send your clothes to you there. Your other effects and your room in Fiume will be preserved. The admiral will advise you on when you can return to Fiume. Do not count on that being anytime soon."

Sean clutched the rail and stared over the side, his back to the young man. He watched the waters begin to churn as the ship began to move away from the dock. "I'm being deported. Is that what you're telling me? Deported like Marinetti. Why?"

"You might like it in Zara," the young man said. "I understand they have some lovely old churches."

Sean spent most of the seven-hour voyage in the bowels of the ship mulling his banishment, grateful for the relative calm compared to his previous boat rides. As the ship approached Zara, he came up to the deck in time to witness a brilliant orange sun dropping behind the hills of the nearby island of Ugljan, lighting up the waters of the Adriatic and painting the sky.

Admiral Millo greeted the arrival of the ship and escorted D'Annunzio away amid a coterie of senior officers. Sean and the other passengers were directed to the barracks in the old *Arsenale* by the pier. He found an empty bed and arranged to borrow some clothes until his arrived.

The next day, D'Annunzio was honored with a military parade along the Promenade that ran along the canal separating Zara from the mainland. Sean remained in the barracks until D'Annunzio took his leave and departed for Fiume. Someone had left a well-thumbed copy of the 1905 Baedeker for Austria-Hungary in the barracks. The pages describing Zara included a map of the town as well as brief descriptions of its attractions. Mostly medieval churches, Sean noted. Some Roman and Venetian antiquities.

By the third day, Sean's clothes had not arrived. Worse, he had no art supplies. He went to the admiral's office to complain and was turned away by a sneering junior officer. The next morning he rose early and walked out onto the Promenade. Three naval vessels were docked in the port. The morning sun illuminated the harsh hills and Croatian villages on the mainland that surrounded Zara. He turned back toward the center of town in search of anything modern that didn't float on the sea, any attractions besides ancient buildings that Futurism wanted to destroy. He hoped at least some things in Zara had improved in the fifteen years since the guide was published.

San Donato was the first of the advertised attractions he came across. A round two-story building that had once been a church but was later turned into a museum, it combined in a single building two things Futurism loathed. Sean declined to pay the admission fee and moved on. Nearby was a tall column with a Corinthian capital and a griffin on top. His guidebook said the column has been used as a pillory. He tried to picture sinners or criminals tied to it, enduring whatever savage punishments were meted out in those days.

Circling around an old stone wall he came upon the imposing cathedral, which the Baedeker dated to the thirteenth century. The façade had three portals, with carved wood doors flanked by colonnettes and capped by compound arches. Statues of religious figures adorned the façade. Above the central portal were two rose windows. Sean was examining the craftsmanship of the twisted spiral colonnettes in the smaller left portal when a young couple came out of the church. "Such a beautiful church," the young woman said to her companion, her accent recognizably Philadelphian. Turning to Sean, she asked, "Have you been inside yet?"

Sean shook his head. He walked away quickly, heading past some unearthed Roman ruins. He passed more churches and, overlooking the town's library, a Venetian-style clock tower he found inferior to the one in Fiume. At the end of the street he came upon the *Cinque Pozzi*, five stone wells dating back to the sixteenth century. Beyond that stood the Porta di Terraferma, the old Venetian gate to the city, with the winged lion of San Marco over the central archway. Bored, he sat down in the little park at the southern end of the peninsula for an hour before making his way along the Promenade back to the *Arsenale*. The twentieth century, he concluded, had not favored Zara with any of its blessings.

The following day, his clothes arrived, along with the notebook holding the latest draft of his manifesto and a copy of Mazzini's *Duties of Man*. At his request, Renzo had seen to the packing. Sean spent three days indoors reading and rereading Mazzini, intrigued by the author's argument for defense of one's country as a prerequisite for man's paramount duty to humanity. He began to see why Kochnitzky believed D'Annunzio's nationalism was consistent with the League of Fiume. Sean started a new draft of his manifesto.

At the beginning of his third week, he took his notebook and a pencil with him on a walk around Zara, scouting for locations to draw. What he had seen of the town to date was hardly the stuff of Futurism. No smoke-belching factories, no shipyards blazing with electric lights, no racing automobiles, no planes, no locomotives. Just quiet, static things crafted centuries ago. Still, the people who had done the crafting had imbued their work with a creativity that he grudgingly admired. In any event, he needed to work on his drawing. He went back to the Romanesque cathedral and stood before the three portals, sketching the intricate play of the stone colonnettes and arches. After an hour, weary and hot from the summer sun, he went inside.

Sean was struck by the similarities to the Capuchin Church in Fiume that he and Chesa had visited so long ago. The interior was typical of Romanesque design, with heavy arches on either side of the nave that rested on columns and piers arranged in arcade fashion. He walked to the front of the nave and studied the carved wood stalls in the choir. The high altar beyond the choir was undistinguished, in Sean's opinion, but a side altar on the left aisle was richly decorated with colored marble columns and sculptures of the four evangelists. An image flashed through his brain, Chesa darting out from the side altar with her camera like she did in Fiume and taking photos of him in the pews. He dropped his notebook and raced out of the cathedral.

SIXTY-TWO

April 10, 1920. What the hell is wrong with me? Stuck in this forsaken pit of antiquity, I took my notebook to the cathedral yesterday to do some sketches and what happens? I go inside and I think of Chesa. Her and her camera and how excited I felt when we were inside the church in Fiume. This wasn't any religious experience or spiritual or anything like that. It just grabbed me in the gut. I couldn't stay there. The feeling was too strong, like she was there staring at me, taunting me about what I once had and would never have again, that feeling that something great was about to happen. I don't know. I just had to leave. I didn't realize I had left the notebook behind. When I went back hours later to get it, the notebook was outside, leaning against that nasty pillory.

Who moved it? Probably some tourist or a priest who was closing up the church. I don't know. I dreamed about this last night, except that in the dream it was Chesa who brought the notebook outside, and I was chained to the pillory. She laid it at my feet and told this huge, masked man to punish me for my sins while she took pictures.

I don't know if I can stay here much longer.

April 16, 1920. I'm making the best of my time here. Trying to, anyhow. The bad dreams have eased up. There's a lot to be said for the artistry that went into the old structures here, I have to say. For the past three days I have sketched the clock tower. I'm getting better at capturing the lines of its quoins, the balustrade beneath the clock face, and the layers of molding in the cornice. The undulating surface of the panel at the top of the tower still gives me trouble. I'm sure Chesa could take a couple of photographs and capture it straight away. I wonder what she's photographing these days.

Sometimes I try my hand at landscapes, especially those hills over on Ugljan. I stay as far away from that cathedral and the pillory as I can.

May 2. 1920. I haven't had anything to write about until today. Marinetti sent me a message via the admiral that he is coming to Zara for a short visit in the next few weeks. Maybe he can get me out of here. I have a new draft of the manifesto to show him. Lots of drawings, too, but I don't think I'll share those with him. They're not bad, but they are all sketches of old things.

SIXTY-THREE

JH: The loss of your brother must have been a terrible blow to you and your parents. Can you tell us about the funeral?

DK: They held a big funeral mass up at the Church of Our Lady of Trsat. That was my father's idea. I was glad he chose Trsat. On our side of the river, you see? The Croatian side. Not in one of those Fiume churches, with all the Italians around.

I sat in the front row, next to my mother. My father was on the other side of her. They were both crying. I tried to feel the same sorrow, but mostly I felt anger. I was angry about Veselko getting killed, but it was more personal, like I was the intended victim, and Veselko got in the way. It sounds crazy today, I know, but I was so full of rage at the time. I saw everything as an attack on me, and I had to respond.

JH: Was it a nice service? That is such a beautiful church.

DK: It was hard to sit through. The air was hot from all the people and the burning candles. The incense made it hard to breathe. It felt like the walls were too close together. And the sounds, they got in my head and were driving me crazy. All the people weeping, and the priest and the altar boys droning on back and forth. The monks were making noise, too; I forget what. Probably some Latin chant that nobody but them understood. I covered my face with my hands and forced myself to inhale. I thought, when they get to the sermon, if I have to hear about God's will or God's plan or the dead at peace or anything that tries to make something positive out of my brother's death, my head would explode. The smoke from the incense got thicker and thicker, like a cloud inside the packed church, covering everyone. I needed air. So I got up and walked out.

Once I was outside, I went down the path toward the top of the stairs, the five hundred steps down to the streets of Sušak. From this point, I had a clear view of Fiume. I wished I had a big bomb I could drop on it.

JH: Did you know at that time who the killer was?

DK: Not right then. But as far as I was concerned, all Italians were responsible. They all loved their *Comandante*, you see? They supported him and his pirate raids. They lived off those raids and off the backs of the Croatian people who had built this city. None of them were innocent.

I felt like I needed to do something bold, terrible, something that would shock the Italians out of their smug complacency. Show them Croatians couldn't be murdered with impunity. Make them see us as human beings willing to risk their lives to be free. Croatians needed to be shocked, too. People like my father who had it easy, who had lost the craving for a national identity, whose sole interest was making money. They needed a jolt. Something that would unite us all in a national identity as Croatians.

JH: And that national identity has now been achieved, thanks to people like you who fought for it. What kind of jolt were you contemplating?

DK: At that point, I hadn't come up with anything specific. But I knew it would have to be big and public. And I'd probably have to do it by myself.

SIXTY-FOUR

June 3, 1920

Marinetti arrived in the afternoon on a flying boat, an SIAI S.16, courtesy of the manufacturer, which sought a share of the publicity Marinetti always attracted. Sean watched the seaplane make a perfect landing in the waters between Zara and the island of Ugljan. After meeting with Admiral Millo for two hours, Marinetti sent for him. They met in a small office overlooking the customs house.

"I need you back in Fiume," Marinetti said. "Mario Carli left the city. His journal irritated the sensitive *Comandante*. Especially his articles about the silly League of Fiume. He'll resume publication from Milan, where we are free."

"The League of Fiume is not silly. It's an excellent plan for pursuing Futurist goals," Sean said, dredging up language from the latest draft of his manifesto, one Marinetti had not yet seen. He straightened in his chair. "It pairs our duty to humanity with recognition of those who seek essential nationalist unity. It is the foundation from which we can launch the social revolution that Futurism pioneered and do so on a worldwide basis. The stage is set for wiping away the imperial forces of tradition and oppression in the struggle for a future both electric and free." To Sean's ears, it sounded like what Carli had written, only better and with a touch of Mazzini. He hoped Marinetti would be impressed.

Marinetti puffed on the cigar, without taking his eyes off Sean. He said nothing. A new cloud of his smoke billowed forth, filling the room and catching sun rays streaking in through the window. After a long minute, Marinetti burst into an extended bout of laughter. "I sincerely hope," he said when he recovered, "the latest draft you are writing for me is not filled with garbage like that. It reminds me of the paintings you showed me when you first came to Milan. Remember?"

"You told me they were shit, and I should burn them quickly before they contaminated anyone."

"I said that, did I? Well, as I recall, you accepted our criticism, and your painting showed modest improvement. Let's hope your writing can do the same."

Marinetti relit his cigar, and Sean told him what he had learned about Piero. He hoped for an explanation of why Marinetti had not said anything about him back in Trieste. "Most unfortunate about Piero," Marinetti said. "But, after all, what business did a man with his poor eyesight have trying to hike on a mountain slope? A tragic accident, to be sure." He waved the cigar and the subject was dismissed. "Is D'Annunzio still begging for cash?"

"The banker Conte had tried to raise funds on the mainland but without much success."

"Are you joking? Conte collected over two hundred thousand lire. People lined up to give him money for the *Comandante*."

"That can't be true," Sean said. The idea that Conte diverted funds came as no surprise—Sean thought Conte was sleazy from the moment he first encountered him in Wickson's office—but the amount staggered him.

"I gave him five thousand myself," Marinetti said. "Instead of action, D'Annunzio asks for more. Anyone who has any lire left and feels like parting with it will give directly to the Fascists."

"Fascists? Mussolini's gangsters?" Sean had no idea Mussolini had such appeal. The Fiume newspapers described him as a fringe player in Italian politics who polled embarrassingly few votes in the elections the previous November. The papers carried tales of his followers' bloody attacks on strikers and Socialists, but nothing suggested a rising political force.

"Those whom you choose to call gangsters, I would refer to as the less enlightened of our war veterans. Mussolini, well, he is admittedly a bit of a reactionary. Jealous of my expensive coat and shoes. He has no soul and little imagination, and the men around him are hardly the people I'd choose to lead the country. But Mussolini radiates enough electricity to power a factory. He has big dreams too, like D'Annunzio, but the man is much tougher. It's been bad in Italy since the war. People are sick of watching strikers and foreigners and a do-nothing parliament. They're tired of waiting for D'Annunzio to pull his pants up and accomplish something, so they turn to the Fascists. Italy needs a strong man as its leader. I'm afraid D'Annunzio's day may have passed."

"Are you serious, Filippo?" Sean asked. "You would consider aligning with these goons?"

Marinetti flashed a tight smile, the one he employed when, after saying something outrageous and offensive, he wanted to keep the listener grasping for what he meant. His lips stayed closed, the corners of his mouth tilted ever so slightly upward and his cheeks pinched in. The look discouraged challenges to his cryptic pronouncements.

"You need to get back to Fiume," Marinetti said, "and get busy with what I asked you to do. I can fly you up to Abbazia, but you'll have to make your way to Fiume from there on your own." He handed Sean a sealed envelope. "This is addressed to you."

Sean returned to his room, the envelope in hand. He had immediately recognized Chesa's handwriting. He tossed it onto his bed, unopened. What could she have to say that would interest him? His resistance lasted five minutes.

> Dear Sean,
> I hope this note finds you well. Assuming it finds
> you at all, that is. I have no idea where you are.
> Renzo told me you were back among the Futurists,

but he, too, didn't know where. I hope Filippo does.

Tom has been hurt again. He tried to stop a gang of marauders who attacked a defenseless old man and was badly beaten himself.

I am afraid for Tom. He is too injured to defend himself. His so-called "friends" at the garage won't help, as they are scared. Horrible men.

I hope my letter hasn't disturbed you, but I thought you would want to hear about Tom.

Chesa

PS: I miss you, Sean. You are a good man in a very bad world.

SIXTY-FIVE

From SEAN REILLY'S JOURNAL

June 3, 1920. Chesa. The ghost in the cathedral reached out to me with a letter. Awful news about Tom. I'm glad somebody let me know, but why did it have to be her? Three months since I last saw her, two of them in exile here, yet I can't get my feelings straight. I never want to see her again, but I have to see her again. She says she misses me. None of this makes any sense.

Poor Tom. Of course I'll do everything I can for him. Marinetti talked to the admiral and says we can leave tomorrow morning. I can't wait to go.

I considered showing Marinetti the latest draft of the manifesto, but after his reaction to what I said about the League, I thought better of it. I have more work to do.

I'm still thinking about our conversation today. Marinetti and Mussolini in agreement? Keller was right. And where does that leave me? Since the end of the war, I have tried to imagine a brighter future in which I could paint again. In my most hopeful moments, I imagined progress and prosperity in a new world inspired by artists. But if Marinetti is serious—something that is always impossible to tell—Futurist artists will have to get in step behind the skull-bashers and brawlers to change the world. Have I misread all his manifestos? Or are the times changing, as Tom had predicted? *The future will be more machine guns than paintbrushes.*

Marinetti's lack of interest in the League of Fiume puzzles me.

The League seems perfectly in accord with the tenets he articulated in his political manifestos. Granted, I hadn't expressed myself very well to him about the League's goals. Nonetheless, I took for granted he would have a more enthusiastic reaction.

Both D'Annunzio and Marinetti seem preoccupied with Italy as a great power. But D'Annunzio, the decadent poet, spoke of a future worldwide order, while Marinetti, the Futurist, is focused on Italy's position in the current one. I would point the irony out to Marinetti, but I don't want to say anything that may jeopardize my ride back to Fiume.

Why do I feel like a man with poor eyesight hiking on a dangerous hillside?

SIXTY-SIX

From *Memories of a Fascist in Fiume*
by Tenente Lorenzo Guidici

After the unfortunate incident in Sušak, raids were once again directed toward the regular army depots. These went much better. Sean was not available, of course, having been removed to Zara. Around this time, I received word of the glorious attack on the Milan offices of *Avanti!*, the Socialist Party newspaper. Its success prompted me to organize a show of Fascist strength in Fiume against strikers holding a rally in Piazza Regina Elena.

The crowd filled the piazza in front of the Adria Palace. Most of them were Croats. Pathetic. They were lucky to have any jobs at all in Fiume. It was an Italian city, and there weren't enough jobs there for Italian men. The blockade had seen to that. I will not sully these memoirs with an account of the strikers' ludicrous attempt at extortion. Suffice it to say they shared the same outrageous demands of their Socialist cousins in Milan and Turin: jobs they did not have to earn, pay in excess of what they deserved, and a say in the employers' businesses that they were not smart enough to understand. My homeland had been wracked by these pernicious strikes. I knew the right way to deal with them.

I stood a short distance away, on a balcony above the piazza. Twenty good Arditi legionnaires were down at street level out of sight, waiting for my signal. They were dressed in civilian clothes, which took considerable effort on my part to procure and even more to convince these boys to don. I had to take away their firearms and grenades. My intention was to intimidate the strikers, not make martyrs of them.

One of the Croat agitators began a wearisome harangue about how the workers' strike was necessary to assert their "rights." He was greeted with a great deal of shouting and cheering. The speaker stood in the middle of the square on a little stone structure, about four or five meters high, surrounded by dirt and grass. The structure is hard to describe but I will try. It was like a tiny amphitheater with wide steps leading up to the top. Picture the magnificent National Monument of Victor Emmanuel II in Rome, without the impressive columns, of course, and then scale it down in the same ratio as Rome bears to poor little Fiume. That will give you an idea of this humble pile of stones. Trolley tracks ran along its northern edge.

As I waited for the right moment to turn my legionnaires loose, I spotted Chesa snapping photos. The spy, ever at work. She was talking to the young Croat who bought the Russian rifles from me. He would point at something—a person or spot in the piazza, it was hard to tell—and she aimed in that direction. Blink went the shutter. The presence of these two in the piazza was cause for concern, as I had no desire for any harm to befall the lovely lady, and I had other plans for the young Croat and those rifles he had purchased. Neither of them were likely to be left unscathed once my legionnaires rushed in to teach the strikers a lesson.

I made my way down to the street to caution the squad. Just as I got there, the speechmaker's rhetoric reached its most incendiary point and the police stepped in. There could not have been more than ten of them. The policemen wore blue uniforms that looked like they had never been dirtied and certainly never bloodied, and they carried rifles they barely knew how to hold (what would Tom Delancy have said to that?) and couldn't be expected to fire or, if they fired, hit anything. They marched in and ordered everyone to disperse. I naturally assumed my men would have to go rescue the police from the mob, but to my utter astonishment the crowd backed off.

The police started climbing up the little stone structure. It was quite funny watching one with a huge belly try to make it up the stairs. The Croat who had been spewing nonsense to the crowd jumped off the monument into a ring of his listeners, whom he must have anticipated would remain in place to cushion his fall. Unfortunately for him, his audience gave way, and he hit the ground hard. I could tell he was hurt. Three of his comrades picked him up and carried him away while he continued imploring the crowd to fight for their rights. Meanwhile, the police were staring down helplessly from the top of the structure, watching him escape, since none of them had considered the rather obvious possibility that the troublemaker might jump. They raced down the steps past the portly one who was still puffing his way up. At street level, they looked around in every direction and tried to figure out where the injured man had gone.

I was laughing so hard at this point I nearly forgot what I had to do.

The police, clearly afraid to go back to their station empty-handed, started grabbing some of the people who had been standing in the piazza listening. I thought perhaps there might yet be an opportunity for my legionnaires if the masses rose up against the police. At that moment, a trolley came up and rang out four bells. Everyone scattered out of the way.

Once the trolley passed, the battle was over. The remnants of the crowd dispersed, and those who remained meekly surrendered. Police began marching their prisoners away. Chesa photographed them. She moved rapidly and relentlessly all over the square and captured the police in action. The portly one was stupid enough to try and take her camera away. I hurried down to the street to intervene before that cretin did anything regrettable. But I needn't have worried; she was far too quick for him, darting in and out among the stragglers in the square, taking pictures while he puffed after her. I suspect he was about to give up or maybe fall over when I arrived and escorted her to the safety of the Corso. But before I reached her,

I walked right past the young man to whom I had sold the rifles. At this point, I did not know his name. He didn't see me, or if he did, he wisely gave no sign of recognition.

It was a little disappointing, I must admit, not to be able to watch my squad battle these strikers.

When Chesa and I had a chance to speak, I asked her what in the world she was doing there, risking her life taking pictures of that mob instead of photographing more pleasant sites in the city.

"That mob," she answered, breathing heavily from her encounter with the police, "they are the city. Those speakers were airing legitimate grievances before the police came charging in. No legionnaires tried to help them. Help the workers, I mean." She gave me a strange look as she spoke. I later learned that she not only knew about my squad, she had photographed them at the start of the rally. She even got them to pose for her. What a marvelous woman.

Chesa and I had dinner together the next evening. I asked if she knew any of the people in the crowd of strikers the previous day.

"Just one," she said. "Gaj's older son. His name is Dušan. Nice young man. He went to school with the twins."

I asked her what she intended to do with the photographs she had taken.

"Add them to the other interesting ones," she said. "I took a bunch up at Trsat Castle. It's a lovely view from up there. You can see the whole city, the bay, the islands, everything."

Everything, indeed. I was worried she might suffer an injury or take photographs of things that I didn't care to have recorded. "Dear lady," I advised, "you need to be more careful around the Croats. With those people, there's no telling what could happen."

She laughed. "You sound like Sean. 'Those people.' Who'd want to bother with a crazy Englishwoman who talks to herself and photographs everything? Most people shy away."

I once hoped that Tom, Sean, and Chesa might be convinced to join in what I and others were trying to accomplish. It wasn't so different, really, from what they desired, each of them. We all wanted prosperity and progress. But unfortunately, they didn't see it that way. What they failed to comprehend was that the values of Fascism— faith in and obedience to the state as the basis for a productive soci- ety—were superior to their self-interested individualism. These were stubborn people.

SIXTY-SEVEN

June 9–10, 1920

Capricia unlocked the door and let Sean in. Tom lay in bed, head and upper back propped up on a pillow. "*Ay, amigo, buenos dias,*" he said. "Welcome back to the front."

"General Villa says we move out in twenty minutes," Sean said. "Grab your gear."

"I ain't moving out so well these days. Old Pancho's gonna have to fight on without me." Tom coughed. "It's good to see you, buddy. I heard you was entertaining all the ladies down in Zara." Capricia smiled for the first time since Sean arrived. She went over to the door and secured the deadbolt.

The apartment was a shabby single room lacking kitchen or bath, one of several carved out of a large house in what had once been a fashionable neighborhood. A single round window let in a shaft of light. The room's furnishings consisted of an old table, a thin wood chair, and a sagging bed, on which Tom reclined. Clothes were piled on the floor. Yellow wallpaper that at one time might have been elegant now peeled off in strips from the walls.

"Sorry the place is a mess," Tom said. "I moved in the day before all this happened. I needed to get out of the barracks because, well, me and Capricia. She don't like the place, but it's all I can afford. Grab the chair."

Sean brought the chair over to the bed and eased himself onto it. He surveyed the damage to his friend. Bruises on his face, a black eye, and a swollen jaw. Bandages were visible under his thin nightshirt.

Tom's pallid visage and vacant eyes reminded Sean of how injured soldiers looked in his ambulance when vital fluids were leaking out of them. He glanced at Tom's sheets to check for discoloration.

"I'll tell you all about my conquests," Sean said. "But first, tell me what happened to you. I have to say, you look like crap."

"Yeah, I wish I felt that good," Tom said. "I'm working my way up to crap." He took a deep breath, held it for a second, and released. A shudder of pain followed. "Two busted ribs. They hurt pretty much all the time. My right ankle and knee are both messed up."

"I'll tell you what happened to him," Capricia said. She stood at the foot of the bed. "I was there. Tom and my sister and me were all knocking around on the street near the big theater. Tom sees a gang of men pounding the stuffing out of some poor man. A Croat, I think, but even so. They kept hitting him and kicking him. It was horrible." She twisted around to face Sean, her face and neck flushed red. "A lady going by said something to them, and one of those scum went running after her like he wanted to hit her. Right there on Via del Porto, in broad daylight! She ran into a shop to hide. I told Tom, 'Let's get out of here,' but he had to be the hero. Look what he got."

"Not a hero," Tom said. "I figured I'd make the fight more even."

"Your math is a little off," Sean said. "One plus one doesn't equal five."

"That's what Annalisa told him," Capricia said, "but he didn't listen. He never listens. He told me and my sister to go home as fast as we could. But we hid in the meat shop and watched. We don't listen, either."

Her comment made Tom smile. "Ah, there was only four of them when I ran up, and the Croat guy started to get to his feet, so things looked pretty good. I messed up a couple of them and squared off against this big oaf. But then I got hit in the back of the head by something, probably a bottle. Knocked me off my feet. It was the son of a bitch who ran off after the lady, like Capricia said. I guess I lost track of him in all the action. Once I was on the ground, they forgot about the Croat and went to work on me."

"Tell him about the police," Capricia said as she passed between Tom and Sean. She punched up Tom's pillow and hovered over him.

"Yeah, not much to tell. A couple of them stood around, but they didn't do nothing until the bad guys finished with me and walked away."

"Walked away," Capricia said, waving her hands above her head. "Didn't hurry at all, like they had nothing to worry about. That's when the policemen finally came out. We saw them watching the fight."

"So did they go after the culprits?"

"No," Tom and Capricia said simultaneously.

"Wait, let me tell it," Capricia said, her hand on Tom's shoulder. "You were half dead lying there on the ground. Me and my sister ran over and started screaming not to let them get away. But those fucking policemen, excuse me, just stood there looking at Tom. One of them said he must be drunk, and they should arrest him for disorderly conduct."

"Sounds familiar," Sean said.

"I let him have it. I said to him, 'You'll do no such thing. My sister and I saw you two hiding and not doing anything to stop that fighting at all.' Annalisa called them all kinds of names and said she knew their captain real well and would tell him everything."

"Is there anybody in the city you two don't know?" Tom asked. His voice was soft and raspy.

"Hush," Capricia said. She glared at him sternly, but her expression changed upon seeing his ashen face. "Honey, lie down and rest. This is too much for you."

Sean excused himself and promised to return the next day. At the door, Capricia thanked him for coming by. Her eyes were reddened. "He missed you. I think he's tired of having us women fussing about all the time."

"I'll be back, don't worry," Sean said. "Soon you'll both be tired of me. And listen. What you did for Tom was incredibly brave, staying there and confronting the police."

Capricia flipped a balky tendril of dark hair off her face. "Fiume women are tough. We don't run."

Sean went to the Governor's Palace the next morning to see Kochnitzky. As he approached the front door, Wickson and Conte stepped out. "Look at what washed ashore," Wickson said. "Sometimes one can't throw the trash out far enough."

Sean strode past him, brushing Wickson's shoulder hard enough to spin him around. Sean didn't look back. Conte blocked his path forward.

"You ask a lot of questions about things that are none of your business. You're like a blind man trying to hike on a mountain." Conte pointed a finger at his chest. "Stay out of areas where you don't belong. A man could get hurt. So could his friends." Sean felt his jaw tighten and warm blood rush to his forehead. He let Conte strut past him.

Kochnitzky's door was open. Inside, he was bustling about. "I must warn you, Mr. Reilly," he said, "I have little time to talk. Please state your purpose."

Sean asked about Piero.

"Yes, I recall your question about the dead Futurist. No one at the Palace seemed to know anything, and I could locate no one interested in exploring the matter any further. For your protection, I did not mention your name, but several people, unprompted, asked if I had been talking to the crazy artist who tried to steal an airplane. You, for your part, agreed to collect information for me. I gather you were not successful in the short time before you ran away from Fiume."

"I did not run away," Sean said. "The *Comandante* sent me on a mission to Zara."

"A mission. Indeed. I shall tell you what I know. Perhaps if you stay here the information will be useful, but if you are smart you will be on the train out of the city tomorrow morning. Do as you please. I learned of some activity, strictly off-limits, in the hills beyond the castle near where your friend had been hiking. Perhaps he saw it. Airplanes, even those allowed to fly, are not permitted to go there. I couldn't find out more."

"But why that area? What could be so important there?"

"I do not know, Mr. Reilly. I have told you all I learned."

"There must be more. Think. What could possibly be up there?"

"Mr. Reilly, you are as tedious as everyone says. Please show yourself out."

SIXTY-EIGHT

From SEAN REILLY'S JOURNAL

June 12, 1920. An airplane buzzed over my head today before disappearing beyond the treetops. Whatever rules prevent me from getting a plane obviously don't apply to everyone.

I am stunned by how bad Tom looks. He jumped into a fight against a pack of thugs to save a stranger and, as a result, suffered the entirely predictable consequence of being badly hurt. Yet Tom saw nothing strange or heroic about what he did. I cannot picture myself doing anything like that, even in moments of fantasy. I am an artist, and I ran away when the old Croatian man I gave a leaflet to was knocked down in front of me on the Corso last October even though the other Futurists and I outnumbered the attackers. I flinched when I faced Conte the other day.

Were the hoodlums who beat up Tom the same men who gave me the castor oil?

SIXTY-NINE

From INTERVIEW WITH DUŠAN KCLEŽA (1992)
[UNEDITED TRANSCRIPT]

JH: Around the time of your brother's death, things were getting harder in Fiume for everyone. Food was in short supply, the currency was increasingly devalued, and jobs were hard to find. Why was the economy so bad?

DK: Why do you think? With a poet running the city? That clown knew nothing about governing. He couldn't even govern his own behavior. But it wasn't equally bad for everybody. No matter how tough things were for Italians, it was ten times worse for Croatians. Italians always seemed to get better meats from the butchers, and that's only one example. And when jobs were cut, guess who got fired?

JH: My research mentions a workers' strike that April to address working conditions. Were you active in that?

DK: I didn't have a job, so I couldn't go on strike.

JH: Good point. Were you present when the police broke up the strike rally in Jadranski trg?

DK: I was there and saw the whole catastrophe. The square was called Piazza Regina Elena back then; they had Italian names for everything. The crowd was mostly Croatian. A few decent speeches about guaranteed hours and higher pay and other things people still want today. The crowd made a lot of noise and waved their hats around like the Italians did whenever D'Annunzio paraded through the streets.

There was a photographer in attendance, a nice lady. I remember her name: Chesa Rei. She took a lot of photographs during the rally.

JH: How did you know her?

DK: I don't remember where I first met her, but I used to see her taking photos all around the city. We talked at the rally. She was British and didn't buy into all the Italian bullshit. My father helped her set up a little darkroom.

She was photographing the rally. I pointed out the figures on the Adria Palace. A lot of people, even those who have lived here for years, don't notice them. Did you?

JH: No, I confess I didn't.

DK: You should go see them. Look for the beautiful building with the big "Jadrolinija" sign on the front. On the side facing the square, you'll see four columns in the middle section of the building, and on top of each of them there's a sculpture. They're up pretty high. On the far left, the Egyptian-looking lady represents Africa. Next to her is an Asian woman, Japanese, likely. Then a woman with a feathered headdress, for America, of course. And on the far right is Europe. I could never figure out which country she's supposed to be from, but if you look at how she's bundled up in a heavy coat, she sure as hell isn't from Italy.

Chesa said they show the city's world culture, and she was right. It's funny, isn't it? The Italians desperately wanted to make Fiume a part of Italy. They said the culture here was Italian, but when I look at that building and those sculptures, none of that ever made me think of Italy.

She seemed interested in hearing more about what the city was like before the Italians invaded, so I invited her to tour the Old Town with me. That's when the police came crashing in to break up the rally.

The strike leaders, for all their fine words, ran away at the first sign of the police. All those years of foreign rule had made us weak as a people, and passive. Our people had suffered for centuries under Hapsburgs and Hungarians. We were beaten down and hadn't yet learned how to link up and fight together. We needed the right spark to set off the fire.

JH: Did the police arrest you?

DK: They tried. I was far too fast for them. All I had to do was keep moving, not even leave the square. With decent leaders, the whole crowd could have run circles around the police that day. It was a missed opportunity.

SEVENTY

June 15, 1920

On his next visit to Tom, Chesa opened the door. After a few seconds of silence, she invited him in. Sean forced a smile. He thanked her for sending him the note about Tom and hurried over toward Tom before she could respond.

"Tom," she said, "I'm going to pop out and get a bite while Sean's here to keep you company. Capricia should be along in an hour or so, but I'll be back before then. Will you need anything while I'm out?"

"Nah. Thanks. I'll be fine."

She stopped at the door, started to say something, and then disappeared.

Tom looked better although his face lacked its usual ruddy color. Sean picked up the chair and brought it over to the side of the bed. He glanced over at the door.

"What's on your mind, buddy?" Tom asked. "Her? Listen, she comes over to sit with me when Capricia needs a break. Nothing else."

"It's not a problem," Sean said. "I don't care what she does."

"Sure." Tom fidgeted on the bed, adjusting the pillow so he could sit up higher. "I didn't tell her nothing about that night. Chesa knows you and I went on the raid, but she don't believe either of us had anything to do with what happened to Veselko. She says you never touch a gun."

"Good." Sean tried to sound indifferent.

"Gaj don't know, either."

"Good," Sean said again. He told Tom about the unpleasant exchange with Conte, including the part about friends getting hurt.

Tom reached under the pillow and pulled out a heavy revolver. "Don't worry about me," he said. "I can handle squirts like Conte. Just you watch your step."

"Which reminds me," Sean said. "I have your old gun at my place. I'll bring it to you. My shooting days are over."

Tom coughed and clutched at his ribs. He slid down in the bed with a low groan he couldn't bite off. Sean took the revolver from him. When Tom was settled, Sean sat back in the chair. The air in the room was sleepy warm. Only a sliver of sunlight filtered through the tiny round window. They chatted a little more before Tom dozed off.

A knock on the door woke them both. Tom reached under his pillow for the revolver and looked puzzled when he discovered it was missing. Sean took the gun from his lap, laid it on the bed, and went to answer the door. Chesa came in carrying a huge platter of food.

"Sorry I took so long, but Gaj made me bring this to you two. His favorite Americans, he calls you. He wanted to give me more, but I insisted this was all I could carry."

Sean went to look for plates, but Chesa pushed him out of the way and found two in a box on the table. He piled grilled pork and pasta onto them and brought them over to the bedside. Tom attacked the food on his plate and thanked Chesa in between mouthfuls.

"Thank Gaj," she said. "That man you defended was an old friend of his. I don't imagine you will ever be able to pay for a meal in his restaurant again."

After he finished eating, Tom said he wanted to go back to sleep. Before leaving, Sean told him what Kochnitzky had said about the activity in the north. "Must be pretty damn important if nobody can get near it."

"Do you mean the thing behind the castle you had me take photos of?" Chesa said. "I'm sorry, but Gaj couldn't make them any clearer when he enlarged them. Too bad you can't get a plane and go see for yourself."

"I tried that once already," Sean reminded her. "There's no way I can get to a plane."

"Maybe I know where you could get one," Tom said.

SEVENTY-ONE

June 15, 1920. I showed Chesa my sketches from Zara and she loved them. She asked if I would continue now that I'm back in Fiume. I said I might, but honestly, I think I'll stick to painting. Pencil drawings can be useful to get a work started, but they won't make me a great artist.

I can't explain why I care so much what Chesa thinks, but I do. I hope she doesn't ever hear what happened on the raid. There's little chance of that happening, I guess. Only Renzo and Tom know. And D'Annunzio, of course. They won't talk. It's just that no amount of explaining and justifying would ever shield me from her judgment if she found out the truth.

I've been thinking more about Tom. What could possibly be worth the cost of the pain that he suffered? His beating was a lot worse than my castor oil attack. What does he see in Fiume that keeps him here and gets him in fights protecting people? Answer that one, Sean, and you'll have your manifesto. Or get yourself killed.

I did risk my life all the time during my ambulance driving days. I took chances to rescue soldiers and kept driving even after I learned what the war could do. Men screaming, ripped apart by lead from a machine gun or shrapnel from a shell, entrails hanging out holes in their bellies, bones shattered. Twice I picked up a boot that was in the road and found part of a leg sticking out of it. Everywhere I had to look at slaughter and smell the stench of death, hear the men begging for death to stop their pain. But the whole time I never gave a thought to quitting.

Sometimes, I think, people do things, and long after they are finished doing them, they learn why they did what they did.

SEVENTY-TWO

From *Memories of a Fascist in Fiume*
by Tenente Lorenzo Guidici

Santo flew in regularly with instructions from Mussolini along with supplies with which to carry them out. I would drive out to the little hidden landing area to meet him. I liked to watch the airplane take off and land. It amazed me that something so sleek and fast could lift the weight of a man—and more—into the air.

Sometime in May or June, I forget which, Santo arrived in a new plane. I don't recall what it looked like, but it came in fast and dropped suddenly, slamming the tires into the grass and bouncing up slightly before settling down. The back end stayed in the air for another second or two and then hit the ground, dragging the tail while it raced along the landing area toward a thick oak tree. I was afraid the machine would not slow in time. Right before the end of the clearing the tail of the plane swung to the left and the engine accelerated, pulling the plane through a 180º turn. I parked my car by the plane and watched Santo emerge from the cockpit.

He wore the proud look of a man who had just gotten lucky. "New plane," he said. He laid a leather bag on the floorboard of my car and climbed in. "She is fast, believe me. Nothing in the air can catch her. I'm still getting used to the throttle. Tight landing, wasn't it?"

"I thought I would have to pull you out of that tree," I said. "Let's get our business done so you can go home."

He produced a thick envelope from the bag and handed it to me. I put it in the pocket of my tunic. Then Santo reached back into the bag and pulled out five vials of cocaine, which he put inside a little canvas pouch I handed him. At the Governor's Palace, cocaine was worth more than gold. I paid him in lire.

"I'm not going back tonight," he said. "I'm gonna lay over here and share some powder with the local ladies. Give me a ride into town?"

On the drive back into the city, we talked about Italy. He brought news of the good reaction Mussolini was getting from crowds when he told them it was time to cleanse Italy of foreigners as well as Socialists. The message was effective as long as it was delivered often enough and loud enough.

I pulled the car into the warehouse. The door closed behind us. Four men dressed in black came out from behind large crates and approached the car. Santo pulled out his pistol and took the safety off. I told him to put it away, that he was not in any danger.

"You know these guys?" Santo asked. "They don't look so wholesome. Four of them and only two of us."

"Five, actually," I said, without looking at him. "Don't forget the man who opened the door. Fatal mistake, forgetting the man at your back. But these are my men. You met two of them last fall when you brought the rifles. They're not very bright, but they follow orders these days. Usually. I'd keep that cash out of sight if I were you, however."

We got out of the car, and I handed the leather bag to Luigi to put with our other supplies. I warned him to be careful since it held enough explosives to destroy a city block. The canvas pouch stayed with me.

I left Santo with my men and climbed the back stairs to my little office. With the door locked, I opened the envelope Santo had given me and read the letter of instructions. When I finished, I set the paper on fire and dropped it into an empty trash can.

This latest assignment called for the use of all five of my squad. They were getting harder to control, however. Their latest transgression was a midday assault on my friend Tom Delancy on a busy street.

The Arditi in me wanted to choose one of them at random and put a bullet in his head to get the others' attention.

This may sound harsh and unnecessary. Discipline is never pleasant, but it is important for progress, especially in a military situation, and by this stage of the Fiume occupation it was essential, especially when the subordinates were of such limited intelligence. I could not have men under my command carrying out unsanctioned operations on targets of their own choosing. Fascist goals permitted and sometimes required the use of force to achieve legitimate objectives, but there had been nothing to justify the beating they delivered to Tom. I had been lenient with them after the castor oil attack on Sean because they were deceived into following instructions from Wickson, but the assault on Tom was a sign that my little band was veering out of control.

Unfortunately, discipline would have to wait. Due to the time constraints imposed upon me by the instructions in the envelope, I had to prepare them in a different way. I took five bottles of grappa from a crate on the floor and brought them down to the ground floor. I handed a bottle to each of them. They looked at me with eyes of oafish gratitude. "Drink up," I said. "I've got a project for you."

Santo gave me a funny look. The less he knew, as usual, the better.

SEVENTY-THREE

June 16, 1920

The airplane was a beauty, a late War SPAD S.XIII with green fabric-covered spruce fuselage, black engine, and a black exhaust pipe streaking along either side. It sat right where Tom said it would be, in a field northwest of the airport. Tom, the old soldier, always seemed to know things, including which car Sean could borrow from the garage.

The controls of this plane were a little different than he was used to and took some study, but he quickly figured them out. He opened the water radiator control, set the fuel mixture, and started her up. The plane made a beautiful throbbing sound as he guided it to the far end of the clearing. He turned it for takeoff into the wind. It was then he noticed the old oak tree, looming huge at the other end of the field. The plane had to be at least fifteen meters off the ground when it reached the tree, or the wheels wouldn't clear. If this plane was as fast as it looked, he would be at the tree in no time at all.

The grass field had a mild uphill grade until about halfway to the end. He fixed his sight on that point and opened the throttle. With a roar, the plane leaped forward and raced through the clearing. The tree came at him fast, like he and it were in a jousting tournament. The machine and Sean became one, its wings his limbs, a union of flesh and metal in a battle against a static wooden enemy blocking the path. He pulled hard on the stick. The nose of the plane tilted upward fast, too fast. To keep the engine from stalling, he leveled off. The steady pulsating beat of the motor reassured him. Another pull on the stick and the plane rose sharply again until all he could see was blue sky. He waited for the sound or feel of contact with the branches, contact that would send him crashing down to earth. The engine whine got louder and higher pitched. He felt a thud of tree limbs hitting against the wheels. The plane shuddered for an instant and then muscled its way free. Sean was flying.

The SPAD handled beautifully. He dipped the wings first to the right and then to the left and after leveling off, shot upward to two thousand meters. The rapture of speed flooded through him like hot oil in the motor. Violent throbs of power raced through his hands and feet. Speed conquered time and space, like Futurism promised. Modernity scorned obstacles, gave birth to courage. *Put that in the manifesto.*

Cleansing air whipped against his face. The blue of the bay and the greens and browns of the earth under him appeared muted and soft like a matte finish, free of the smoke and stench and noise of people. Everything appeared in focus, which Sean guessed was proof he was inside the circle of confusion, with his eyes opened to a tiny aperture. He wished Chesa were up in the air with him so she could behold with her own eyes what the dirty streets and buildings looked like from up high.

Somewhere on the ground in those hills behind Trsat Castle lay something important that he needed to find and capture with Chesa's camera. He banked the plane over the Governor's Palace and proceeded north, following the chain of hills. Shadows stretched out below him over swaths of farmland and slopes of untamed shrub. Nothing resembled what he hoped to find.

He pointed the nose of the plane upward and for a moment seriously considered attempting a loop. Recovering his wits before it stalled, he rolled the airplane to the left with a hard kick to the rudder and then used the joystick to pivot the nose in the same direction. The plane dropped out of the climb and leveled off, heading back in the direction from which he had just come. His instructor in Philadelphia would have applauded. A slow banking brought him over the Governor's Palace once again.

The sun had reached its zenith, making the shadows shorter and exposing more of the ground to his vision. As much as he enjoyed flying, he needed to put the airplane on the ground soon. He navigated north once again, keeping the mountains to his right. The plane responded with the precise movements of a ballet dancer. The boundary where earth met sky went from horizontal to diagonal, like somebody tilted the world while he flew, maybe to sweep the earth clean. That, not war, would be the world's true hygiene.

He spotted a small gap bisecting a grove of trees. He had missed it on his first pass over the area but now the shadows were a little shorter, exposing more of the ground. The gap went on for a few hundred meters, a thin cavity carved into the grove. He scrambled to pick up the camera, but by the time he had it in his hands, the target was well behind him.

Sean banked the plane once more, sweeping over the edge of the bay and back toward the hills. He pulled out the camera's bellows to the maximum and set the aperture and shutter speed.

People on the ground were gaping up at the plane. Three times over the same area had to raise suspicion. He couldn't risk a fourth. This time the gap was easier to locate. He pointed the camera in its general direction, aimed as well as he could, and pressed the shutter button. He advanced the film and pressed again, hoping for the best. Then he sat the camera on his lap and took a quick look. The gap was like a long furrow in the densely wooded part of the hillside, straight, and uniform in width. Marks of human engineering. This wasn't a deer path. It trailed on to the north, through the mountains for a good length, disappearing for a stretch under a tight canopy of trees, only to reappear and fan out. Beyond, he could detect faint lines in the dirt that suggested ruts. The nearest road was about three kilometers away.

Sean turned the plane toward the landing area and descended

gently for the approach. Everything looked perfect until he saw the clearing where he intended to land.

Two cars were parked in the middle of the field. He pulled on the stick and aborted the landing. Where else could he go? The airport was out of the question, given his previous experience there. He did not want to be caught with this plane. He needed to get it on the ground quickly. He flew out toward the bay. The sea was a lovely shade of blue, highlighted by small whitecaps near the shore. The main shore road below him was empty, no cars for as far as he could see. He straightened the plane and landed, skidding once, twice, coming to a stop on a tight stretch of the road a short distance before a curve. It would take whoever was at the clearing at least ten or fifteen minutes to find the plane. He climbed out and ran.

SEVENTY-FOUR

From SEAN REILLY'S JOURNAL

June 16, 1920. Flying again! It was wonderful, beyond words. I have not felt so free and exhilarated in so long. What a plane. The future is most definitely in the air. If only I could capture that spirit in my painting. I'll give the canvas a try tomorrow morning.

That gap I saw is a pass through the trees. I don't understand what it's for, but now that I have seen it, perhaps I can get some answers to what happened to Piero. And find out who is behind all this, and why.

SEVENTY-FIVE

THE NIGHT OF TWO EXPLOSIONS
June 19, 1920

"What is your plan for tonight?" Andrej asked. "Do we march over into Fiume and start shooting women and children?"

"My brother was a child," Dušan said. It was past time for challenges from Andrej or anyone else. He picked up his rifle and caressed it. "He's dead. We are not going to suffer quietly anymore. The Italians must pay for what they did. We'll make them regret ever coming to Fiume."

"They will pay us, certainly," Andrej said. "They have a lot more guns to pay with."

Dušan pulled back on the rifle's bolt handle. "That means we need to be smart. And fast. Do any of you lack the guts to fight?"

"I'm talking about not taking stupid risks," Andrej said. "I saw stupidity over and over again in the war. Outgunned men get slaughtered."

Dušan reached into his pocket and pulled out a brown stick of gelignite. "This will help make up for guns we are missing."

Renzo and Santo dined at a café off the Corso and then visited a nightclub Renzo knew would appeal to Santo. "Drinks are good," Renzo told him, "and the women are outstanding."

"Too bad it's in this shithole city," Santo said.

"Not to worry, Santo. You will not need to come here much more."

"How are we going to get into Fiume?" Andrej asked. "Do you suppose the guards on the bridge will let a bunch of rifle-toting Croats from Sušak march into Fiume at night? Or do you expect us to swim?"

Dušan peered down the sight of his Mosin-Nagant, one eye closed. He put his finger on the trigger and tried to imagine the sensation of firing the rifle at a human, something he had never done. His imaginary target let out a cry and fell over dead. Satisfied, he raised his head. Yellow light from a gas lamp danced on the faces of the other men. "Why swim?" he said, passing the rifle to the man next to him. "I found a boat this afternoon we can 'borrow.' We'll sail over and tie up at the Fiume pier like we're fishermen coming home after a long day at sea."

A robust Saturday evening crowd packed the club. The house band attempted American jazz tunes at ragged tempo and high volume. Young patrons danced not unlike at the festivals, writhing and sweating, intoxicated, crisscrossing the crowded dance floor in a paroxysm of shared madness. Renzo spotted two young women near the door and called out to them. "Annalisa," he shouted. "Over here." He didn't recognize her friend. It was unusual to see Annalisa without her sister.

At the same moment, Luigi and the squad followed Renzo's map down a small street near the eastern end of the Corso to a building that housed an outspoken Croat newspaper. Luigi expressed a fondness for newspapers, even though Renzo suspected he was illiterate. "There's so much to break and burn."

Dušan led his cadre off the pier. Two of them carried a long basket reeking with the odor of fish. "You know," Andrej said, "the stink will never come off the rifles."

"Shut up," Dušan said. Andrej always had to have his say. "Would you rather be parading around this nice neighborhood showing everybody our weapons? We're supposed to be fishermen, remember?"

Luigi shattered the glass in the newspaper's storefront with a rock. He told Ugo to overturn desks and tables. Two of the others ran through the offices in search of any workers. Another tore down everything hanging on the walls. Ugo went over to one of the tall, heavy cabinets and, with one hand, pulled it over, causing the cabinet to fall face down. "Impressive," Luigi said, "but dumb. Now pick it up and pull the drawers out so the papers will burn."

The two who went to the back emerged, dragging an old man in an ink-stained apron. He screamed for help. Luigi told Ugo to make him be quiet.

Dušan's objective was a secondary school near the old tobacco factory. The school taught students who required extra attention, especially troublemakers. Dušan had been sent there after being expelled from his Fiume high school and lasted all of three days before being expelled from it also. The school made a perfect target, not just because of his bad memories of the place. The dark neighborhood would provide good cover when the Italians heard the explosion and came running.

The street they followed came to an abrupt dead end. "We're lost, aren't we?" Andrej said. "I thought you knew the area, Dušan."

"Shut up," Dušan said. He had only ever been in this part of the city during daylight hours. This wasn't Old Town. "We need to keep going. It's near here."

"No. We're through following you," Andrej said. "I'll find us a target. I spotted one right before we started up this street."

Ugo dragged the unconscious old man out into the street. Luigi considered leaving him inside to burn but thought the man might turn out to be another one of Renzo's friends from the war. Once everyone moved outside, Luigi went back in. He pulled a gelignite stick from his pocket, inserted the detonator, set the explosive inside the printing press, and lit the fuse.

Andrej demanded the gelignite stick Dušan carried. "There," he said. "On that corner. When they come to see what happened, we can take our shots."

"Not here," Dušan said. "Too many lights."

"Give him the goddamn stick," said one of the others. "Let's not argue in the street."

Dušan passed the gelignite and the detonator to Andrej and went searching for cover.

When Renzo heard the explosion, he acted surprised. "That sounded like a bomb," he said. "I better go see."

"Wait. There's a second one," Annalisa said. Her face turned ashen. She squeezed her drink glass with both hands. "What is going on?"

She was an attractive girl, Renzo observed. Maybe even prettier than her twin sister. "Stay here with Santo," he said. "You'll be safe here."

Dušan found a spot where he could see and shoot but not be seen. Andrej and the rest scattered to his right, a few meters away. Dušan heard the blast from the east and saw the smoke. Trouble in Old Town. He wished he had ten sticks of gelignite.

The explosion at the newspaper blew through the roof and shattered glass in neighboring buildings. Flames shot out through broken windows. "Beautiful," Luigi said to the others. "Now we hit anybody who don't speak Italian."

The blast from the other end of the city momentarily got their attention. Ugo demanded to know if Renzo had another squad working for him.

"Maybe Renzo thinks we need competition," Luigi said. "We better do a good job here."

Smoke billowed into the street in front of Dušan. Flames lit up the area behind the gray cloud. Men coughed and shouted. Four or five of them stumbled out into the street. Uniformed and armed, Dušan noted.

He stood and fired. Bullets came at him from inside the smoke. Two ricocheted off the wall inches above his head. Sounds echoed off the other buildings around him. Suddenly Dušan recognized their location. "Fucking brilliant," he yelled to Andrej. "Of all the targets in Fiume, you had to pick the legionnaires' barracks."

Renzo mingled with the crowd staring at the burning newspaper office. He hadn't orchestrated the attack on the other side of the city, but he had a good idea who was behind it and wasn't at all displeased with the result. This was precisely the kind of action he intended when he sold the weapons to the young Croat. The timing came as a minor surprise, though.

Luigi and the others stood in position as close to the newspaper's front door as the fire permitted. The old man lay at their feet, unconscious but not dead. "Anybody wants to put the fire out," Luigi announced to the crowd, "you got to get past us."

Ugo spat. "Past us? Not likely." He pulled a small wooden club out of his pocket.

The shouts from inside the smoke curtain grew more organized. Dušan heard orders being given. Smoke melted away and lights came on from the buildings surrounding the barracks. A volley of bullets flew at one of Dušan's cadre who, despite instructions, stood upright. The man dropped his rifle and fell to the ground.

Smoke poured out into the street in front of the newspaper building. Light from the raging fire illuminated the smoke, imbuing the scene with an eerie quality. People shouted in two languages. "Italians of Fiume," Luigi announced. "Tonight we strike against enemies of Italy. It's a night to celebrate."

Three men advanced toward the door of the burning building. "Ain't nobody going to put this fire out tonight," Ugo shouted as he charged at them. He swung his club into the face of the closest man.

A light came on behind Dušan. He dove to the ground and crawled into a darkened portico. His breath came in short bursts. "Fuck. Everybody get out of here."

A patrician-looking gentleman with silver hair approached Renzo. "What on earth is going on?" he asked. Renzo recognized him. One of the prominent Fiume citizens who served on the city's Italian National Council.

"I don't know, Your Honor," Renzo said. Flames inside the newspaper office shot higher. The two men drew back and shifted their gaze to the plume of smoke rising into the night sky from the west of the Corso. Renzo shook his head. "Two explosions in one night. Your city is out of control. It needs a strong hand."

SEVENTY-SIX

June 23, 1920

A week after his flight, Sean went to see Tom. "He's not here," Chesa greeted him. She paced furiously from door to window and back. "The police came and dragged him right out of the bed." She nodded over toward Capricia, who sat on Tom's bed, doubled over, crying. "Capricia and I were both here, and we couldn't stop them. They searched the room and found his gun. Then they found a rifle under his bed."

Sean was stunned. The arrest made little sense, but the rifle even less. Tom liked pistols, Sean knew, especially old revolvers, and he loved machine guns but had no use for anything in between.

"He tried to tell them it wasn't his," Chesa said, "but they didn't listen. They kept shouting at him and saying he was a terrorist who stole a car and an airplane and shot soldiers. Then they took him. Capricia and I did everything we could. We used every name we could come up with, even D'Annunzio." She went over to Capricia and rubbed her back gently. "It's all a big mistake, love. I have no doubt. We'll get it straightened out."

"Did you tell them Tom never left the room, and you two were with him all the time?"

"What do you think?" Her tone was dark, indignant. "But when they found the rifle, everything went crazy. I was afraid they might kill him there in his bed. Sean, you've got to go straight away and do something. Talk to the police. Maybe they'll listen to you."

"Of course," Sean said. The last place he wanted to go was the police station. They would be investigating the theft of the car and the plane. Tom, the old soldier, would never give them Sean's name, but if he showed up asking about Tom, how long would it take them to associate the airplane theft with him, the crazy artist who already tried to steal a plane from the airport? "Did you get the name of the sergeant?" he asked.

"Oh, hang the names. They didn't stop to introduce themselves. I wish I had my camera so I could've taken pictures of them."

"Where is your camera?" Capricia asked. Her face was buried in her hands.

"I loaned it to someone," Chesa said. She shook her head discreetly when Sean started to pull the camera out of his leather bag. "I don't recall ever seeing these policemen before. But it all happened so fast."

"I recognized one of them," Capricia said. She sat up and wiped her eyes. "He was one of them who stood by when Tom got beat up. He wanted to arrest Tom back then. He grinned at me the whole time today." She started crying again.

Sean stood there for a minute, pondering what to do. "Pack his clothes," he said. "This may take a few days to get sorted. Do either of you have any cash? I only have a few hundred lire on me. It will help if I can spread some around to the guards."

Capricia sprang to her feet and gathered a pile of Tom's garments. Chesa grabbed her purse and dug out five hundred, all she had.

It took ninety minutes and most of the lire before Sean was allowed to see Tom. He followed a guard through a narrow corridor, reeking of industrial cleaner, urine, and sweat, to a cell at the end, where Tom lay sleeping. The guard went off to find a chair. He returned in a few seconds with a small stool, which he placed outside the iron bars of the cell door. He said Sean could stay twenty minutes.

The cell held a small cot, with an uncovered mattress on which Tom lay, and a pot over in the corner. The stone walls were bare and gray. Sean didn't want to disturb Tom, but he hadn't much time. "Tom," he said, first in a whisper and then louder until his friend woke up.

"Shit, I just got to sleep," Tom said. He looked frail, curled in a fetal position on the cot. The stubble beard, previously a mark of his ferocity and steel will, reminded Sean of homeless men he had seen in Philadelphia begging for cigarettes and spare change.

"Did they hurt you?"

"Nah. Not much. They yelled a lot. It was almost funny. How did you find out?"

Sean told him about going to the apartment and his conversation with Capricia and Chesa. "It's a good thing Capricia didn't get her hands on your gun, or there would be a couple of dead policemen."

Tom chuckled weakly. "Did you see anything while you was in the air?"

"I'll tell you tomorrow. After I get you out of jail."

"Tomorrow? It ain't going to be tomorrow or any time soon. Renzo says besides stealing the car and the plane, I'm supposed to be the leader of Croat terrorists who blew up the front of the barracks and shot a couple of legionnaires. It'll be a while before I see sunlight."

"Croat terrorists? You must be kidding. What in God's name gave anybody that idea?"

"They found a Russian rifle in my room, under the bed. 'It ain't mine,' I told them. First time I ever seen it. But they was all excited and jabbering away so fast I couldn't hardly understand them. My Italian ain't *that* good. One of them was ready to shoot me. He kept shouting '*Americano, Americano,*' like that was bad. Good thing Capricia and Chesa were there." The lines on his forehead multiplied and deepened. "Is she safe? They didn't—"

"She's fine," Sean said. "Chesa and I walked her home. She's worried sick about you. And God help the police chief, the National Council, the *Comandante,* even the League of Nations because she will raise hell with all of them. President Wilson can look forward to a call."

Tom smiled briefly, but the creases did not go away. "She needs to be quiet, for her own good. You got to talk to her. Tell her to stay quiet. I'll deal with this, but I don't want nothing happening to her." He shuddered and clutched his ribs. "Tell her for me. Please."

"I will," Sean said. The man was incredible, he thought. Broken ribs, in jail for something he didn't do, yet still protecting others. "And I'll do everything I can to get you out of here," Sean said with more bravado than bravery. "It's my fault. They just grabbed the wrong *Americano*. The car, the plane, pissing people off. They never would've gone to your place if I hadn't taken the plane up."

Tom gazed at the ceiling. "I know you'll try, but I don't guess it will help. Somebody went to a lot of trouble to plant a rifle on me. But talk to Renzo, and see what he says. Maybe the two of you smart guys can figure out what's going on."

The guard returned and told Sean in a hostile tone that his time was up. Sean didn't argue. Tom was ready to go back to sleep. "Behave yourself in here," he said. "I'll do everything I can."

"Thanks, buddy," Tom said. His voice was little more than a whisper. "Look after Capricia."

Sean trudged out the front door of the jail. Tom's pallor troubled him. Sean had seen strong men in weakened condition before, and they didn't always survive the ambulance ride. There was a limit to what even a man like Tom could endure.

SEVENTY-SEVEN

From SEAN REILLY'S JOURNAL

June 23, 1920. Ten weeks in Zara did nothing to improve my manifesto. I can't seem to drum up that Futurist zeal I need for my painting. Am I good at anything?

When I heard about Tom's getting hurt, I had this absurd idea I could help. Instead of helping, my actions landed Tom in jail. My attempts to help people too often lead to their getting hurt again, and worse. I always think of that corporal.

Soon after my transfer to the Asiago region, I picked up a wounded corporal, a funny young man. Nigel something. I can never remember his surname. His wound was serious—a machine gun bullet in the thigh—but not life-threatening.

Nigel started joking with me while being placed in the ambulance and kept it up when we reached the clearing station. We were told to wait outside for his field hospital assignment. "Congratulations on hitting every rock and pothole in the road," Nigel said. "You drive like my grandmother, and she's eighty years old and almost blind. You need a plow horse, not a truck. I can run faster than you drive, even with this bullet in my leg. Want to race?" He wouldn't stop talking.

I told him I was a Futurist. Nigel thought that was funny. "Futurists should be flying to the moon instead of driving ambulances on earth. But if you fly the way you drive, you'll be three hundred years old by the time you get there."

An orderly came over to the ambulance with the hospital assignments. Good fortune shined on the corporal. His destination was one of the nicer facilities. "You need to go to Brescia and see the automobile races," Nigel said as I started the engine. "You'll see some real driving. I will take you there when the war is over."

I raised my voice so he could hear me over the sound of the engine. "I've been to the Brescia races. Twice. And to the air show. I got to fly one of the airplanes at the show." Corporal Nigel was awed into silence.

When we reached the field hospital, we shook hands. I wished him good luck with the doctors and a happy recovery back home. He made me promise to meet up at Brescia after the war.

In the spring, heavy artillery barrages came back. I picked Nigel up again in my ambulance. This time his leg was blown off, and guts dangled from his torso. Blood spewed out in all directions. No talk of Brescia. He kept screaming for God to let him die. While I drove, I pictured his leg, the one with the scar from the bullet wound, lying out on the side of a hill somewhere by itself. I started to laugh. Not an amused laugh, and none of the other drivers or the doctors and certainly no civilians would have seen the humor of a leg fixed up and saved by military doctors only to be blown off by an Austrian artillery shell four months later. Such humor is reserved for people who let themselves care about the men in their vehicles, and who can appreciate the role they play in pushing the good fortune of those men to the point where their luck runs out. I should have driven the corporal into a ditch somewhere the first time. Or to a train station instead of the hospital so he could get the hell away from the war.

After that experience, I loaded the wounded in the ambulance, slammed the door shut, and drove as fast as I could. I didn't look at their faces or even talk to them. I refused to listen to their stories about how they got injured or about their villages or sweethearts back home. If I ever had to pick them up again, I didn't want to recognize them and feel guilty for my part in cycling them back to the war. I didn't want to consider what might happen to them if they were sent back to the fighting.

But I can't ignore Tom. Now I have to figure out what I can do to help him.

One bad thing about flying is that your airplane always has to come down and land on the ground. Landings can have unpleasant consequences. Earth is full of them.

SEVENTY-EIGHT

From *Memories of a Fascist in Fiume*
by Tenente Lorenzo Guidici

Not long after the two explosions, I was summoned to the Governor's Palace to meet with the *Comandante*. Although I was no stranger to the Palace, the summons left me a little uneasy.

I had ample time to mull my fate. Anyone who desired to meet with D'Annunzio, even if they were invited or, as in my case, ordered to appear, had to wait. Hours, sometimes days, went by before one was finally granted an audience with the *Comandante*. Some were dismissed without ever seeing the man. D'Annunzio wore his vanity like another medal on his chest.

The hours spent sitting in the two-story atrium cannot be described as pleasant. Seated around me were assorted supplicants, some seeking favors or relief, others looking for tidbits to include in newspaper or magazine articles. Minor literary celebrities sat next to unwashed, sweating workers. Poets mingled with peasants. The thoroughly democratic summer sun blazed through the skylights and warmed us all equally. It was a Socialist's egalitarian dream, all happening inside a Hungarian palace built to celebrate a now-defunct empire.

My uneasiness stemmed from the street altercation after the explosion at the newspaper office. The squad I entrusted with the mission had, in their enthusiasm, done more damage than I anticipated. There were civilian injuries, although to my knowledge none of them fatal.

Let me be perfectly clear. I had no regrets about what they did and have none today. When a mother gives birth to her child, there is always pain. It is how nature works. So with nations. Italy was giving birth to a new order, in which its unity and energy and strength would be made visible to the world and especially to those who would dare to deny our nation its rightful rewards from the war. Even Marinetti agreed with that. Of what concern were a few bruises on the part of our enemies? Luigi and the others reacted to the disorder around them. They had ample provocation. Illegal strikes by the Croat workers, insults in the Croat newspapers and on the street, threats of Jugoslav violence everywhere. Italian women feared for their safety, lest some ignorant Slavs molest them in broad daylight. These provocations could hardly fail to arouse strong passions on the part of Italian men. The Croats had only themselves to blame, just as they bore full responsibility for the cowardly and deadly attack on the legionnaires' barracks on the same night. Stern justice, applied without mercy, was needed to deal with terrorists and maintain the peace. Many people in fact questioned why harsher measures were not taken.

A word should be said about the weapons. After my current imprisonment began, some ill-intentioned individuals alleged that weapons used by the Croat terrorists in the barracks attack were obtained from me. It is true that I sold a few surplus rifles to a young Croatian man but only after obtaining assurances that they would be used solely in defense against the Serbs. Given that D'Annunzio's League of Fiume was busy arming virtually everyone who promised to shoot Serbs, my error (if indeed the weapons I sold were the ones used in the attack on the barracks, a point that was never proved) paled in comparison to that of the *Comandante* and the communist Kochnitzky.

While my conscience was—and is—clear, I harbored doubts that the *Comandante* would view the situation in a dispassionate manner and react with approval. What type of bizarre edict would be forthcoming? After three hours baking in that sitting area, I was in such a state that I nearly used my dagger on an irritating Frenchman who simply would not shut up. Before I could do him any justifiable harm, Guido Keller emerged from the *Comandante's* office, took me by the arm, and escorted me outside the Palace. We stood over by the east wing where no one could overhear us. My concern deepened, for obvious reasons. I asked Guido if I were in trouble.

"You? Why, what have you done? No, don't tell me. I've heard enough crazy things already today." This, from a man who sat naked in trees talking to owls. "It's about your friend, Sean Reilly. The *Comandante* suspects he is working for the Foreign Ministry in Rome and has been stirring up the Croats to make the Command look bad. He wants you to keep an eye on your friend and report back."

From where we stood, I could look out onto the bay. The afternoon sun had turned the water a shimmering silver white. I remember this because things looked so different from that angle, at that time of day. Wait an hour or move a few steps away, and the blue water of the bay looked greenish-brown. "Sean?" I said, in disbelief. "You're telling me that D'Annunzio thinks Sean Reilly is a secret agent. Sean, a spy for Rome? You certainly have heard some craziness today, Guido."

Guido shook his head. "I did my best to calm him down. At first, he wanted to arrest Sean or deport him. Or worse. I convinced him that we should keep Sean here and watch him closely. Better the enemy that you know. Honestly, I have my doubts about D'Annunzio these days. He needs to cut back on the cocaine."

"Who gave him this idea about Sean?" I asked.

"Wickson. And Conte."

I told Guido that I would make the reports to keep the *Comandante* happy. I was curious, though, about what other crazy things Guido had heard. The paranoid *Comandante* might well have assigned someone to keep watch on me, too.

"He has this idea to reform the military," Guido said. "A new code. All officers save one are to be of the same rank. Guess who the supreme officer would be?"

Word of the proposed military reforms leaked out the next day. Two colonels and one general left Fiume within a week. I turned in the requested reports on my friend Sean Reilly. And the *Comandante* never figured out the real spy was Chesa.

SEVENTY-NINE

Sean returned to the jail the next morning prepared to do whatever was necessary to free Tom. The morning taunted him with a warm breeze and cloudless blue sky.

Before he made his confession, Sean wanted to talk with Tom and make sure their stories were consistent. He told the guard at the front desk he was there to see Tom Delancy. The guard dropped the newspaper and disappeared. Soon another guard appeared, a burly giant who said only, "Follow me." It didn't sound like a suggestion.

Sean followed him, scrambling to keep up. How would it feel, he wondered, to be locked up and helpless before men like this one? This wasn't the new order he had in mind when he came to Fiume. The future crashing down on him was dark and had bars on the windows and locks on the doors. They passed through the corridor between the cells to a door at the end, where the guard stopped. Tom's cell, Sean noticed with horror, was empty. "Come on," the big fellow said.

"What did you do with Tom Delancy?" Sean demanded. His hands shook. "If you hurt him—"

"This way," the guard said. He opened the door to a stairway and began climbing. Sean glanced again at the empty cell and then followed him up. At the top, the guard pulled a key from his pocket, unlocked a metal door, and held it open. "Welcome to the penthouse," he said, surprising Sean with his sudden eloquence. His tone changed, too, like he was sharing a little joke with a friend.

Sean immediately saw the humor. There in the jail, one floor above the filthy, claustrophobic cells, was a room that looked indeed like the penthouse of a luxury hotel. An antique cushioned sofa faced two plush chairs likely borrowed from the Governor's Palace, and by the wall stood a beautiful mahogany credenza like the one Sean's parents carefully selected for their Rittenhouse Square townhouse. Two brass lamps topped by multicolored lampshades sat on the credenza on either side of a large wood box with a single knob on the front. Framed landscapes of Tuscany adorned the freshly painted walls. A white upright piano occupied the far end of the room. It seemed to Sean that D'Annunzio must have designed this part of the jail himself.

"Mr. Delancy," the guard called out. "You got a visitor."

"One minute," came Tom's voice from somewhere Sean couldn't see, immediately followed by the sound of a toilet flush. "But remember, the name's Tom. Mr. Delancy is my father, and trust me, you would not want him here. He's a tough son of a bitch."

Tom emerged, dressed in blue silk pajamas. "Ask them to make it a light lunch, Tomaso, will you? That breakfast was huge."

"I'll tell them," the guard said, with a gruff laugh, not unpleasant. "But it won't do no good. You'll see." He left by the same door through which he and Sean had entered. From the other side came the clinking mechanical sounds of a key being rotated in the lock.

"Ah, Sean, good morning," Tom said. "Like my new home?" He clutched his ribs for a second, face contracted in pain. He let out a long exhale and straightened up.

"I thought you were in jail," Sean said, trying to comprehend the incongruity. A minute before, he had been worried about Tom's safety—to say nothing of his own—and now he found Tom in a luxury suite, although one with a door that locked from the outside.

Tom chuckled, leading to a cough. "I got moved to the cell of honor. Remember when Guido kidnapped that army general and brought him to Fiume? D'Annunzio said he couldn't let a general sit in one of those shitty cells like they put me in last night, so he had this furnished. See the box on the, uh, what's it called?"

"Credenza."

"Yeah, I guess. That box is a radio. Can you believe it? Marconi fixed that one personally for D'Annunzio. I don't know what to do with it, but I'm staying in a room that's got one."

Tom eased himself over to the dining table and into a padded chair. He motioned for Sean to do the same and poured each of them a cup of coffee.

"Honestly, this is Renzo's doing. He raised hell with somebody. In the middle of the night, Tomaso—did I tell you that's the guard's name?—he comes to my cell and tells me to get up and grab my things. You saw him. He looks tough, and I was in no shape to argue. I figure it's not gonna be good, and he don't say anything. We go through the door and start up the stairs, and I'm trying to plan what I can do to defend myself. Which is not much, because my ribs are killing me. He opens the door and I'm in a fucking palace. He goes away and comes back first thing this morning with a huge breakfast. I was hungry because I couldn't eat the slop they tried to feed me in the cell downstairs. Even so, the breakfast was too much. I made Tomaso sit and eat some of it. We started talking. He's a good guy. Same name as me. Fought in the war, too. He's an Italian version of me."

"Scary thought. I guess it's good at least one of you is locked up," Sean said before he considered his words. "Sorry. That wasn't funny. You're in jail. I need to get you out of here." He couldn't resist more humor, however. "Maybe you'd like a few more meals first? Any of the *Comandante*'s women up here?"

Tom slapped the arm of his chair. "No," he said, "and good thing because Renzo is gonna bring Capricia here this afternoon. She scares me more than Tomaso."

After half an hour, Tomaso returned to end the visit. He escorted Sean to the front desk, where Renzo stood.

"You know it was me who borrowed the plane," Sean whispered to him. "I'm going next door to the police building to confess. I'd like you to come with me and put in a good word so Tom can get released." Renzo sighed and motioned for Sean to follow him outside.

"I know Tom is innocent," Renzo said. "He didn't steal the airplane. You couldn't get him in one of those machines at gunpoint. And he's plainly in no condition to drive a car. But he did possess keys to the garage, and someone used them to take a car and drive to the plane."

"They got the car back. And besides, it wasn't a military plane," Sean said. "It wasn't taken from the airport."

"Doesn't matter. Somebody used the car and stole the airplane and then landed the plane in the middle of a public street. That is one problem."

"I can solve that problem," Sean said. "Let them put me in jail. How long can they hold me? But first I need to tell you about what I saw while I was up there. I can show you photographs once they're developed."

Renzo's eyes narrowed at the mention of photographs. "Tell me later," he said. "But listen to me, please. Abetting the theft of an airplane is bad, but they wouldn't have dragged Tom out of a sickbed for that. Somebody told the authorities Tom was mixed up with bad people. I didn't believe it—let me rephrase that—I don't believe it. But they found a rifle in his room, a Russian rifle. The kind the Croats use. And here is the bad part. The rifle is exactly like the one they found on the dead Croat after the attack on the barracks a few nights ago. Do you see? They're convinced Tom is in league with those Croat terrorists."

"Tom? A terrorist? Seriously?"

"I know, Sean. Be that as it may, they did find the rifle. Tom had no explanation. And remember, last week he rushed out to defend the Croat who fought with a few citizens. To a lot of folks, that shows he's switched sides."

"This is beyond insane," Sean said, sputtering. "Tom sees a gang of hoodlums beating up an old guy, five against one, and he tries to help the man, so people assume he's a terrorist?"

"Calm down. I'm on your side. And Tom's side, too, of course. You have to appreciate how it looks, though. The point is, he took the side of the Croat in the fight, and later he had a Croat rifle under his bed. Two Italian soldiers were shot with that exact kind of rifle. And on top of all that, he's connected to an airplane spying on the city."

Sean was not ready to give up. "OK, how about if I confess about the plane and the car and say he had nothing to do with it, that I stole the keys, and then we get him out of the city? Get him expelled. I hate to see him go, but maybe it's for the best."

"Right now, jail is the safest place for him," Renzo said, shaking his head. "People are angry at the Croats, and he is seen as one of them."

"Well, then I need to be in jail, too," Sean said.

Renzo brushed the front of his tunic and pulled it straight. He sighed. "One American in jail suspected of helping the Croats is bad, but two would be dangerous. Tom is safe and comfortable where he is. It's a much better place for him. You've seen his apartment. I had to call in a lot of favors to get him in that suite. If the wrong people suspect the two of you are in league, both of you will be in the bad cells where they lock up the Croats. Tomaso is a good guard, but I understand he can be quite unpleasant at times."

That made Sean shudder.

"Look, people have a lot of anger toward America these days. Your President Wilson has tried to deny Italy everything we fought for, including Fiume. So if two Americans were jailed for conspiring against Italy, a lynch mob could not be ruled out."

Sean contemplated the broad boulevard that ran past the Governor's Palace. His attempt to help Fiume cost Tom his freedom; now, from what Renzo said, making a confession and going to jail could get Tom killed.

"How long do you figure he will stay locked up?" Sean asked, trying not to sound relieved about dodging jail time.

Renzo gave no estimate. He promised to do everything possible to get Tom released, and headed off to the Palace.

Sean wandered down to the Piazza Dante even though it lay in the opposite direction from Tom's apartment. He couldn't face Capricia yet and tell her the bad news about Tom.

Yet another festival had taken over the piazza, celebrating the feast of something or other with the usual dancing and drinking. Torches and banners and flags once again decorated the streets, like on the day he first arrived in Fiume. Music blared. Bullets and rockets shot into the air. The crowd was smaller, however, and the dancing seemed more frenzied than at previous festivals. Perhaps people were making up, with ferocity, for the steady decline in the city's fortunes and resources or clutching at the fantasy that fueled the city for so long, the end of which they must know was coming, even if they could not say when. They shouted and swore like the soldiers on the train at Trieste. Sean hated them all. *You didn't want to come to Fiume, did you?* He needed to get as far from the crowd as he could.

When he arrived back at Tom's apartment, Chesa greeted him with a hug. "My God. I didn't expect you. So they let both of you go? That's wonderful. I was straightening up here, getting the place ready for Tom. Didn't imagine you'd be here so soon, so I made Capricia go home. Where is Tom, anyway?"

Sean told her Tom remained in jail. "But in a really nice section. They call it 'the penthouse.' It's the room where they keep generals and other important guys. It even has a radio."

Chesa backed away from him. "He's still in jail? What did the police say when you told them you took the car and the airplane?"

For several long, miserable seconds, he could not speak. The answer he had rehearsed seemed now too pathetic. "It was—I didn't talk to them." He sat on the bed, head down, eyes glued to the floor. "I think it was for the best."

"You think it was for the best?" Her voice assumed a squeaky tone. "You leave your friend rotting in jail, and you say it's for the best. Best for you, I'm sure. Sean, I can't believe you."

"Sit down and let me explain." He patted a spot on the bed.

"No, I won't fucking sit down. Look, I understand it can't be easy to turn yourself in and get put in jail. The idea is frightening. But Tom is already in jail, and you come in here talking like it's nothing, talking about what, a radio?"

"You don't understand." Sean's voice became squeaky as well. "I'll make things worse." He told her what Renzo said. "And, when you look at it, jail is the safest place for him." He was immediately disgusted with himself. He glanced over at her, hoping for a signal that she understood or at least didn't hate him.

She sat on the bed beside him, her eyes boring into his skull. "You poor wretched thing. What happened to you? Or is this who you truly are, and I just imagined you were someone else?" She paused. "That sounds like what you said to me a few months ago. You held up a mirror in which I had to see what I truly am, without all the pretty words and lies I told myself. Now I will do the same for you."

Sean could not speak. He leaned forward, hands on either side of his head. Chesa laid her arm on his back. "What are you going to do?" she asked softly. The squeak was gone.

"What can I do?" he said without raising his head. He couldn't look at her. "Renzo's right. If I confess, that won't get Tom out. I'll just get locked up, too, and he will go back to the shitty little cell again. He might not survive. It's a rough place."

"But you've got to do something. He needs you."

He jerked his head up. "You make it sound like I could snap my fingers and it would all be fixed. Well, I don't see anything I can do." He knew he should stop talking. "What would you do, go sleep with the *Comandante*?"

"Yes," she said, without hesitation, without indignation. "I would, for you." Her tone was matter of fact, like she was ticking off errands she would need to run. "If you were in that situation, I'd fuck D'Annunzio again. Then I would hold his dick and stroke it until he agreed to do what I asked, and if he refused, I would squeeze harder and harder until he did agree. And I would hate myself the whole time and maybe never get the stink out of my body. But I would be able to look in that mirror."

Sean buried his head again, trembling, ashamed to let her see his face.

Chesa slid off the bed and knelt before him. She grabbed his head, a hand clutching each ear. No tenderness in her touch. She was a rough mirror. "What are you going to do?" she asked. "Tell me."

He tried to pull her hands off, but she refused to let go. He covered them with his own and forced himself to look into her face, her beautiful, fierce face.

"I'll do it," he said at last. "I'll go fuck D'Annunzio."

"Stop the asinine jokes." She squeezed tighter and moved her face closer to his. "Now. This is your last chance."

Another ultimatum, like Marinetti's. Last chance for what? Happiness and self-respect? Any future with her? It seemed he needed ultimatums imposed on him to force him to act. He reached out and laid his hands on her head, gently, in contrast to her tight grasp. He couldn't look away. Dared not.

"I'm sorry," he said at last and took a deep breath. "Two things. First, I'm going to gather all the evidence Tom is innocent. Capricia can testify she's been with Tom all the time, and she never saw any rifle here. I'll get the guys at the garage and the barracks to give statements about how they never saw him with any terrorists. That will help him, without implicating me or creating an American-Croatian conspiracy."

Chesa squeezed tighter. "And?"

"Ow," he said. "And when that doesn't work, I'll go to D'Annunzio and—wait, don't do it, this is not a joke—I will swear Tom is innocent and say I need him to go raise funds for the League of Fiume. Tom's father is a big shot union leader in New York, so it's plausible. I'll dress up the story a little." Sean exhaled. "I'm glad it's just my ears you have your hands on."

EIGHTY

June 24, 1920. I wanted to make love to her right there in Tom's apartment, hold her tight for hours, and feel her holding me, our bodies locked together like in our good lost days. I craved her warmth, her scent, the feel of her cunt, the touch of her fingertips, the graze of her hair on my face and chest, her whisper in my ear. Instead, she went to her hotel room and I returned to my apartment.

The sky this afternoon, unmarked by clouds, was the blue I need for my painting, the perfect shade to capture the freedom and joy of a pilot in the air, free of the dirt and pain of Earth, expressing through color what I had dreamed of finding in Fiume. That blue exceeds my grasp. I can't buy it and can't mix it. I stood staring at the sky, ruminating over color while my friend remains locked in a jail cell.

Tonight, I tried to paint. In the dull light of my apartment lamp, none of the colors seem right. And the lines are weak. Painting requires hard choices, and courage to create new images. I am weak. No Futurist message, no League of Fiume ever made me stronger. A fighter is needed to free Tom, and I am not up to the task despite what I told Chesa. Oh, I will try. I will talk to them all now that Chesa has prodded me. I'll do what I can for my friend, for the man who came to my rescue when I needed help. But what chance of success do I have? The canvas mocks me.

Tonight I took a long look in the bathroom mirror and tried to figure out how Chesa could see in me some good quality I cannot find.

EIGHTY-ONE

From INTERVIEW WITH DUŠAN KCLEŽA (1992)
[UNEDITED TRANSCRIPT]

JH: There were two separate attacks in the city on June 9. Italian criminals destroyed a Croatian newspaper and beat several people senseless. At approximately the same time, you and your squad were involved in a battle on the other side of town. Can you tell us about your fight?

DK: The Italians had pushed us and provoked us and assaulted us. My brother was killed by one of their raids. A line had been crossed. We had no choice but to respond. I don't want to get into all the particulars.

JH: Were you concerned about casualties?

DK: It was something we had to do, do you hear me? Liberation is a nasty business. It always is, always has been. You have to use every means available. People get hurt. That's the way it goes. The Italians oppressed our people through naked violence. They were only going to give way when they faced greater violence. If you don't believe me, look at 1945. The important thing was to act. You don't scare anybody with just talk.

JH: Your June action must have caused quite a stir. What did you do next?

DK: Next? We scattered and hid. This was guerilla warfare. Attack and hide. The Nazis were constantly chasing us.

JH: I think you mean the Italians, don't you?

DK: Yeah. [Inaudible] The Italians.

JH: You went into hiding after the attack on the barracks. Did you return to Sušak?

DK: Where else would we go? Every Italian soldier in Fiume, every policeman, they were all on alert, looking for us. And they wanted blood. We made it back to Sušak somehow, I don't remember exactly. It was the next morning, I know that. First, we spent the night at my father's restaurant.

JH: Was your father happy to see you were all safe?

DK: No, no, no. You're not listening. Or I'm getting confused. This was seventy years ago. Let me think. We did meet up at my father's restaurant after the attack, but there were only five of us. We had to leave one guy behind. He was dead, I know that. The rest of us made it to the restaurant like I said, but we started splitting up right away. Andrej was the first to go. Then the others. They said they didn't want to fight no more. They wouldn't even take their rifles. I don't know how they got back to Sušak. I hid the guns and took off before my father showed up.

JH: Quite an uncomfortable night, I imagine. What was going through your mind?

DK: It was like a long fuse burned inside me, endlessly creeping toward something that was waiting to go off. I wanted to punch someone, something, it didn't matter. Punch the wall. But I was afraid of hurting my hand. Can you believe that? All these years, I never admitted that to anybody before. I was afraid to get hurt, and that made me embarrassed, and being embarrassed there in my father's restaurant made it even worse.

That was the lowest point of my life. The young man who wanted to be a leader in the freedom fight was worried about his hand. All my passion and energy had been spent on that barracks action, and my hand was like a fuel gauge showing the tank was empty.

JH: Were you tempted to give up?

DK: No. Absolutely not. Never. I needed to rest. After a couple of weeks, I forced myself to act. Little things at first. I went out on the streets at night and set a few fires. Italian places, especially restaurants and cafés. A few Croatian places, to punish folks I thought were too friendly with the Italians. Nothing big. Just something to keep the fight alive. I nearly got caught a couple of times.

I was building toward something. I promised myself that when I killed the bastard who shot my brother, I would do it in the most public way so everybody, Croatians and Italians, could see who did it. If I got killed in the process, I would die with honor. Croatians would respect what I did and be encouraged to rise against those who oppressed them. Italians would learn fear.

Funny, huh? One day I was scared to get hurt, but a little while later I was ready to die. That fuse inside me had burned all the way to the end.

EIGHTY-TWO

June 26, 1920

Tom had made clear he didn't want Capricia involved in the effort to free him. Sean went to see her anyway. He was determined to use every resource available, and that meant Capricia as a witness. Chesa insisted on accompanying him.

The twins lived with their mother in an affluent section of the city. The walk from Chesa's hotel was pleasant, shaded in part by a long canopy of thick oak trees. Large, detached houses had manicured hedges and front-yard gardens of irises and roses and camellias. It brought to Sean's mind the nicer parts of Philadelphia out by Fairmount Park.

They were admitted to the house by the girls' mother, who was on her way out. She insisted Annalisa stay with Capricia during the visit. "Annalisa's the sensible one," she said. The sitting room was warm and sunlit. Chesa and Sean seated themselves in stiff armchairs, leaving the settee to the twins. No refreshments were offered.

"Capricia," Sean began, "Tom needs your help. You were with him pretty much all the time after he got hurt, were you not? So you can testify the rifle wasn't his, and he never met with any Croatian terrorists."

"Is he still in jail?" Capricia said, surprised. She looked quickly from Chesa to Sean. "I thought you took care of this. Chesa told me you went to the police yesterday to get him freed. She said it was some heroic action you were taking."

Sean explained he was doing everything he could to help Tom, but first he needed evidence to prove his friend's innocence. "One can't march into the police station and demand somebody's release from jail, you understand. We need to make preparations." All of this was true but in the sitting room, the message was not well received.

"He's saying he hasn't done anything to help Tom," Annalisa said. She laid an arm around her sister and, having scorched Sean with her words, stared brazenly at him. "Right?"

"Girls," Chesa said softly, "Sean is trying—"

"I want to hear him say it," Annalisa said. "Let him give us his excuses." Sean could tell her days of wanting to model for him were in the past.

Chesa gave him a look that was sympathetic but made clear the next steps were his. "Annalisa is correct," he said. "I haven't yet spoken to the authorities. I promised Tom I would do whatever is necessary to get him out of that jail cell, nice as it is. But I need your help. You will be perfectly safe. I must know if you will be available."

"Available for what?" Capricia asked.

"To testify, as I said."

"And who am I supposed to testify to?"

"To the, uh, well, I'm not exactly sure. To the police, I guess, and the court if he goes on trial, maybe to somebody in the Command or the National Council. I guess it depends." His brilliant plan somehow lacked critical details. He wondered whether his fatuity was obvious to everyone or if only women could see it.

"So they can put me in jail, too? They might say, 'Capricia, you must be helping those Croats, too.' Who's going to testify for me?"

"Not him," Annalisa said. She aimed a withering glare at Sean. "He's afraid to do anything. Sean will go look for somebody else. Or more likely he'll run away, like he always does."

"Annalisa, stop it," Chesa said. "Sean is trying to help. That's why he came here. Tom is his friend."

Annalisa's face showed no hint of relenting. She knew something, and in an instant Sean saw it too.

"Capricia," he said in as gentle a voice as he could manage, "did the police or anyone else talk to you about Tom? Did anybody threaten you?"

Capricia wiped her eyes. "A man came here yesterday. He told me I needed to stay out of this for my safety, that it was dangerous, and I couldn't do Tom any good. He said Tom was safe there in jail, in a nice suite, but a lot of angry people were mad at him and wanted to hurt him and me too." She tilted her head, and the gesture reminded Sean how young and vulnerable she was. "Why do they want to hurt me? I didn't do anything."

"Did you recognize the man?" he asked. "Did he give his name?"

"No. He said he was a friend and was trying to help Tom but needed me to stay quiet. I never saw him before."

The advice this mystery man gave Capricia sounded like what Renzo had told Sean. The visitor could not have been Renzo, of course. Capricia knew him well.

"Did you see this man?" Chesa asked Annalisa.

"She wasn't there," Capricia said. "I'm the one who answered the door. Even my Mom doesn't know."

"I saw him," Annalisa said. Capricia swiveled on the couch to face her sister, eyes wide open. "I peeked out the front window. His name is Santo. I don't know his last name. I met him at a club not long ago. He was with Renzo. It was the night those two bombs went off and the fires and stuff. Sleazy guy. Tried to give me cocaine."

Annalisa took Capricia's hands and squeezed them. "Sorry, sister. I should have gone to the door with you. But I figured since he was a friend of Renzo's, you were safe."

"He didn't say anything to me about Renzo," Capricia said. "He said he was from the Security Department or something like that. Not the police. I thought he meant from the Governor's Palace. Now that I think of it, if he worked there, I would have recognized him."

"Santo is a pilot," Chesa said. "He flies in every few weeks or so. He tried to give me cocaine, too."

Here, at last, Sean thought, was a lead to whoever might be

behind the frame-up. The plane that Sean took, did that belong to this Santo? What connected Santo to Tom? Or Santo to Renzo? Sean couldn't make sense of anything, sitting there in the living room under the scrutiny of the three women. The only thing certain was he could not risk their safety. The people behind Tom's arrest showed they would go to any lengths to prevail.

"This changes things completely," Sean said. "Capricia, forget what I said about testifying. It's too risky right now, and Tom wouldn't want it." Chesa slid forward in the chair and gave him a quizzical look. He didn't stop. "What you told me about this Santo character is a big help. Believe me, I will keep working to make sure Tom is safe and gets released. And I'll keep you out of it."

They all stood up. Annalisa came over to Sean, put her hands on his shoulders, and leaned into him as if she were going to kiss him. She didn't. "Promise me," she whispered, "whatever you do, you won't let them hurt my sister." He promised.

Back outside under the oak canopy, he pondered how he could convince anyone of Tom's innocence when two of the people who knew Tom best, himself being one of them, declined to bear witness on the man's behalf. Futurist principles were no help.

Chesa and Sean drifted back in the direction of her hotel. He suggested they sit among the roses in the public garden adjacent to the Teatro Giuseppe Verdi. The idea was good but unfortunately shared by many. They could find no place to sit. Chesa suggested they try for a spot along the sun-splashed canal. One bench came open, and the two of them ran to grab it.

They sat facing east, toward Sušak. Directly in front of them, small boats knocked up against the canal's walls, lashed by bowlines to cross-shaped bollards. The odor of brackish water and fresh fish was strong but not disagreeable. He wanted to ask Chesa how she met Santo but decided against it.

"I was under the impression you hated the water," Chesa said.

"I hate boats, or more specifically, I hate being on boats while they're in the water. I don't mind looking at them from dry land. They can't harm me then."

Sean knew the real question was coming, the one he did not want to answer. Out it came. "What are you going to do next about Tom?" The woman was relentless. She demanded answers and action. He had none of the former and little enthusiasm for the latter, given his failures thus far.

"What about reaching out to Gaj?" she suggested. "He adores Tom and I'm sure would be happy to help. With all Gaj's friends in the Croatian community, I'll bet he could round up many of the leading citizens to step forward. They could testify to the police or whoever that neither Tom nor they have been involved with any terrorists, and Tom has only ever tried to help people who were attacked."

Chesa had been taking a lot of photos lately in the Old Town section, Sean knew. In Sušak, too. Croatians from all walks of life, in everyday occupations and leisure. He asked her why she cared so much about those people.

"Because they *are* people," she said. A little ringlet of hair crept down the side of her face. "I want everybody to see them as I do."

More boats coasted into the canal. Beyond them, the factories and warehouse buildings in Sušak stood out against the blue sky. "Who do you think would listen to them?" Sean said. "Just look at the newspapers. Some anonymous Croats claimed responsibility for the attack Tom is supposed to have led. If Capricia needs to be quiet, so do they."

Chesa shifted around on the bench, and for a minute he was afraid she would get up and walk away. Instead, she lifted her head and perused the hills where the castle loomed. "You don't like anyone telling you to be quiet," she said.

"That's different." She did not demand an explanation of how it was different, to his relief. He had been exposed and humiliated enough for one day.

"Gaj told me something the other day," she said. "He heard it from Rabbi Kleinzeller, from the synagogue over on Via del Pomerio. This is second hand, keep in mind, so I may not have it exactly right. 'We all have a vision of perfect order and goodness. But in the real world, there's much evil as well as good. We will find the perfect future only when we help everyone else enjoy those things we demand for ourselves.' A beautiful ethic, isn't it? It's in their prayers, I gather." Her hard gaze dared him to contradict wisdom more than two thousand years old.

"I wish things were that simple," he said. "Those are old words. Today is a new age, ruled by speed and machines and young ideas." Even as he spoke he wondered if some platitudes might be embedded too deeply in his brain.

She looked askance, lips pursed. That told him everything she was thinking.

"Maybe this is a new age," she said finally, "but I'm not sure it will be a better one. I have trouble seeing the improvement, anyway. Did I ever tell you why I stopped painting and took up photography?"

She hadn't. For a long time he had wanted to ask about her painting days but didn't dare, even in the early days when they were so close and spoke intimately to each other. She'd made clear she didn't want to talk about her painting and he had let it go.

"It happened before the war, before I came to Italy. I had just turned eighteen and was living with my parents back in England. My father paid for my art classes and encouraged my progress. Even set me up in a little studio. One day he asked me to paint the portrait of an old mate of his. The man came to my studio and sat for several days, and we talked about his wife and his children and my father while I painted, and then on the last day he raped me."

Sean recoiled, his eyes opened wide. "Raped you? Oh my God, that's—that's awful."

"More than you could know. The thing is, I felt guilty afterward. Not that I encouraged him. Not one bit." She paused and drew a deep breath. "While I painted, I saw nothing ominous about him. He was the man who for years came to visit my father. But when he left and I fixed my clothes, I studied the portrait—it was almost finished—and I could see the evil, clear as I see that boat. I must have seen it before he touched me because I painted it. I saw his wickedness and put it in the portrait and did not recognize it or the danger it represented. I kept on painting, all innocent, until he forced himself on me. What it was I saw—the eyes, the curl of the lips, maybe the way he held his chin—I can't describe it today, but I remember perfectly the sick feeling I had looking at his portrait when he was gone. The signs were subtle, but they were there. I should have looked more carefully while I painted, but I was too enchanted by my art. Then it was too late. I threw the canvas into the fire, along with my brushes, and never told anyone. You are the first. I made up some excuse about not wanting to paint anymore and bought a camera."

Sean grabbed the back of the bench to steady himself. The evil she described eclipsed anything in his experience. He had seen and heard terrible things in the war and insulated himself by keeping people away. Only his painting suffered. Chesa, in contrast, had no chance to distance herself. She had suffered in a way he couldn't conceive. And much as he wanted to, there was nothing he could do about it. He couldn't go back in time and rescue her in an ambulance. She hadn't needed saving, though, by him or anyone else. She fixed herself up, changed her life. Her pain lingered, however. Why hadn't he seen it before?

"Jesus, I don't know what to say, Chesa. I'm sorry—"

"Don't. Just listen to me."

"Yes."

A small boat navigated into the canal, silently, tying up a few meters away from where they sat. Green water lapped noisily up against the concrete walls. "Evil is out there, Sean. Speed won't make it go away. Maybe Rabbi Kleinzeller's way will. I don't know. I just can't accept your vision of human perfection and harmony in the land of fast machines."

"I know there are rotten people out there. I get that. But things will get better when culture and industry move forward. You have to believe in progress, don't you? We'll be able to see what needs to be done and fix things."

She looked at him with soft green eyes. "You think you can see everything like an artist, but you can't. Not while you are painting, anyway. If you are looking close, you only see a part. The rest is a blur. You miss a lot in that blur."

Two fishermen emerged from the boat and climbed up on the quay. Each carried a basket that looked heavy. Water dripped out and left a trail. Sean followed their progress past the row of benches and down toward the Mercato.

"What do you see?" he asked quietly.

She gazed absently at the water. Reflected images of clouds and blue sky dissolved in the wake of a passing vessel. "I take photos from a safe distance, so I don't get that look into the subject's ultimate truth, their soul, you might call it. You've criticized my photos for precisely that lack, and you're right. But I see other things, more than I'm looking for. It's all in focus, Sean. The bad and the good. No blur."

She stood up and rested a hand on his shoulder. "Your art versus my photographs. We're on different sides. How will we ever bridge that divide?"

EIGHTY-THREE

From **SEAN REILLY'S JOURNAL**

June 26, 1920. She asked how the divide between us would ever be bridged. An excellent question. While I fumbled for an answer I had no hope of finding, a tall boat entered the canal and blocked the view we had been enjoying.

I have trouble even thinking about her getting raped. It's overwhelming. How could somebody do that to her? I think instead about what she has schooled me about photography and how it applies to our relationship. Small aperture is good for things far away but forces the camera to tell lies. Too much is in focus, so depth is distorted. What's close and what isn't? Truth reveals itself up close, when the lens is wide open. But up close only part of the truth is visible. You best be careful what you focus on because danger lurks in the blur.

Boccioni would have disagreed. The woman on the balcony in his painting was supposed to convey all the visual sensations she was experiencing, no matter how close or far away. That was intoxicating for Boccioni and his buddies. Chesa would have none of it. She traded the canvas for the camera. Adjusting her lens, she could control how close she would get to her subjects, how much confusion she would allow in her photos. All the depravity and shit and everything else, kept at a distance, in focus but at the cost of veracity. Always a little off. Now I understood why she bore that cost.

She's right. The circle of confusion traps us on opposite sides. No fine words from Marinetti or D'Annunzio will close the distance.

Except, she has tried to get close to me. Hasn't she?

EIGHTY-FOUR

From *Memories of a Fascist in Fiume*
by Tenente Lorenzo Guidici

After Tom was arrested, I presumed Sean would learn the obvious lesson and quit causing trouble. Instead, he became more agitated. It was difficult to keep him from meddling. I explained to him that the arrest was complicated, and he didn't want to make matters worse. Sean could hardly listen, he was in such a state. He was ready to throw himself at the Fiume authorities and wanted me to help him.

The reader might imagine some parallel between Tom's imprisonment and my own. In reality, they could not be more different. My freedom has been lost due to the lies from my enemies, some of whom brazenly call themselves "Fascists." The struggle for power in a young movement like ours creates opportunities for abuse. In Tom Delancy's case, his jailing was in his best interest and that of Italy, too. Certainly, his accommodations were infinitely nicer than my foul, overcrowded cell.

It had not been easy to arrange what happened to Tom. Sean wanted to free him and have him deported, but the artist simply did not appreciate how relentless a true soldier is. Tom would never leave until he found who was responsible, and even if he were deported, he would return in a heartbeat, angrier and more determined than before. I finally was able to make Sean understand the risks to both Tom and himself. I told him, truthfully but perhaps not for the reasons Sean understood, that jail was the best place for Tom, at least for a while.

Sean had given me another concern, though. He saw something from the airplane. If it was what I thought, and if he possessed photographs of it, I would have to do something about him, too. I could not under any circumstances let such photographs reach Rome.

And then there was Chesa, Rome's secret agent. She continued to take pictures all over the city. I could do nothing about the photos she had already passed on, but I didn't want new ones to find their way into the government's possession, especially if they showed my little squad in action. Giolitti, the new prime minister, was a shrewd old politician, and the wrong evidence in his hands could prove embarrassing. We were getting too close to risk that.

EIGHTY-FIVE

July 9, 1920

No one at the garage or the barracks would speak to Sean about Tom. The consensus seemed to be that Americans were bad, Americans of Irish ancestry were worse, and anyone of any ethnicity who helped Croats or Tom Delancy deserved whatever might happen to them.

Sean tried the Governor's Palace. After being denied admittance to the *Comandante*'s presence, he went to seek help from Léon Kochnitzky. The man had been curt and obnoxious, but he did give Sean the clue about the mystery in the hills. Sean hoped he could convince Kochnitzky to put in a good word for Tom with the *Comandante*.

He found Kochnitzky in his office, alone, shoving papers in boxes. Kochnitzky ignored his presence until Sean got in his way and asked him what he was doing.

"What does it look like I am doing, Mr. Reilly?" he said. "Packing. I am leaving Fiume. Unlike you, with no intention of returning."

"You can't leave. What will happen to the League? And to Fiume?"

"The League will go the way of other quixotic ideals," Kochnitzky said. "A victim of greed and corruption and lack of funds. Our vain and blind *Comandante* wills himself to continue, but quite frankly, Mr. Reilly, the League is dead. No nation or would-be nation will follow Fiume when Fiume cannot live up to its promises. I leave tomorrow and suggest you strongly consider doing the same."

Sean followed him to the far side of the office. Kochnitzky pulled a batch of files from a large cabinet and stuffed them in a box. "Surely more could be done to save the League, even without money," Sean said. "We could still crusade for justice. Narrow it to a single fight. Take on the Serbs, for instance."

Kochnitzky shook his head without looking up from the box. "The League is dead. Killed by a cancer here in Fume. Watch behind you, Mr. Reilly. You are not safe here. No one is. Not even the *Comandante*." He sat down at the desk and began emptying its drawers.

Sean tried unsuccessfully for several minutes to get Kochnitzky to explain what he meant about D'Annunzio. He left without asking for help with Tom's release.

Sean saw no alternative but to go directly to the *Comandante*. He crossed the atrium and mounted the stairway to the upper level, the same stairway he had seen Chesa climb on that awful night. A sour taste filled his mouth as he climbed. When he reached the top, he swung around and ran down a long corridor, at the end of which stood a guard with his back to the door.

"Stop," the guard ordered. "No admittance here. You have to go around the other side and speak to them. No one gets in this side."

The guard was a young man, possibly a local Fiume recruit fresh out of high school. His uniform was vintage Fiume irregular: a gray tunic too large and decorated with medals he could not possibly have been awarded, and pants of a different shade at least one size too short. His boots were scuffed and falling apart. He held no rifle, and the leather holster attached to his belt was empty.

"I must see the *Comandante* immediately," Sean said in the most authoritative voice he could muster. "Open the door."

The guard didn't move, but he started to apologize rather than yell for assistance. Sean pressed on.

"Soldier, I said open the door. I have an urgent message for the *Comandante*. Do you understand? News he needs to hear immediately. I'm going in there even if you try to shoot me."

The guard rubbed his hands on his upper arms and glanced down the hall. "But sir, my orders are not to let anyone pass here."

"Unless the *Comandante* gets this message, the whole city of Fiume will be in grave danger. And everyone, those left alive anyway, will want to know why the message didn't get through in time." He paused for a few seconds to let that sink in. "Make a field decision, soldier. Like the Arditi."

The guard pulled a key out from his pocket but made no move to unlock the door. Sean heard voices from out in the atrium heading in his direction.

"Move," he yelled at the young guard. "The *Comandante* is in danger. Open the door and let me in. Then let no one else pass. Do you hear?"

"I hear you," the guard said miserably. He moved to unlock the door, saying over his shoulder, "Wait here while I check with the *Comandante.*"

The other voices drew closer. Sean grabbed the keys out of the young guard's hands and opened the door himself. Once inside he slammed it shut and locked it from the inside. Fists pounded on the door. The shouting was intense. Exulting in his success, Sean spun around and beheld a naked woman kneeling on a large unmade bed. *Comandante* D'Annunzio stood nearby, wearing nothing but her wide-brimmed plumed hat.

Four hours later, sitting in a cold jail cell, the same one Tom originally occupied, Sean still laughed about the hat.

"You got a visitor," Tomaso called out from the far end of the hallway. "A real pretty one. Twenty minutes."

Sean raised himself from the bare cot. The clicking of a woman's shoes on the stone floor grew louder and faster until Chesa appeared. She wore a chic blue satin dress, pearls, and gloves. The look was stunning.

"You bloody stupid clown," she said. "What on earth were you thinking?"

"I heard it was pretty funny," Tomaso said. He came up behind her, carrying a wooden stool he placed before the bars of the cell. "The old *Comandante* standing there at attention." He lumbered away, laughing crudely.

"Please, take a seat," Sean said, extending his arm as if he were receiving her in the parlor of a sumptuous villa. "Welcome to my new world. You look lovely tonight. Do you have a date?"

Chesa narrowed her eyes and frowned. "I don't perceive anything funny about all this, despite what Tomaso says. And no, I don't have a date. I dressed up because I thought it might help get me in here to see you. The jailors might mistake me for someone important. And don't you dare say a word about me and D'Annunzio, or I'll leave right now."

He returned her serious look, chastened, holding it for a minute. Then he burst out in uncontrollable laughter. Chesa's frown deepened as she sat down, watching him clutch his sides. She tugged at the hem of her dress and looked over at the stone walls of the cell. He had started to recover his composure when he saw her face. A smirk had appeared, which she tried to swallow but could not. Within seconds she progressed to brief chortles before exploding in shrieks of wild laughter. That got Sean going again, and the two of them sat helpless for several minutes.

Finally, Chesa was able to speak again. "Was he really 'at attention,' as your jailor so delightfully put it? I can imagine the look on his pompous face."

"Oh yes. When I turned around and faced the two of them, the lady screamed and then scrambled under the covers. D'Annunzio stood there, her feathered hat on his head and his dick aimed at me like a rifle. All I could think was, *Don't point that thing at me, it might go off.*" Chesa started laughing again, her face completely red as she bent over. She put a gloved hand over her mouth.

"By this time the guards were banging at the door, and I was afraid they would break it down. I said to him, 'Sir, I need to talk to you about Tom Delancy. He's innocent. And there's a gap in our military defenses along the ridge on the north side of the city.' He just stared at me, goggle-eyed. The *Comandante* couldn't speak. The man of all those words couldn't make a sound. I added, 'And you personally might be in mortal danger.'

"D'Annunzio says, and he's spitting as he says this, he is so mad, 'Go in the next room and wait for me there.' The lady was screaming again but from under the covers. And yes, D'Annunzio was at full salute.

"I couldn't handle looking at that sight any longer, and the banging on the door got pretty loud, so I went to the next room. In retrospect, I should have stayed where I was because the other guards wouldn't dare come into D'Annunzio's bedroom. I could at least have explained myself more to the *Comandante* before they arrested me. But once I was in the other room, the guards came in the door on the far side and grabbed me, and here I am."

"Yes," she said. "Here you are. You've had quite a day trying to help Tom even though your efforts don't seem to have borne much fruit. That was a good idea, by the way, reaching out to Kochnitzky. I'm a little surprised you didn't try Guido Keller. But all things considered, you deserve a reward. I brought you these." She handed him his journal and the notebook containing his drawings and the drafts of the manifesto. "To keep you busy for the next couple of weeks. Someday when your opus is published, I will read it closely, looking for a sign of how today's activities fit in with your visions of Fiume." She put her fingers to her lips. "I'm sorry. I wasn't trying to be mean. Forgive me."

"How is Tom? Is he—"

"Tom's fine. Yes, he is still in his deluxe cell. Capricia talked to him late this afternoon. He, too, saw the humor in your sorry episode. He said to tell you he will get a message to you soon. Did Tomaso or anyone advise you of what will happen in your case?"

"No. I figure they will be hard on me. I may as well confess about the plane and the car and get Tom out of here. I'll even say the rifle was mine."

"Don't be so hasty. You always want to react too fast. Did you recognize the lady who was, ah, entertaining the *Comandante*?" He shook his head. "She's the wife of one of the National Council members. Yes. Consequently, no one is particularly interested in putting you on trial. That news came from Tom, who I assume heard it from Renzo. So keep quiet and you will be out of here in two or three weeks. They need to charge you with something, but it's being treated as a nuisance matter. It's a lot better than assault on the *Comandante*, which is what certain people wanted to charge you with."

"Time's up," Tomaso called out. "Sorry, Miss. You have to go. He'll be here tomorrow."

"Thank you, Tomaso," Chesa said. "You've been very kind. I wonder if you could give us sixty seconds to say good-bye properly." She gave him a shy smile. It worked.

Chesa reached through the bars with both hands and held Sean's head. "Be careful, please," she said, with a tenderness that shook him. "I beg you, don't do anything else stupid. You've quite filled your quota already."

EIGHTY-SIX

From SEAN REILLY'S JOURNAL

July 9, 1920. Chesa made fun of my manifesto but I don't mind. I am too exhausted to take offense or think about it or Fiume or Futurism or how the naked *Comandante* might carry on without the League. I can't tell whether my actions will help create a golden future, but I have taken action. So what if Kochnitzky wouldn't help? At least I planted the thought in D'Annunzio's head about Tom and the gap out in the hills behind Trsat Castle and the risk to his own person. Maybe he will take action, too.

D'Annunzio stopped writing novels and plays when he took up his military adventures. Mazzini gave up his literary dreams for the political struggle. I wonder what kind of art they could have produced had they tried to do both.

July 10, 1920. I've been looking over the sketches I did in Zara. They're not bad. I don't have much else to do for the next three weeks, so maybe I'll try some more. I can't see outside, but if Chesa can bring me some of her photographs, I can at least try. Better than working on this stupid manifesto.

EIGHTY-SEVEN

From INTERVIEW WITH DUŠAN KCLEŽA (1992)
[*UNEDITED TRANSCRIPT*]

JH: How did you go about finding your brother's murderer?

DK: Oh, let's see, I walked up to people at random and asked them if they did it. No, I stood up on a table at one of the Corso cafés and yelled out, "Whoever killed my brother, Veselko, please come forward and identify yourself." Then I went to the Governor's Palace and politely asked Mr. D'Annunzio if knew which of his Italian friends had pulled the trigger.

Dumb fucking question.

[Inaudible]

All right, I'll behave. There wasn't much I could do, since all my confederates had abandoned me, and the police and the other legionnaires were extra suspicious of all Croatian males after our fight at the barracks. Asking questions about Veselko to the wrong people would call too much attention to myself. But no other Croatians would admit they knew anything, and the Italians who might know weren't about to sit down and confide in me. That's when I went to the last person I wanted to see because I had no other choice.

JH: Who was that?

DK: My father.

I tried to be respectful, but we started having words even before I could ask him for assistance. I said to him, "I didn't come to argue with you, Father."

"You never come here for anything else," he said to me. Threw that in my face. "All you talk about is the terrible Italians, and oppression, and—"

"Freedom," I said. "Freedom and independence. You used to talk about such things. Remember? Before you got fat and rich from your stupid restaurant." Yes, I said that.

He slapped me in the face.

JH: He hit you?

DK: He did. Looking back, I guess I deserved it. He said, "You dare to talk to your father like that? What do you know about freedom? You don't even know about work. You are an embarrassment to me and your mother." To me, his oldest son, he said that. The pain of the slap was nothing compared to those words. I feel it now, all these years later.

JH: I'm sure. How did you react at the time?

DK: Oh, I was mad. "So be it," I said. Well, I shouted it, actually. "For Veselko, then. He was always your favorite. I'm going to avenge his death." I let that sink in while I rubbed my stinging cheek. "Just tell me who was responsible. I'm sure you know. You hear everything."

He didn't react like I thought he would. He gave me the whammy eye like the boxers do before they fight, and then he told me I was responsible. That's right, me. His voice was bitter. He said, "Veselko would never have been there except for you and those crazy ideas you put in his head. The boy should have been home studying or here at the restaurant working."

"You sent him home, didn't you?" I said. I wasn't shouting now, but my tone was hostile. Disrespectful, yes. I said, "He came to me when you dismissed him. Why did you do that? I never would have seen him that day if he had stayed at work."

"Now you accuse me?" my father said, so loud that I swear the dishes were rattling. "Get out of here. Now. And don't come back."

JH: That sounds heartbreaking. It must have been so hard to hear it from your father. Did you leave at that point?

DK: No. I wasn't ready to go. "I am not accusing you, Father," I said. "It's not your fault, and it's not my fault. We didn't shoot him. A yellow bastard shot him, and I will find out who. Nobody in Fiume or Sušak has done anything about it, so I will. Help me find that Italian."

"So the killing can continue?" he said. "Anyway, it wasn't an Italian."

"You know who it was?" My voice rose again. I couldn't control it. "Tell me now."

"I don't know the name," he said. "All I have heard is that the shooter wasn't Italian. Could be English, could be American, or French or whatever." I remember that while my father was saying all this, he was cutting the tentacles from a squid, slashing at them with one of his sharp knives, and dropping the ink sacs into a nearby jar. Funny how I remember that. He pulled out the innards and began cleaning and slicing. That poor squid never stood a chance. "That's all I overheard from the tables," he said. He wasn't shouting at me anymore, but he wasn't encouraging me either. "Are you going to kill all the foreigners?"

I told him, "I'm not a murderer, like the Italians and their mercenary friends. All I want is justice. And, not that it matters all that much to you, I'll be careful."

JH: I can imagine that must have had a powerful effect on him.

DK: We stood looking at each other and didn't speak. A voice from the front shouted, "Customers." My father looked away, and then turned back to me. Still no words came out. The whammy, again. I flinched like I did when I was little. But his eyes told me he accepted what I was saying.

JH: What do you mean, "accepted"? That he agreed with you, and wanted to go after the killer?

DK: No, no, no. You don't understand my father. Not many people did. Most people only saw the smiling fat guy welcoming people into his restaurant. Jolly Gaj. What I saw in his eyes was that he, too, wanted justice for Veselko, but it was complicated. That's what I read from his eyes. Maybe I'm wrong. He threw me an apron. "Go help out for a while," he said. "A little work won't hurt you. Justice belongs to people who get their hands dirty."

JH: Did you do it? Did you stay and work?

DK: Yeah. I put the apron on and set to work. I figured maybe I might hear something.

It was hard working there, I can tell you. I washed dishes and cleared the tables and sometimes helped serve the meals. No one seemed to notice me, much less recognize me. I was just another young Croat, invisible to the Italians unless they wanted someone to beat up. Only my father drew their attention, and everybody loved him. Smiling, jolly Gaj.

EIGHTY-EIGHT

October 19, 1920

Sean's time in the jail cell exceeded Chesa's prediction due to his quarrels with a couple of the guards. Not with Tomaso, of course.

Once freed, he visited Tom. The months of incarceration showed on his friend. Tom had been drinking heavily, and despite the nice facilities in his suite, his hygiene suffered neglect. He stank. Sean tried talking to him about the League of Fiume. Tom yelled that it was all bullshit and politicians were bloodsuckers and so were all those who supported them. At least, Sean thought that's what he said. Tom's rant was difficult to decipher. He wondered how all the liquor made it to his room.

Sean tried painting again, with limited success, and became a regular at Keller's Union of Free Spirits meetings. He enjoyed the clash of ideas in these meetings, where he could put forth the Futurist case for a progressive future and suffer nothing more serious than ridicule. Speaking out helped sharpen his thinking. He still wanted to be a great artist. In a better world, he would be. Painting was bound to come easily in a better world, and Futurism laid out a path to get there although a few detours might be necessary. The Free Spirits talked about publishing a journal, and they invited Sean to submit an essay.

He planned to tell the truth about Fiume, describing the battle that raged between those who coveted the status quo or worse and those who aspired to the crusade for the new world. His essay would place Futurism in the vanguard of the crusade, provided it first shed all links to Fascist thuggery. Speed and machines retained their importance but must be subordinated to justice.

Chesa gave guarded support to the idea. She suggested a climb to Trsat Castle as a way to get fresh air and recharge his brain after the stay in jail. He quickly agreed. What he had written for his manifesto after the previous climb to the castle was, he had to admit, not very good, but the exercise had stirred up ideas. He hoped a second climb would do the same for this essay. And he wanted more photos of the hills. Those he took from the plane were blurred; even Gaj couldn't fix them. Her Kodak lacked the higher-speed shutter required for aerial photography.

They crossed the bridge into Sušak without difficulty and mounted the stairs leading to the castle. He found the climb longer and more difficult than he remembered, in part due to the speed at which Chesa took the steps. She seemed to fly up them.

About a third of the way up, she stopped at a landing and waited for him. When he caught up, she was holding the camera against her body and pointing the lens into a little chapel. "It's beautiful inside," she said. "So pristine and understated. Look at that fresco. A heavenly place to take refuge on your path to the top."

"I didn't know you were so religious," he said. She was full of surprises.

"Not religious. Spiritual, maybe. Tell me you don't sense something here. Something warm that touches you inside." His face answered for him. "Oh, forget it. Move on. Maybe a few hundred more steps will help your senses."

"I'll sense Jesus, Mary, and Joseph and all the saints and apostles by then."

She let out a quick snort. "For you, the reception line will be quite different, I suspect. And warmer. Let's get cracking."

Chesa stopped at a few more chapels to take photographs. Watching her in action, crouching, leaning, angling for the best light, the best view, alternately smiling and frowning, Sean imagined one of those Madonnas from the chapel paintings coming to life and descending from the canvas, smile brighter than their halos, frown that would terrify the most brazen sinner. How could he not idealize her as a goddess?

They spent two hours exploring the castle, laughing and concocting fantasies before making their way to the tall turret. From its heights, they took in all of Fiume and Sušak. Chesa employed her camera in every direction while Sean surveyed the mountains to the north, searching without success for the pass he had seen from the airplane. The mountains melded together in the distance like clay smoothed over. He located the landmarks he used from the plane and moved around to get a better angle until he spotted the entrance to the trail.

"Chesa," he called. "Would you mind bringing the royal camera here to take pictures exactly where I point?"

"Gladly, milord," she sang. She took three photographs in the direction where he pointed, steadying the body of the Kodak on one of the merlons of the battlement. "There," she said. "If developed properly, I believe these won't be as blurry as the last time. I may need to ask Gaj for help again. He knows so much about developing and enlarging."

She pointed the lens at him. He smiled in the most formal pose he could muster but nothing happened. "Damn it," she said. "The bleeding thing is out of film. I have another roll in my pocket, so bear with me. Stay where you are and keep that expression on your face. It's priceless."

She disappeared into the shade. Minutes passed. Obediently, he didn't move.

"Fuck. Get in there, you little bugger." Chesa's voice carried and tugged at him like the song of a siren, except he didn't believe sirens cursed as frequently or with quite the same gusto. "There, that's got it." A grunt. "Now we're ready."

She stepped out of the shade and snapped several shots of him with his frozen smile. That accomplished, she went back to photographing the city and the port.

"I'm ready to go," Sean said.

Chesa wheeled around. "Are you truly ready to go? Leave Fiume, I mean. We could go to Florence or Venice. I'll even go to the States with you if you prefer. Show the photos to whomever at the Palace, let Renzo get Tom out of jail, and let's go."

A year ago, James challenged him about going to Fiume, and more recently Gaj questioned why he wanted to stay. Now Chesa pushed him to leave. He wrapped his arms around her. From this height, Fiume was small and unimportant, a little village governed by a buffoon. Why stay?

It wasn't that simple. "Let's talk about it tonight," he said.

"That means no," Chesa said with a sigh. He felt her body droop. She freed herself and attacked the camera, contracting the bellows and latching the lid with jerky movements. "Of course. The stairs, then. Are you ready?" She patted the pocket of her jacket to make sure the exposed roll of film was still there. The camera hung from her shoulder on a long, thin leather cord she had tied to the hand strap on the case.

They began the descent without speaking. The late afternoon sun brought out the harsh ugliness of the old stone walls lining the stairs.

"How far along do you suppose we are?" he asked. "Halfway?"

"I haven't been counting," she said.

She had barely finished speaking when two masked figures darted out onto the stairs and blocked their progress. Sean whirled around. Three men, similarly masked, one of them slim, another quite large, towered a few steps above them.

The slim man made his way casually down the stairs. He leaned close to Chesa and said, "Give me camera." His accent was unrecognizable, the words snarled, almost unintelligible. "We don't like foreigners come to Sušak and take photographs." He reached out and grabbed at the camera case.

Sean pushed the man's arm away. "Get your fucking hands off her," he shouted. The other four men closed in. The two from the steps below grabbed him and pinned his arms behind him.

"Mr. Tough American, eh," said the slim man. The accent grew even more confusing. "You shot the boy Veselko. You killed our brother." He yanked the case from Chesa's shoulder, breaking the leather cord.

"Ow! You fucking pig," she shouted, and kicked the assailant in the leg.

"You're a vicious little cunt," the man said, hopping on one leg. The funny accent disappeared. He slapped her hard in the face, sending her staggering down several steps.

While the other men laughed, Sean leaned back as far as he could and pushed off the stair riser with both feet, causing the two men holding him to release their grasp as they all fell. He landed on top of one of them, allowing him to get up first. He grabbed Chesa's hand, and the two of them raced down the steps. The men pursuing them closed in quickly. "Go, go, go," Sean yelled at Chesa and pivoted to confront them.

"You're gonna wish you hadn't done that," the slim man rasped. He nodded to the large man, who stepped down to Sean's level and knocked him down with one punch. Other blows followed before and after he blacked out.

He came to sometime later, not sure for a moment where he was. The sky had darkened. His nose and jaw ached, and he felt stabbing pains in his ribs and knees. As his mind cleared, he grew alarmed about Chesa's fate. Had they caught her?

He struggled to his feet and immediately fell. The pain in his ribs was excruciating. He noticed blood on his torn jacket and reached up to his nose. Dried blood had caked all over his face. He got up, slowly this time, and worked his way down one agonizing step at a time. "Chesa," he called out. "Where are you? Chesa?"

No answer. He limped down to the next landing and called her name again. What had they done to her? He heard a muffled sound coming from a dark chapel on his right. Its heavy wood door was shut. "Chesa," he shouted again. "Are you in there? Come on out."

"Sean," he heard her say. "Oh thank God it's you." She opened the door and stepped out, glancing around cautiously. "Are you sure they're all gone?"

"They got what they wanted. Can you give me a hand?"

"Oh my God, what did they do to you?" she said. She put her hand to his face but pulled away quickly when he cried out in pain. "Oh God, oh shit, let me help you." She put his left arm around her shoulder and moved where he could grab hold of the stair rail.

The dark staircase seemed endless. He barked at her several times to slow down. They staggered over the bridge and made it to the hotel, where Paolo, the night clerk, greeted them in the lobby. "Mr. Reilly," he said. "Again?" He ran over and put Sean's arm over his shoulder.

"Getting to be a habit with me," Sean said, "coming here all busted up. At least tonight I'm not shitting my pants. I hope, anyway."

"Quiet," Chesa said. "Save your jokes for later." The three of them squeezed into the tiny elevator. She turned to Paolo. "If you could help get him to my room and then get me some towels, I will be forever in your debt."

Sean was deposited in the bed to a chorus of grunts and curses, most but not all of which came from him. Chesa began taking off his shoes. The clerk stood by, appraising the damage. "Can I ask a question?" Paolo said. "Why does this keep happening to Mr. Reilly?"

"The towels, please, Paolo," Chesa said, pulling the second shoe off.

"Yes. Sorry, Miss Rei. Right away." The young man scurried out.

"Nosy little shit," Chesa muttered.

"He's a good kid."

"You're right, he is. He's been a great help. But I didn't like his question. Mostly because it's the same one that keeps occurring to me."

Sean tried to find a comfortable position he hoped would shield him from any more questions.

"I need you to tell me the truth," she said. "This is a terrible time to ask, but I have to know." She paused. He was afraid of what was coming. "Those men. One of them said you shot Veselko. Did you?"

He started to rise in the bed, but the pain stopped him cold. He sank back, closing his eyes. When he opened them a minute later, her fiery eyes and her question hadn't gone away. "I'll tell you exactly what happened," he said. The pain had burned away his ability to tell lies or dodge her question like he had when she asked about the war wounded months ago.

"Please." She helped him shift in the bed to elevate his head.

"Remember when I talked about going on that raid? You thought it was a bad idea. I decided to go anyway and asked Tom for a gun. He didn't want to give me one and said so. He said I didn't know how to shoot and—"

The door burst open. "I've got the towels," Paolo said, out of breath. "And some washcloths. I also brought you a bowl of hot water. Watch out, it's really hot." He set the bowl on the floor by the bed and stood staring at Sean. "He looks bad, Miss Rei. Want me to call a doctor?"

"No," Sean said. "I don't want anyone to know I'm here. Understand? Anyone. Promise?"

"Yes sir." The young man reached into his pocket, pulled out a small vial, and laid it on the table next to the bed. "Here's some pills to help with the pain. It's for our special guests for when they don't feel so good." He turned to Chesa. "Anything else I can get you?"

"No, Paolo. Thank you ever so much. You are a dear."

Paolo didn't seem to want to leave. "Don't worry," he said on his way out. "Your secret is safe with me."

Chesa laid a hot wet cloth on his face. He yelped from the sting of the heat and the soreness of his bruises. "Don't be a baby," she said. "You'll be fine. I need to wash the blood off." She wiped his nose and mouth and cheeks with firm strokes while massaging his forehead with her left hand. "Let me lay the rag over your whole face. Pretend I'm going to give you a shave."

"Ow. Gently, for Christ's sake. Didn't you ever do any nursing, like during the war?"

"No. I was asked to help, but I didn't. It's terrible, but I couldn't stand to see all that . . . You understand. I hope. Now, where were we? You went to see Tom and asked him for a gun. What a silly idea. I bet I've had more experience with guns than you. You've never shot one, have you? Not even in the war."

"I figured having a gun would maybe, I don't know, give me confidence or courage. Silly, I guess."

"Did he give you the gun? No, of course not. He's too smart. So he refused and you went out on the raid, and Tom felt guilty and protective of you because he didn't give you the gun. That's so, isn't it? And when he got shot, you came to his aid."

"It was dark, so dark." Sean pictured that night from beneath the cloth draped over his face. "I ran over to Tom and could tell he'd been shot. People were shouting. Somebody came running toward us, and I stood up and looked where I heard the steps coming from, but I couldn't see."

"But you had no gun. So, one of the others must have fired. Tom had a gun, I'm sure. My God. How horrible, if Tom shot Veselko." She fell silent and pulled the cloth away.

"I shall never look at Tom the same way again," she said. "Poor dear Veselko. But you said it was dark. Tom wanted to protect you, I'm certain. You, standing there, and a dark figure running at you both. Tom couldn't see, and he had just been shot himself, so he fired."

She handed Sean three of the pills, along with a glass of water. Then she reached down and loosened his belt. This was the time to correct her about who pulled the trigger.

"Do you mind if we only do it three times tonight?" he said. "I'm feeling a little tired."

"Shut up, you clown," Chesa said, giving his pants a rough tug. "Things are all starting to register. Those Croats on the stairs accused you. But I'll bet they couldn't tell one American from another. Especially in the dark. And when you puzzle it out that way, perhaps it explains why Tom is in jail. It's for his protection. Didn't Renzo say something like that? Yes, that's why he's in the penthouse."

"They're not Croats," Sean said. "The men on the stairs who attacked us, I'm pretty sure they were Italian." The pills started to work. Confession time had passed.

"Well why did they pretend to be Croats, and why would they hurt you so badly? Oh, Sean, you were incredibly brave there. You stood up to five monsters so I could get away. I don't understand why you didn't come with me to that chapel. We both could have made it. But you were a hero today. I love you so much, my silly, brave clown hero." She leaned over and kissed him. "You are my prince, knight, and jester, all rolled into one. Now just sleep."

EIGHTY-NINE

From SEAN REILLY'S JOURNAL

October 19, 1920. I didn't actually lie to Chesa. I allowed truth to slip away and get lost in a blur. There is a difference. Sean Reilly is a mere ghost, too insubstantial to do anything like steal a plane or shoot a man. The altar boy might light the candles, but only a priest can say Mass.

I don't care. I will never regret not correcting her about Veselko's death. It was a good bargain. I traded truth for the chance to hear Chesa tell me I was her silly, brave clown hero. I will say or risk anything to hear it tomorrow and every day after that.

NINETY

From *Memories of a Fascist in Fiume*
by Tenente Lorenzo Guidici

I summoned Luigi to my office in the little row building at Viale XVII Novembre. He entered slowly, looking nervous, no doubt sensing my anger. I had given strict orders how I wanted him to get the camera, and my instructions did not include assaulting either Sean or Chesa, nuisances though they both were. He and the others in my little squad were like the oafs who, a few years later, manhandled Matteotti, whose death led to the uproar that has emboldened my enemies.

"You jackasses have made a mess of things again," I said to Luigi. It is necessary to speak in a coarse manner to a man of this sort. "You beat up my other American friend—that's the second time for him— and topped it off by hitting a woman. She is a friend, too. All that and you did not get the film I asked for."

Luigi started to say something, but I warned him to be quiet. I did not care for the defiant look he gave me. It was the feral glower I recalled from the day I first caught him trying to steal a truck from the barracks. Unfortunately, I lacked the means and the time to administer the discipline deserved. I needed the squad to complete a pressing task.

"The photos I seek are not in the camera you brought me," I said. "She must have replaced an old roll of film in the camera with a new one. You didn't ask before you hit her, did you? Of course not. I want the old roll. Understand? Now go get it. In fact, get all of her film. Prints and negatives, too. But be gentle this time."

It was like giving guidance to children. One can only highlight the path for them to take and hope they stay on it. I gave him the address of Chesa's darkroom. The photographs she was passing on to the Rome government represented a threat to what I was trying to accomplish in Fiume and, beyond that, to Fascism itself. Action had to be taken to stop the flow. But I had no desire to hurt her. "If you take Ugo," I stressed to Luigi, "leave him outside."

In the years since my departure from Fiume, I have been forced to listen to complaints about alleged atrocities committed by men who worked with me or under my supervision. These accounts are predictably sordid, and the sheer number of them can only be understood in connection with the natural tendency of the Croats to blame everyone but themselves for anything bad that happens. Action and retaliation were the norm in Fiume in the last days of the occupation. Everyone was on edge. What response did the Croats expect to their terrorist activities?

I could never have accomplished all those things I have been accused of. Although I was an officer, my influence within the city was limited by the few people who worked for me and by my well-known intolerance of criminal behavior. While occasional excesses by those carrying out my instructions may have taken place, they were always corrected and usually punished. With better men to command, no injury to Sean or Chesa would have occurred. Sadly, good men were not available to me.

As a loyal and obedient Fascist, my response to Croat violence was at all times measured by what was necessary for the good of Italy, not by any base feeling of hatred. I challenge my accusers to demonstrate their hands are as clean.

NINETY-ONE

November 8–9, 1920

"I need to get out," Sean said.

Three weeks had passed since he and Chesa were attacked on the Trsat stairs. "The medicine must be working, finally," Chesa said. "Getting out of Fiume will do you good." She sat on the edge of the bed in her red robe, hair wrapped in a towel. *A fine way to dress for an argument,* Sean thought.

"Will you stop?" he said. "I'm not leaving Fiume." Her hotel room had been his refuge while he recovered, and even after he felt better, he was wary of returning to his apartment. The attackers probably knew where he lived. He doubted they would trouble Chesa at this hotel.

Chesa took the towel from her hair and pulled her robe tight. "You don't owe this city anything. And it's destroying you. How many more beatings before you suffer permanent damage? Or get killed? It's only going to get worse, you know. My friend Nina says the new prime minister will crush D'Annunzio and his faithful. He's going to send the army in here."

This mysterious Nina again, whoever she was. Sean added her to the growing list of those questioning his presence in Fiume. "I have to stay. For Futurism. And to free Tom. You're the one who pushed me to do something for him, remember?"

Chesa's glare was scathing and relentless. "So let me see if I have this right. You have to stay here and keep doing the same things that didn't succeed before and only got you hurt and your friend locked up, because repeating what didn't work before will now somehow lead to a different result, maybe after your head gets bashed to pieces. Forget what I said about those pills working."

An altar boy's lot was not easy, Sean thought. Light the candles, snuff out the candles, fetch this and that for never satisfied priests. Hurry, hurry. Do whatever they tell you to do. *Marinetti wants you to go to Fiume and you don't want to go, do you?* The pain in his right knee flared. "I've got obligations," he said.

"Your bloody obligations. Listen. You have your art. Your ideas are in your paintings and your manifesto. You can paint and write somewhere else besides Fiume. Anywhere else, in fact. You'll certainly paint better without getting pummeled every few months."

"Let me ask you," he said. "Why haven't you left? You've seen the danger here."

She shook her head. A clump of wet hair dropped between her eyes. She rewrapped the towel, securing all the hair in place. "The things I capture on film are here. But your art is different. It's in your head, and your head goes where you go."

He reminded her she had been attacked, too, and the hooligans had taken her camera. "I'd feel a lot better if I knew you were safe."

She exploded. "Are you trying to get rid of me? That's what this is about, is it? Pack me off so you can play around. Maybe you can pick up with some of the *Comandante's* other leftovers."

"No. Please. You know me better. I just don't want anything bad to happen to you."

"Then let's leave together." Her voice became pure silk and honey. "Tonight. I'll go settle my hotel bill straight away, and we can be on the train in a few hours. I'll go anywhere with you, I've told you many times. We'll make Marinetti put us up until we get settled somewhere. I'll need to get my negatives from Gaj. Please say yes."

"I can't." He stepped over to the mirror and glanced at his reflection. "I'm not going to run away. I won't leave Tom in jail or go anywhere before I deal with the people who did all this to him and me. To us."

"Revenge," Chesa said. Sandpaper and vinegar replaced silk and honey. "It's the first thing you've said that makes any sense. Wait, not that pursuing revenge makes sense. These people you want to 'deal with' use guns and daggers and masks. You don't have a gun or even know how to shoot. But I can understand your wanting revenge. Yes, that's the American in you, or maybe your Irish blood or both." She lay back on the bed and closed her eyes. "Or just the man in you."

"I didn't think you'd understand. But I have to do it."

"Why?"

"Huh?"

"Why do you have to? Why this need to avenge? Don't play games with me. You did nothing after you got the castor oil except hide in your apartment and mope. Now you need revenge. And don't tell me that it's because that man hit me."

"It's different now." He knew it was time to shut down the argument before it got worse, like the night when he read her his manifesto. "I'm going out. On the street. Here in Fiume. Is there someplace you could, um—"

"Shut up and get out," Chesa said. She did not stir from the bed. "I'm not going anywhere."

He visited Tom for the first time since the attack on the stairs. Tomaso let him in. Sean was staggered by how bad his friend looked. Tom hadn't shaved for quite a while, and his hair, always thin but usually slicked back, pointed in all directions. Empty whiskey bottles lay scattered on the table and the floor. A couple of fist-sized dents marked the walls. He was seriously drunk.

"Finally remembered me, huh?" Tom said. Sean glanced over at Tomaso, who shrugged and shut the door on his way out.

Sean described the brutal attack that kept him away while he recovered. "Probably the same bad guys who put you out of commission back in June. Today is the first day I've been outside since the attack."

"You think hiding in your woman's bed for three weeks makes you some kind of fucking hero, do you? Look at Sean, everybody, the tough guy. Gets the shit kicked out of him, *again*, and didn't have nobody to come along and rescue him because he left me in this stinking jail. He cried all the way home, except he didn't have the guts to go home. He went and hid out at his woman's place, which put her in danger too but he don't care because he can fuck her while he hides." Tom reached for the bottle Tomasso had laid on the table and took a long drink.

The comment about putting Chesa in danger stung. "Look, I'm sorry I didn't get out earlier. But I'm here today and will be working every day to get you freed." Tom took another drink and looked away.

"How is Capricia?"

"She ain't been up here for a while," Tom said. "We had a big argument. I'm an asshole and nobody wants to be around me anymore. Even Tomaso can't get out of here fast enough." Another swallow. "You know what I'm gonna do? When I get out? Yeah, I will get out one of these days, and I'll walk all the streets in this town, and anybody even looks at me funny, I'm gonna hurt them bad, and anybody wants to fight, I'm gonna kill them. And when I find out who set me up, that person is dead, too, I don't care how many of them there are. *Muerte.* Or *morte,* however the fuck they say it here."

Sean did not need Chesa's canvas to detect the virulence in his friend. It ran deep, made worse by drink and too much time alone. He changed the subject. "I'm looking for the goons who assaulted Chesa and me," he said.

"You?"

First Chesa and now Tom. Sean had gone from clown prince hero three weeks ago to merely a clown, and now to a nobody who couldn't take care of himself and hid behind a woman's skirts and got told to run away. Exactly the advice Tom now gave him.

"Here's what you need to do," Tom said. "Get the fuck out of Fiume. Go somewhere else. You're useless here, and just asking for trouble. Take Chesa and go. You hear me?"

Sean told Tom he was staying and had a score to settle. "I've got that Bodeo you loaned me for the raid."

Tom looked at him like he was the stupidest person on earth. "You don't know how to shoot. Don't be fooled by the fact you hit the kid. Firing a gun at someone who's shooting at you ain't nothing like that. One guy with experience can take out a hundred guys like you in a fight. You got to use your strengths, not your weaknesses."

"So, what are you saying? I should go after them with a paintbrush? Or bore them to death with my manifesto?"

"Why should I be the only one to suffer, listening to that shit?" For the first time this visit, Tom seemed amused. "No, if you want to go after somebody, you're gonna need a weapon but, in your case, not a gun. Didn't you play baseball or stickball? I thought every kid in Philadelphia did. Can you swing a bat?"

"Oh yes," Sean said with pride. "I can hit with power. Never hit a person, though."

"They're easier to hit than a little ball. The thing is, can you make yourself do it? That's the real question, buddy. When you gotta get close and swing at a man, can you do it? If you can't smash his head with a bat and see his blood and brains spurt out and splatter all over you and keep on going, you don't want to ever start. Don't figure you can scare off any of these guys."

"You're saying I'm going to have to kill somebody?"

"Don't kill nobody you don't need to. But when you threaten a guy with a bat or a pipe, he's going to reach for something to stop you, a gun, if he has one, or a knife. And you're gonna have to hit him hard enough to stop him from hurting you. The shit builds and builds until one of you stops breathing. And I don't want that to be you. These are tough boys. But you are smarter than them."

Sean pumped Tom for a few tips about how to trap and overcome enemies but Tom soon shut down, like a car that ran out of gas.

"You want my advice, though?" Tom said. "Forget the bat, forget the gun. Forget me. Just leave. You and Chesa. This ain't no place for you. It's not a battle you're gonna win."

NINETY-TWO

November 9, 1920. I couldn't explain my not leaving Fiume to Chesa or to Tom. Where does a person draw a line and decide *no more*? Somewhere on the boundary between *I'm afraid to do anything because I'll get hurt* and *If I don't act now, the consequences will haunt me for the rest of my life.* Too many bad things have happened. The castor oil, the attack on the old Croat taking the leaflet, Tom's beating, and what they did to Chesa and me on the Trsat stairs. She was right. It's not about advancing Futurism or helping Tom. I have crossed the boundary. I'm more afraid of what will happen to me if I don't do something than what could happen if I do.

Nobody understands. Or they think I'm not capable of anything besides drinking and lousy art. They may be right.

Poor Tom. He looked awful. But I think our talk was therapeutic for him. Tom needs to take his frustration out on somebody, and I'm an easy target. An appropriate one, too, since I had everything to do with his being in jail in the first place. He gave me some good advice. Now all I need to do is find the leader of these goons and get him alone and ask him a few questions, baseball bat in hand. That's all.

November 10, 1920. What is wrong with Chesa, anyway? She's a puzzle. First she says she can't leave Fiume because of her camera work, which seems strange because she doesn't even have her good camera anymore, just the old Nattia she doesn't even like, because of its poor lens. And by now she must have photographed every street in Fiume and every legionnaire. But then she turns around and says she's ready to leave Fiume in a couple of hours if I agree to go with her. Does her photography matter or not? There is something she's not telling me, and I cannot figure out what.

NINETY-THREE

Letter from Filippo Marinetti

October 26, 1920

Sean:

I have become thoroughly disenchanted with Mussolini and those who follow his lead—all drawn from the lowest levels of intelligence, culture, and breeding. Reluctantly, I am determined to dissociate myself from the Fascists at the next national conference. Without Futurist leadership, the whole Fascist movement will quickly wither and die.

Concerning the current situation in Fiume, your lack of progress is a major disappointment to me. While D'Annunzio and his coterie continue to beget headlines, our message has not received the widespread attention our movement deserves. This state of affairs I can only attribute to your lack of effort. Your commitment to Futurism has evidently wavered.

I shall say this plainly, lest there be any misapprehension. Should you leave Fiume before the task I set for you has been accomplished, you may consider all ties between yourself and Futurism to be forever severed. There is simply no place here in our movement for Futurists who can neither paint nor follow instructions.

Filippo

NINETY-FOUR

From INTERVIEW WITH DUŠAN KCLEŽA (1992)
[UNEDITED TRANSCRIPT]

JH: You went back to work at your father's restaurant, listening for clues to who killed your brother, Veselko. With all the legionnaires and such dining there, you could have been discovered at any moment. How did it work out?

DK: I learned things, little by little. One of my friends dropped by the restaurant to visit. He had been arrested and held in the jail for a couple of weeks. He told me something I didn't know. He said that there was an American in jail, but he was being held in a deluxe cell that was reserved for special prisoners. This American wasn't a general or anything. Just a rough looking guy. It was the talk of the whole jail, guards and prisoners alike. Nobody could understand why an American, of all people, got treated like a prince.

I figured that if the American was being held in a fancy jail cell, it was probably because he killed my brother, and the bloodthirsty Italians were rewarding him. The man probably killed a lot of other people, too. I remembered Andrej saying something about how he thought the man he shot during the raid spoke English. It all began to make sense. This American, whoever he was, started shooting after he got hit. Not wanting to face Andrej's shotgun, he fired his pistol at my unarmed brother. The coward. I figured he was probably hiding there in jail, not even under arrest at all.

See, at the time, I didn't know that the guy in the deluxe cell was the same guy who tried to save Mr. Mesić and got beat up by five thugs. Had I known that, my thinking would have been different. But I didn't know.

JH: What did you do next? Try to get to the man in the jail?

DK: I wanted to be sure it was the right guy. Besides, I couldn't get near him in that jail.

I kept working, clearing tables and washing dishes. Did you ever work in a restaurant? No? It's an awful job. I hated it. The customers made a mess. Food all over the table, on the chairs, on the floor. I heard a little of this and a little of that but nothing that I needed to know.

One afternoon, the lady photographer I met at the strikers' rally came in for lunch, along with three other women. I knew two of them: the twins Annalisa and Capricia. I never knew their last name. Back in high school, Annalisa sometimes talked to me, unlike the other Italian girls. One of the few nice memories I had of school. The fourth lady I didn't recognize. She was a little older than the photographer. In better times, I'd have shoved the other waiters out of the way and insisted on serving the ladies myself. In better times, understand, when I wasn't busy trying to track down my brother's killer.

I heard the photographer lady call me before I could disappear into the kitchen. "Dušan? Please, can you come over here? There's somebody I would like you to meet."

I set down the tray of dirty dishes I was carrying and went over to them. I felt like I had been summoned by a call of those Greek sirens.

"Remember me?" the unforgettable lady said. "Chesa Rei. You gave me a cultural lesson some months ago, during a rally in Piazza Regina Elena. And of course, you know Annalisa and her sister, Capricia." The twins smiled, and Annalisa waved her hand at me like we were back in school. "And this distinguished lady is Nina Giovanitti. She's a journalist in Rome for one of the major newspapers. They've asked her to do a story on Fiume. I'm wondering, would you be able to show us around a bit? You promised me the tour if you recall." She nodded toward the twins. "I might even be able to persuade these two to join us."

Annalisa gave me a big smile and said, "Hi, stranger. Haven't seen you in so long. Listen, I'm so sorry about your brother. We used to see him here all the time. He was such a sweet kid."

"Yes," Chesa said. "Please accept my condolences, too. We're all devastated. It's good your father has you to help him."

"Chesa took a lot of photos of your father and Veselko," Annalisa said. "Really good ones."

The idea of those photographs disturbed me, and I couldn't explain why. "I have to get back to work," I said. "Enjoy your lunch." I hurried back to the kitchen, forgetting the plates I had been carrying.

"See, I told you he was cute," I heard Annalisa say. But I didn't stop.

Leading four women around on a tour of Fiume and Sušak was tempting, especially with Annalisa. That group, however, would draw way too much attention, right when I was trying to be discreet. I felt pretty safe in the restaurant, but out there on the streets lots of eyes would be on us. On them, mostly, but then people would notice this Croat kid with the ladies and not be too happy, do you understand? Anyway, what did they want to go sightseeing in Fiume for? With a journalist, for God's sake. Those Rome newspapers didn't want to hear about the real Fiume and the atrocities being committed daily by their countryman. She could go sit in a café on the Corso and hear all the Italians praise D'Annunzio and argue for annexation. She didn't need me.

Later, after they left, I thought of one thing I should have asked them. Maybe they knew about the American in the jail. I cursed myself for missing the chance. But I got lucky the following week.

Three Italian officers came in for a late lunch. The place was almost empty, and I had to finish cleaning up before I could take a break. They were loud. I heard them say something about a raid in Sušak, and immediately I got all interested. I figured, *What the hell, let me see what I can learn.*

JH: Weren't you afraid? You could have been recognized and arrested yourself.

DK: Are you kidding? I had shit coming out of my pants as I walked up. I went over to their table and started clearing off the dirty plates, and they stopped talking for a minute. That got me even more nervous, but I took a chance and said, as politely and humbly as I could, like I'm some dopey little Croat, "I hear the guy who shot the kid at the Sušak warehouse got locked up." I'm figuring they will either pull out their guns or daggers, or they will confirm what I said. Maybe they're proud of him, being in a deluxe cell and all.

"No," one of them said. "The American in the jail didn't shoot anybody. All he did was help somebody steal an airplane. The dumb ass."

"Well, that's not all he did," another officer said. He sounded like he had drunk more wine than the others. His companions looked daggers at him, and he shut up.

I picked up another plate and pressed my luck, since these guys obviously were well informed. "Sorry," I said, "I must have heard wrong. I thought it was an American who shot the kid."

JH: Whew! You had guts.

DK: The drunk officer looked at me funny and said, "You hear a lot of things, do you? Maybe too much. Get the fuck out of here."

The first officer told him to relax, and said I was a good kid, I must be a good kid because I worked for Gaj, and Gaj was a good man even if he was a Croat. He turned to me and said, "The shooter was an American but not the guy in jail."

"It was the artist American," the drunk officer said. "A fucking painter, can you believe it? One lucky shot and *blam*, he drops the kid." He said this to his fellow officers, and then he turned to me and said, "Now clear the fucking table and get lost."

JH: I'm sure you were quite happy to get lost at that point.

DK: I couldn't get away fast enough. Right then my father called out from the kitchen, "Dušan. Hurry up with that table." I threw the dishes on the tray and carried them back to the kitchen. I put the tray down, tore off the apron, and ran out the back door.

JH: Now you had the information you needed.

DK: That's what I thought. How hard could it be to find an American artist in Fiume? Only, those officers at the restaurant didn't give me the artist's address.

It would be different today, right? It's a lot easier now to track somebody down. Government records, phone books, and whatever. I had nothing, not even a name.

NINETY-FIVE

December 8, 1920

hesa stepped around empty bottles and piles of dirty clothes on the floor of Sean's apartment, picking her steps as though she were in a cow pasture. Cleaning had not been a priority for Sean in the weeks since she had last visited. Seeing the look on her face, he suggested they go out. She quickly agreed.

The sky loomed gray with the threat of a nasty storm. Sean gazed at a particularly ominous cloud while they walked until he stumbled on a curb and made a graceless effort to keep from falling. Chesa smiled at his stagger. That was nice. If he could not be the prince hero anymore, he was grateful at least to be her clown.

They made their way to Piazza Cesare Battisti, by the Capuchin Church, and sat on a bench where they could see the fountain and, past it, warehouse buildings and cranes on the pier. The cranes made him think of giant giraffes that escaped some mechanical zoo. They chatted. Her friend Nina had told her about the crazy Fascist violence in Trieste and Florence and up in Milan. He said he hadn't heard. The pauses between their responses grew longer, and she filled each gap by wriggling her shoe, which, after crossing her legs, extended out straight in front of her. He stared at the shoe as it made little circular motions. When she put the shoe on the ground, he knew a moment of truth was coming. *She's ending it. Us. Permanently.*

She pointed to one of the warehouses, a corner of which he could see from his spot on the bench. "You needn't get up," she said.

"It's the one with the broken upper windows. You'll find what you are looking for in there."

What he was looking for was something to make him a great painter. And clues about how to free Tom. And the key to letting him spend forever with Chesa Rei. Those things didn't usually come in warehouses.

"The men who attacked us," she said quietly.

Impossible she could have found those men, when he had been unsuccessful in his search. "You saw them once," he said, irritation not disguised. "They wore masks and spoke with funny accents. You thought they were Croatian."

Chesa dropped her gaze. It was a gesture she had used on him a number of times, averting her eyes but somehow fixing him more perfectly than if she were staring at his face. He couldn't move even if he tried. Then, when she did raise her head to behold him, he was reduced to jelly. Her eyes tunneled right through to his brain. She employed magic or sorcery or something. There on the bench, with the church at their backs and the port laid out before them, he sat in the early immobilized stage, fixed, set up for the look to come.

She didn't get mad, which scared him. Maybe she didn't care enough about him anymore to react with anger. He was grateful they were outside and not confined in her hotel room, where arguments always seemed amplified by the walls. Here in the piazza, his ugly remark melted away into the clouds overhead.

"I got the information at the Governor's Palace, so I'm confident it is accurate," she said. "Now don't say anything. Just listen for a minute. Please. I went there with Annalisa. She wanted to press Renzo for help with getting Tom out of jail. The whole thing is driving both Tom and Capricia crazy. I agreed to escort her. Renzo wasn't at the Palace. We found Guido Keller, though, and spoke to him. Quite an unusual fellow he is but friendly without being . . . you know. He promised Annalisa he would speak directly to the *Comandante* about Tom, maybe try and get him transferred to the barracks, if not outright released. We thanked him, and I took a chance and asked him if he knew about a gang that terrorized people. He gave a little boy grin and said, 'Which one?' I described them the best I could. I mentioned the huge fellow and three others and the slender one who was the leader, and Guido shook his head up and down like a jack-in-the-box, just like Renzo described him. Guido said the slender man's name is Luigi, and he's a nasty one who likes setting fires. I immediately thought yes, that's the one."

"And did you ask him for Luigi's address?" Sean's tone had an acrid quality he felt powerless to tame. She had asked the right question to the right person and found in minutes the information he'd spent weeks searching for.

She continued staring at the ground. The look was coming, he knew, but she wasn't ready to unleash it yet. "That warehouse," she said, her voice sounding weary, "is where he and his gang spend most of their time. If you want him, you'll find him there."

"Why are you telling me this?" he asked.

She lifted her head and fired the jelly-creating stare at his brain. "You're not going to move on until you confront this man," she said. "I know you, Sean. You are a good man. Renzo said that about you the night of our first dinner at Gaj's, and I saw it for myself straight away."

He started to say something but sensed she wasn't finished.

"You are stubborn, though. You won't let this revenge obsession go, and you will never leave Fiume unless you achieve some resolution. I don't know how else to help you. I'd bash this gang for you if I could. I'd chase the lot of them out of the city. But this is the best I can do. So take what I'm saying and try not to get yourself killed. I hope you find peace with whatever you decide to do. Come see me afterward, and we can talk about our future, if we're to have one."

Hot blood flooded into his face. He looked straight into those green eyes. He knew he should thank her. He said, "Did you see the *Comandante* while you were in the Palace?"

She slumped a little on the bench and picked at a button of her coat. "Yes. He came upon us while we talked with Guido, and he invited Annalisa and me to stand out on the balcony with him while he gave his speech. Quite spectacular, to tell you the truth, being up there and seeing all those people in the crowd below, watching their faces and hearing them respond to him. I can see how making those speeches must be addictive for him. Like sex, I suppose, except with thousands of partners at once."

NINETY-SIX

From SEAN REILLY'S JOURNAL

December 8, 1920. Thank you, Chesa. Thank you thank you thank you. I said it over and over after she walked away and couldn't hear me. What I was unable to express to her while she was sitting next to me came spilling out. I apologized as well, again too late. I hope one day I can work up the courage to tell her face-to-face how really grateful I am and how sorry I am for saying these awful things I say to her. But that kind of courage belongs to great painters, ones who would not fear looking squarely into the mirror Chesa holds up.

December 9, 1920. I could have asked Guido and maybe got the same answer Chesa did. Why didn't I? Maybe because he wouldn't help me get the airplane last year and the things he said about Futurism and Marinetti. I don't know if I can trust him.

Tonight when I opened my notebook, I skipped over the manifesto drafts and looked at the sketches I did in Zara and in jail here. The drawing of the cathedral is the best one. What caught my eye was the pattern of the seven colonnettes and arches on the central portal: round, flat, twisted spiral, flat, round, flat, round. I can't figure out the thought behind that pattern. I wonder if some symbolic meaning was built in. The seven virtues, maybe. The twisted spiral could represent fortitude. Or something else.

There's an enduring beauty that comes through, whatever it means. To think this was created over five hundred years ago. Some amazing artistry.

NINETY-SEVEN

From *Memories of a Fascist in Fiume*
by Tenente Lorenzo Guidici

A week had gone by, and I did not yet have those photos Sean took from the airplane. The denouement of D'Annunzio's adventure was fast approaching, and the longer those photographs remained in existence, the more likely it was they would find their way to Rome. I can say without exaggeration that the success of Fascism and indeed the future of Italy were at risk. Had I been aware of the state of incompetence that pervaded the Rome government at that time, I would not have been as concerned. Lacking the luxury of that knowledge, I was anxious to retrieve the film.

Adding to my unease, I learned Chesa had recently visited the Governor's Palace accompanied by young Annalisa and had been asking for me. Asking questions of everyone about everything, I'm sure. I was surprised at first to hear she inquired about Luigi. The last thing I wanted was for her to send reports back to Rome about someone who could be tied to me. Was her spying getting closer to my activities? Of course when I learned later what Sean did to the man, that explained it. It disturbed me that she would abet such violence. She should have left Fiume by then and taken Sean with her, for both their sakes. That was the advice I gave her when we dined after the strikers' rally. I explained the danger Sean faced and promised I would look after Tom. Unfortunately, my offer to help went unheeded.

Around this time, Mussolini sent me a message. The new Italian prime minister, Giolitti, was negotiating a treaty with the Jugoslavs that would give Italy most of what was desired but leave Fiume a "free city," at least for a while. D'Annunzio and his friends would have to leave. Mussolini said he was going to support the treaty. He didn't need D'Annunzio returning home to lead a disaffected mob thirsting for revenge over another mutilated victory. D'Annunzio may have been a dreadful *Comandante,* but he was still a potential rival capable of performing magic with his oratory.

I knew what had to be done. For Italy, for Fascism, for the Italian race.

NINETY-EIGHT

December 1920

Sean arrived on the Corso early in the morning and set up a blank canvas on his easel opposite the city clock tower. The shops hadn't yet opened. Few people strolled on the Corso at that hour, and those who ventured to the open cafés didn't notice the artist at work in the shade. After a few preparatory sketches in his notebook, Sean began painting the tower.

The large stone blocks that made up the portal arch were relatively easy to capture, but the relief above the arch contained images of emperors Leopold I and Charles VI and proved more difficult. Higher up and highlighted by the morning sun, twin pilasters flanked either side of the clock face, and a pediment curved over it. Getting the right proportions was tricky, but the sketches helped. The biggest challenge was the ribbed copper dome that topped the tower.

A thought occurred to him while he mixed paints for the dome. What if Mary Cassatt hadn't anointed him as a prodigy on that day long ago when she visited the Academy of Fine Arts? Maybe she was trying to draw his attention to a flaw in his depiction of the lilacs. That encounter with her had fueled his dedication to art and set him on the path he followed to this day. He laughed and let the thought pass.

His brush strokes plumbed the inner essence of the tower with shades of light and shadow, unlocking its secrets and giving it an unsettling, dreamlike effect. The work had a detached simplicity and stillness. No airplanes, no automobiles, no simultaneity. No force lines to show motion and speed.

At noon he packed up and returned to his apartment. It had been a solid morning's work, without the agonizing moments that accompanied his attempts at Futurist painting. He set the painting up on the easel. He wouldn't mind showing this one to Chesa, maybe when it was a little further along. After a quick lunch, he headed out to Piazza Cesare Battisti.

Sean surveilled the warehouse with the broken upper windows over the next three afternoons. Luigi and his cohorts came and left each day. Wickson visited once, as did another man Sean figured might be Santo.

The warehouse faced the main street running along the quay. The right side of the building stretched halfway along an unused wharf. It lacked windows on that side but did have a solid-looking metal door. He had seen the gang exit this door onto the wharf, to smoke cigarettes, jostle, and argue. As sundown neared on the third day, he had seen enough. All visitors were gone and the five he was interested in were inside the building. Their truck was parked by the side door. He crossed the street, armed with a club the size of a regulation baseball bat.

Stopping at the truck, he pulled a long rag from his pocket and opened the vehicle's petrol tank. He forced one end of the rag into the tank, struck a match, and lit the rag. Patiently, like someone making a delivery, he rapped on the door with the club. When the voices inside got close, he ran as fast as he could toward the street, turning the corner just as the door opened and the truck exploded into flames. Sean entered the warehouse through the front door and locked it behind him.

Inside, boxes of fruits and sacks of scarce wheat were scattered all over. Mountains of clothes lay alongside greasy automobile parts. His apartment was tidy by comparison.

Sean moved quietly through the squalor toward the open side

door. Flames from the truck cast dancing shadows on the far wall and ceiling, reminiscent of the images that greeted Sean in Piazza Dante the day he arrived in Fiume. As Tom predicted, all of the men save one had run out to the burning truck. There, watching from a safe spot inside the warehouse, stood Luigi, shouting to the others. Sean recognized the voice. How could he ever forget it?

Staying behind Luigi and to his right, carefully hidden, Sean got as close to the opened door as he dared. He picked up a carburetor and heaved the heavy piece behind Luigi, creating a loud crash. Luigi spun around. As soon as he did, Sean ran to the door and slammed it closed. He slid its iron bar across to lock it, then turned around in time to see Luigi lunge at him with a crowbar. Baseball time had come.

Sean swung his club like a bat, aiming for the arm holding the crowbar. He hit the arm dead on. The crowbar went flying. Luigi screamed in pain as he fell to the floor, the bone in his arm shattered.

"That's one arm," Sean said. His voice sounded calm, masking the adrenaline rush surging through his body. "Let's try a leg." He gave a full two-handed swing, stepping forward into the motion for additional power, and drove the club into the fallen man's shin. The bone snapped with a loud crack, eliciting a piercing scream. "Would have been good for a double, maybe," Sean said, "but I can do better." He circled behind Luigi's head.

Luigi curled into a fetal ball, trying desperately to shield the broken limbs. "You fucker. I'll kill you." He reached out to one of the stacks of wood behind his head. Sean brought the stick down hard on his hand, eliciting another scream.

"That's one arm, one leg, and one hand," Sean said. "Forgive me, what were you saying? Wait, there's another bone I need to address." With a quick short swing, he hit the ankle on Luigi's unbroken leg. "OK. I've taken care of the limbs. Now I can work on the parts that hurt a lot more."

Luigi wailed in pain, calling helplessly for Ugo and the others. Sean didn't think he needed to worry about them yet but went to check the iron bar on the door to be certain. Satisfied, he returned to Luigi.

"You have about one minute to tell me what I want to know before your friends wise up and come to the front door and break it down. I will be gone but you will be buried under a pile of clothes I set on fire. Light you up like a candle." Sean had been waiting almost a year to say that to him.

"I won't tell you nothing," Luigi said. "My boys will kill you. Burning you will be the mercy part after they get finished."

"Ah, Luigi, you're trying to get me angry," Sean said. "You make this too easy for me. But please, let us get to business. First, tell me who was responsible for the attacks on me and who framed Tom. If there's time before you start roasting, I want to hear what you know about Piero Terruzzi, the guy hiking in the hills, and about the two pilots who crashed last year." He tapped the end of the club on Luigi's ear. "Speak up."

"Wickson. He's the one who told us to give you the dose. Everything was his idea."

Sean tapped the ear again, harder. "Come now, Luigi, you can do better. Wickson may have asked you to go after me that first time. I believe that. But when you were giving me the castor oil, one of your chums said the boss didn't want you to use gasoline. Remember? Nobody has ever called Wickson "boss." And Wickson didn't tell you to frame Tom or kill Piero and the pilots. He doesn't have the brains or the nerve. So don't act like I'm stupid." He swung the stick at Luigi's elbow. "Hurry now."

Luigi eventually gave him a name.

On the morning following his *recontre* with Luigi, Sean went to see Tom and shared the details, proudly, like he had medaled in an athletic contest. "Don't be so happy," Tom said. "I warned you, those are tough *hombres*. Did you find out anything?"

"After I broke a few bones, I got the name of the person responsible for what's happened to us."

Tom gave him the same look as when Sean once said Fiats were better than Fords. "Who?"

"Guido Keller. He takes orders directly from the prime minister."

It was as if Sean had said mules were better than Fords. "Let me get this straight," Tom said. "Luigi told you Guido ordered the attack on you and had me arrested. And you believe him?"

"I hurt him pretty badly," Sean said.

Tom shook his head. "And that made him tell you the truth? If you'd hit him a couple more times, he'd have told you it was Sister Mary Frances, taking orders from the Pope. Did Luigi give up anything else?"

Sean did not say anything. His gaze drifted over to cold gray ashes in the fireplace. Luigi gave him Guido's name and he, reveling in the violence, had believed him.

"Nah, it don't make any sense," Tom said. "Guido's the one who told Chesa Luigi's name and the address of the warehouse. Besides, if Guido wanted you and me gone, we would disappear. He's not gonna send clowns like Luigi and those others. You think Guido would kill pilots? Or listen to the prime minister? Why would the prime minister give a fuck what happens to you and me and that blind guy?"

Sean remembered something else Luigi said. "We are all on a list. Me. You. Even Chesa. Christ, what have I done?"

"Shit," Tom said. His voice rose. "Get Chesa out of Fiume. Do you hear me? Today." His eyes bulged. "She is in more danger than you can imagine." Minutes passed before he said anything else. Intense, painful don't-you-fucking-get-it? minutes. Then Tom confessed he had given Renzo the address of Chesa's darkroom.

"Why is that a problem?" Unless. Unless Tom suspected Renzo planned to harm her. How could Tom think that about Renzo, the man who saved both his and Sean's lives and who had been saved by each of them? Impossible to believe such a thing. Yet not five minutes before, Sean believed Guido was the evil mastermind. Fiume was the city where anything could happen.

"Luigi is the link," Tom said. "He's been on several of the raids, and he listens to Renzo. But I never knew he was part of that gang that hit you and me. Not until you told me that big bruiser was with him. Luigi is the connection between Renzo and the bad shit going on. I didn't know that when I gave Renzo the address he asked for. I'm sorry. Renzo's got some explaining to do."

"Renzo has another bad friend," Sean said. "You know the guy whose plane I took? Santo? Annalisa saw him in a nightclub drinking with Renzo on the night of those explosions. A couple of days later Santo tried to intimidate Capricia into not doing anything for your release."

Tom stood and grabbed the front of Sean's shirt. With one hand he pulled Sean up and forced him to lean over. Their faces nearly touched. "Find Chesa," he said, "and both of you get the fuck out of Fiume. Renzo is up to something, and he ain't gonna stop. You hear me? Go."

NINETY-NINE

December 12, 1920. I took more pleasure in beating the crap out of Luigi than I should have. Chesa's words: "Yes, that's the American in you, or maybe your Irish blood, or both. Or just the man in you." But at least I could claim a legitimate reason for what I had done to Luigi. I sought information and succeeded in obtaining it. Or so I imagined. Tom made me see the error of my thinking.

Revenge. Oh, you're wrong, Chesa. It's worse. It's the human in me, something primitive, a corruption your painting would have spotted in an instant. It grew quietly, veiled by Futurism, but now it bursts forth with all its stench and ugliness. Revenge is what remains in a dirty warehouse when a man's hopes and dreams and ideals—and his art—have ebbed away.

I have trouble believing Renzo could be part of what happened. We had been through so much together during the war, the three of us.

ONE HUNDRED

JH: Before the break, you told us you had learned the killer was an American artist, but you didn't know his name or address. Your next step was to track him down. How did you find him?

DK: Well, I didn't have an address. Or even a name. Minutes after rushing out of the restaurant, I began to regret my haste. That American went to the restaurant all the time. Instead of searching the streets of Fiume for him, I could have simply waited for him to show up for a meal. Can you believe the insolence of this guy, to have his food cooked and served to him by the father of the boy he murdered? I pictured the son of a bitch, body slumped forward on a table, pieces of his brain mixed in with the pasta on the plate before him. But my father would have been mad. Bad for business.

JH: Could you have gone back to work there?

DK: I suppose. But honestly, that would have been a disaster. Having to put up with my dad preaching about the wonders of hard work was bad enough, but listening to the Italians who rattled on and on about glorious Italy and their mutilated victory in the Great War and how the bastards in Rome were leading the country straight to hell, it was driving me crazy. If they loved it so much, why didn't they go back there and leave Fiume to the Croatians? I couldn't take any more. Anyway, shooting the murderer in my father's restaurant would get me killed and my father killed, too.

This was about justice, not suicide. And, to be perfectly honest, restaurant work was hard.

The only thing I knew about the American painter was that he was friends with the other American who was locked up in the jail. Not much to go on.

JH: How did you learn the killer's name?

DK: From Andrej, who had been arrested on some pretext and spent a week in jail. His cell was across the corridor from an American who told everybody he was an artist. Sean Reilly was his name. But Andrej didn't have an address for me, so I kept looking.

Once the American got out of jail, he seemed to disappear. I figured he would return to the jail to visit the other American locked up in there. He may have, but I couldn't get anywhere near the jail without being chased away by the police. With all the Croatian prisoners inside, they did not want to see a Croat like me hanging around outside the place.

I searched everywhere else, listening for an American accent because I had no idea what he looked like. I went up and down the Corso, checking out the customers seated in the cafés and the crazy men and women making speeches in front of the shops. The piazzas, too. I wandered through the Mercato and squeezed produce while checking out the shoppers. I scouted down by the waterfront, near the warehouses, but hurried away when some ugly characters started to harass me. Even though I was armed—I had a pistol by this time—I didn't want to use my weapon on them. Sean Reilly was my target, first and foremost.

One evening I followed the crowds that were heading to the Governor's Palace, hoping maybe the American would show up to hear his *Comandante*. He didn't show up, but standing there gave me a new idea.

JH: A new place to look for the American?

DK: No. Something else. I'll tell you how it came to me. These yokels were all over the garden and driveway and out into the street, you see? I worked my way to a spot close to the corner of the Palace itself. D'Annunzio started speaking. I forced myself to clap and cheer when the others did so I would not look suspicious. I tried not to yawn. How did this short funny-looking man attract all these people?

The speech did not make much sense, so I quit listening. Sean Reilly did not show up. I was frustrated. I had wasted weeks in the search. I had to do something.

Watching D'Annunzio on the balcony face the crowd, surrounded by other important looking people, a picture unfolded in my mind, and it was perfect. The damage would be spectacular and even give me a decent chance to survive and fight again. I exited the crowd and went back to Sušak. Too much time had already been spent chasing the American.

JH: What was your idea? To assassinate D'Annunzio?

DK: Yes. Yes. Yes. There on the balcony at one of his speeches. In front of everyone.

Listen, those people didn't think twice about using violence on us to crush us. That gave us the right to defend ourselves. Like I said before, those who fight for liberation have to use every means available.

JH: But why D'Annunzio instead of the man who killed your brother? You said you were looking for justice.

DK: You don't think killing the man who led the occupation of my city was justice?

Let me put it this way. If somebody had shot Ante Pavelić before World War II, then he and his Ustashe Fascists wouldn't have seized power here in Croatia, and hundreds of thousands of Croatians and Serbs wouldn't have been murdered. If somebody had killed Hitler in the 1920s, then millions of Jews and other people don't get killed, and Pavelić and the Ustashe never get to power. Mussolini started Fascism, so if somebody had killed Mussolini early on, then Hitler would never have learned it. Now guess who Mussolini's teacher was? Those black shirts and the big rallies and the castor oil and the beat-up squads, that all started with D'Annunzio. Count up all those people whose lives could have been saved if somebody killed D'Annunzio, and then ask me again about justice. It's just logic.

JH: So you forgot about pursuing Sean Reilly?

DK: Sean Reilly was a nothing, a nobody. My insight was that I could do more for my brother and my homeland and my people by killing this *Comandante* who invaded our city. I would go down in history like that Bosnian Serb, Gavrilo Princip, you know, the one who shot the Austrian archduke and set off the First World War. They worship him in Serbia as a freedom warrior. Always have. Killing D'Annunzio would show the world that Croatians are not afraid to fight for their freedom.

Besides, once D'Annunzio was dead, there would be plenty of opportunity to go after Sean Reilly in all the confusion that would follow.

JH: You mentioned Gavrilo Princip. What if someone had shot him before he could kill the archduke and, therefore, the First World War didn't happen? Maybe none of those others would have risen to power in the first place.

DK: What? Fuck you. I'm done talking. [Inaudible]

January 1918

The story took shape in the ward at the field hospital after the Battle of Tre Monti. Renzo would start telling it, only to be interrupted by Tom and Sean, who added details in increasingly loud voices until the nurses came and told them to be quiet. The laughter would start, and the storytelling continued. By the time Renzo and Tom were transferred to the hospital in Milan, it had been recounted so many times Sean could tell the whole thing himself.

The tale begins with Renzo leading his platoon of elite Arditi assault troops down the snow-covered west slope of the Col del Rosso. Snow in the Tre Monti region has been falling heavily for days. Footing is treacherous. Renzo's assignment is to seal off a narrow pass that runs through the foothills to prevent the Austrians from executing a flanking movement around the Italian garrison high on the mountain. Rommel had used the flanking maneuver successfully during the Caporetto rout to capture thousands of Italian prisoners by attacking from their rear. A repeat at Tre Monti would be disastrous.

When Renzo's platoon gets close to the bottom of the slope, the enemy's rifles roar to life. Pinned down, the Arditi scramble for cover behind boulders and inside shell craters, suffering heavy casualties from the merciless fire. Renzo is directing the placement of his men when he feels a mind-gashing pain in his leg and falls. His foot is caught in an Austrian bear trap buried in the snow. A bullet strikes his arm; it stings like a cigarette burn. Another hits him in the thigh, and one gets him in the chest. Those last two are agonizing, like the trap on his leg. He waits for the inevitable shot to the head. Snow and intense enemy fire cut off any chance of help from the garrison on the Col del Rosso.

A blast of sudden machine gun fire from Renzo's left draws the enemy's attention away. A squad has descended from out of nowhere. ("From Monte Valbella, you ungrateful bastard," Tom would interject. "It was a long way down to save your ass.") The newcomers open fire on the Austrians. One brave soldier runs over to where Renzo lies and opens the bear trap to free Renzo's leg. Ignoring enemy fire, the soldier carries Renzo on his back. Only when they reach safety does Renzo notice this soldier has suffered several bullet wounds himself. To Renzo's astonishment, his rescuer is an American.

The American introduces himself as Tom Delancy, a machine gun specialist attached to the IV Brigade. ("Yes, on Monte Valbella," Renzo would agree, "where they managed to get through the whole war without getting their uniforms dirty.") Renzo has trouble believing what he sees. The hero who saved him is comically unheroic looking: a short, stocky plug of a man with a head too large for his body, wearing a filthy coat that would have shamed the meanest peasant from the Po region.

Renzo is bleeding badly and understands that without medical attention soon, he will not survive. He also knows the enemy will attack again, and there's little chance of his getting away. He orders what's left of his platoon, those not hurt, to retreat a thousand meters to the south, where they will enjoy the advantage of good defensive bulwarks and still protect the Col del Rosso garrison. Renzo remains with a few others to cover the retreat. Tom insists he, too, will stay. He tells Renzo his machine gun can keep the Austrians at bay for a short while. (Tom: "If there had been two of me, we could've held them off till hell froze over.")

Before long an ambulance unexpectedly appears. Unexpected because ambulances usually go no farther than the dressing stations, several kilometers away from the front line. (Sean: "But even there we were never safe from artillery.") Out steps another American, this one a gangly young man wearing denim overalls and a heavy, dark wool coat, without helmet or cap to cover his mop of red hair. (Sean: "If I wanted to wear a uniform, I would have joined the college boys in the Red Cross.") Tom yells for the driver to take Renzo, but Renzo refuses to go. He insists the driver take other wounded. Renzo is certain he will die right where he is. The driver shouts he will be back after he drops the load off at the dressing station. Renzo doesn't believe it. He can hardly believe the ambulance made it this far in the first place. Who would risk driving those ten kilometers again, especially in the declining daylight and blinding snow?

The driver does come back, twice more. On the last trip, Renzo allows himself to be taken, along with Tom. It's dark, and the shooting is now only sporadic. Renzo and Tom are in bad shape. Renzo, in particular, is fading fast. Tom hands his pistol, a fierce .45 caliber Colt, to Sean for safekeeping. Sean takes the gun reluctantly (Tom: "Like I had wiped my ass with it.") and starts the ambulance. The enemy's big guns are hurling shells in the truck's direction. The shriek of those huge shells is terrifying, even to the battle-hardened warriors in the back of the ambulance. The road, already in bad shape, gets worse. Sean drives like a madman, knowing the men need emergency care soon if they are to survive.

They make it through the artillery fire, but less than a kilometer from the dressing station, the ambulance is stopped at a Carabinieri roadblock that has just been set up. An officer insists Sean get out of the ambulance. He says he has orders to shoot anyone not in uniform. By this time Tom has passed out. Renzo shouts from the back of the ambulance to shoot the carabinieri and drive on. Instead, Sean steps out, leaving Tom's pistol behind on the front seat. The carabinieri keeps shouting at Sean, saying he was either an Austrian spy or a deserter, and it doesn't matter which because both are subject to summary execution.

Somehow, with all his wounds, Renzo manages to open the back door of the ambulance and stagger to the side with his rifle. Mustering what little strength he has left, he shoots the carabinieri. Sean helps Renzo back into the ambulance, and they race off.

When the ambulance reaches the dressing station, Renzo is barely conscious. The orderlies are about to leave him for dead, but at Sean's insistence, they put him on a stretcher and take him to the operating theater. Sean finds Tom at the end of a long row and has to fight to get him treated. (Sean: "Nobody believed he was a soldier. I mean, look at him.") Sean returns to Renzo, who asks Sean to stay with him during the surgery. The sight of the ether mask as it is lowered onto Renzo's face triggers a violent reaction in his already pain-befuddled brain, causing him to lash out with both arms. Sean cradles his arms and helps restrain him until the ether takes effect.

Sean spends the night at the dressing station in a tent, trying to sleep on a stretcher. The next morning, he goes out in the ambulance to pick up more injured soldiers. In a couple of days, after their conditions stabilize, Sean drives Renzo and Tom to the field hospital. Each evening after he delivers wounded to the hospital, he visits the two men. Sometimes they talk about the war, but most times it's about women, wine, and food. Always, though, before Sean leaves, they talk about what life after the war will be like. Everything will change, they agree. The world will get better.

Months later, Renzo was awarded the Silver Medal of Valor for his heroic action during the Battle of Tre Monti. He gave the medal to Tom. When Sean found out, he smiled.

ONE HUNDRED & TWO

December 13, 1920. Renzo and Luigi. Impossible. The more I think about it, the less it makes sense. I saved Renzo's life and he saved mine. Yet there's no denying what Tom said.

I now have to look at everything Renzo has said and done, and everything he will say and do from now on, in a whole different light.

What am I supposed to think when someone I trusted more than any man alive, except maybe Tom, could be responsible for the attacks on me and Tom? And on Chesa, for Christ's sake. Chesa.

I can't just let this go.

ONE HUNDRED & THREE

From *Memories of a Fascist in Fiume*
by Tenente Lorenzo Guidici

do not exaggerate when I say panic prevailed among the denizens of Fiume, including many of the remaining legionnaires, after news reached us that a military action was coming. True, that had long been a possibility. The Italian Army remained camped on both the east and west Fiume borders since the start of the occupation, and the navy enforced a blockade. But given the lax attitudes of both branches of the armed forces, the city had mostly forgotten about them. Now that the treaty was signed, people got nervous.

Santo is a good example. He came to visit me about this time at my office on Viale XVII Novembre. He burst in unannounced, which was dangerous in those days after what happened to Luigi. I drew my pistol before I recognized him. "Did you hear?" he asked. "The army and navy are coming to clean out D'Annunzio and all the legionnaires. What are we going to do?"

I cannot imagine what plans Santo thought I might share with him. "Are you aware," I asked him, "that an angry man is out there in the streets looking for you? The man who beat poor Luigi half to death now wants to play baseball with your head. Had you heard that?"

"My head?" Santo repeated. "Why me? And what is baseball?"

"An American game. The players swing a large stick at a little ball and sometimes at each other. It's a dirty game played by sneaky little bastards like yourself."

"But why me?" Santo asked. His voice rose in pitch to a childlike whine. "Can't you take care of this? Tell that big gorilla Ugo and the others to get rid of him."

I laughed, which seemed to upset him. "Why you? I suspect Luigi, tough man though he is, or was, implicated you when he was being used for batting practice. It seems the baseball man now blames both of you for bad things that have happened in Fiume. He's looking for more names."

"You mean, like yours?"

Santo was becoming a genuine irritation. "Poor Luigi," I said. "He really is a mess. If he were a horse, I'd have him put out of his misery. Quite useless now, all those broken limbs. I believe the baseball man—the hitter, that's what they call the man who swings the stick, or maybe it's the batter, I'm not sure—knows what you look like. I'm sure he knows what your plane looks like and where it sits. Do you know how I know that?" I did not pause for an answer. "Because he borrowed it once for a little ride. Left it in the middle of the road when he was finished. Quite inconsiderate of him, don't you agree?"

"That bastard. You mean that American, the painter?" Santo started shaking with anger. "I will go shoot him myself. Where is he? You seem to know everything. Tell me and I'll go kill him, and then we can have dinner and go back to that nightclub."

Santo was no use to me at this point. He had made all the deliveries I needed. If anything, he presented a risk of exposing my plans. How long would it be before Chesa caught up to him? Not something I could permit.

"Santo, Santo," I said. "You let passion get in the way of your brain. The best thing you can do is to get out of Fiume. Tonight. Ugo and the rest of the crew are out looking for the American. But in the meantime, you don't belong here any longer. Especially with the army on its way."

"But if he's loose, running around the city looking for me, he could be waiting for me at the plane."

"Exactly. And he knows a lot about airplanes. I imagine he could nip a wire or fuel hose or tamper with something else, and you might not even notice until you were up in the air. It's been known to happen."

"But if you're telling me—"

"You need to get going quickly," I said, cutting him off. "Before he gets to your plane. I'll see you back in Milan soon."

"That's it? That's all you have to say?" Santo's voice was that of a schoolboy hit by the teacher with a pointer when he had been anticipating a candy reward. "You want me to run away. What's going on? What the fuck have you been doing here for the past year?"

That was more than I needed to hear. "The less you know about what I have been doing, the safer you are," I said. "Do you understand? Now go to your plane. Immediately. I don't want to see you again in Fiume. If I do, I will have Ugo come visit you, and then we'll ship the pieces back to Rome."

Santo stood there, mouth open but speechless.

"Please check your machine before you take off," I said. "I would rather not have another plane crash right now." He scurried out the door, and I got back to work.

ONE HUNDRED & FOUR

December 16, 1920

ean raced over to Chesa's hotel. She was going to leave Fiume whether she wanted to or not. The short December day had faded into a chilled evening under a clear sky. When he got to her room, he demanded she get on the train the next morning. He promised her he would follow soon.

"I'm not going," she said. "Can we please not have the same argument again?"

He didn't want the argument to escalate, but she needed to hear about the danger. She had to take the threat seriously.

"You don't want to know all the details," he said. "Trust me. You need to go. I whacked Luigi with a club and broke a few bones."

"Oh, Jesus."

"Then I set him on fire."

"You did what?" She raised her hands to her cheeks. "Oh, God. You are serious. Why did you do something so foolish?"

Sean grimaced. It was a little late for this reproof. She knew he was a fool when she gave him the address. What did she think he would do?

"Those friends of his will hunt you down. Goddamn it, Sean, *you* need to leave Fiume tonight. You should have stuck to your painting. And I never should have told you about the warehouse."

"All I want is for you to get on a train as soon as possible and wait for me somewhere safe," Sean said. "Let me do what I have to do. I need to fix things."

"Fix what things? You won't tell me."

"No."

"Can you at least finish by Monday?" she asked. "You go do whatever you have to do before then, I'll close up here, and we will leave together."

Sean couldn't look at her. He went to the window and gazed out at the lights on the Corso. "You need to go right away. I'll catch up, I promise. But I can't give you a date. Trust me, please. You must get out of here. Your name is on the list."

"Oh, for the love of all that's holy, what are you talking about? Sean, you always do this."

"Luigi told me that you and Tom were on a list to be dealt with. I'm on the list, too, of course."

"That's just fucking wonderful," she said. "And why me? I understand how you would be in danger. I can even empathize with them on that score, whoever they are. But why me?"

"I don't know. I guess . . . because of me." He put both hands on the window frame. He hadn't protected Chesa, and now she was a target.

ONE HUNDRED & FIVE

From SEAN REILLY'S JOURNAL

December 16, 1920. Chesa thinks I should have been content with painting and left well enough alone.

Mazzini would respectfully disagree. I have been reading him again. He wrote that if people don't have freedom, they may talk about art, but they are unlikely to produce "vital" art. But isn't vital art—art that incorporates and addresses real life—what Futurism preached? That's what attracted me to the movement in the first place, back in Paris. Boccioni and Carrà produced works that certainly looked vital to me back then. Futurism these days seems more talk than anything else. All those stupid manifestos.

Had I stuck with my painting, where would I be, Chesa? Miserable, that's where. When I was back in Trieste, my mind was a mess. I believed Futurism would help my painting, get me past what I saw in the war. Futurism and Fiume. But Futurism hasn't helped and Fiume fought me, taunted me, bruised me. Robbed me of my scruples and left me worse than where I started. Or perhaps it isn't fair to blame Fiume. I wasn't robbed; I traded those scruples cheaply in pursuit of artistic fame.

However one looks at it, Fiume has brought me no closer to my goal. The only thing I truly understand at this point is that anyone who shoots an innocent young man in a panic and later maims another man in cold blood, and who brags about the latter while concealing the former, lacks the soul of a great painter.

I cannot figure out how to explain to Chesa that, while both of us are in danger, only she is worth saving.

ONE HUNDRED & SIX

Mr. Kcleža, my name is Stanko Bešlic, and I am the deputy supervisor of the State Archives. On behalf of the Archives, I want to apologize for what happened yesterday with Mr. Horvat. With your permission, I'd like to continue the interview, and I promise the questions will be more respectful.

DK: Go ahead.

SB: Thank you, sir. Now Mr. Kcleža, you were—

DK: Call me Dušan.

SB: Yes, sir. Thank you. Dušan, you were telling us that you had decided that for the good of the Croatian people you would take action against the dictator D'Annunzio. Can you tell us what happened next?

DK: I wanted it to be spectacular, in front of all of those people who worshipped him, and the newspapers and such. Something that would capture the world's attention. A political act, do you follow me? I didn't want this to look like the revenge of a jealous husband. This was something I wanted to do for Croatia, like you said.

SB: That sounds brilliant. What method did you decide on?

DK: Well, I don't want to give out too many details, because of who might be listening to this interview. Kids can do wacky stuff, you know. They like to try things they hear about, especially if it sounds dangerous. Don't give them any more bad ideas. And the Serbs, too, they might be listening. We have a truce these days, but the fight is not over, not while a part of our country is still in Serb hands. I'd like to say right now to my brothers and sisters in Krajina: we will never rest until you, like the people of Rijeka, have been liberated.

SB: Inspiring words, sir, from a venerated hero like yourself. I believe all Croatians join you in those thoughts about Krajina. Now, is there anything you feel is appropriate to tell us about your plan for D'Annunzio?

DK: I'll tell you my plan involved the gelignite I had left over and a torpedo.

SB: A torpedo? That would certainly be spectacular. Where on earth would you get one of those?

DK: You need to learn more of your country's history, young man. The torpedo was invented at the Whitehead Torpedo Works here in Rijeka, not too far from the Governor's Palace. The factory built them for all the big navies around the world. Go take a look at the Palace. There are a bunch of torpedoes on display on the grounds still today. Trust me, it wasn't hard to find one back then.

Finding a powerful enough detonator was more of a challenge. I got help. Remember me telling you about Andrej, the veteran in our little group of fighters? [Inaudible] Oh, that was the other interviewer. Anyway, Andrej worked at Whitehead before it closed down like all the other businesses those Italians ruined. He knew where they kept everything, including the detonator charges. I tracked him down in a tavern in Sušak. He was his usual unpleasant self. He never liked any idea that came from me. "You are insane," Andrej said. "A torpedo? On dry land? Do you think these are toys you can play with?"

I bought round after round, plying Andrej with drinks and hitting him with questions. How did the triggering mechanism work? How much explosive would be needed? Were parts still there in the abandoned factory? Most importantly, how could the torpedo travel over a dry surface with enough speed to reach the target and then explode? Andrej insisted the whole thing was impossible. We drank and talked more. It was difficult and impractical, Andrej kept saying, but I kept pushing. It was a dumb idea, he told me, and would probably blow up in our faces. By closing time, Andrej had agreed to help.

SB: Please go on. This is fascinating.

DK: We broke into the factory the next evening and got what was needed: an old torpedo casing, a detonator pin, and fulminate of mercury for the secondary charge, to set off the primary. We couldn't find any guncotton, the usual primary charge, but I had one stick of the gelignite, which I figured could be used instead. "Does it have a chance, damn it?" I asked. Andrej shrugged. That was good enough for me.

Shit. I've said too much, haven't I? Can you edit some of this out?

SB: Certainly. But please continue.

DK: We assembled the torpedo but had not worked out how to propel it with sufficient force. So back we went to the factory, keeping a close watch for any guards or legionnaires, and dug through heaps of trash. We must have pried open a dozen or more wood crates until we got lucky. Inside a large crate we found a testing launch.

Some tinkering was needed to adapt it for land instead of water. Andrej was pessimistic, as usual, but allowed that, given the short distance the torpedo would need to travel, it might arrive at its destination with enough force to set off the internal firing. I held the torch while Andrej did the necessary modifications.

Then I went out and scouted the grounds of the Governor's Palace to make sure no patrols were guarding the area.

SB: I imagine the device was far too heavy for even two men to carry. How did you manage to get it all the way from the factory to the Governor's Palace?

DK: With great difficulty, I'll tell you. Andrej rigged a cart for the transport, and then the two of us lifted the torpedo and the launch platform into the cart.

Andrej was complaining the whole time. "You know, if anybody sees us, we will never be able to explain."

"If anybody sees us, it will be too bad for them," I told him. I had my pistol inside my coat. "Let's get moving."

It took us the better part of an hour to cover the half mile to the Palace. We set up the torpedo and the launch on the lawn to the right of the portico. We made it look like a little monument. I stole some flowers from a nearby garden and planted them around it. By the time we left, dawn was only a few minutes away.

SB: Didn't anyone from the Palace notice a torpedo on the lawn?

DK: Who knows? Their headquarters was a pretty disorganized place, from what I heard. Lots of drinking and drugs, too. We left it there for a couple of days, unarmed, to see if anybody would do anything, and nobody did. Then we went back, Andrej and me, and we armed it and aimed it right at one of the columns that support the balcony where D'Annunzio always gave his speeches.

Then we waited until the next rally. Actually, I waited by myself. Andrej didn't want any part of it after we did the arming. He said a lot of people were going to get hurt, not just D'Annunzio, and he didn't want to be around when the explosion went off. Crazy, you see, because he gave me all this help up until that point. A lot of people can't handle seeing something through to the end. Of course there would have been casualties, a lot of them. At the time, I thought it was worth it, but looking back, ah, maybe he was right. It's always hard to say how much is too much when you're talking about fighting for freedom.

SB: You've got the torpedo armed and ready. Everything is in place. The next rally is held. What happens?

DK: The crowd shows up at the Palace to hear the latest speech. D'Annunzio comes out on the balcony with a bunch of his generals and flunkies, and I take up a position by the torpedo. I wait for D'Annunzio to speak. I want the crowd's attention focused on the balcony as I send the people up there to hell. Then I see the women.

On the balcony, standing right behind the *Comandante*, I see the lady photographer and Annalisa whatever-her-name-was, the girl I went to school with. I don't know what they were doing there, because I can't figure either one of them would give the time of day to D'Annunzio, even if he was supposed to be this great sex god. But there they were, and I couldn't do it with the two of them standing there. Those women were good people.

All these years later, even after all the things I did during the Second World War, and there are some things I don't talk about, I remember that moment and how I felt. It was the hardest decision I ever made.

I was so close, do you see? All I had to do was launch the torpedo, and the world would change. This was the moment I planned and worked for. Rid the world of the invader D'Annunzio. Wake up the Croatian people. But I hesitated. I knew all along there would be casualties when the torpedo got fired. Like Andrej said. But the casualties would now have a face. Two faces. Two women I knew. D'Annunzio started another one of his endless speeches, and I walked away.

SB: You walked away without trying to fire it. Did you try again the next day?

DK: I didn't get the chance. That night I retrieved the gelignite and the detonator so nobody would accidentally set it off. The following day I guess somebody at the Palace got suspicious. They put guards out all over the grounds and pointed my torpedo away from the Palace and toward the bay. I never got a chance to get back to it. I suspect Andrej leaked word about the device, but I was never able to confirm it.

It wasn't all in vain, do you hear me? The Italians got the message. A threat planted by Croatians aimed right at the heart of their Command. Even if it didn't go off.

While I was trying to think up another way to get at D'Annunzio, something else came up to make me reconsider my plan.

ONE HUNDRED & SEVEN

December 22, 1920

Tomaso handed Sean a handwritten note from Tom that looked like it had been penned by a five-year-old. The note said, as best Sean could decipher, "Go away and don't fucking come back. If Chesa don't leave, tell Guido to deport her. Goodbye. Tom."

He tried to persuade Tomaso to let him go up to Tom's rooms. The big guard shoved him out the door.

Not knowing what else to do, Sean went to the Governor's Palace and found Guido Keller. They pushed their way through legionnaires who scurried about in relentless irresolution. Boxes of papers spilled onto the floor where, ten months earlier, there had been formal dancing. Guido looked tired. His impish grin was missing.

"Deported? Tom wrote that?"

"Yes."

He motioned for Sean to follow him into a red-walled parlor. "I guess we can make that happen," he said. "You're certain she's in that much danger?"

"Yes. Tom thought so, too." Sean didn't mention the list.

"It will take a few days," Guido said. "Even here we have paperwork. Why don't you take her over to Abbazia for a little holiday, and we'll not let her back in? Of course, she could probably talk her way past any guards we have. She will hate you forever, you understand."

"I know," Sean said. But she would be safe.

"Is staying here worth losing her? She's a nice lady. You and she should leave together. And not come back."

Sean glanced over Guido's shoulder and noticed a gilded rococo wall mirror, not unlike the one in Tom's luxury jail cell. The wood had pleasant carvings of leaves and flowers, but what drew his attention was the shape of the frame: wide and rounded at the top and pinched-in about halfway down, the outline of a fleshless human skull. Glancing back at Guido, he said, "Do you trust Renzo?"

"You should go," Guido said, and walked out of the room.

ONE HUNDRED & EIGHT

December 22, 1920. Tonight, I pulled out and examined each of the canvases I had started. I'm not sure what I hoped to discover, and in any event, no answers were there to be found.

Tom's note shook me, and Guido wiped away any remaining illusions about Renzo by refusing to answer my question. Both men warned me to leave in the strongest possible terms.

I have told Chesa I need to stay here in Fiume to fix things. Like that was possible. What could *I* fix?

D'Annunzio's tenure in Fiume is likely measured in weeks or days. Rumors are that the Italian military forces are prepared to shoot their way in. The Croatian terrorists will likely strike again soon. Chaos is coming. Blood will be spilled. Not the Futurist fantasy kind. Real blood.

It comes down to this. I can leave with Chesa and, by doing so, save her and myself from very real and very likely violent harm. Marinetti won't be happy, but then again he never is. Or I could stay in Fiume and risk Chesa's life and my own in a pathetic and probably hopeless attempt to prevent I don't know what, exactly, connected with that gap in the hills behind the castle.

Leaving Fiume is the smart thing to do. Of course if I leave, I'll be turning my back on Tom and severing my ties to Futurism. What then of my dream to become a great painter? Forget great. I probably couldn't even eke out a living through my art. Who would buy this shit? I'd have to find a job. Perhaps I could drive a taxi. Or teach English to spoiled children of rich folks. Or maybe—it might take some getting used to—I could drive an ambulance.

ONE HUNDRED & NINE

From *Memories of a Fascist in Fiume*
by Tenente Lorenzo Guidici

Fiume was about to face the combined might of the Italian Army and Navy, forces that brought down the entire Hapsburg Empire at Vittorio Veneto. D'Annunzio's adventure was about to end. I had to ensure that the *Comandante* did not pull off yet another bravura performance. With his silver tongue and his audacity, he was quite capable of recasting capitulation into triumph, at a cost too heavy for Italy to bear. Many people, including many Fascists, idolized him. That was not in Italy's best interest. Notwithstanding his heroics in the Great War, the man had proven himself to be a confused and incompetent leader over the sixteen months of his reign.

The *Comandante's* behavior became even more erratic after the treaty was signed. One minute he screamed that the defenders of Fiume were invincible gods who would rain death and destruction on any who dared attack us. Seconds later he spoke rapturously about the glorious and no doubt painful martyrdom we were about to experience and for which we would reap everlasting acclaim. Seriously, if we were invincible gods, how could we be martyred? Then he would turn around and declare that, like in our march from Ronchi, the army would never fire on us. Instead, he promised, they would lower their weapons and join us. We should prepare to welcome and feed them.

I had no illusions of invincibility and was not ready to be a martyr, at least for Fiume. I lacked the *Comandante's* faith that the army's allegiance-switching would be repeated. My only hope was that both sides would minimize the fraternal bloodshed. For the good of Italy, Italian soldiers should be fighting Croats and Serbs, not legionnaires. I did what I could to ensure that happened. First, though, I had to make sure that Chesa's film didn't reach Rome.

ONE HUNDRED & TEN

Sean drifted off to sleep in his chair. He woke a couple hours past midnight, the details of his dream still sharp and clear in his mind.

In the dream, Chesa was sitting on the edge of her bed, wearing a soft white robe he hadn't seen before, cinched tightly at the waist but loose enough at the throat to allow him a pleasant peek at her breasts. Her hands were folded in her lap, and she smiled. "Oh Sean, I'm so happy we're leaving at last. It won't take me but a few minutes to get ready. Then we'll be off to the train. I can hardly believe it. Where shall we go first? Let's spend a few weeks in Venice if you don't mind. There won't be crowds this time of year, and I do so love the place. Just you and me. I love you so much, darling. What photographs I will take! I'll pop round to the darkroom to get my camera." She rose and headed out the door, clad in the white robe. "No. Wait," he called to her. "Come back, Chesa. Please come back." But she didn't.

Sean bounded out of the chair, wide awake, breathing rapidly. *No hesitancy now. No indecision. They needed to leave together on the first train of the day.* He couldn't wait to give her the news. He ran down the stairs and out into the street. It was raining, cold and hard. His hat and umbrella lay on the floor up in his apartment, left behind without a thought. He took the same route to her place as on the night he suffered the castor oil attack, past the fountain where he had stopped to wash his face, and through the warren of little streets in the Old Town. When he got to her hotel, he was soaked. Paolo greeted him.

"Sorry, Mr. Reilly, but you just missed her. She said to tell you if you came by that she had work to do."

"Any idea where she could have gone at this hour?"

"Her darkroom, probably," Paolo said.

Sean raced out the front door of the hotel and turned right. The blast knocked him off his feet.

ONE HUNDRED & ELEVEN

From INTERVIEW WITH DUŠAN KCLEŽA (1992)
[UNEDITED TRANSCRIPT]

SB: You said that while you were trying to find another way to eliminate the dictator D'Annunzio, something happened. What was that?

DK: The Serbs in Belgrade and the Italians in Rome made a treaty to carve up Croatia. They called it the Treaty of Rapallo. They decided that the best thing for us Croatians was to hand over to Italy a huge mass of our land, including most of Istria. Fiume, they said, would be an independent state, and the League of Nations would look after us. Nobody bothered to ask Croatians what we wanted.

SB: What did you think of the treaty?

DK: Me? I thought it was bullshit. They gave away a big chunk of our country, don't you see? I didn't trust Rome or Belgrade, and the past seventy-some years have proved me right. Neither of them could keep their hands off us.

What time is it? I'm getting hungry.

SB: It's a little after four. We have a car waiting to take you to dinner in just a little bit. But before we wind up, I would like to ask you a few more questions, if you don't mind. Can you tell our listeners what it was like in those last few weeks of 1920? Did things quiet down in the streets after the treaty was publicly announced?

DK: Of course not. Those legionnaires never stopped harassing us. Why, a few days before Christmas, they blew up one of my father's properties, a nice building on the edge of Old Town. Completely leveled the place.

SB: Were many people hurt?

DK: It was at night, the building was mostly empty. Only one person was killed. These people would stop at nothing to get their way. That building cost my father a lot of money.

SB: Was your father the intended target?

DK: Who knows? By that time, all Croats were targets.

ONE HUNDRED & TWELVE

October–November 1918

n October, Sean made his arguments again for the ambulance plane. The tide of the Great War had turned in late 1918. The Italian Army raced eastward in pursuit of the retreating Austrians, erasing the bitter experience of the Caporetto disaster. The army's hospitals could not keep up with its advances. Sean went to see Captain Fabi again and argued that those badly hurt might require an ambulance trip of a hundred kilometers or more to get proper medical care. A five- or six-hour ride in an ambulance was a death sentence. The army needed an ambulance plane. Finally, the captain listened.

Sean was allotted an old two-seater Caproni Ca.18. The machine, a prewar production reconnaissance plane, had seen little use since the early days of the war but seemed in decent condition. Sean supervised the necessary modifications. Mechanics removed the rear seat to make room for stretchers and moved the gauges and re-rigged the controls for the wings, rudder, and throttle to allow the pilot to sit in front, in what had formerly been the observer's seat. The arrangement was cramped for someone of Sean's height, and the alterations put him closer to the noise of the motor. He didn't mind. He was going to fly.

Correspondents from the Milan newspapers interviewed Sean while the work on the airplane moved forward. "The ambulance airplane is a Futurist idea," he told them. "Futurism is the greatest thing to happen to medical care since anesthetics. After my flight, no one will have to suffer because they are too remote to get treated. Every part of Italy will be within reach of a good hospital, and it is all thanks to this vision." He hadn't checked with Marinetti before speaking so boldly, but when the story came out in the papers, Sean thought it sounded good. Futurism would get credit for an innovation that saved lives. He made sure Captain Fabi saw the articles.

He worried that the modifications were taking so long, the war might end before he got the chance to show the world what an ambulance airplane could do. Sean badgered the workers until the plane was ready. A small crowd showed up to watch him take off. One of the army pilots loaned Sean his goggles. The morning sky was a little cloudy but calm. He flew off toward the front and landed the airplane in a grassy meadow that had somehow eluded the Austrian artillery. Two injured captains were brought from the dressing station on stretchers and loaded in the rear of the fuselage, sheltered by blankets and sheets of plywood. *Disturbingly coffin-like*, Sean thought. He kept this thought to himself.

Once aloft, he felt movement in the back of the plane, causing an imbalance like one might feel on a motorcycle if a passenger behind the driver leaned the wrong way in a turn. Sean compensated by banking the plane slightly to one side or the other as necessary. The wind picked up. Lightning flashed in the mountains to his right. Or perhaps it was artillery. He couldn't tell.

A light film of engine oil began to accumulate on his borrowed goggles. He wiped the lenses with his finger, lamenting the absence of a windshield, and searched for landmarks pointing toward his destination, a half hour away. He pictured the amazed reception he would get when he landed. A perfect Futurist act—using an airplane to rescue the war's wounded fighting men. Marinetti had served in a bicycle brigade, and Boccioni joined the cavalry and got himself killed falling off a horse. Now came Sean Reilly, blazing across the October sky in the speedy machine of the future.

The engine coughed once, and again, and resumed its buzz but at a lower and deeper pitch. According to his map, he was forty kilometers from where he needed to land. The winds were stronger than on the two practice runs, and in neither of those had he been carrying extra weight as he was now. He wiped more oil from the goggles. Once news of his success spread, he would get his own pair.

At ten kilometers out, he felt the plane shaking in an unfamiliar way. He heard screams from his passengers. Only a few minutes more to the hospital. A sharp gust bumped him off course. He banked the plane over to the northwest but could not straighten up. A stream of hot oil sprouted from the engine onto his face. The engine quit, and the plane began to dive. He fought to level it and overcorrected. The ground came at him quickly. The left wing dipped and touched the ground first, then the propeller. The plane flipped over.

He woke up in the field hospital a day later, shoulder and hip dislocated, one arm broken, spleen punctured. Pain in his back and knees. Both of his passengers were dead. No one spoke to him except the nurses, who gave him terse commands in broken English. The doctor visited once after the surgery and did not return. Soldiers in the ward, like the ones in the enlistment station, spoke about him in Italian, assuming Sean couldn't understand. He wished that were true. When he left the ward for X-rays, he returned to a bed that had been urinated on.

After a month, he was transported to the American hospital in Milan. The war was over. Captain Fabi came to visit. The captain didn't smile. He asked how Sean was feeling.

"Horrible," Sean said. "I hurt everywhere. I wonder if those damn doctors in the Italian hospital fixed anything. At least here the doctors talk to me. They say I am recovering."

"Your recovery will take a long time. My leg is proof of that." The captain pulled up a stool and sat. He glanced around at the empty beds in the ward. "You will go home to America like the rest of them once you are healed, yes?"

"Possibly." Sean called for the orderly and asked for water. "They won't allow me alcohol here, and I haven't been able to bribe any of the orderlies to sneak any in. I want you to know, Captain. I did everything I could. One minute I was in control of the airplane and getting ready for landing, and then . . ."

"And then two officers died. I wasn't the only one who thought your idea for this ambulance plane too dangerous. After the crash, my superiors wanted to court-martial you. I had to explain you were not in our army. They didn't care. Lucky for you General Diaz now runs the Supreme Command, and he quashed such talk. Had Cadorna still been in charge, I fear you would be in serious trouble today."

"The plane was old. The engine leaked oil. It lacked enough power to—"

"Stop." The captain held out his hand and then rested it on Sean's arm. "It was too dangerous. I should never have let you fly. Maybe in America, when you get there, you can convince your authorities to try airplane ambulances, if you continue to believe it is a good idea. Here in Italy, we are slow to appreciate such things."

"They're already testing airplane ambulances in America," Sean said. "In Texas. I read it in the American newspapers. They use bigger planes, new ones with powerful engines."

The captain stretched his bad leg and rubbed it with both hands. "I will send you some grappa. Discretely. I knew the ambulance plane was dangerous. We all did. You were not ready. We were not ready. Maybe someday there will be ambulance rescues from the sky, even in Italy. When are you leaving?"

"As soon as they let me out. What will you do, Captain? Stay in the army?"

"I don't know. Many of us will be discharged, looking for work. Who can predict what the future holds? Perhaps your Futurist friends can tell us."

Sean looked up at the ceiling. "My Futurist friends want nothing to do with me. They accuse me of setting the cause of Futurism back by many years. They're probably correct."

"Too dangerous," the captain said as he stood up. "It was a good dream, though. Perhaps someday."

ONE HUNDRED & THIRTEEN

From *Memories of a Fascist in Fiume*
by Tenente Lorenzo Guidici

The explosion was most unfortunate. Things of this sort happen when one is forced to use men who are not very smart and who have been made rabid by a violent attack against one of their number. Passions escalate, and harm occurs that was in no way the objective. It was not possible for me to prevent it. And while the last thing I wanted—in fact the very thing I cautioned the boys against— was for anyone to get hurt, I sincerely believe that what happened was directly linked to Sean's lawless and violent action against Luigi. He cannot have failed to foresee that the others would retaliate.

When I met Sean at the site of what had been Chesa's darkroom, it was raining heavily, and despite the December chill Sean wore only his light jacket. He refused my offer of the umbrella I carried.

The blast site was by a dingy courtyard in the Old Town area, a few blocks north of the Corso. Little of the building remained standing, as the concussion had ripped through the entire structure, and fire had consumed the rest. The acrid smell of burned wood assaulted my senses and made me cough. I spoke to a couple of policemen, who filled me in on the details, and then returned to Sean.

"Is she safe?" Sean asked me, and I had to tell him the rescue workers had found no trace of her. There was still hope. We both stared at the smoldering remains of the building.

"Listen, Sean," I said, "the police believe the Croats did this. They believe they know exactly who. The same ruthless terrorists who blew

up the barracks a couple of months ago and shot several of our people. The firemen said this explosion was caused by gelignite. There's
more to tell, but I don't think you want to hear it."

He insisted I tell him.

"The leader of those terrorists is Dušan Kcleža." I paused to let
that sink in. "Gaj's son. The brother of the boy you shot."

To my surprise, he didn't react, at least physically. His eyes remained fixed on the ashes, where some embers still glowed. "The
other day a vagrant down by the warehouses was brutally attacked," I
said. "Had his arms and legs broken. A truck was set on fire, too. Must
have been those same Croats. For your own good, Sean, you should
leave Fiume right away. I have a friend who can fly you out."

Sean turned and looked at me. He was shuddering, most likely
from the cold drops of rain rolling down his head and neck. He didn't
say a word.

After a while, I left him there and returned to my little office,
where I resumed preparations for what came next. So much de-
pended upon the well-timed use of that defile in the hills beyond the
castle. Above all, I had to be certain that all of Chesa's film had been
accounted for.

ONE HUNDRED & FOURTEEN

t rained through the night. Sean stood at the edge of the charred area that was once Chesa's darkroom. The site reminded him of damage caused by artillery shells during the war. Rescue workers pulled away rubble.

In the morning, they uncovered a familiar looking shoe and a few scraps of clothing. They could not locate a body. Sean ached for a miracle. Then one of the workers emerged carrying a silver necklace. Sean had given it to her a month ago, and she had never taken it off. He took the necklace and put it in his pocket.

He remained at the site for several more hours before ending his vigil. He didn't feel like going to his apartment, so he drifted over to the piazza by the Capuchin Church, settling on the same bench where he had so often gone to escape his troubles. A steady wind pelted him with rain and cold air, bringing on a shiver he couldn't shake. When he couldn't stand any more, he went inside the church and took a seat in a back pew.

The interior of the church was empty. Only a few lamps were lit, creating a gloomy place to grieve. He did not pray. Seated on the hard wooden pew, he tried to empty his mind. Thoughts came anyway.

How ludicrous to suspect that Renzo, his good friend, could have anything to do with Chesa's murder, no matter what else he might be involved in. And yet. *Don't think of Renzo,* he scolded himself. *Focus on Chesa.* He groped for the necklace in his pocket. Remembering her right now hurt too much. *Try someone else.* He looked up at the ceiling. For a long time he had mourned the effects of the ambulance plane crash on Futurism. Sitting there in the church, he thought of the two wounded captains who died in the crash. He had never learned their names. Never asked. He pictured Chesa again and wept. He lost track of time.

A woman entered the church and sat silently at the far end of the pew. Being in no mood for conversation, he ignored her. "You are Sean Reilly, correct?" she said. She slid over next to him. "I'm Nina Giovanitti, a friend of Chesa's. May I offer you condolences?"

Chesa would not have wanted him to insult one of her friends. He let out a long breath, leaned back, and nodded by way of response. *Couldn't friends of the deceased grieve privately?*

"I knew Chesa from Florence. Such a beautiful, wonderful woman. I can't believe she's gone."

Nor could Sean. He wanted this woman to leave.

"I don't suppose she talked much about me," Nina said, "but she told me a lot about you. I've seen so many photographs she took of you."

Photos of him? He peered at the woman for the first time. She was an attractive woman in her late forties or early fifties, with dark hair tied up in the same way Chesa used to do hers. She wore a long wool coat with a fur collar. The coat opened to reveal a smart skirt and blouse, appropriate for a woman in business. Why would Chesa send her pictures of him?

"I'm sorry," he said. "I don't know who you are, and I don't feel much like talking."

"I understand," she said. "You miss her. I do too. In fact, the reason I came to Fiume was to get her to come back to Florence. Or Rome. She used to send me these lovely letters telling me all about Fiume and this marvelous man she had met and how happy she was. The last couple of letters, though, she didn't sound so happy. I begged her to leave, but she wouldn't do it. I told her how dangerous the city was going to get."

"She knew. She saw it every day," Sean said.

"No, there were things she didn't know. I'm a journalist in Rome, and I could see what was coming. The government's new treaty with the Jugoslavs means they have to get D'Annunzio out of Fiume. They want to do it quietly, to keep peace and stability. But Mussolini and his Fascists are dead set against peace and stability. They've been rampaging all over Italy with their *squadrismo*, trying to make the government look weak. They'll do everything they can in Fiume to sabotage a clean exit. I tried to warn her. I told her she had done enough.

"And listen, I'm sorry if this hurts, but Chesa said she would only leave if she could convince you to go, and you were being stubborn. That's why I came here. I hoped the two of us could change your mind. Failing that, I planned to drag her out of this doomed place."

Was this woman trying to make him feel worse than he already did? What did he care about a treaty or Fascists? Chesa was dead. He had lost her forever, and he needed to mourn. Had they left together when she asked, she'd be alive today. "What do you mean, drag her? Who the fuck are you?"

"Like I said, I'm a journalist. I can be quite persuasive." She surveyed the empty church. "You should have left with her when you could. I know this must be painful for you."

Sean stood up. He had enough guilt already. Nina stood up, too. He could see she was crying. He didn't think journalists were supposed to cry.

"I'm going to find out who killed her," she said.

"Go fuck yourself," he said.

ONE HUNDRED & FIFTEEN

From INTERVIEW WITH DUŠAN KCLEŽA (1992)
[UNEDITED TRANSCRIPT]

SB: One of the terms of the Treaty of Rapallo was that D'Annunzio had to leave Fiume. I'm sure he didn't agree with that.

DK: He was supposed to get out. That's right. Of course D'Annunzio raised a holy fit and screamed how he was going to die to defend the right of Italy to annex Fiume, and all that other nonsense he had been saying for so long. He wasn't ready to pack up and leave his comfortable life in our Governor's Palace, where he lived for free. He needed to be encouraged, so Rome finally got serious and sent the real army and navy to throw his ass out. Which, mind you, was something they could have done any time in the preceding sixteen months.

SB: What did that mean for you personally?

DK: It meant I didn't have to kill D'Annunzio and risk my life, because with any luck the Italian military would do it for me. I was happy to let Italians kill Italians, do you see? The fewer of them left standing, the better for us. And if they didn't kill him, at least they were going to chase him out of here. One way or the other, he wasn't going to be a problem for us anymore.

SB: You didn't feel bad about not acting against him yourself?

DK: Not too much. Oh, it would have been nice being the one to kill him, but I had to consider what was best for our people. If I had killed D'Annunzio after the treaty was announced, then that'd make him a martyr and all military forces headed to Fiume would start shooting Croatians instead of D'Annunzio's people.

Anyway, my original plan was to kill the American who shot my brother. If the Italian Army and the legionnaires were busy slaughtering each other, they wouldn't notice what happened to the painter.

ONE HUNDRED & SIXTEEN

December 23–24, 1920

ight snow was falling when Sean left the church. It melted fast upon touching the street, but traces lay visible on the trees, roofs, and shutters. He scuffed his way around the back of the church and headed to his apartment. Heavy gray cloudiness blanketed the late afternoon sky and begat an early dusk.

From the sidewalk in front of the food store, Sean noticed a light had been turned on inside his apartment. He didn't need Tom or anyone else to explain that meant danger. He scurried to the alley at the side of the building and hid in the dark recess of a doorway. Before long, four men came out onto the street, one of them, predictably, very large. They lumbered past the alley but did not look Sean's way.

When he got to his rooms, he found them in shambles. Clothes were strewn about, canvases slashed. His easel lay in pieces. The stench of urine permeated the apartment.

His journal, curiously, survived untouched. He stuffed it and a few clothes into his duffle bag and left. On the street, he faced the question that confronted him the previous December after the castor oil attack: where could he go? He came up with the same answer as on that night: Chesa's hotel room.

He feared being seen going in the hotel's front door, so he circled around to the courtyard behind the hotel and pounded on the door. Paolo let him in, closed the door, and quickly fixed the deadbolt latch.

"I need a big favor," Sean said.

Paolo gave a nervous look to the front of the hotel and whispered,

"Sure. I'll do anything I can." The clerk scouted the area around the front desk before leading Sean to a spot less visible from the street. "I am so sorry about what happened to Miss Rei. It's awful. Did they figure out what happened?"

"You might get a visit from some violent men," Sean said. "Let me know if you do."

Paolo's eyes opened wide, like he had conjured up a demon. "You just missed them, and it's probably a good thing because those were nasty fellows. Four of them. They said they were special police on an important investigation, so they needed to see her room. One of them asked if you were around. I said, 'You guys don't look like police. How come you're not wearing uniforms?' The biggest guy, and I mean he was huge, he goes over to the little table in the front and picks up a lamp with one hand, smashes it, walks over to me, and puts the broken edge at my throat. He says, 'Now do you see my uniform?' They went upstairs for about half an hour. I made sure to stay out of their way until they left. At least I hope they all left. I'm afraid to go up there."

"I want to see her room," Sean said. "If I'm not down in ten minutes, call the police. The real police." Paolo gave him the key. Sean climbed the stairs and stood outside her room, listening. Hearing nothing, he went in.

The damage was worse than in his apartment. Her mattress lay askew on the floor, joined there by clothes, broken furniture pieces, toiletries, and anything else that previously resided in drawers or on shelves. Her red robe lay in the bathroom, desecrated with a stain and a foul odor. He sifted through the wreckage with his foot, unable to bear touching any of it with his hands.

He returned to the lobby, eyes damp. His body felt heavy. Paolo offered to let Sean stay at his apartment. "It's small and not too clean, but you should be safe there. I don't get off work until 7:00 a.m., so you won't be bothered."

Paolo had not misrepresented the condition of his apartment. Dirty clothes littered the floor. Papers, boxes, toys, and books—flotsam, discarded or forgotten by hotel guests that became treasure for the clerks—sat in piles. One area, however, was tidy enough to have delighted even Chesa. A six-foot easel stood there, holding an unfinished watercolor. Next to the easel, on a small, battered game table, a wooden box held liquids and paints. Cleaned brushes were laid out like silverware at a grand restaurant.

Sean fell on the bed, exhausted. Sleep was slow to come. He worried that Chesa's image would fade from his memory, no matter how hard he fought to retain it. He visualized her exquisitely beautiful face, long neck, and lean body. One of her eyes had a brown tint mixed in with the green. *The left or the right?*

He realized he had no photographs of Chesa. All of her work at the darkroom was destroyed, and he hadn't found any photos or negatives anywhere in the debris scattered around her hotel room or his apartment. He had taken pictures of her, though. Chesa had allowed him to practice on her camera. She posed as his model. So beautiful, so exquisite. That roll of film was still in the Kodak when they went to Trsat. The pictures she took of the gap in the hills were on the same roll. When the roll ran out, she replaced it with a new one. So the thugs who assaulted the two of them on the Trsat Stairs got the new roll inside the camera, while the roll with the photos of her and the gap was safely stored in her pocket. Perhaps Gaj had that roll of film.

Before falling asleep, he vowed to go visit Gaj.

The late morning sun woke Sean. He struggled to orient himself. *Strange apartment.* As he got out of bed his feet came in contact with Paolo's snoring head. The young man was asleep on a bed of dirty laundry.

Sean remembered his urgent need to go see Gaj. But by this time Gaj would be busy preparing the day's meals, if not already serving them. Better to catch up with him at night, after everything had been cleaned and put away. Gaj would have more time to talk then.

Sean found a day-old local newspaper on the floor. One story dominated the front page:

ITALIAN ARMY, NAVY HEADED TO FIUME. Reports reached Fiume yesterday that the Royal Italian Army and Navy are proceeding to Fiume to arrest Comandante D'Annunzio and crush his regency. The army is already massing in Trieste. Six ships, including the battleship *Andrea Doria*, are steaming in this city's direction and could arrive at any time.

In response, the Comandante pledged he would stay in Fiume to his last breath. He called upon all citizens and legionnaires to join him in defending Fiume against the impending attack. "Let the city be painted red with my blood and that of other noble warriors. We shall sacrifice ourselves in glory to safeguard its sacred flame. Let this flame cast its accusing light on the vile dogs in Rome, who shiver and cower in their filthy kennels."

The Comandante vowed to blow up bridges and mine the harbor to impede the advance of the attacking forces. He assured the crowd gathered at the Governor's Palace that the entire perimeter of the city had been meticulously surveyed, and that fierce defenders have been stationed at each possible point of attack. As he spoke, squads of legionnaires were observed moving rapidly to their positions at barricades on major streets. All borders were sealed at 6:00 a.m. today.

While these precautions are essential, Comandante D'Annunzio predicted that true patriots in the Italian military would never fire on him or the brave legionnaires. Instead, the soldiers will rush to join the Fiume legionnaires, as thousands did in the sacred march from Ronchi.

Residents were advised not to be alarmed by recent atrocities, including a vicious beating in the vicinity of the harbor, believed to be the work of roving bands of Croats. The police obtained several leads on the identity of the culprits, thanks to the assistance of concerned citizens, and will make arrests soon.

Sean threw the paper on the floor. Did the *Comandante* seriously believe the ragged bunch of legionnaires who remained could stand against the army and navy? D'Annunzio had succeeded before, and no one questioned his courage, but times had changed since the march from Ronchi. Even if the army declined to shoot D'Annunzio because of all the medals on his chest, Sean figured they would not hesitate to fire on everyone else, including any American reckless enough to be in the wrong place at the wrong time.

He opened his journal and looked around the apartment for a pen.

ONE HUNDRED & SEVENTEEN

From SEAN REILLY'S JOURNAL

December 24, 1920. It's a miracle I was able to salvage this journal. Everything else I owned has been ruined.

I haven't had much time to write in you, journal. And I haven't felt much like writing when I did have the time. But what that newspaperwoman Nina said about Chesa, it keeps ringing in my head. I've got to write this down. I can't tell anybody. Nobody around here to listen.

This is what I should have said to that bitch. No, Nina, you don't have any fucking idea how painful it is for me. I know full well what I have done. And did not do.

My hands are shaking. If ever I had illusions about deflecting from myself the blame for Chesa's death, they have been shattered by this woman who came over to Fiume to steal my Chesa. Now that she can't do that, she saw fit to punish me. Chesa never mentioned anything about a journalist, although I did recall her mentioning the name Nina a couple of times. Chesa seemed to know so many people in Florence and Rome, Futurists and other artists. I never inquired too much. Didn't want to know. It was always too intimidating for me. Now I learn she had a running correspondence with a journalist who she shared photographs and commentary with about me. And what did this woman mean, Chesa had done enough? Enough what?

Here's what else I should have said to Nina. If you want to blame me in your newspaper for what happened to Chesa, go ahead but tell your readers that I was a man who "loved not wisely but too well." My poor, beautiful Desdemona.

I can't imagine I'll have much more to write.

December 24, 1920. One more thing I need to write down, this time about Renzo. He said something when we were standing there looking at what was left of her darkroom about how Dušan was a terrorist who blew up the barracks. I asked him why Dušan hadn't been arrested if they suspected him. Why was Tom in jail and Dušan not? He didn't even answer, like he was insulted.

December 24, 1920. I have to put this down, or I will forget it, too. One night, weeks ago, after we made love, Chesa lay completely at rest next to me, eyes shut. Face serene like the Madonna in a Fra Lippo Lippi painting. "Sean," she murmured, "what's it like? Flying?" She didn't move any part of her face but her lips. I couldn't look away. Shameless of me to stare at her like that, but it would have taken a lot more than shame to shift my gaze away.

"Have you never been in an airplane?" I asked her.

"No. Tell me about it." The words stretched out for several seconds, as in a song. "You love it so. It must be grand."

I told her about the rush of air as the plane gathered speed for takeoff, objects on the ground racing past in a blur, and then the magical moment when the noise and rumbling of the tires cease like some giant picked the whole machine up as if it were a toy. I described as best I could the feel of climbing into and above clouds, of banking into tight curls, of diving to pick up speed, even rolling, sometimes staying upside down. That drew a small gasp from her and a tiny hint of a smile. I told her about the landing, how on the approach you enter the no-man's-land between earth and sky, between the unlimited freedom of the air and the small, hard clearing you have to drop into, between the fantasy of height and the reality of the ground. How navigating that border was terrifying but also exhilarating. The tiny smile on her lips broadened into the most beautiful expression, surpassing any Madonna ever. Staring at her had been more sublime than flying. Better than painting or anything.

There. Now that I have written it down, it's there forever. I will remember that moment for the rest of my life.

December 24, 1920. One final last thing. Today is Christmas Eve. D'Annunzio's Fiume adventure is quickly coming to an end. Santa will not bring any presents for the *Comandante.* That is clear. No annexation of Fiume to Italy, no crusade to unite the downtrodden peoples of the world. Futurism hasn't taken root here in Fiume. Nothing worthy has been accomplished. No epic took place. As Chesa put it so long ago, this wasn't the *Iliad.*

But if nobody pays attention to that gap in the mountains beyond the castle that I discovered, perhaps the real meaning of Fiume remains to be written. I don't believe the tale will be a happy one.

I try to think how things could have been different. Imagine if Mazzini had kept up his literary ambitions and had been able to communicate his ideas of independence and liberty more widely in popular fiction. Maybe art cannot lead the masses—the Futurist Political Program seems proof of that—but at least art can offer hints to a better future that doesn't involve screaming for war like Marinetti and D'Annunzio. Imagine art and real life, working together, keeping ideals alive, acting without killing anybody. Art's Christmas gift to life.

ONE HUNDRED & EIGHTEEN

From *Memories of a Fascist in Fiume*
by Tenente Lorenzo Guidici

Sean was my biggest concern at this point. He either had Chesa's film or knew where it was. My assistants had been unable to locate him. When they appeared in my office, I expressed to them how disappointed I was in their failure. "Let me guess," I said. "You went quietly to that woman's hotel room and searched it carefully, like I instructed, leaving no trace of your visit, right? No, you did not. You wrecked it, like a pack of hyenas. Now you can't find him or the film I asked you to retrieve. Splendid work, gentlemen."

One of the men started to explain but was silenced by Ugo's elbow to his throat. For a few seconds the only sound in the room came from the man who was fighting to breathe. Ugo asked for instructions on what to do next.

"You need to split up," I told them. "Forget the hotel. He's not going back there. Same with his apartment. And he won't be dining at that Croat restaurant—it's off limits to you boys, understand?—because the proprietor now knows, thanks to me, that Sean killed his son. But look for him everywhere else. This isn't a big city. Remember, I want the roll of film and any negatives or photographs he might have. If you kill him when you first see him, he won't be able to tell you where they are. Ask politely first, before you begin persuading." I stopped speaking to let that advice register. It was not easy for me to give orders that could cause harm to a friend. What choice did I have? My loyalties to

Italy and Fascism went beyond friendship. "There isn't much time left," I warned them. "In a few more days the army and navy will be here. The film could end up in the wrong hands, in the uproar. If that happens, well, there will be consequences for the four of you. Unpleasant ones. Now get to work."

Judging from the anger I saw in Ugo's eyes, it was good that my need for these four was about at its end. They were nearly uncontrollable at this point.

After that, I went to a briefing at the Palace that Guido Keller was giving to the few senior officers who hadn't deserted Fiume yet. A map was tacked to the wall showing defensive positions around the city. Guido pointed to the key roads and harbor access points that were likely to be used to attack the city. Assignments were handed out.

I was pleased to see that responsibility for the northwest sector was given to Colonel Albertini, a former member of General Cadorna's staff and a mandarin of the first order. He was a short, plump man, nearly bald, with gray- and white-hair circling above his ears like an old laurel crown. Having seen him in action during the war, or should I say inaction, I had a good appraisal of his worth. At my request, I was assigned to assist him.

Keller gave special instructions to the colonel that I did not like. "You will have several machine gunners. Deploy them as you see fit, Colonel, but leave a few to cover this area here." He pointed at the mountains west of Trsat Castle. "The *Comandante* reckons we might be vulnerable up there."

I stepped up close to the map, in front of the senior officers, and offered a simple suggestion. "This area in the north," I said, sweeping my hand in an arc from the castle to the airport, "is defended for us by the mountains. The main attack is certainly going to come from the south on the road running by the bay. It's the only one, realistically, that the army can use." I reassured Guido that I had personally inspected the area in the hills. "There's no way anyone could get over those mountains, I promise you."

Keller did not look convinced. He reminded me, as if I needed reminding, of the officers who said the same thing during the war about the hills around Caporetto, right before the Austrians and Germans came pouring over them into our flanks. He warned the colonel to keep the sector adequately defended.

I moved closer to the colonel, who was staring at the map. "I know the area well, Colonel, and will be honored to help in the deployment of the men under your command."

"Yes," the colonel muttered. "That may be useful. So much ground to cover."

He was correct. He had much ground to cover and only one small area I needed him to neglect.

ONE HUNDRED & NINETEEN

December 24, 1920

I

Gaj switched off the lights in the dining area after the last employee left and then locked the front door. At the sound of Sean's voice, he grabbed the back of the chair closest to him.

Sean stepped out from a darkened corner. "Please don't be alarmed, Gaj. I need your help. Don't turn on the light. I don't want anyone to see me."

"In the kitchen," Gaj said. "I'll put the light on in there. Wait for it."

Sean waited. His mouth was dry. He didn't like the tone of Gaj's voice, the absence of the usual hearty greeting. When he entered the kitchen, Gaj was standing by an open drawer, holding a cleaver.

"One question I will ask you," Gaj said. His forearm muscle quivered. Sweat beaded on his forehead. "Did you kill my son? Give me an answer. No bullshit."

Sean had hoped to ask him about the photographs before any talk about his son's death. No point in lying to the man, though. The knife in his hand proved Gaj already knew what happened. Sean's eyes darted back and forth between Gaj's face and the gleaming blade of the cleaver. "Let me explain," he said. "A man came running at me. It was dark. I thought he had a gun, and I didn't know it was Veselko. My friend Tom had just been shot, so I reacted and fired."

Gaj squeezed the knife hard, the trembling blade scattering reflections in all directions. Sean felt like a rack of lamb on the cutting board.

"You come in here asking for my help? Like you come to my restaurant how many times since my son died, eat my food, and talk to me, but you never say anything about my son? Nothing except, 'Sorry for your loss, Gaj.' What's there to be sorry about? Just another dead Croat kid. You know what? Maybe I'll dismember you and serve your parts to my customers tomorrow. I'll send a special plate over to your beloved *Comandante*. Let him chew on that."

Gaj was not a large man, but he seemed frighteningly huge in the kitchen. Sean's knee began throbbing, causing him to flinch and reach behind for the counter to steady himself. Gaj pulled the cleaver back slightly. Sean raised his hands. "I'm not moving, Gaj, not doing anything. I can't stand still very long since I got beat up." His words sounded like a cheap ploy for sympathy, but the pain was nonetheless real. "I didn't come here with any weapon."

"Then get the hell out. Don't ever come back."

Sean didn't move. "I need your help, Gaj. Please. I need it for Chesa. Let me finish what I have to say."

"Don't talk to me about that beautiful lady." Gaj's fingers tightened around the handle of the cleaver, turning white.

"Please, just listen." Sean stared at the floor. "I am so sorry about what happened to Veselko. If I could change any moment in my life, that would be it. I didn't know the man running at me was him. I reacted. But I had no—"

"Your time is up. Get out." Gaj let out a long howl and hurled the cleaver in Sean's direction. It stuck in the wall inches from his head.

Sean shuddered. "Listen to me. Chesa gave you some film. She had problems developing the photographs and said you would be able to help with enlargements. I'm pretty sure the film is what got us attacked on the stairs and got her killed."

"I don't know what you're talking about. I said to leave." Gaj's tone retained the menace, but the volume dipped.

"Damn it, Gaj. She's gone. The darkroom, her camera, and her pictures, all destroyed. Those murderers even went to her hotel room and wrecked everything there. The film is all that's left of her." He raised his head. "That and a necklace. Please. I'm begging you. I need the pictures on that film."

Gaj squinted in Sean's direction and then walked over to the wall where the cleaver was embedded. He pulled it out and examined it. "At least I now know what happened to my son. Every day I get the plates out, I miss him. I think, my boy works for me, helps me, but before long he will leave, go to university maybe, get a good job. Then the truth hits me in the head." He turned his back to Sean. "Follow me," he said. His voice was hollow.

They exited through the rear door of the restaurant into a dark, odd-shaped courtyard. At the far end stood a tall, rusticated building topped by a frieze showing what looked like dragons on a gold background. The structure lacked any Futurist aesthetics, but Sean found it striking nonetheless. Gaj unlocked the front door and led him down a hallway to a ground floor office. "Wait here while I get her photos," he said. "And don't touch anything."

Gaj disappeared into an alcove hidden by a heavy black curtain that stretched from ceiling to floor. Sean turned to the wall of photographs on his left. He recognized several distinguished visitors to Fiume, including Marconi and Toscanini. Marinetti, too, in full dramatic pose, eyes opened extra wide and arms extended, looking like he had been hit by a jolt of electricity. Other pictures showed ordinary folks shopping or dining in Gaj's restaurant. He spotted one of Chesa. The photo caught her coming out of her darkroom. She wore a long white apron and had her hair pulled back and collected in a scarf. Her eyes displayed the intense all-business focus Sean knew well from whenever he foolishly tried to interrupt her, but here her lips showed the beginning of a shy smile, caught by the camera doing something she loved but a little embarrassed to show how much. She was wearing the necklace.

Sean heard noises from the alcove and pivoted to see the curtains being separated. Gaj emerged, followed by a young man holding a rifle.

II

"This is perfect, Father," the young man said. "I'll bet no one saw either of you come in here. No one will see when we carry his body out, either." The young man pointed the rifle at Sean. "You're gonna die," he said, "for what you did to my little brother."

Gaj lured him into the darkroom so he and this young man could kill him, Sean thought. No, he realized, that was ridiculous. He'd come to the restaurant uninvited and unwelcomed. Sean labored to breathe. "You're going to kill me? Did you kill Chesa too?"

"Put the gun down, Dušan," Gaj said.

"No," Dušan said. "Father, don't listen to him. I did not blow up the woman. I still have my last stick of gelignite. Anyway, I had nothing against her." He waved the rifle at Sean. "Just this American. Just him."

"You killed Chesa," Sean said, trying to sound defiant, "and the two of you want to murder me."

"You accuse my father?" Dušan shouted. "I should shoot you just for that. He never killed anyone. He's not like you."

"What I did was an accident," Sean said.

Gaj let out a roar, the sound ringing off the walls of the small room. "Shut the fuck up, both of you. Nobody is going to die in my studio." He turned from Dušan to Sean and then back again. "You two, you are so much alike. Both too quick to speak and to act. Neither of you stop and think first."

Gaj moved over to Sean, so close that Sean could feel the warmth of the older man's breath on his face. "What you did was no accident," Gaj said. "You pulled the trigger on your gun. My son Veselko died. You intended to shoot him. You maybe did not know it was my son when you fired. But don't ever say what you did was an accident. Don't insult him or me.

"And you," he said, wheeling around toward Dušan, "playing with guns and explosives. You imagine that will be the end, everything will be solved." He paused and then, sounding like a father talking to a ten-year-old child, said, "Where did you get the gelignite?"

"Just like old times, Father," Dušan said. "You want me to confess and expose all my friends. I don't mind this time, though. Maybe you will find this amusing. I got the gelignite and the rifles from the American's friend."

"You mean Tom?" Gaj asked. "The one in jail?"

"No. Not him. An Italian. Always in fancy uniform." He nodded toward Sean. "You stood next to him yesterday. The soldier with the umbrella."

Renzo. Sean swayed slightly and caught himself before falling. His knee throbbed. "Why should I believe you?" he asked, but knew all too well why he should. "Renzo is my friend. He saved my life."

Dušan shrugged his shoulders. "He had goods to sell. I gave him cash and took the guns. We needed them. The gelignite was a little bonus."

Amid thoughts of castor oil and beatings and explosions, a riddle surfaced in Sean's mind. *Why would a good soldier like Renzo sell weapons to a Croat, knowing he would likely use them to attack Italians, the people Renzo came here to defend?*

Dušan spoke again in a matter-of-fact voice. "He insisted we use these guns. Nothing else." The vicious tone quickly returned. "But back to business. I will kill you with one of the weapons he sold us. You shall inherit the Italian wind. For my brother." He nodded his head toward Gaj. "For the son he loved."

Gaj moved over toward Dušan. "Put the rifle down," he ordered. "He's unarmed. If you kill him, I will lose another son. And I cannot bear that."

"He's right," Sean said. Dušan's sneer displayed the full ugliness of revenge.

Gaj spun around. "Shut your mouth," he said. "I want so much to shoot you myself. You killed my son. You come here to my city, you and those arrogant legionnaires who marched in here with their guns and trucks, bringing along the scum from the Italian jails and sewers, and you all do anything you want. Tell everyone what to do. Kill us whenever you like. You assume because you come here with weapons Fiume belongs to you. You're wrong. The city belongs to the people who work here and who build things here."

Gaj grabbed the rifle out of Dušan's hand and laid it on the desk. "Listen to me, both of you. You are young and stupid. Like me, once. Now I am old and not much smarter, but I know this. Revenge earns no honor. Revenge is the path followed by the weak. A stronger man will walk away. Even run away, yes, if that's what it takes."

"You can't run away from justice," Dušan said. "Justice is what I want."

Gaj seemed to be growing taller, beyond what the small room allowed. "I did not fight in the Great War," he said. "I was too old, thank God. But I have seen much killing and many other things I didn't want to see, and I know what justice looks like. I dream about it. It's not killing. It's a place where anyone can live, where we share with everybody what we claim for ourselves. In peace and with respect." He let out a long, whistling breath. "If we must run away sometimes to get there, well then, we must run."

What a dream, Sean thought. *What a contrast to the Futurist ethos of war and aggression and destruction, or the nationalism and ethnic purification that Fascism urges, or the violence favored by Dušan.* He knew what Chesa would say.

Gaj laid a hand behind Sean's neck and pulled him close. "If I'm going to pass my dream on," he said, whispering, "I must have grandchildren." He breathed harder, forcing the words out and shoving them into Sean's brain. "And for grandchildren, I need my son to be free, alive, and out of jail."

Sean's leg felt on fire, but he dared not speak or move.

"I was blessed with two sons," Gaj said. "You robbed me of the younger one, but before you did, I drove his brother away. And for that, I can blame no one but myself. That is my shame and my sorrow. You and I, we have each sinned against my grandchildren. We have time to make amends."

"How can we?" Sean asked, his voice barely audible.

"Help me get my older son back."

"Very touching, Father," Dušan said. "A bit late, though. I'll tell you what. After I send the American to hell, I'll go shoot the Italian who sold me the weapons and dedicate the act to you and your dream. Before I kill him, I will say, 'Hey everyone, I'm doing this for my father. Not for the Croatians who were killed or maimed or whose houses and shops were destroyed or who rot in the stinking jail. It's for Gaj, my father, so he'll have something to tell his grandchildren when they suffer the same oppression. Although, he is not likely to see any grandchildren, because one son was butchered by an American he wanted to defend, and the other, yours truly, will be hunted by the police and the entire Italian Army and go down in a blaze of glory.' You see, that's how *fighters* pass their dreams on."

"You will not suffer alone for your deeds, my son," Gaj said.

"Perhaps not, but a price must be paid for killing my brother. The American and his Italian friend are responsible. They will make the first payment."

Sean's mind raced back to the moment he heard Renzo say the dead body was Veselko. He saw the gun in his hand where a paintbrush should have been. Then Gaj's voice brought him back to the room.

"I am responsible," Gaj said. A long silence unfolded. The three men exchanged glances. "I let him go that afternoon, to protect him. I thought it was dangerous for him, a healthy young man, to be around those lovely women. But I didn't know what was going through his mind. He never talked about things like freedom and independence, even when he heard me arguing with you, Dušan. He must have shared my thinking. I assumed so. But when I gave him the week off, he didn't go home and study or play or chase girls. He joined his brother to fight against the men who steal from us. The same ones I feed in my restaurant. And I didn't know him. I didn't know who he really was. How could that be? What kind of father does not listen to his son and find out what is on his mind?"

Sean reached down and rubbed the inflamed area of his leg. Honesty has a painful yet salutary sound, he thought. Why had he not been honest with Chesa? "The fault isn't yours, Gaj," he said. "I'm the one who pulled the trigger. I will go to the police and tell them what I did." He had a sudden vision of Chesa, smiling, holding a mirror up for him.

"Shut up, both of you," Dušan yelled. He lunged toward the table and grabbed the rifle.

"Please, lay the gun down, son. I beg you," Gaj said, his voice like a dull knife.

Sean took a step closer to Dušan. "I understand revenge, Dušan," he said. "I really do. I wanted vengeance myself. But the future—"

It was the last thing Sean remembered before he passed out.

III

When Sean came to, he felt water hit his face. He opened his eyes and found himself lying on his back on the floor. Dušan stood over him, shaking a wet hand, causing drops to fall on him. Gaj's voice called out from somewhere he couldn't see, "Do you need more water?"

"No," Dušan said, peering down at Sean. "He's coming around. He looks like shit, though. I don't know if your idea will work. I promise you, I am not carrying him."

Sean's hands probed his chest for any gunshot wound. None. He had survived so far. He tried to stand but his leg buckled under. He lifted himself to his hands and knees and began crawling away from Dušan and toward a door. From behind, he heard a laugh.

"Father, come see this," Dušan called out. "He's trying to crawl into the closet."

"Don't play games," Gaj said, coming out of the darkroom carrying a chair. "Here, help him up." He put the chair on the floor. "Sean," he said, "come back. We want to talk to you."

Sean scouted around for the real door. He had to get away. Only a few more feet.

"Stop," Dušan said. "Don't you want your photographs?"

Sean's knee gave out again and he slipped. A hand reached out for him, and he accepted the assistance. He rose and found himself eye to eye with Gaj.

"Please," Gaj said. "Come sit down. I have an idea for you and Dušan. It's foolish and risky, probably suicidal, so it should appeal to both of you."

Gaj's plan was based on his experience seventeen years earlier during the Zagreb riots. He and a small team of fellow Croats rescued five of their comrades taken prisoner by the Hungarian authorities. "Confusion is your friend," Gaj said. "It worked for us. Just keep your escape route open and watch behind you."

Good advice. It sounded like something Tom would say. Although if confusion were really his friend, Sean thought, he would no doubt be the most popular man in the world.

The plan was simple and well designed. Dušan had already given his assent while Sean lay passed out. Sean quickly agreed. The three worked well into the night on preparations. Dušan and Sean crafted documents and Gaj made prints of photographs. Shortly after two, Dušan excused himself and went off to recruit a few trusted friends to assist.

Sean would have liked to sleep, but Gaj wanted to talk. Despite the man's gentle words and his help with all the preparations, Sean was scared. Could he trust Gaj? The man had already thrown a meat cleaver in his direction earlier that evening, even before Sean provoked him with his ill-judged remarks. How should a man act around his son's killer? Sean had no idea.

IV

"You and your ambulance during the war," Gaj said. "Chesa talked about that all the time. So admirable, she thought. She used to tell me, 'Gaj, he has a beautiful soul. He drove out to the battlefields and rescued the wounded and risked his own life.' She was embarrassed she did not volunteer during the war. Perhaps that was just as well. I don't believe she would have made a good nurse. Do you? She was a bit too fastidious. Had to do everything her own way. Maybe I'm wrong. But she never forgave herself for not trying, and she worshipped you for what you did during the war. Does that sound too strong? You never told her you shot Veselko, did you?"

Sean looked down at his hands. He did not want to discuss Veselko with Gaj, even though no knives were nearby. Not for a moment did he presume that Gaj had lost any of his anger.

"I didn't think so," Gaj said. "She would have been cut to the heart, but she would have forgiven you even for that. Maybe you won't accept this, but it wasn't Sean the artist she loved. She loved the ambulance man who saved other people. The man who defended her on the Trsat stairs. She said, 'If he can ever see what I can see, then his painting will flow like wine.' I don't know. I never saw your art. You hide your light under a bushel, as they say. Anyway, I never cared for Futurism myself. Pretentious crap, in my opinion. You could do better."

This was almost worse than talking about Veselko. His Chesa, so beautiful, so full of love. Gone. He missed her more than anything. He doubted, however, she ever said anything so optimistic about his painting.

"You are a complicated man, Sean Reilly," Gaj said. "Chesa told me much. You didn't want to come to Fiume, but you did. You knew what soldiers were like, yet you got on the boat and came here, and you stayed here, and for one terrible night, you joined with them on a raid, surrendering all those reservations you had. You put on the uniform for the raid—oh, not literally the tunic and such, but you know what I mean—and became one of them. And you have found it hard to take the uniform off since that night, much as you may want to."

Sean gazed at a photograph on the wall. Four smiling faces, three men and one woman, seated around a table. The first dinner together at the restaurant, Chesa's hand resting on his.

"I joined them," Sean said. "Yes. Tom is my friend. Renzo is— was—a friend."

"And Tenente Guidici is a soldier. He fights for a new kind of army. One I'm afraid will bring more misery and destruction than either of us can imagine. I don't know what can stop an army like his."

"Nor do I," Sean said. He kept staring at the photograph.

"You drove an ambulance during the war. And you came to Fiume to advance the cause of Futurism. That took courage."

"I don't look at it that way, but I did have Futurist dreams in those days."

"And you have them yet?"

"I have dreams about the future. Better ones now."

"Better Futurist dreams or different?"

"Some ideas I take from Futurism. Modern machines, minimum wage, end to illiteracy, things like that but without all the aggression and the 'Italy above all' craziness. I like D'Annunzio's ideas about the League of Fiume, about the crusade for justice around the world, but in my dream, people don't resort to war to achieve the goal. And I like what you said about everyone being welcome as long as they work. Less aggression, more cooperation. End to nationalist hate."

"You put my poor words on the same plane as those of Marinetti and D'Annunzio? I suppose I should be honored." Gaj handed Sean the photographs he had come to the restaurant to get. "It is difficult to find all the answers in a single place, I agree. A narrow viewpoint leads to trouble."

Chesa understood that. *When you narrow the aperture, you get more information, but the photo starts to tell lies.* Knowing which aperture to use and when—that was critical.

"Precisely," Sean said. "Nothing has all the right answers. Not even the catechism. A friend of mine in Trieste once said Futurism was like the Catholic Church."

"Be careful. I am devout Catholic."

"No offense intended, but many good people have done terrible things because of what's in that catechism or, just as bad, what's not in there. I know. I was raised Catholic myself."

"I see." Gaj paused. Sean hoped he hadn't offended him. "I am glad you and my son will cooperate tomorrow," Gaj said at last. "It's time to let the dead bury the dead. But let me ask you this. What if these dreams you have today don't come true?"

So many of his dreams of a better world had included Chesa. They were never going to come true. But if he let go of them, he would be losing another part of her and the mirror, too, and what she and he were, together. All lost forever, beyond the power of any photographs to recapture.

"Do you believe in heaven, Gaj? I do, but it's probably not what you have in mind. It's not a place you go when you die. For me, heaven is where good dreams go when they don't get a chance to come true. They still exist. You can visit heaven and find those dreams. Not just your own. Anybody's good dreams. Someday, somebody will make use of them. The better the dreams are, the longer they will survive."

"And these dreams you have today, they are good dreams? Good enough to be found in your heaven?"

"I think so."

ONE HUNDRED & TWENTY

From SEAN REILLY'S JOURNAL

December 24, 1920. Gaj is quite a man. I killed his youngest son, yet as angry as he deserves to be, he gives me a gift no other could: Chesa's mirror. Chesa, by way of Gaj, showed me what a blithering idiot I've been for twisting my ambulance experience into a torment I needed to forget and move on from. Futurism preaches moving on, rejecting the past. But when has Futurism ever accomplished anything as worthwhile as saving lives in an ambulance?

Chesa's mirror is a relic I can cling to, along with her necklace and the photos that Gaj gave me.

Why do I abide in Fiume?

Because Chesa Rei is here. Was here.

ONE TWENTY-ONE

From INTERVIEW WITH DUŠAN KCLEŽA (1992)
[UNEDITED TRANSCRIPT]

SB: **The American brazenly visited your father, demanded some photographs, and accused your father of wanting to kill him. That must have infuriated your father.**

DK: It infuriated me, I'll tell you. Nobody can say shit like that about my father and get away with it, if I'm around. But old Gaj started to get preachy, as usual. People liked him for that, the way he could find a good moral lesson out of anything. He said something about how people would be remembered and why we do the things we do. Even I got caught up in it. My father had always told us—told me and Veselko—when we were kids, "You act for your children and their children." I didn't have any idea back then what he meant. Veselko probably did. He was smarter than me. But I see it now. It's taken me a while.

SB: It sounds like your father took the long view.

DK: You can say that, certainly. Really long view. He knew we would be free one day, even though he would not live to see it. "My dream," he used to say, "is for Fiume to be part of a strong, independent Croatia. No more Italian or Serb or Hungarian master. Sušak and Fiume will be united. No guards on the bridge." He knew troubles lay ahead, do you see? But he was determined to keep his dream alive and do what he could so that his grandchildren, or maybe their grandchildren, could see it come true. "If I let that idea go dark in my head," he used to say, "how will it ever shine for them?"

He really wanted grandkids. In the end he got them. Too bad he didn't get to see any of my grandkids, but you know what, I'm glad he died before the Second World War because that might have been too much for him. Those were really tough times. Bad things happened, and he might have given up hope. Where was I?

SB: Your father was talking about the future.

DK: Yes. I think he felt guilty about the way he had treated me and didn't want me to get hurt. The American ran off at the mouth until finally he passed out, crumpled up on the floor of the darkroom.

SB: Did you shoot him then?

DK: When he was passed out? Obviously, you never knew my father. Or me.

My father came up with a plan for us to work together. He was really something, my dad.

ONE TWENTY-TWO

December 25, 1920

ean peered out from behind the stone fence. Behind him, Dušan and four other men waited and shivered in the predawn cold. Each held a Russian rifle. The jail across the street was quiet. "Any sign of him?" Dušan whispered. "Maybe he's already inside. Or it could be his day off. You should get moving."

"No," Sean said. "Not until I see Tomaso go in the door. He has to be upstairs with Tom and me when you enter."

Sean went over the plan again in his head. As good as it sounded hours ago when Gaj laid it out, he feared the scheme had only a small chance of success, depending as it did on a high degree of coordination. They had no opportunity to rehearse and hardly any time to discuss. And these four men Dušan brought along were strangers to Sean. Could they be counted on in a fight? He twisted around to check them out. Silent and alert. Good. He looked at Dušan, the man who, a short while ago, pointed a rifle at him. Dušan gave him a reassuring nod. Gaj's magic had paired them, convincing Dušan that by working with Sean instead of killing him, the two could free a jail-full of prisoners, Croats as well as Tom. Sean hoped the magic worked even without Gaj's presence. Sean and Dušan had both insisted that Gaj retreat to safety in Sušak.

"There he goes," Dušan whispered. Tomaso marched deliberately to the stairs leading to the jail's front door and labored his way up. *Moving slowly this morning,* Sean noted. Something to be factored in. "Ready?" he said when Tomaso unlocked the door and entered the building. "I'll need eight minutes before you light the charge. No more, no less."

"The plan was five," Dušan said.

"You saw Tomaso. He's not moving too fast."

"I don't like changes to my father's plan. Don't try any tricks, understand?"

"I'm not changing any of the steps. Only the timing of the first one. I can't keep Tomaso out of your way unless he's upstairs with Tom."

"You got eight," Dušan said. He looked back at the others, who were checking their weapons. "But no more changes. They make me suspicious."

"Just give me eight minutes and then do everything else as we planned. I won't get out of there alive without your help at the right time, and I don't have any better ideas."

"Stick with my father's plan, and you won't need any better ideas."

It occurred to Sean how exposed he was. Behind him, armed and with a clear shot, stood a young man still angry about his brother's death. In front, guards at the jail would be quick to shoot Sean the minute they suspected what he wanted to do. Somewhere in the city roamed a band of thugs who attacked him twice before and were now crazy with rage over what he did to their comrade Luigi. Futurists despised him for the ambulance airplane crash. And Nina, the newspaper lady, blamed him for Chesa's death. Sean had succeeded in uniting hostile forces from all over the region, something the League of Fiume was never able to accomplish. He had created the League of Anti-Sean. Maybe the Serbs would come after him as well.

He took a long breath, inhaling the cold salty air sweeping in from the bay. Back during the war, he always observed a ritual before getting into his ambulance. Eyes closed, wrists behind his back, chest out, and face tilted to the sky. For fifteen seconds, regardless of rain, snow, sun, or falling shells, he thought only of the work he was about to do. Nothing was allowed to interfere. He commenced the routine now, for the first time since the war. Fifteen seconds of quiet concentration. Then he stepped out from behind the stone wall and crossed the street.

When he reached the heavy front door, he discovered to his horror it was locked. Panic hit him like one of the kicks from Luigi and his friends. He spun around, wildly searching for Dušan, but quickly caught himself and turned back. *Don't give them away, in case anyone is looking.* He pounded on the door, again and again. He regretted not clarifying with Dušan that the eight minutes would commence *after* he went inside. A voice behind the door called out, "Too early. Come back later."

"Open the door," Sean shouted. "Tenente Guidici sent me with a message from the Command. Open up." He hoped Renzo was not inside.

He heard no sound from the other side of the door. Seconds went by. He stopped breathing. How many of those eight minutes remained?

A series of clicks and scraping metal came from inside the door. To his relief, the door creaked open a tiny bit. He leaned into the door and pushed it open all the way. The guard, a young, skinny man, stumbled backward.

Sean positioned himself between the guard and the door and set to work distracting the young man so the door did not get relocked. "Two more army divisions arrived at Trieste," he said, pumping a fist to his chest. "With artillery regiments. They could be here by tonight, maybe late this afternoon."

The young man looked stunned. "Is that true? You don't think they would shoot at us, do you?"

"They might." Sean strutted forward in the direction of the front desk, staying between the guard and the door. The guard retreated, having no choice. "If they do, we'll need good men like you out on those front lines to defend the city. Not everyone can face the deadly fire and suffer agonizing death to protect the honor of Fiume. Although of course, we are all anxious to." He stopped, concerned the boy might run around him and lock the doors out of fear of invading hordes. "But not to worry yet," he added. "Like you, I don't believe they want to fight us. Now, I need to see the prisoner Tom Delancy. Please ask Tomaso to escort me up there immediately."

The guard disappeared. A few minutes later, he returned wearing a bright smile. "Tomaso's busy with a little disturbance, so I'll take you to Mr. Delancy. Since you are from the Command."

They walked quickly through the familiar corridor. Cells on either side were crammed with Croatian prisoners. A bilious taste entered Sean's mouth. Tomaso was not behaving the way the plan anticipated he would. The clock, in contrast, was doing its job with lethal efficiency, counting off the remaining minutes until the next part of the plan commenced. He checked his watch. Three minutes left. Unless the countdown didn't start until he went inside the front door, in which case he had five minutes, maybe six. Either way, he needed to get Tomaso up to Tom's cell fast. But Tomaso was not likely to leave off whatever crisis he was dealing with to come and say hello. Sean needed an emergency serious enough to drag the big fellow upstairs in time.

When they reached the door to Tom's suite, the young guard pulled out his keys and began fumbling with them. Sean grabbed them and put the correct one in the door himself. He flung the door open, and shouted, "Tom Delancy, you cheating, murdering, Irish bastard," in his loudest and angriest voice. "Where are you?"

Tom pushed his chair from the breakfast table and stood up. "What the hell?" he said. Sean reached inside his coat and pulled out a gun, the Bodeo he used on the raid and never returned. He pointed it at Tom and screamed, loud enough for Tomaso to hear no matter where in the jail he might be, "Tom, you fucked my woman and killed her. I'm going to kill you."

Tom took a step in Sean's direction but froze as Sean raised the gun. "Are you crazy?" Tom said. "Honest, I ain't seen her in weeks. You know I'm stuck in here. How could I—"

"Shut up. You did it." The young guard stood frozen in place. Apparently, Sean had to spell out for him what to do. "Nobody is going to save you, Tom. Not even Tomaso." The young man still didn't move. He was slow. Or terrified. "Even if Tomaso was right here in the room. Two of you against me." At that, the guard fled down the stairs.

"You can't be serious," Tom said.

Sean put a finger to his lips and whispered, "When Tomaso gets here, we need to be fighting. Don't ask. Follow my lead. You're getting out."

"You're not going to hurt Tomaso," Tom said.

"No. You're going to take my gun. Come over here. You need to be visible when he comes through the door. I want him to see you in peril."

"That wasn't a question." Tom shook his head. "I'm telling you. It's not even a warning. Just a fact. I don't figure you could hurt him even if you shot him."

"I have no intention of trying to hurt him. All I want to do is keep him here long enough for the rest of the escape plan to get started. He's the only guy here capable of screwing things up. Well, except me."

Tom tilted his head to one side, his face white and pasty. "You better start shouting again because I hear footsteps. I sure hope you know what you're doing."

Sean put the gun inside the waistband of his pants. The footsteps grew louder. At last, plans and dreams and poetry and manifestos were about to square off with grim reality and a really big guard. "I'm going to kill you with my bare hands," Sean screamed. He threw himself at Tom, who stepped backward, letting Sean fall to the floor.

"Sorry," Tom whispered. "Couldn't help it." He picked Sean up. In a loud voice he yelled, "Yeah, you little *cabrón*," and landed a jab on the side of Sean's mouth. "I fucked her. So what? You couldn't do nothing for her."

Blood trickled from Sean's lips. He swung at Tom, a long roundhouse arc Tom patiently allowed to land. The punch caught him on the jaw. Tom shook his head sadly. "Artist," he muttered. Sean waited for Tomaso to step into the room and then kneed Tom in the groin.

Tom crumpled to the ground and Sean dove on top of him. He wrapped both hands around Tom's neck, pushing down on his throat. Sean heard Tomaso yell, "Hey. Get off him."

Tom broke the chokehold with a quick left hand to Sean's nose, starting a stream of blood. Sean pulled back his right arm for another long punch, but the arm felt paralyzed for a second, suspended in the air like it was frozen. His arm then started moving in the wrong direction, slowly at first, followed by an agonizing jerk up and across his back. The force of the jerk lifted him off Tom and into the air for a quick second, before dropping him to the floor.

"I thought you could fight," Tomaso said, staring at Tom and sounding more puzzled than contemptuous.

Tom struggled to his feet. "I didn't reckon nothing like that from a friend. You can't trust friends these days." Sean scrambled to sit up.

After an awkward pause, Tomaso seemed ready to walk out, leaving Tom and Sean to settle the matter themselves. Where was the damn explosion? Did Dušan not know how to tell time?

Sean climbed to his feet slowly, feeling lightheaded. He forced himself to focus on one thing. Whatever happened next, he needed to keep Tomaso on this floor.

Mustering what strength he had left, he said to Tomaso, "You keep out of it. It's him I came here to fight. I'll deal with you afterward if you want a piece of me—" Sean never saw the fist that knocked him down. He was on the floor, dazed but conscious, when the blast shook the entire jail.

Tomaso buckled, stepping backward and forward. Tom did a similar dance but he regained his balance faster, and by the time Tomaso recovered, Tom had the gun pointed at him. He had taken it without Sean's ever noticing.

Sean stood up, stumbled to the door behind Tomaso, and descended the stairs as fast as he could. The grogginess from Tomaso's punch slowly wore off. He found Dušan standing by the now-empty cells. "Is everybody out? Guards accounted for?"

"Yeah. All done. Like my father said. It was easy. These guards didn't know what was going on. We put them in cells in the other wing."

"You got their uniforms? And the face masks?"

"Of course. They're up front, near the door. We got their rifles, too. Do something for your nose before you bleed all over the mask. Where's your friend and the big guy?"

"Upstairs. Tom has a gun on him, but even so, Tomaso scares the shit out of me. I don't want to bring him down here until everybody is in position, and we're ready to march out the door."

"Yeah, all right." Dušan wore a smile. "Relax. Everything is working. We got a good plan. Just follow it." He ran on ahead, shouting orders, herding the men to the front.

Dušan and his men put on guard uniforms, and each held a black balaclava in his hands along with an M91 rifle taken from the guard's arsenal. Dušan pointed to a small pile of clothes on the bench by the door. Sean stared at it. Several seconds went by.

"What's wrong?" Dušan asked. "Put the fucking uniform on and get moving."

"I just . . . Never mind." He donned the pants and tunic and picked up a rifle. Tom was not going to act on any signal other than Sean's. That meant another trip up the stairs.

Dušan opened the front door a crack, peeked out, and shut it quickly. "Lots of people out there," he said. Sean nodded and headed to the stairs. "You got two minutes," Dušan said.

The plan and its ruthless timetable. Sean opened the door to the stairs and started the long climb. *Two minutes. Eight minutes. Everything on schedule.* But life doesn't always happen on a schedule. If it did, he would have scheduled intercepting Chesa before she went to her darkroom. Losing his balance momentarily, he grabbed with his right hand for the rail to steady himself, which made his shoulder come alive with a bolt of pain. He let go and fell.

Above him, the door opened. Before he could get to his feet, he saw the hulking figure of Tomaso filling the doorway, hands at his sides. The big man did not look happy. He moved down the stairs toward Sean.

"Tom? Are you there?" Tomaso moved faster. "Tom?"

"I'm here," came Tom's voice from somewhere behind Tomaso. "You better get down the stairs before you hurt yourself. Tomaso, hold up a minute, and let Sean get out of the way." Tomaso halted. His expression did not improve.

Grateful not to have to climb anymore, and relieved not to be tossed by the menacing Tomaso down the few steps he had climbed already, Sean hurried out into the front desk area where he joined Dušan and the others. "Here they come," he said.

"Are you all right?" Dušan asked. He and the others had donned their balaclavas, pulled down to expose only their eyes.

The stairway door banged open, and a large fist pinned it to the wall. "Shit," Dušan said in a low voice, scanning Tomaso up and down. "I hope my father knew what he was talking about."

The group filed out the front door of the jail and down the steps to the street. Tomaso led, followed by Tom and the Croatian prisoners. Dušan and his four friends patrolled the sides of the group along with Sean, all wearing masks and carrying their rifles as Tom had shown them.

Smoke poured out of the courthouse building adjacent to the jail. Firemen struggled to get through the crowd gathering in the street. Armed men swarmed around, yelling out orders and curses.

"Look at all these people," one of the newly freed prisoners whispered. "You guys blew up the building next to the jail and brought everyone here. Whose smart idea was that?"

"Shut up," Dušan said. "Fool, if all these police and soldiers are next door, they won't be in our way when we go the opposite direction, will they?"

A truck stopped in front of them. Out climbed an officer. A squad of legionnaires scrambled from the back and assembled to his right.

The officer, who bore captain's stripes, inspected the prisoners and their guards. Dušan fingered the trigger of his weapon and signaled the others to remain silent.

Sean stared at the captain and felt sick. Little more than an arm's length away stood the man he had kissed and started to undress at Casa Piacere.

The captain stopped in front of the big man. "Tomaso, what the devil is going on here? Where are you going with these prisoners?"

This, Gaj had warned, would be the most dangerous part of the escape. If Tomaso did not cooperate here, they would need to shoot their way out, and the odds of surviving such a fight with a heavily armed group of legionnaires were not good.

Tomaso broke the silence. "Taking these prisoners to the barracks down by the canal so they don't get away."

The captain glanced behind Tomaso to the jail. "Why? Was the jail damaged? From what I can see, only the court building got blown up."

Dušan moved his finger to the safety but did not release it. "Captain," called out one of the legionnaires. "We're ready to move out."

"Just a minute, Sergeant," the captain said. He studied Dušan and Sean. "Why are these men in masks? And where is Farrelli? How come he's not leading the move?"

Sean felt sweat running down his back. He didn't want to risk letting the captain hear his voice, but Dušan's accent was worse, and they needed to get past the captain and keep moving. "From the Command," Sean said through the mask. His words came out slurred, muffled by the mask.

The captain took two steps over toward Sean and inspected his headgear. "What the hell happened to you?" He shifted his gaze to the ill-fitting uniform. "I don't know what the fuck he said, so will one of you please explain why masked men are escorting this scum out of a secure jail?" The captain cocked his head and moved over to Dušan. "You. Speak up."

"They're from the Command," Tomaso said. "Renzo sent them. Farrelli's inside but he's hurt. Things got a little rough in there."

The captain looked at the damaged courthouse and then to Sean. He stepped back to face Tomaso. "So I see. All right, Tomaso, carry on. Need some help? I can spare a couple of men."

Sean kept picturing the captain in that dress. *Piacere. No, I don't need anything you have to offer, sir. A great artist does what he must. I told you that back at Madam Christina's.*

"We're good," Tomaso said. "They ain't stupid enough to try anything now."

The captain turned to his squad and directed them to the courthouse.

With Tomaso in the lead, the group marched on. They turned right at the corner and headed south past St. Vitus Church. "We're just about home," Dušan said, sounding jubilant. "A couple more blocks and we're on the boat." He patted his rifle affectionately.

The street narrowed until it was little more than a lane. Shadows draped over its entire width, but somehow a glare of morning sun reflected off the glass windows of the shops right into their eyes. Dušan looked back at the man behind him. "Until last night I didn't even know my father owned a boat." He bumped into the man ahead of him. "Look out. Why is everyone stopping?"

Four similarly masked men, one of them even larger than Tomaso, blocked the lane. Sean recognized them right away: Ugo and his buddies. Each of them wore a holster in which rested a large pistol. Ugo also carried a rifle, one of the Russian Mosin-Nagants. "Jail scum, huh?" Ugo said. "Where you boys going?"

No one spoke. Sean was afraid his voice would be instantly recognized, and he knew what to expect at their hands. Neither Dušan nor the other masked Croatians could risk speaking. That left Tomaso. He had cooperated so far, but how much longer could he be counted on? Sean glanced at Tom and saw him staring at the revolver he returned to Sean before they left the jail. Tom had warned him before about using a firearm. In a battle with experienced men, Sean was certain to lose. He might as well have been carrying a paintbrush instead of a gun. Dušan's cocky attitude was gone. He looked less like a guard than an uncomfortable, fidgeting prisoner.

"Get out of our way," Tomaso said finally, in the tone of one who tells rather than asks and who seldom saw the need to repeat himself.

Ugo moved forward and stood face to face with Tomaso, like two huge wrestlers about to contest. "You're Tomaso, from the jail."

Tomaso nodded.

"Where you going with them?" Ugo pointed toward the prisoners.

Tomaso moved to his left slightly, enough to block Ugo's view, causing the latter to retreat a half step. "To the pier. Orders are to put them on a boat and send them back to Sušak."

Ugo seemed to think that was funny. "You can give them to us," he said. "We'll take care of them." He looked over his shoulder." We got orders, too. Don't we?"

Sean could see the canal from where he stood, one short block away to the east. A hard gust of wind made him close his eyes for a second. When he opened them, he turned to glance at Tom, carelessly. Tom lowered his head quickly, but too late. Ugo spotted Tom, and he closed in.

Tomaso stepped with him, moving backward, a half-second too late. "The American," Ugo said. "Boys, look who they got. It's the American from the jail. Tell you what, Tomaso. You can keep the Croats. Put them in a boat, drown 'em, I don't care. We're taking Yankee boy. I got questions to ask him."

Sean tried to get in front of Tom, but Tomaso got there first. Ugo scowled at Tomaso, standing eye to eye as if looking in a mirror, and twisted around to face Sean. "This one's bleeding all over himself," Ugo said. "That don't look right." He squared up against Sean. "What's your name?"

Before Sean could react, Ugo ripped the mask from his face. "The other one," Ugo said with glee. "We're taking him, too. The rest of you can get the fuck out of here."

Sean raised his rifle, but his movements seemed frozen in contrast to the tumult around him. Ugo swung in the direction of his face but before the punch could land Tomaso struck Ugo with a crushing left fist, staggering him backward; one of Ugo's men fired his gun at Tomaso; Tom grabbed Sean's revolver and pushed him down while firing at the shooter; Dušan emptied his rifle at another of Ugo's men; Tom picked off a third who was trying to get his gun out of its holster. Silence followed. Ugo started to get to his feet. Tom put a bullet in the center of his forehead.

Sean stood up and tried to make sense of what had happened. Five men lay on the ground. Marinetti used to say that poetry was a violent attack on unknown forces. There on a little street in Fiume near the canal, the punch-and-slap fantasy of Futurism gave way to dead bodies. Sean saw no poetry in the carnage, no beauty. He heard Tom shouting his name.

"Help me with Tomaso," Tom ordered. "Wake the fuck up!" Tom stepped over Ugo's body without looking down. "Dušan, you and your buddies make sure those guys don't get up. Move the bodies someplace where they can't be seen. Then get out of here."

Sean squatted alongside Tomaso and found his wound. Blood rushed out of his abdomen. "He's hit pretty bad," Sean said. "He needs help right away." A few meters behind them, shots rang out.

"We're going to get help for him," Tom said. "Hang in there, Tomaso, you tough old bastard. Me and Sean ain't leaving you."

Sean stood up. "Tom," he hissed, "we have got to get out of here. Every legionnaire in the city is going to be looking for us, and probably half the Italian Army too."

"Listen to me," Tom said in a level voice, without taking his eyes off Tomaso. "We are not leaving him. Understand? Now, go steal a truck or a cart. Move."

Sean commandeered a battered truck from a surprised local

painter and backed it into the tiny lane. The bodies of the dead men were already gone. Dušan and the others had vanished as well. Sean didn't get to say anything to Dušan. Perhaps that was best. What would he say? Maybe just this: your father's plan was perfect.

The truck bed was cluttered with old clothes, paint cans and brushes, a tarpaulin, and a couple of ladders. Sean pulled out everything save for the clothes, which he spread out on the floor of the truck bed. Tom positioned himself by Tomaso's head and reached under the groaning man for leverage to pick him up. "Look out," Sean said, "you'll kill him that way." Tom let go.

"Do like I tell you," Sean said. "Take the tarp and wrap it around the ladders like a stretcher." While Tom set to work, he examined Tomaso's wound again. Grabbing the cleanest of the discarded clothing, he pressed it on the bleeding spot. "Hold the rag here while we get you on the truck," Sean said. "You're going to be fine."

Tom brought the improvised stretcher over and laid it alongside the injured man. "When I raise him," Sean said, "put the stretcher under his back. Ready?" He reached over and rolled Tomaso onto his side. Tomaso roared out in pain but did not resist, much to Sean's relief. Sean had no wish to receive another punch from Tomaso, even given the man's injured state. Tom shoved the stretcher under his back. Sean gently let Tomaso down, drawing a loud groan. Sean checked the wound, and then he and Tom hoisted the stretcher into the truck. Tom started to climb into the truck's cab, but Sean told him to ride in the back with Tomaso and keep the cloth on the wound.

It occurred to Sean, as he eased into the driver's seat, that he was about to drive an ambulance for the first time since the war. He put the truck in gear, thinking: *this time I'm in uniform.*

A few minutes later he stopped to pick up the doctor, the same one who operated on Tom after the raid, and then drove to the hospital by the barracks. They rode in silence, Tom now in the front seat and the doctor in the back with Tomaso. Legionnaires ran by them in all directions. "You did good with the stretcher," Tom said. "I guess you had lots of practice with stuff like this in the war."

"I did. I certainly did," Sean said. "You did pretty good yourself. I don't know what would have happened if you and the others hadn't finished those guys off. How did you usually deal with prisoners in your years of fighting?"

"I never took any prisoners," Tom said, looking out the window.

ONE TWENTY-THREE

From *Memories of a Fascist in Fiume*
by Tenente Lorenzo Guidici

The military attack on Fiume commenced the day before Christmas. At my direction, the legionnaires set up roadblocks in perfect positions, but we had too few men to make a proper defense of the entire city. I am proud to say that despite our limitations no breakthrough occurred in the sector where I was assigned, and casualties were kept to a minimum. The Arditi I brought in under cover through the carefully constructed defile in the hills fought bravely, deterring widespread attacks on Italian civilians. The fighting was over in less than a week, after which I returned to Milan, where I could openly and proudly carry out Fascist activities and share in the Party's success.

D'Annunzio soon returned to the mainland, but not as a conquering hero. My efforts in Fiume contributed to that. As everyone knows, the *Comandante* left Fiume and retreated quietly to a villa up by Lake Garda, while Mussolini stepped forward and led our Fascist Party to victory and control of the government. Three years after D'Annunzio's left Fiume, the Duce forced the Jugoslavs to recognize Italy's historic claim to the city. Fiume was finally annexed to our country by the actions of a strong leader.

I never saw Ugo or the others again. I heard reports they were butchered by a gang of angry Croats, but their bodies were never found. Such vicious lawlessness is unfortunately to be expected where order has not been imposed.

I've lost contact with my American friends. Tom Delancy seems to have disappeared around the time of the Christmas fighting. More is known about Sean Reilly, and it confirms all the good qualities I had always admired in him. It seems that some treacherous Croats were roaming the Governor's Palace during the last days of the fighting, intent on mayhem. They killed Wickson and looted the entire Fiume treasury. One can only imagine what torment they put him through to get him to open the safe. While several of them escaped with the money, the rest were looking to murder *Comandante* D'Annunzio when Sean burst into the Palace and intercepted them. I am told he held them off long enough for the Arditi guards to arrive and save the day.

I truly miss those Americans. While some of my actions may seem shocking, even barbarous, everything I did was in the best interest of my country. I tried to shield my friends to the maximum extent possible. Fiume was a place for men of action, however, and sometimes dreamers get hurt.

Finally, it is impossible to recall those months in Fiume without mentioning Chesa Rei. The tragedy of her death at the hands of those Croats cannot dim the memory of her beauty and brilliance. After the Duce's rise to power, I was able to access the government's file on her. The file contained the materials she had sent from Fiume during the occupation. As I had feared, her intelligence was excellent. Among other things, she had supplied photographs and descriptions of barracks, ammunition depots, and locations vulnerable to attacks. Worse, she captured on film some ill-advised activities by individuals that our enemies would no doubt have used against us. Fortunately, the government minister whose duty it was in 1920 to receive and analyze the materials was a dotard who dismissed outright the idea that any intelligence from a woman was worth looking at. He buried them in a file, where they sat unused. For the good of Italy, I destroyed them all prior to my unjust arrest.

Fiume will forever stand as a lodestar for Italy. Its legacy is how it showed the world that, after years of submitting passively to internal chaos and the whims of other Western powers, our nation was ready to rise up and take by force what was rightfully ours. *Comandante* D'Annunzio demonstrated what could be done when the people's will was properly harnessed. Following that example, Italy has prospered in the ensuing years under the Duce's strong rule. Italy will continue to rise, as it must. The force of our race that forged a glorious empire in ancient times will shake the earth with its thunder once again.

ONE TWENTY-FOUR

December 26, 1920

I

Sean returned to the barracks hospital early the next morning, dressed in civilian clothes. Tom had spent the night watching over Tomaso and somehow managed to acquire pieces of a legionnaire uniform. Sean found it curious that Tom, lately incarcerated in the city jail, had not been challenged by any of the legionnaires who came into the hospital. But then again, Tom was not a man one lightly challenged, and besides, the legionnaires seemed more concerned about the fast-approaching armed forces. Tomaso was in stable condition, Tom reported. Sean's shoulder hurt simply thinking about him.

"He saved our lives twice during the escape," Sean said, "when he could so easily have handed us over to the captain or Ugo. Why?"

Tom stretched out his arms and leaned his head back, mouth open in a drawn-out yawn before answering. "If you'd ever been a soldier, I wouldn't need to explain it to you," he said. "And since you wasn't, no amount of explaining will ever make sense to you."

Sean told Tom he was going up to the gap in the hills he had spotted from the airplane and the castle. "It must be important. I still can't figure out why," he admitted. "But I'm going there."

Tom demanded to see the photographs. After studying them for a couple of minutes, he tapped the one on top with a stubby forefinger and returned the stack to him. "I know."

Sean couldn't imagine what Tom could tell from such a short look at the photos.

"It's a defile, the kind military use. Somebody's gonna come through it in numbers, looking for a fight and wanting to surprise people."

"The Italian Army?"

"Nah, not them. The defile ain't big enough, and anyway, you would've seen them massing behind it, pulling up their trucks and big guns. This is for a small stealth force, maybe forty or fifty tops."

"Then who? Serbs?"

"Probably not. They'd be there in greater numbers, too, if they wanted to come in and mix things up with all the other fights going on. They don't. The Serbs are gonna stand back and let Italians shoot each other. This trail is for somebody to sneak in and raise hell. It's an Arditi style maneuver, but Arditi are not gonna sneak in to fight legionnaires. A lot of the legionnaires here are former Arditi, and they won't fire on each other. No, this is a small company of guys coming to do some dirty work. Who their targets are, I don't know. You're the smart one. You tell me."

Sean harbored no illusions about being the smart one. The mystery of the defile had eluded him for over a year. A small, stealthy force was coming to Fiume in the middle of a big fight with the army, and they would not attack legionnaires. What did they intend to do?

When Nina talked to him in the church before their conversation got nasty, she mentioned that Mussolini and his Fascists were stirring up Slavs to make trouble for the weak government in Rome. Fiume was the perfect place for such trouble. That treaty with the Jugoslavs looked like a government success. The last thing the Fascists wanted to see was a strong show of military force followed by a quiet D'Annunzio exit.

But the legionnaires defending D'Annunzio were Italians, for the most part. That brought Sean back to the riddle that stumped him in Gaj's darkroom. The brutal violence of Luigi and those others in Renzo's squad inflamed Dušan and other Croats, but at the same time Renzo sold weapons to Dušan that Dušan used against Italian targets.

That was the whole point, Sean understood now. Renzo's goal was not to protect Italians. He *wanted* lots of Italian casualties, with blood on Croat hands. And if this force about to pour through the defile was coming to torch the Croatian community, it would start an ugly battle, Italians versus Croats, from which Rome couldn't back down. What if something happened to D'Annunzio in the ensuing melee? Kochnitzky had hinted the *Comandante* was not safe. In that case, the treaty would no doubt be scrapped, and the resulting turmoil would provide an excuse for a Fascist coup back in Rome.

"They're going to massacre Croats," Sean said. "I've got to stop them."

Tom grabbed the photographs out of his hands. "You need to find yourself a safe hole to crawl into and stay there for the next week or two. Things are gonna get rough. There'll be serious fighting here."

Sean didn't answer. His brain was heated with thoughts about the impending slaughter.

"Look, you did a good thing yesterday," Tom said, "getting me and them other guys out of the jail. It was a smart trick. But the time for tricks is over."

"Maybe so," Sean said. "But I made up my mind last night when I talked with Gaj. I have to act. Lots of people will get hurt."

"You're not gonna stop them with a paintbrush and a couple of pictures," Tom said. "Two or three well-placed machine guns on either side of this," he pointed to a spot on the photo, "and nobody will get through. Let's go. You can guide me to the right spot. Then get out of here."

After making sure Tomaso was comfortable, they borrowed a truck. Tom got behind the wheel. He drove like a Brooklyn cabbie, one of the jobs he had attempted unsuccessfully in between fighting campaigns. Tom said they needed machine guns and a few men to fire them, and he knew where to find both. He parked the truck on a street at the western edge of the city and disappeared into a throng of armed men. Sean limped after him. By the time he caught up, Tom was deep in conversation with a lieutenant and pointing into the hills. Large crates were stacked high blocking the width of the street. Four machine guns lay on the ground nearby.

"Captain Keller came by here yesterday," the lieutenant said, "and told us to look out for enemy forces coming from the direction of those hills you pointed at. But Colonel Albertini insists we all stay here. He says he's not taking military orders from a character who sleeps in trees. The colonel is sure the whole Italian Army is coming up this street. It's crazy, but that's what your friend Renzo assured him."

Tom shook his head. "One machine gun and five good men with rifles could hold this position. And anyway, the main thrust will come on the road south of here. Let me talk to your colonel."

"Tom, it's hopeless," the lieutenant said sadly. "His mind is made up. What's more, he's scared. He doesn't want to have to come running down a hill like he did at Caporetto. There's nothing you can do."

Tom insisted on trying and told Sean to back him up. Sean had no idea what help he could give, but he followed along. Perhaps nothing was hopeless.

They found Colonel Albertini staring out defiantly at an empty street beyond the barricade. Tom respectfully requested a word. The colonel glowered. "Speak up," he demanded. "You look familiar. Name?"

"Thomas Delancy, sir. I had the honor of serving under you in the IV Corps during the war. This man," he nodded at Sean, "is a top aide from the Command."

The colonel gave Tom a hard look. "Yes, I recognize you. In jail for aiding the Croats who attacked the barracks. How did you escape?" He turned to the man at his left. "Sergeant. Two men."

Sean started to speak, but Tom cut him off. "Colonel, you are well informed. As always, sir. But I can now reveal, and Mr. Reilly will confirm, the Command put me there to listen to the Croat prisoners talk about their plans. I can't even begin to tell you, sir, how hard it was, pretending to be a prisoner, listening to that scum whining. But

I learned many important things."

"It's all true, Colonel," Sean said. "Absolutely."

The sergeant appeared at the colonel's side, trailed by two legionnaires.

The colonel remained fixed on Tom. "Why should I believe you? Do you recall the penalty for escape in wartime? I should have you shot."

"Colonel, the Command thought you might be up there in those hills. They sent me to warn you about the enemy's plan to break through right up this street. But I see you already figured that out. A brilliant military move, if I may say so, sir."

Sean nodded gravely. "Brilliant. Yes."

"Colonel?" the sergeant said.

"Stand down, Sergeant," the colonel said, "and keep quiet." To Tom, he said, "Tell me more about the attack."

"The Serb army, guided by a group of those traitorous Croats, plans to attack here, at the same time the Italian Army moves on the main road by the water. Another small force will attack from the north, over in the hills. A diversion, making a lot of noise to get you to expose your men. The enemy underestimates you, Colonel."

"Tragic miscalculation," Sean said. "Fortunately, the *Comandante* does not make the same mistake."

"Right through this street?" the colonel said. He cleared his throat with a long cough. "I thought so. The Command would put me in the path of the greatest danger. How many?"

"Could be a whole brigade. Perhaps more." Tom convinced the colonel to set up his command headquarters ten blocks east, in a piazza by a church. "That area has a commanding view, sir. From there you can keep us all under your watch and guidance."

"Machine gunner, weren't you, Delancy? A decent one, as I remember, for an American. You can help man those guns here. Get moving. I will send instructions from my command post." He glanced once more at the street and called for his car.

"Very brave, Colonel," Tom said. "Putting yourself at risk if that diversion in the hills breaks through."

The colonel brooded. He told Tom to take a few men and one of those machine guns to stake out a defensive position in the hills. "Hold until you are relieved. Understand?"

"I'm sure the *Comandante* would agree," Sean said and started to move out. But Tom hadn't finished.

"Yes sir," Tom said. "And sir, let me assure you if they get past us, it is because we, the few men, are all dead. We will fight to our last heartbeat to keep those screaming savages from overrunning your headquarters."

The colonel climbed into the car and sat for a moment eyeing the hills. He thrust out his lower lip. "Delancy, you had better take several of those guns. And as many men as you need. The lieutenant can manage here."

Sean stood in awe.

When the colonel disappeared, Tom picked three men and two machine guns, and settled them in the back of the truck. He again suggested Sean make his exit.

"Shut up and get in," Sean said. "I'll drive you up there, but I need the truck."

Sean drove hard through the streets, past ramshackle houses and untended fields and groves of leafless ash trees. The road ended at the edge of a meadow. Tom checked the photographs and looked up. "To the right, about forty-five degrees, and then north." Sean gunned the truck into the grassy field.

Driving triggered memories. Like in the war, the ruts and craters in the overgrown field threatened to jerk the steering wheel from his grip. Mud caked on the tires and weakened traction. Rocks and boulders, hidden in the grass yet big enough to upset the truck, had to be dodged. The only thing missing here was artillery shelling. He forced the truck to its maximum speed and licked his lips. He felt sorry for the men in the back. At least they weren't wounded.

"Like Tre Monti," Tom said.

Sean nodded. "Except today I'm taking you to the front, instead of away from it. Try not to get shot, will you? I can't be rescuing you all the time."

Sean brought the truck to a halt at the edge of a creek. "This is as far as I can go," he said. The men in the back got out and unloaded the guns. "I got a question for you," Sean said as Tom climbed out. "When we pretended to fight yesterday in front of Tomaso, you called me a '*cabrón*.' What the hell is that?"

Tom laughed. "Probably better you don't know. But let me warn you. If you're in Mexico, don't ever call somebody a *cabrón* unless you learn to fight a whole lot better than you did yesterday."

II

The truck ran out of petrol a half kilometer from the Governor's Palace. Sean ran the rest of the way, carrying the rifle and pistol Tom had taken from Ugo. The sound of machine guns and small arms firing gave notice of the army's advance. A huge gray battleship, larger than any ship he had ever seen in the Fiume harbor, lay at anchor offshore, menacing the city with its long guns. One of those guns appeared to be pointed directly at the Governor's Palace. *Nothing good came from the sea.* He wondered whether D'Annunzio even knew about the battleship. The damage that ship could do to the Palace—and the city—was unthinkable.

Tom had said long ago if he shot enough bad guys, that should make the world better, and he would rely on smart guys like Sean to tell him who the bad ones were. Sean left Tom in the hills with assurances that anybody trying to get through the defile was a bad one. Tom's machine guns might or might not lead to a better world, but they would prevent those would-be attackers from making the current one a whole lot worse.

Renzo's hooligans were dead, and his invading Arditi would not get past Tom, but Renzo was certainly capable of wreaking havoc by himself. As Tom had pointed out, the man did not quit. Sean needed to warn the *Comandante* and talk him out of this futile battle with the Italian military.

A few sulking legionnaires guarded the portico at the front of the Palace. They leaned on sandbags piled six feet high and seemed more interested in trading rumors about the approaching forces than in protecting the occupants of the building behind them. He hurried through to the front door without challenge. Once inside, he ran up the stairs to the sunlit atrium.

Papers and cigarette butts lay scattered among greasy plates of half-eaten meals and wine bottles spilling their contents into puddles on the marble floor. Men in military garb ran back and forth, oblivious to the mess and each other. No one tried to intercept Sean this time. He ran toward Wickson's office; Sean wanted to settle with him before going to see D'Annunzio. Wickson's door was closed but not locked. When Sean barged in, he found Wickson lying on the floor in front of an open and emptied safe, an expanding pool of blood by his head. Sean clutched the rifle tightly and hoped he wasn't too late for the *Comandante*.

He opened the unguarded doors to D'Annunzio's suite and crept through the anteroom. Two steps from the arched entrance to the main room, he heard Renzo's voice.

"You have served Italy in many ways, *Comandante*," Renzo said. "Consider this as one more sacrifice you are called on to make. In those endless speeches of yours, you often boasted you would gladly die defending Fiume. Now you are going to get your wish. Except your death will be for the glory of Italy instead of Fiume or that ridiculous League. Not so bad, is it?"

"Drop your gun, Tenente," said D'Annunzio. "That's an order. Fiume needs its *Comandante*."

"Sorry. Italy needs you, too, but in a different way. Your passing will be an inspiration to the nation. All over Italy, people will mourn your death at the hands of those treacherous Croats. When they rise against the prime minister and his broken government, they will demand Mussolini step in and take charge to avenge your assassination. You were brilliant in the war, *Comandante*, but here in Fiume, you lost sight of who you needed to fight for. Instead of Italy, you wanted to lead the world's rabble. So we Fascists will restore you to your purpose, posthumously. Imagine. You will be a hero forever in the history books of Italy."

"Quite a plan," Sean said. He stepped into the inner room. The *Comandante* and Renzo stood on the far side, near the piano, a few meters apart. Sean moved slowly toward them but halted upon hearing the click of the safety on Renzo's pistol, which was pointed straight at D'Annunzio's head.

"Stay there, Sean," Renzo said. "No closer."

"I don't see any treacherous Croats here," Sean said. "Only a treacherous Italian. A treacherous friend."

Renzo took a few steps backward until he could keep both D'Annunzio and Sean in his sight without moving his head. "They will be here any minute. My men are collecting them from the jail. Ugo and his chums are quite angry about what happened to Luigi. I can hold them off, my friend, if you join us. Otherwise, I can't let you leave, and I won't stop them."

D'Annunzio took his eyes off Renzo and glared at Sean, affirming wordlessly that the only thing worse than being rescued by an unworthy savior like Sean was the ignominious prospect of being betrayed by him. "Preposterous," he said. "This is like a bad opera. The people of Fiume need—"

"Shut the fuck up," Sean said. "The people of Fiume needed you to be out protecting them, not hiding in your Palace fucking their women."

"Well said," Renzo agreed. "Now use your head. Is this man worth dying for? When he sent you away to Zara, he did it so he could make another attempt on Chesa, may she rest in peace."

Sean bristled at the mention of Chesa. He fixed his eyes on the white wall behind the *Comandante* where framed portraits of the old Hungarian governors hung. Beneath them, D'Annunzio looked small, shorter than he seemed on the balcony of the Palace. Smaller than on the ship to Zara.

"They're not coming," Sean said.

"Stop talking crazy, Sean, please."

"Your boys are dead, Renzo. The Croats from the jail are back in Sušak. They won't be available for sacrifice."

"Impossible," Renzo said. "You don't expect me to believe you did this yourself."

"I had help. Recognize the rifle? The Russian one you gave Ugo, like the ones you sold to Dušan. Here's Ugo's pistol, too. It's a long story, and I don't feel like telling it."

Renzo drew in a deep breath. "You have proved to be a major nuisance, Sean. I should never have let you stay in Fiume. Once you got caught up with the League of Fiume and the death of that Piero whatever-his-name-was, you just would not stop. I had hoped you were smarter. You had every possible warning. Tom and I both told you to leave. As did Chesa. I told her she needed to get you out because you were in danger. I know she tried to convince you."

Sean rotated the rifle's bolt handle, pulled it back and shoved it forward to chamber a cartridge. The sound echoed in the room. He pointed the rifle at Renzo.

"Don't be crazy." Renzo's voice sounded level and cool. "From that distance, you couldn't hit anything you aimed at."

Sean kept the rifle pointed at Renzo. Throbs of pain in his jaw and shoulder and knee rumbled on inside him at different speeds.

"I am deeply sorry about Chesa," Renzo said. "I meant her no harm. The men were only supposed to destroy the photographs. No one knew she'd be in the darkroom that late. But she was there, and it was dark, and Ugo was too brainless to make sure the place was empty. Luigi would have been smarter, but he wasn't available, thanks to you. Why was Chesa in the darkroom, or still in Fiume at all? Because you wouldn't leave. You see, everything comes back to you."

Sean's arms shook. First Nina, now Renzo. The barrel of the rifle wobbled. Perhaps he couldn't hit Renzo from this range, but everything urged him to try. He saw for the first time the large brown canvas bag at Renzo's feet. The zipper on the bag was closed, but Sean guessed its contents. "Killing Wickson and stealing the funds in the safe—is that my fault as well? Or is that for the glory of Italy? How about Bini and Zeppegno? I wasn't even in Fiume when their plane crashed."

"If you want the money, take it," Renzo said. "All of it, if you want. There'll be plenty more when we rule Italy. Take the cash and join us." He waved the pistol at D'Annunzio. "The *Comandante* doesn't need the cash. He wanted to give it away to every grifter who promised to start a war of liberation. Be sensible. I can cover things up here. Take the money, leave. It's what Chesa wanted you to do.

"If you say her name one more time," Sean said, "I am pulling the trigger."

Renzo sighed.

"I came here to warn the *Comandante* about you," Sean said. "The beatings, the castor oil, the bombings."

D'Annunzio shook his head in short, deliberate movements. "Those pilots were beautiful."

"Who are you going to pin the *Comandante's* murder on now?" Sean asked.

"That will be you, of course. Sean Reilly, the crazy American who broke in here a couple of months ago, today came back to kill the *Comandante*. He fired the same rifle used in those other Croat attacks. He was a terrorist, known to be working with the Croats. I shot the assassin, but too late to save our heroic leader." Renzo shrugged his shoulders. "I will feel bad about what I have to do."

"So this is how it all ends," D'Annunzio said. His face tightened like he had drunk something bitter. "To be sacrificed, my bullet-punctured body used as a stepping-stone for that fat hyena Mussolini. It is better I shall not live to see such a world. I detest vulgar comedy."

"Time has run out, gentlemen," Renzo said. "I salute you, *Comandante*." He bowed slightly. "And Sean, my friend."

"Wait," Sean said. "You should see the pictures first."

"You never quit, do you?" Renzo said. "I'm sure your photographs of the mountains are quite beautiful, but they don't matter. By now, a squad of Fascists, real Arditi veterans, is marching through the defile up there and will soon stir things up in the Old Town. The Croats will go crazy and retaliate by assassinating the *Comandante*, led by their notorious American friend Sean Reilly. No one believed you. I'm curious though. Where did you hide the film?"

"What treason is this?" D'Annunzio said. Spit flew from his mouth. "I gave orders to cover that sector of the mountains."

Sean pulled a packet of photographs from his coat pocket and flung it at Renzo's feet. "These pictures are different. You should take a look before you do anything stupid. Anything else stupid, I mean."

Renzo lowered his head and glanced at the packet, but made no attempt to reach for it. He kept the pistol trained on D'Annunzio. A look of uncertainty crossed his features for the first time.

"I did have photographs of the pass," Sean continued, "but Tom has those now. And yes, *Comandante*, you gave orders, but you didn't follow through, as usual. Renzo countered those orders and moved the troops away. But Renzo didn't follow through either. I did. Tom Delancy and some legionnaires are guarding the defile with two machine guns, and they'll pin down anyone who tries to get past them. Caesar himself couldn't get through there. But that's not what I want Renzo to see." Sean pointed toward the packet on the floor. "Go ahead. They're good. Chesa took them. And you are in them."

"Photographs of me?" Renzo said. He picked up the packet. "How kind of you. But it's not going to change anything."

"Let me see those," D'Annunzio said. "I demand to know what is going on."

Renzo untied the string and sifted rapidly through the photographs, using both hands but managing to keep his gun in a threatening position. He glanced up every second or two. "Impossible," he said. "These pictures are false. I don't know how but they are."

"Not impossible," Sean said. He felt like smiling for the first time in a long while. "You look quite dashing in them, with your perfect uniform, standing with Dušan, leader of the Croatian terrorists. I don't know how far away you were from each other at the time, but in these photos, it looks like you stood right next to him. It's the angle, maybe. And both of you are perfectly in focus. Chesa once explained the effect to me. The circle of confusion, she called it. What's in focus depends on how open the aperture is. The more you try to see, the less accurate your picture is. I don't understand the physics. But I can see the result. And so will everyone else. Copies are already in a safe place. Such a smile on your face, like you and Dušan are great friends hatching plans for an attack. Anybody looking at the photos could conclude you two are conspiring."

Renzo's face betrayed his concern, but the tone of his voice didn't. "What good are they going to be to you?"

"Give them to me," D'Annunzio demanded.

"They're going to keep me and the *Comandante* alive," Sean replied. "As long as we are both still breathing, the pictures stay secret. But if either of us were to suffer some harm, newspapers all over Italy and France will get copies, and Mussolini will have some embarrassing questions to answer about why his trusted lieutenant consorted with those vile Croatians on the assassination of the beloved war hero Gabriele D'Annunzio. Oh, I also have a letter you sent Dušan arranging for the sale of the guns. Even a receipt you gave him. Forged, of course, but it will take months, maybe years before anyone figures that out. You won't have that much time, I suspect, before Mussolini gets rid of you."

Renzo examined the pictures, and then looked at Sean. "How do I know," he said softly, "you didn't already reveal these photographs and your phony documents?"

"You don't. I would say trust me, but we're a little past that now, aren't we? But trust this: the pictures and the papers are what will keep me and the great poet alive. As soon as they go public, I'll become the next target, right after you. These pictures have power only if they are not seen."

Renzo reached to pick up the canvas bag and froze. "You're not going to try to shoot me?" he said. "I would defend myself."

Sean did not answer. His mouth was dry, and he wasn't sure words would come out properly.

"Not that there's much risk of your hitting anything," Renzo said, but he seemed to regret his taunt. "I am sorry about, oh, things. But you have your dreams, and I have mine."

He stood up, canvas bag clutched firmly in hand. "The cash will help back in Milan. Good thing no one knows how much is in here, except the late, unlamented Mr. Wickson." He pulled the bill of his cap down slightly, shading his eyes. "*Comandante*, it has been an honor serving with you. For all of our sakes, for me and all of Italy, be careful, and don't get yourself killed defending Fiume. *Ciao*."

Renzo vanished through the door at the far end of the room. A minute later the heavy thud of the front door of the Palace jolted them both. D'Annunzio crumpled onto an ornate high-backed chair, his head sunk to his chest.

At last, Sean thought, a chance to talk to the *Comandante* about putting an end to this senseless fighting. He walked over to the window and pulled the heavy curtain aside. Staring out at the bay, he saw a flash of orange-red and a column of smoke rising out over the water, and then heard a familiar screaming sound.

ONE TWENTY-FIVE

Letter from Gaj Kcleža

January 20, 1921

Dear Mr. Marinetti:

I regret to advise you of the passing of our mutual acquaintance, Sean Reilly. He had the misfortune of being present at the Governor's Palace last month when it was shelled by your government's battleship. The shell slightly injured *Comandante* D'Annunzio. Tragically, the blast killed Sean.

Sean dreamed of a better world. He once told me that heaven is where good dreams go when they don't come true. I maintain a more traditional Catholic view of heaven, but I find great appeal in the thought that Sean's dreams survive him somewhere, in a place where they can be embraced by others and perhaps come to fruition when the time is right.

Sean left with me several photographs and papers and gave instructions that in the event either he or D'Annunzio suffered untimely deaths, I should make them public. Due to the tragic circumstances of Sean's death, I have decided to keep them locked up at present. I would appreciate it if you would contact Renzo Guidici, formerly of Fiume, and let him know those items are securely conserved in accordance with Sean's wishes. Please inform him that should anything unfortunate happen to D'Annunzio or to me or my family, he can count on the items being widely disseminated. He will understand. Tell him also that Tom Delancy would like a word with him.

If you ever travel to Fiume, Mr. Marinetti, I hope you will visit my restaurant again. I will serve you a good meal, and we can discuss photography and poetry.

You humble servant,

Gaj Kcleža

ONE TWENTY-SIX

From INTERVIEW WITH DUŠAN KCLEŽA (1992)
[UNEDITED TRANSCRIPT]

SB: Your goal of a free Croatia has finally been realized in this year 1992, thanks in no small part to your efforts and your courage over the past seventy-plus years.

DK: And the men I fought with. Don't ever forget them. Women, too.

SB: Absolutely. You do them great honor by your remembrance. Tell us, please, what do you think the future holds for our nation?

DK: More fighting. We have to stay vigilant. There will always be people who want to take our freedom away. Look, this goal of free Croatia goes back over a thousand years, and how many of our people do you think had to fight and die over that time so you could ask me that question? My father kept the goal alive for me and my children and their kids. I've passed it on. Now maybe some things I did, if I could do them over, I might not do the same way. You understand? But we did what we had to, for Croatia. What was your question again?

SB: What will Croatia be like in the future?

DK: A beautiful land full of free Croatians, ruled by Croatians. And lots of complaining.

SB: You mentioned your father's dream of a time when men and women of all ancestry, even Italians and Serbs, could come to Fiume and live and work together as equals.

DK: My father was a dreamer. It's a nice dream. I'm a fighter. That's the difference. Maybe my grandkids can figure out how to be both. One of them is an artist, can you believe it?

THE END

AUTHOR'S NOTE

iume Restoral is a work of historical fiction set in the city known today as Rijeka, Croatia. In September 1919, newspapers around the world covered the story of its occupation by Gabriele D'Annunzio and his legionnaires. It became a major issue discussed at length at the Paris Peace Conference.

D'Annunzio was an internationally celebrated poet, novelist, dramatist, and Great War celebrity. He remained as Fiume's *Comandante* for sixteen months until he was forced out by the Italian military. He spent his remaining years in a villa overlooking Lake Garda, at the expense of the Italian government. Guido Keller was a decorated Great War pilot and D'Annunzio's eccentric "Action Secretary" in Fiume. Fillipo Marinetti founded the Futurist art movement in 1909 and, in the years after the Great War, tried to turn it into a political movement. Léon Kochnitzky, the Belgian poet and devoted D'Annunzio disciple, worked tirelessly on the League of Fiume. After leaving Fiume he became a noted art critic. Luisa Baccara, the pianist and D'Annunzio's mistress, followed him from Fiume to his post-occupation villa. Marconi and Toscanini did visit Fiume during the occupation. Mussolini needs no introduction. James, who appears in Chapter 4, is loosely based on a famous author, but I leave it to the reader to recognize him.

These were real people, but their dialogue and behavior in the novel have been invented by the author. The other characters are purely my creations.

ACKNOWLEDGMENTS

There are too many people to whom I am indebted for their help on this novel. Without meaning to slight anyone, I want to mention some of the people who made this possible.

I am grateful to my brilliant editor, Laurie Chittenden, whose insightful suggestions improved and deepened the novel. Thanks also to Chuck Dennis, Sheena Auroa, and Carla LoCoco, whose invaluable comments helped so much on drafts. I am indebted to Stacey Swann, Ron Nyren, Thomas H. McNeely, Deborah Johnson and Nami Mun, each of them published novelists and instructors in the Stanford University Online Certificate Program in Novel Writing, for their wisdom about writing and their comments on the text of my novel. Anamyn Turowski, from the Writers Studio, guided my early efforts at fiction. Her lessons on tone, mood, and voice helped liberate me from years of legal writing.

I'm grateful to Kimberley Cleland for all her help with social media and so much else. And thanks to copy editor Robert Kenney and book designer Ian Koviak for their work preparing the book for publication. It did turn out rather nicely.

Thanks to my parents, George and Rita Dennis. They taught me so many things, including the love of reading.

And finally, I owe more than I can ever express to my loving wife, Cheryl. Her advice and support improved this novel and my life.